DRIVE ME

TO

THE MOON

Drive Me
To
The Moon

By

Mike Baines

ISBN9798815449602

Drive Me To The Moon

Mike Baines

Dedicated to all who are

Wildland firefighters

Or have been

Wildland firefighters

And to those who support

Wildland firefighters...

Dear Reader,

Let me say this at the very start for those who skip over things like the Foreword without reading it: There may be an event described in this book that screams at you – "this is about me!" Let me assure you that it is not. You may have experienced something very similar, but I have gone to great lengths to make non-fictional events fit into fictional circumstances and dress them up to be unrecognizable. As an example, I might write about a person who crossed a street in the middle of a block – a blatant jaywalker. At some time in your life, you may have crossed the street in the middle of the block, but I am not writing about you.

That being said, there are three insertions that are included verbatim and not disguised. The first is a text or email to the mechanic who inspected a driver's pickup. The second one is a question about planning one's life that a young person asked many people in order to get as many ideas as he could. The third is a Viet Nam vet's description of what it was like for him to be on a fire suffering from PTSD. I am hoping that anyone with PTSD might benefit from reading what this vet wrote. I also hope that the vet himself would reconnect with me.

I have also used the actual names of some towns, landmarks, highways, and establishments. My reasons to do so was to give my story structure and for my own enjoyment. All the places mentioned are places I am very familiar with.

I would like to add one last note on the events and characters described in this book. People can only write about what they have learned or experienced. The wildest fiction that has ever been written was only written because the author had some reality to launch his or her imagination from. My reality started with my first assignment on a fire as a crewmember of the Cannell Meadow Helitack on the Sequoia National

Forest in 1974. Since then, I've held many different fire qualifications. For the last 20 years, I have limited myself to Liaison Officer (LOFR) and Human Resource Specialist (HRSP). This last qualification, or job, has allowed me to work with the social fabric that makes up our wildland firefighting forces. I get to deal with both the positive and negative attitudes and actions that people bring to a fire. Drive Me to the Moon is the product of my 48 years of involvement with the fire militia, 34 years as a Forest Service employee, 12 years as a hostile work environment mediator, and my lifelong faith in Jesus Christ.

I have many people to thank that came along beside me in this creative endeavor. I cannot list them all due to the role they played, but for those I can, I've listed them in the order as they chimed in.

First I want to mention Tracy Larsen for providing me with particular background information. If I need to learn how to drive a truck with multiple trailers, I'll call her first. Thank you, Tracy!

Stew Souders, a fellow HRSP, gave me initial encouragement that I might have a book worth writing. I thank him for his patience and forbearance as he had to read the humble 2 and 3-page genesis of Drive Me To the Moon several times! Thank you, Stew!

It seems important to me that every author has someone who will be brutally honest when critiquing manuscripts. It should be a person who is confident in their own skills and abilities. I was fortunate to find such a person who didn't mind bending low to help one of his minions out. I appreciate the encouragement and misguidance I received from Ken

Arbogast, a fellow veteran of the U.S. Forest Service and fellow author, in addition to his duties as Supreme Overlord Master, Chief of All Existence. I hope you can tell we have a great relationship! Thank you, Ken!

Coming up through the ranks of the Forest Service, one of my favorite supervisors had a daughter the same age as my son. Time went by and that supervisor moved on; I moved on. Years later the supervisor's daughter and I became Facebook friends. I found out that she had been an English teacher for some 10 years. Providentially, I also found that I needed an editor for this book. Adrienne Del Rio Kingston has saved the reader from endless numbers of mind-numbing paragraphs that begged the question: "where are you going with this?" This book is better by far from her involvement and I can't thank her enough. So, thank you, Adrienne!

I also want to thank fellow author and sister Verda Spice, (get her suspense-filled book, "Fox Hollow" from Amazon.com if you haven't already) and my punctuation master sister Jane Pardue as well as my wonderful wife Paulette for the time they spent reading and checking my manuscript chapter by chapter as they were written. These three ladies helped to put a bow on the finished book. Thank you, Verda, Jane, and Paulette!

Even if you have never been around a large wildfire, I hope you learn something new and worthwhile from this book – and it may not be about fire.

As an old Human Resource Specialist, let me close with this: "Try not to offend anyone. Try harder not to be offended!"
Best Wishes,
Mike Baines

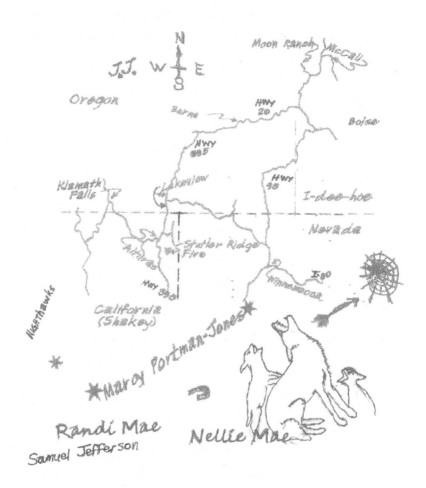

Mike Baines

Chapter One

The Call

The line went dead on the other end. Yet, Marcy stood frozen with the phone still at her ear. What had she just agreed to? Hadn't she promised Jacody they would make important decisions together? How could she spin this so he wouldn't feel she had gone rogue? Goodness knows they need the money! But committing to being gone for one to two weeks on a fire without talking to him first was going to be a hard pill for her husband to swallow.

Marcy put her phone down and walked to the kitchen sink. She stared out the window at the ranch she and Jacody were trying so hard to hold on to. The long rays of the late afternoon sun held that intense quality of light that gave everything a bright golden glow. Across the barnyard and up along the creek, a rainbow appeared from the wheel irrigation system watering the 16-acre alfalfa field, neatly trimmed after its second cutting. Jacody should be finished cutting the 8-acre field and replacing the irrigation lines by supper time. With purpose, Marcy went through Jacody's favorite meals. She wanted to cook one that would put him in the best mood possible before she shared what she had just committed to.

Shepard's Pie surfaced as the winner. As comfort food goes, it is right up there at the top of the list and Marcy was looking for all the comfort she could get to soften the hard discussion that would follow the evening meal. As her hands busied themselves preparing the meal, her mind busied itself remembering how they came into possession of this ranch.

Jacody and Marcy had often marveled about how the stars fell into alignment concerning the ranch. For them to be in the possession of this patch of God's Green Earth was nothing short of a miracle. Maintaining possession of it, however, requires both to do whatever is necessary to pay the bills. Hiram Walker's family owned this ranch since the early 1800s, and Hiram, well into his 80s, has health issues with no family to help him keep things up. Over the years, he came to rely more and more on his lifelong friend Sam Portman and his strawberry blonde sidekick for the help he needed.

Hiram and Marcy, along with Marcy's husband of two and a half years, Jacody Jones, struck a deal. Hiram, with no relatives to leave his property to, wanted to make sure the government wouldn't get their greedy hands on it after he was gone. Hiram was fond of Marcy and came to think of her as his granddaughter too. After Marcy married Jacody they were working on his ranch almost weekly. So, it put Hiram's mind at ease when, several years ago, he had legal papers drawn up giving ownership of the ranch to Marcy and Jacody Jones with the stipulation he could remain on the property and in his house for as long as he was physically able. This came as both a blessing and a bane to the Jones.

The blessing was that, in this day and age, acquiring a 680-acre ranch with a 2,400-acre federal grazing allotment would take more cash than the 2 of them were likely to earn in their lifetime, or, at least, in the next 30 years. But there it was. All nice and legal; I's dotted and T's crossed. If they can make it profitable, Moon Ranch would be all theirs!

The bane, or curse, was that as Hiram's health declined, so too had his industry. He had barely kept enough cattle on his federal allotment to maintain it. That is, if the current permit holder does not put at least the minimum number of cattle designated by the Forest Service's Range Conservationist on the allotment, the permit could be reassigned to another permittee. That alone was an indicator that the ranch's management was in a downward spiral. Irrigation equipment was in disrepair and some of the land had fallen out of production. The fact was, the ranch had been bleeding money for several years as Hiram neglected it. Hiram had borrowed money using the ranch as collateral and those notes were coming due; notes that were now Marcy and Jacody's responsibility to pay.

Marcy was confident that she was more than up for the task. From an early age, she had proved herself to be an able-bodied hand. Like most ranch kids, she had been very active in 4-H livestock. She went through horse, beef cattle, sheep, goats... all but rabbits. What was there to do but shoot and eat rabbits and where was the challenge to that? She helped her family with equal skill moving cattle from winter pasture on the home place to the summer range on her grandfather's grazing allotment he had with the Forest Service. She was accurate with the lasso from horseback and could head or heel calves when it came time to brand, tag, dehorn, and worm them. From the time she could reach the pedals on the flatbed dually, she had driven the truck loaded with hay to do winter feeding. Tall for her age, by thirteen she was driving the ranch's old Dimond Reo semi-tractor, dubbed "Desperado" by her dad, around the ranch. Then, on occasion, late in the evening when she and Grandpa Sam were coming back from hauling hay to the Midwest and he was growing weary, she would take the wheel and bring them home.

At eighteen she was hired by Acme Fireline Inc. as a crewmember on their hotshot crew. On any large fire, one of the first resources called for is hotshot crews. A hotshot crew is made up of 20 highly trained wildland firefighters. They are the boots on the ground; the first line of defense against a spreading wildfire. They start in Arizona/New Mexico and work North as the fire conditions and the fires move North. They usually end the season back down in Southern California where the fire season always lingers longer. They work twelve to fourteen hour days, 7 days a week, 2 weeks at a time. After 2 days off they start another 2-week cycle. That means lots of overtime from late spring to late fall. During her short fire career, she moved from crewmember to squad boss to crew boss. At 22 she tore the meniscus in her left knee and hung up her White logger's boots for good.

During the off-season from fire, she was keeping Desperado, the truck grandpa Sam bought new in 1974, busy hauling grain from the nation's food basket to granaries or seaports on the West coast during harvest. In the fall it might be beef cattle hauled to Kansas and from there, calves back to Oregon where they would be fattened before being hauled back to the Midwest. Big Bud Fontaine Logging and a few construction outfits often called on her to move equipment around for them.

As Hiram Walker's health declined, she started turning down long-haul jobs. If she wasn't there to help on the Walker Ranch, Grandpa Sam would try to do it all and she was worried about him injuring himself, although she would never tell her grandfather

4

that. He would only work harder to prove her wrong. It got better when Marcy and Jacody started seeing each other. Jacody truly enjoyed working on Hiram's ranch.

"Jacody. Yes. I need to deal with Jacody!" Marcy said into the thin air.

Her thoughts returned to the task at hand. Her goal was to keep her husband on an even keel while getting him to see the benefits of the sacrifice. She knew Jacody could relate to the pull she felt to answer the fire call. When she joined the Fireline Hotshots, Jacody was a rookie, just like her. He too had a strong attraction to fighting wildland fire. It was he who designed the crew's logo: Wiley E. Coyote spreading fire with a drip torch that had "ACME" on it in big letters. They liked the joke: "If you play with fire for money, you're an arsonist. If you play with fire for fun, you're a pyromaniac. If you play with fire for money and fun, you're a wildland firefighter!"

If all she had to do was make money, she could do that. What was the point, though, if you never got to enjoy the reason you spent all your time making money? "We need to get ahead of the game so we can have a little fun and enjoyment!", she said out loud to herself. The fact remains, "you have to make hay while the sun shines". Running this ranch and getting it out of the red ink was a 3- or 4-person job. But when it is just the 2 of them, they must work sunup to sundown 7 days a week. They seem to have stopped the bleeding but have yet to start showing a profit. They spend, spend, spend, and eventually, there is a profit – hopefully equal to, or greater, than all the spending.

Her going on a fire right now would be a large infusion of cash that would really help them until they sold off some of their livestock that was ready for market. The catch here was they needed to retain a certain number of cattle to maintain the stocking level on their federal grazing allotment. She needed Jacody to see that meeting her commitment to Big Bud Fontane Logging was a plus for the ranch. All she had to do is to pick up a dozer, take it to the Stutler Ridge Fire and be there to move it as directed by the fire management team. Simple! She would only be gone two weeks... maybe more... but probably only two weeks. Yes, they should have discussed it together so his fragile male ego would not be threatened, but she was sure the decision would have been the same. "That's a fact, Jack!" she mumbled as she took the Shepard's Pie out of the oven to cool.

Marcy heard the side door close and the sound of big boots in the mudroom off the kitchen. Right on cue... supper is ready and so is my man!

"Now that's good timing," Marcy said, "Get washed up and I'll throw a salad together. You set the table and maybe open a bottle of that Blueberry Pino Noir."

"Something sure smells good and if I wasn't hungry before, I sure am now!" Jacody said.

"We've got Shepard's Pie tonight," Marcy said.

"What? Wait! It's not my birthday. I know it's not our 3rd anniversary yet. Is it? Is it our anniversary? I'm sorry! I can't believe...."

"Hold on! Stop!" Marcy interrupted, "Can't I fix a good meal I know you like, 'just because'?"

"Well, sure you can Honey," Jacody said more calmly now. "You can fix good stuff anytime you want. Don't let me hold you back. I'll eat it too!"

"I know you would!" Marcy laughed. "So how's the cutting look on this field? Is it about the same as the upper field?

"It may be a little better. That new irrigation system may be worth the money we spent on it. Time will tell but we sure aren't going to make it back in just two cuttings," Jacody said.

"Well, it might come close if what we get for alfalfa goes up," Marcy said as she set the salad on the table and turned to get silverware.

"Oh sure, that would help," POP! Went the cork out of the wine bottle, "but on the balance sheet, it won't make up for the increase in diesel fuel!" Jacody said as he poured each of them a glass of wine.

After they were seated at the table, they bowed their heads and closed their eyes. Jacody prayed and gave God thanks for the food, for their marriage, for the ranch, and for their families. He asked God to be with Hiram and to heal him if it is in His will. Jacody said "Amen" and Marcy echoed him.

They remained silent for a while; Jacody seemed focused on every bite of comfort food. Marcy ate too, but not with the same vigor as Jacody. She watched Jacody and wondered what he was thinking about. It seemed he could close all the drawers in his mind and be content to think about... nothing. Meanwhile, she was getting knots in her stomach knowing she was going to have to start a conversation she'd rather not have.

"When I was in town today, I stopped by Shady Acres and visited with Hiram," Marcy said, stalling off what she really wanted to talk about.

Jacody said, "Well good! How's Hiram today?"

"Not much better, I'm afraid. "Marcy said. "The nurse told me he is still having mini hemorrhaging in his brain and the hospital says they can only make him comfortable. He wanted to know if I was still selling girl scout cookies. I wonder who Lydia is and if she used to sell cookies to him. I'll have to ask Grandpa Sam if he knows anything about that."

"Yeah. Do that," Jacody said in between bites.

Marcy waited for the right words to come. The silence for her was deafening. Jacody, on the other hand, didn't seem to notice. Again, all the drawers in his brain appeared closed as he happily poked pie in his face.

"This dry spell is really something," Marcy began.

"Yeah. Something," Jacody replied.

"Lots of fires in California, Oregon, and Washington," Marcy said.

"Uh-huh," Said Jacody.

"You ever miss going on fires?" Asked Marcy

"What? No, not really."

"But the money was good, right? Marcy asked.

"Oh. Yeah, good. Would you pass me another biscuit, please?

"You'll never guess who called this afternoon," Here we go Marcy thought.

"Your Grandma Nellie. No. Wait! A guy concerned about the extended warranty on your vehicle running out? Publisher's Clearing House? We're rich! Oh! How about HGTV? We won the HGTV Dream House 2019 in Whitefish, Montana?" Jacody blurted out.

"OK! OK! I think I liked you better when you were just quietly sitting there eating. Marcy said. "I've been

trying to find an easy way to talk to you about something."

"Did your mare get out again? I swear that horse has learned how to open gates! Seriously! I've run that fence line, and I don't find a break in it." Jacody said defensively.

"You are not going to make this easy so I'm just going to tell you what I've done," Marcy said.

Now that she had his undivided attention, she continued, "I got a call this afternoon from Bud Fontaine." Marcy said.

"So what does Big Bud want? A skidder up on a timber landing? Jacody asked, "that shouldn't be a problem."

"No. That wouldn't be a problem." Marcy answered evenly, "He wants me to go down to Ruby Mountain Equipment in Winnemucca, load up a dozer, take it to the Stutler Ridge Fire on the Modoc National Forest in California, and then, he wants me to stay with it until the fire releases it. He's emailing me the Resource Order. The fire is a lightning start from yesterday and is up to around 5,200 acres as of early this morning according to Inciweb. There is a Rocky Mountain Type 1 Incident Management Team in place, and they are hurting for resources. I need to be prepared to spend 2 weeks there and maybe be extended another week. There. I know we said we would not make any big decisions by ourselves... but I got caught up in the excitement of going on a fire again and it could mean as much as $10-12,000, maybe more depending on how long I'm there. We could upgrade the irrigation system on the upper field like we did the lower field. I told Big Bud I'd do it. Please don't be mad at me."

Jacody sat there idly running his finger around the outside edge of his empty bowl making the spoon in his bowl go around and around. He finally spoke, "Well, I am disappointed." He looked up for a moment, and then looked down again. "I'm disappointed that I might not see you for up to three weeks." He paused, then looked up at her and went on. "I'm disappointed that you thought I might be mad at you. I'm unhappy that I will have to feed that horse of yours. You know she doesn't like me at all."

Marcy said, "really? You're not mad. How about your male ego? Is it damaged since I took it upon myself to make this decision?"

"Of course," Jacody answered, "I think we should talk with each other, and we should weigh out the pros and cons together. I could easily get upset with you because this is a big deal; you leaving me alone with everything here on the ranch to do by myself. I'd like to think you gave this careful consideration – that you thought of all the advantages and disadvantages. I'd like to think you considered the impact this will have on me. I'd like to think that... but I'd be wrong if I did. It sounds like Big Bud just told you to go down to Winnemucca, pick up a dozer and go to the Warner Mountains and stay with it until he tells you to go home. I'm wondering why Big Bud can tell you to do stuff and you just say, OK, but when I try to tell you something we end up in a big debate about it and I say, 'Well, I guess we don't need whatever it was after all'. Then you often say, 'No. I think I should do that.'

10

It takes us hours to get to an agreement. But with Big Bud, it's once and done. But this is what you want to do, I have every confidence you know how to do it, and we would have come up with the same decision if we had talked it through. So you are going. We can use the money. Actually, we need the money."

Marcy had brightened up, "Oh J.J., I'm so glad..."

"Whoa, whoa, whoa! Hold your horses," Jacody interrupted, "there's more," he continued somewhat sheepishly, "You see, this afternoon I kind of obligated our contingency fund to upfront much of the water system I'm going to put in over on the Roberts' Ranch and I wasn't sure how to tell you.... being we always discuss big decisions before we make them, and I failed to do that with you this time. I just knew you thought something was wrong the way you just poked at your food and kept looking at me the way you do when you know something isn't right but you're not sure what. I thought my brain was going to burst I was trying so hard to figure out how to tell you. I felt like I had skated out on thin ice by myself. Now I feel like we both are out there on thin ice together. I feel a whole lot better now!"

Marcy's jaw went slack temporarily. "What! You....!" She threw a half-eaten biscuit at him hitting him harmlessly on the chest. "All during supper I thought the drawers in your brain were closed, that you weren't thinking anything, and here you were stuffing your face because you needed to confess sins greater than mine and didn't know what to say! Well, I'd say I sure saved your bacon on this one Sweetie-pie! Furthermore, talk about me and Big Bud, will you? What's Ralph and Rhonda Roberts got on you that you are buying water systems for them with our money?"

Jacody held up both hands as a sign of submission. "Okay, okay! My bad, your good. Whatever you say, dear. Let's call it a draw."

"Your bad and my good? Marcy asked with one eyebrow raised. "Yeah. I can live with that."

"Uh-huh," Jacody said. "God seems to have a way of keeping us on an even keel. Now you know why I couldn't be too mad at you for doing the same thing I just did. The Roberts' job will bring in a healthy check and Big Bud's job will too. I'm glad we didn't let the Road Use Taxes and permits lapse on Cupcake."

Chapter Two
The Pick Up

Marcy came out of the bathroom prepared to face whatever the day threw at her. The rich aroma of hot coffee directed her nose into the kitchen. Jacody had breakfast all but ready: sauteed onions and peppers mixed in with eggs topped with shredded cheese and salsa. To go with the coffee was his recently made Cherry Almond Biscotti, Marcy's favorite.

"You know," Jacody said, "I'd really rather have you here at home than hanging out with a bunch of men I don't even know."

"You and me both," Marcy said. "I'd rather be home with you than anywhere else in the world. But we talked about this. We agreed this is too good an opportunity to pass up. We can really use the money right now and if we don't do anything different than we've been doing we won't get anything different than we've been getting."

Jacody looked at his wife and, with a curled index finger, raised her chin so he could look directly into her clear blue eyes. "Hey," he said softly. "We did talk this out last night, I agreed. So you don't have to keep convincing me. And please, don't feel guilty about leaving us... me and all these animals. Maybe we will have a small, inexpensive party and buy some expensive irrigation equipment after you get paid. It's alright. Remember... I love you."

"Oh..! Now I really don't want to go!" Marcy said as her eyes glistened with tears. She put her arms around Jacody, raised up on tiptoes, and kissed his neck.

Hugging her, Jacody mocked, "Yeah! You say that now, but I saw you out back whacking each tire on your rig and topping the saddle tanks off with diesel fuel. You can't wait to get that antique truck on the road. By the time you get on 95 South and wind old Cupcake up, you won't even hit 50 mph before this ranch and everything on it becomes just a faded memory!"

"Oh stop!" Marcy laughed, "You know that's not true. I'll call you every evening to check in on you and to tell you good night." She gave him a jab in the ribs right where it always made him jump. "Besides, you and that backhoe are going to be digging up Roberts' alfalfa fields for the next two weeks. You and your shadows better be too tired to notice I'm not here."

"Fat chance of that happening!" Jacody mused. "We'll be busy alright. I'll be trying to get home

14

before dark so I can get all my chores done and then when I do get into the house, it'll just be me and the microwave!"

"Well, you are a good button pusher, for sure!" Marcy quipped.

"But" Jacody got serious all of a sudden, "you will be missed. I could never get used to not having you around."

"I know." Marcy sighed. "I know. It's like my life is getting put on hold until I get back home to you. I won't lie. There is a part of me that is excited to be involved on a big fire again even though it won't be like being on a shot crew. But there's another part of me that is going to miss you so much, that I'm afraid I'm going to be homesick until we get back together again."

Jacody said, "I don't want you feeling bad or getting sick. You just give the word, give me a sign, and I'll have an appendicitis attack! I'd do that just for you. I love you that much! They would have to let you come back home to take care of me!"

Marcy laughed out loud, "That is huge J.J., considering you had your appendix out already! But it isn't a life sentence. We can do this for two weeks."

Jacody had already taken Marcy's duffle bag and sleeping bag out and stowed them in the truck's sleeper. Last night he had put a plug-in Yeti Cooler on the floorboard on the passenger's side of the truck fully stocked with cold drinks. Now he picked up her cloth bag with all her toiletries, laptop, charging cords, and other miscellaneous items Marcy thought she might want while on her assignment. They walked out on the side porch and were greeted by Chuck and Chew. They both knew someone was leaving and if it was Jacody, they would be in the back of his truck before he could even get to the truck's door.

Although it was Marcy who usually fed the two Blue Heelers, they were totally devoted to Jacody as his constant shadows, as Marcy often referred to them. When Jacody wasn't available to them, the two spent their time patrolling the perimeter of their domain. Once they were assured there were no trespassers they practiced their herding skills, to the distress of 7 geese and 14 chickens. For some reason, they liked to herd the geese to the East side of the house and the chickens to the Westside. The geese accepted this as part of the give and take on the ranch. The sooner you give the dogs what they wanted the sooner they would leave you alone. So the geese would immediately waddle to the East side of the house and stand there looking at the dogs until they left to "help" the chickens. The chickens, on the other hand, always seemed surprised and confused as if this behavior was all brand new to them. During the fiasco, there were usually two or three renegade chickens who seemed to identify as geese. Neither Chuck, short for Charles Barkley, nor Chew, short for Sir Chewsalot, would have any of that, but they never lost patience with them. They would work slowly and painfully to cut the chickens out of the flock of geese and reunite them with their own kind.

Marcy bent down and scratched both dogs behind their ears. "I'll miss you guys. Are you going to miss me?"

They looked her hands over twice to make sure their noses hadn't missed any morsel of food or some treat. Finding none, they switched their attention back to Jacody.

Marcy wanted to linger there on the porch and soak in this moment. The air was still crisp from the night before. Breathing it in was like a refreshing cold drink of spring water from a tin cup. A covey of quail was calling to each other from beyond the corral. The sun was just rising over the mountain ridge to the East and its light was shining on the uplifted face of the mountain to the West. It was like a blind being slowly opened from the top down. As always, it was inspiring to watch the line, with its light above and shadows below, slide down the mountain. This was a moment in time Marcy would treasure and be sure to recall from time to time. They were both healthy, both of the same mind, and both contributing to the dream. This was a time of optimism! Anything and everything seemed possible!

Marcy and Jacody walked arm in arm back to the implement yard where the truck that used to be Desperado and now was Cupcake waited. Before opening the door and mounting the steps, Marcy and Jacody embraced. After a long kiss, Marcy pulled away thinking that if she let this go on any longer, Jacody would want to say goodbye again. They had already said goodbye last night... not once but twice!

She didn't want to show up at the equipment dealership with a stray stem or two of hay in her hair.

Marcy climbed up into the seat and started the diesel. Jacody handed up the cloth bag to her and pushed on the bottom of the door to close it. Cranking down the window, Marcy looked down at Jacody and said, "I'll call you tonight."

Jacody called up to her, "shoot me a quick text when you get to fire camp just so I'll know you are there and that everything is OK. Then call me later before you turn in. Love you!"

"Love you too!" Marcy went on to say, "Just remember, fire camp may still be in the process of getting set up. They may not have internet or cell service yet."

She checked her brakes to make sure the pressure was up in her air tanks, and as she increased the engine's RPMs she let out the clutch. Cupcake lurched forward. The chains and load binders neatly hooked on the storage rack on the back of the sleeper cab rattled as the semi moved past the barn, the corral, the ranch house, and down the drive. Holding to the left, she swung out wide and turned to the right, giving as much road as possible for the transport trailer's rear tandem axels to travel on as it rounded the turn.

Ten minutes later she was Southbound on US 95 going through the gears and gaining speed. Without a load on the trailer, after she got up some momentum, she could skip every other gear. When she got into 13th gear and hit the make-shift cruise control switch on top of the gear shift lever, she noted that not once had she forgotten Jacody and the ranch despite Jacody's prediction. A bittersweet smile crossed her face.

Actually, it was quite the opposite. There were things she prayed to God that she never would forget. This morning saying goodbye to Jacody, the tender look in his eyes, his voice – so soft and reassuring, the home they were making were all memories to be cherished. Other memories, much older but as permanent as the brand on a horse's hip, seemed to be happy yet sad all at the same time. At the heart of these memories was this old truck. Reo, Diamond, Truck, Desperado, Marcy ticked off the names her truck had been called. And now, making newer, better memories, its name is Cupcake.

Ever since she was thirteen and Grandpa Sam, and later her father after he came back from "the war" or "being lost" or... whatever, took her on runs with them in the old Diamond Reo, there was a sense of excitement and adventure when they first started out. Grandpa Sam would sing Dave Dudley's "Six Days On the Road" at the top of his lungs and she would join in:

> Well I pulled outta Pittsburgh
> A rollin' down that Eastern Seaboard
> I got my diesel wound up
> And she's a runnin' like a never before
> There's a speed zone ahead, well alright
> I don't see a cop in sight....

Having never been there, Marcy could only imagine pulling outta Pittsburgh and didn't care that it takes a lot of "rollin'" before you get over the mountains to the Eastern Seaboard; she just liked the emotion and enthusiasm of the song. She always started her trips with that song in her head if not actually from her voice. She sang it now.

She enjoyed bossing Cupcake's 350 horses around, feeling the power, and listening to the sound of the Cummins diesel engine. Her gauges told her everything she needed to know about the truck and her GPS told her the roads to take to get her where she was going. She was quite content in her little world; 35,000 pounds of steel hurtling down the highway with speeds at times easily over 80 miles an hour. Once loaded she could be piloting 40 – 50 tons.

Before she and Jacody began planning to get married, she had spent most of her extra income updating Cupcake. She had installed an 11-inch screen on the dash where she could monitor cameras fore and aft, Google Maps, text and phone calls, plus a few other apps. She had found an aftermarket air conditioner unit and had that installed. The painted rims on the truck were swapped out for chrome ones. The big-ticket item was the finely detailed paint job. The main cab, doors, hood, and fenders were dark royal blue. Light pink ghost flames were applied from the chrome radiator grill back onto the hood. From the doors around the sleeper unit, she added a waving American flag on each side. The chrome exhaust stacks appeared as large flag poles. The flags wrapped around the sleeper unit and met in the middle of the back. Using a Castellar font, she had "CUPCAKE" in gold letters outlined in white and then outlined in black just behind the ghost flames on both sides of the hood.

After her father handed "Desperado" over to her, she thought the name no longer fit. So she set about coming up with a name that suited her better. One morning over coffee, she finished off the last of the Sea Salt Chocolate Almond Biscotti. Intending to make another batch, she went to her collection of cookbooks to find the recipe and check the ingredients. The need for a new name for the truck was still fresh on her mind and the name of one of her cookbooks was 'Martha Stewart's Cupcake Cookbook'. The word "Cupcake" seemed to stand out for her, so the search was over; Cupcake was the new name for the Diamond Reo.

When Marcy dubbed Cupcake to be Desperado's new name, it seemed such a minor thing. She was shocked at her grandmother's reaction when Marcy brought the freshly painted and lettered truck home and showed it to her. As a grown woman now, it dawned on her that Grandma Nellie believed the transformation of Desperado into Cupcake to be a visible sign that she, Grandma Nellie, had been victorious in the battle she waged with Grandpa Sam in raising their granddaughter. To Grandma Nellie, it seemed Marcy had always gravitated towards her grandfather and her granddaughter wanted to be involved in whatever Sam was doing. That often placed Grandma Nellie and Grandpa Sam in opposite corners. Grandpa Sam would just chuckle when Marcy broke Grandma Nellie's "Rules of Etiquette for Young Ladies". She had warmed Marcy's bottom more than once for such infractions. Marcy got it good for using Skoal, a dipping tobacco, when she was around 13 years old. "It's bad enough you gotta dress like a boy and work like a boy... you sure ain't gonna chew tobacco like a man." Grandma Nellie tried her best to keep the lady in Marcy visible. Getting her in a dress to go to church on Sunday was always a hard-fought battle in Marcy's younger days. So, Marcy's transformation of Desperado into Cupcake made the fact that Marcy was a truck driver much more palatable for her grandmother.

Lost in thought, she was making great time. US 95 was miles and miles of straight-a-ways. Marcy kept the throttle lock on top of the gear shift pressed on most of the time. It served as an early model cruise control. She only had to slow up occasionally like going through Jordan Valley or Burns Junction. There were few small towns to go through. In a little over 5 hours, she was pulling into Ruby Mountain Equipment in Winnemucca.

Following the instructions that came with Big Bud's email the night before, Marcy located Lamont Dollarhide, the sales department manager. They went over the paperwork for Marcy to pick up the D-6 dozer that Big Bud had purchased. Lamont directed Marcy to pull Cupcake around to the back of the shop's service area where they had just finished prepping the dozer for delivery. As she was leaving his office, she heard him on the dealership's PA calling for Del to load Marcy's transport trailer with the dozer.

Delbert Livingston was waiting for her behind the shop to direct Cupcake to where he wanted to load the D6 Cat. He watched Marcy closely as she opened the door and climbed down to the ground.

"Well if you ain't a tall drink of water for a thirsty man!" he said once her boots hit the ground and she turned around. Del was around 6 feet tall, a full 2 inches shorter than Marcy and he eyed her up and down as though he had never seen a woman taller than him before.

Marcy groaned inwardly. Not now, she thought. The hot Nevada sun felt like a blast furnace bearing down on her. Maybe it would have been better if she had not had that air conditioner unit installed in Cupcake. Coming out of the shade of the cool cab into the 102 degrees of glaring sunshine was an assault almost as jarring as Del's insult.

"I can tell you've been watching too many old movies and I gotta say, that line has never worked for me!" Marcy said impatiently. She turned her back to Del and reached up to get the pair of leather work gloves she always kept just under the driver's seat in easy reach from the ground.

"Well now, I can deal with that!" Del said with enthusiasm. "What does work with you?"

Marcy pushed on the bottom of the truck door to close it and turned back around to face Del again. "I think you should ask my husband that after he helps you up off the ground, if, after that, you still want to know", Marcy said as she jumped up on the tractor's deck behind the sleeper unit and started throwing down the load binders (chains, ratchets binders and lever binders or boomers) she would need to secure the dozer to the transport trailer.

Del stiffened, "What makes you think I'd be on the ground...."

Marcy halted him with an upraised hand. "Are you just going to continue to make yourself feel inadequate or are you going to act like a real man and get that dozer loaded on my trailer?"

Hearing a portion of what had been said, Lamont, the sales manager, broke in, "Del! Quit thinking with your little head, get that dozer loaded, and get back in the shop or you can just go down the road for all I care. One more customer complaint and you won't have a choice!"

Del's face clouded over as he stalked off to climb up in the dozer's cab. Lamont grabbed some chains and helped Marcy position them at the anchor points on the trailer; two towards the front, two towards the back, and one on each side in the middle. "Sorry about that," Lamont lamely offered.

"I was handling that you know," Marcy told Lamont.

Lamont straightened up and considered Marcy. She was tossing the various load binders used to hook and tighten the chains onto the locations where they would be needed. He noticed the ease with which she worked that suggested not only strength but skill and experience.

He grinned at her, "Well yes, I'm sure you can take care of yourself. But, you see, my job is to make sure all our customers get what they come for and on their way as quickly and easily as possible. I didn't want to see you get held up explaining why you put Delbert in the hospital. I suspect he was this close to getting a boomer between the eyes!" He said, holding his hands up inches apart.

Marcy laughed, "When you look at it from that perspective, I guess I should thank you for doing your job. But, you know, I get tired of not being able to deal just with what I've been hired to do. That's tough enough by itself. I like my job. I like it enough that I'm willing to deal with all this BS people give me for not being what they expect; all the crap that isn't added onto a man who is doing the same job, but often, not nearly as good or efficiently. How many men come here to pick up a piece of equipment and get hit on? You don't need to answer that, I think you understand. Sorry for venting a little."

"You're not going to be able to tighten that chain if you don't put that boomer's hook on the next link down." Marcy directed.

"No, that's OK. You've got a right to vent!" Lamont noted, "and yeah, I need just a little more slack in this chain to get it to work."

With the D6 on the trailer, Del hot-footed it out of sight back into the shop. Lamont and Marcy finished securing the beast to the trailer, and Marcy climbed back in Cupcake's cab. She noticed she had missed a text from Big Bud wanting to know if things went smoothly at Ruby Mountain Equipment. He didn't need to know any details so she texted him back that she was pulling over to the truck stop for a late lunch and would be back on the road shortly headed for the Stutler Ridge Fire.

Chapter Three
Westbound and Down

Marcy topped off her fuel tanks with diesel at the Must Stop Truck Stop – The Trucker's Home Away From Home. From experience, she knew there may or may not be diesel fuel available at fire camp. After pulling Cupcake over into the parking area, she went into the restaurant to get an overdue lunch. She felt she was doing OK on time; it was around 1400. Might as well start getting used to using military time now, she thought, because once in the fire environment, that's all that would be used.

The special at the Must Stop Truck Stop today was meatloaf, mashed potatoes, and green beans with a dinner roll. About halfway through her plate of food, Marcy started having a lead feeling build up in her stomach. Concerned she might hurt the waitress' feelings if she refused the Styrofoam clamshell for the uneaten remainder, she took it with her after she paid her bill. There was a trash can out in the parking lot where she could dispose of it without being observed, so she used that.

Back in the saddle again, Marcy slowly steered Cupcake back up on I-80 Eastbound. Not bothering to pick up any speed, she eased onto the next exit for US 95 North. Marcy's lips tightened as she put Cupcake through the gears. Just as she was lighthearted on her morning's trip on US 95 South with an empty trailer and horses to spare, now she was all business - purposely shifting gears as she listened and felt Cupcake pull against the weight. With a load on, Marcy needed to get the big Cummins diesel engine up over 2,000 RPMs before she shifted to the next highest gear, or, shift to a lower gear before the RPMs fell below 1700 RPMs on an uphill climb.

Marcy's years of experience had bonded her to Cupcake. She hadn't missed a gear or needed to look at the tachometer to know when to shift up or down since her teenage years. Still, she couldn't afford to be lackadaisical in her driving nor her maintenance of Cupcake. Most vehicles over 40 years old are in a museum, for show, or in a junkyard. Regular maintenance, attention to detail, and sensible driving had prolonged Cupcake's professional life on the road.

"How bout you Northbound?", came a voice over Cupcake's CB radio.

Marcy unhooked the CB mike and keyed it, "Yeah Driver, Come on."

"You got the Hoosier Chigger Digger here. Northbound 3 miles you got alligators. Watch it", announced Chigger Digger.

An alligator is trucker talk for a piece of tire on the road. They look like an alligator and, if run over, they can bounce up and do damage to hoses or belts, fuel crossover lines, or even to the body of the tractor.

"Yeah. 10-4 on the alligators driver. Thanks", said Marcy.

"What's your handle? Come back." Came the voice over the CB.

"You got the Cupcake here", said Marcy.

Chigger Digger responded, "Roger the Cupcake. That's some paint job. Could've guessed you be a lady trucker!"

Marcy laughed, "yeah 10-4. The paint job made my grandma happy!"

"Haha, your grandmother, huh", came back Chigger Digger. "How old is that truck anyway?"

"Driver, if you gotta ask, it's older than you are youngster!" Marcy said.

"Where you haul'n that iron?", asked Chigger Digger.

"Haul'n up into Shaky on a fire," Marcy replied.

"Breaking up... Catch you on the flip side," was the last Marcy heard from Chigger Digger as the two trucks drove further apart and out of CB range.

Thirty-one miles North of Winnemucca Marcy made a left turn onto highway 140 towards Denio, NV. As the miles disappeared under Cupcake's wheels, Marcy let her mind wander back in time. Having just mentioned to Southbound Chigger Digger that her grandmother Nellie liked Cupcake's paint job caused her to think about her grandmother now and the circumstances in which she was raised.

Marcy's mother, Beth, passed away when Marcy was only 3 years old. Her father, Daniel Portman, was distraught over the loss of his wife. He left in the Diamond Reo taking all the cross-country haul jobs the local trucking company dispatcher would give him. Seldom would he stop by the family ranch to spend time with his daughter and parents. He said it only reminded him of what he lost. After a year of being lonely on the road, he joined the Army looking for relief from his troubled mind. The exact opposite happened, however. In Syria and Afghanistan, he saw things he couldn't unsee and participated in horrific events that never gave him peace. Eventually, he was diagnosed with Post Traumatic Stress Disorder (PTSD), and, after he had served his country for 2 years, the Army gave him an Honorable Discharge.

Marcy wondered what her father was like before the nightmares, or night terrors, that often plagued him. His grasp of reality seemed to ebb and flow. Her memories of her father during the "absent" years were sketchy at best. From the bits and pieces she gleaned from her grandparents and what sometimes "leaked" from her father's rants, she had what she knew was only a partial storyline for her father.

When the Army discharged him, she had this vision of him just standing by the road not knowing where to go. In her mind's eye, she saw him as absolutely and desperately lost. He didn't come back home but found his way into a kind of brotherhood of disconnected war vets. They lived in shelters under a bridge in an isolated part of a National Forest in Northern California. Marcy's grandparents got a cryptic note from him when he was discharged, and then, every few months a phone call or a short note, but they never had a way to contact him or locate him. He was always fine... "yeah. Be home sometime." From these brief scrapes of conversation, her grandparents milked every bit of reassurance they could that their son still knew the way home. It was just enough to keep their hopes alive.

Three years later Grandpa Sam and Grandma Nellie were over the moon when they opened the door at 3 in the morning and found that this long-haired, bearded homeless person standing on their front porch was their son. From the very rare occasions when Daniel spoke of what he calls, "the return to the world", he says he needed to live like that to help him get his head screwed on straight. Even the 9-year-old Marcy could tell her father's head was still somewhat cross-threaded.

Marcy had her father back, but she was never sure what to expect. Daniel didn't seem to know how to be her father. His mood swings and occasional loss of reality made it hard for anyone, especially his young daughter, to get close to him. Marcy already had a man who, for all practical purposes, had been her father and continued operating in that role even after Daniel returned.

As far as Grandpa Sam was concerned, the sun, the moon, and the stars were only hanging in the sky above so they could shine on his granddaughter, Miss

30

Marcy Portman. Sam would move heaven and earth just to see her smile. From the time she was born, she was the apple of his eye, and he gave her the run of the place. Even after Daniel came back into their lives, there was little chance Sam would ever be dislodged from his position. It pleased both Sam and Daniel that Marcy wanted to be a big part of the workings of the ranch.

Daniel functioned well on the ranch. If he could keep his hands busy, his mind would stay idle. If his hands became idle, his mind would get busy, and that was seldom a good thing. When the ranch work was done for the day, Daniel built guitars, even though he was not a very accomplished player. He only went into town to attend "Recovery", a weekly meeting at Bible Baptist Church for people struggling with issues like Daniel's.

Of course, Marcy had her chores to do around the ranch. When she was tall enough to reach the pedals, she would drive the one-ton dually flatbed truck with a load of hay out to feed the cattle in the winter. Work is work and kids are kids. When you mix the two you get some "interesting" results. With 3 or 4 inches of snow, a kid can have a lot of fun at work. Marcy enjoyed cutting "donuts" in the snow by cranking the wheel, punching the gas, and swinging the rear end around. She learned that, by counter steering, she could hold the truck in a controlled sideways skid. It was fun unless you lost the skid and the backend spun out of control spilling a load of hay. Then the fun turned into work loading the hay back on the truck. She learned just how far and fast she could go by trial and error. The biggest lesson learned was what happened trying to do the same thing while towing a trailer. The trailer rolled damaging the trailer tongue and hitch. Seeing dollar signs and a repair bill, Uncle Zach was really upset while Grandpa Sam just smiled and said, "Ah, my little girl!"

As she got older, boys started showing an interest in her; tall and willowy, she was a looker indeed. Her grandmother liked to help her choose what to wear when she had a date. It was like Nellie was finally getting the feminine granddaughter she always thought Marcy could be. On the other hand, when a boy came calling, the first thing Grandpa Sam would do is show off his gun collection. Then he would often point out toward a grove of trees just off the driveway and softly say, "that's where the bodies are buried." It was like he was afraid he might lose his little buddy, so he would try to scare off her suitors.

Marcy and her grandmother had many long talks about her father, her mother, and God. Marcy struggled with how God could love her so much and still take her mother away from her physically and her father mentally. She was just a kid when her mother died and her dad left. How did she deserve that? She couldn't blame her mother or her father as this was way beyond their ability to control. She couldn't blame her grandpa or grandma; they were deeply hurt just like she was. Still. She wanted to blame someone... and that someone should have to pay. So far, the only person she found to be guilty was God. If only God would offer up some defense, she might understand; she wanted to understand. It wasn't that she didn't love and adore her grandparents, but other kids had both parents and grandparents, why couldn't she. It seemed that the empty place in her heart where her parent's love should be would never be filled.

Grandma Nellie often told her that there are things beyond our human understanding. It is alright to question and ask God why. It is normal to hurt because of what has been lost. "There will come a day when all the curtains will be pulled back and what has been hidden from us will be revealed," Marcy could hear Grandma Nellie say. She began to hum an old hymn that had always lightened her spirits:

> Tempted and tried, we're oft made to wonder
> Why it should be thus all the day long.
> While there are others living about us,
> Never molested, though in the wrong.
> Farther along we'll know more about it
> Farther along we'll understand why;
> Cheer up, my brother, live in the sunshine,
> We'll understand it all by and by.

Marcy aspired to follow the one line, "Cheer up, my brother (or sister), live in the sunshine". She tried to be content and wait to understand it all by and by.

Things were different now, that's true. She had Jacody who she loved deeply. Her heart swelled when she thought of him and the life they shared. She used to think when she fell in love and got married, her life would be so complete that nothing in her past would ever hurt her again. Well, it didn't work out that way because the empty place – a term she used to encompass all the disappointments of her youth – was always the same anytime she visited it; hollow and cold. Her life, Jacody, her grandparents, even her father, old Hiram Walker, the ranch, was a love that she would always cherish. It seemed that, as her life blossomed with goodness and hope, she was coming to an understanding, as hard as it was, that if she could go back and change all the sad things in her life, the good things she had now and what she hoped for in the future, would not be the same. And in that difference, would the present be this good? Could the future be this bright? She didn't see how it could be better.

The highway broke into Marcy's reminiscing. The long uphill grade had gotten steeper, and Marcy was continually having to downshift. When Cupcake's speed dropped below 45 mph, Marcy clicked on the hazard flashers and grabbed another lower gear. The big motor home she had spotted far behind her on a previous straight away was now gaining on her fast. There were very few other vehicles on this stretch of Hwy 140 and even fewer RV-type vehicles. This was not the road to Reno, the Grand Canyon, or Salt Lake City. Often when people took this route, they carried an extra can of gas because fill-up opportunities were limited. So, it was with interest Marcy watched the vehicle growing larger in her mirror.

Out of habit, Marcy checked Cupcake's passenger-side mirror to see the same report: the motor home was gaining on them. As she brought her eyes back to the front, they lingered on special parts of the interior of the cab. A Shoshone dream catcher was hanging from the dash, a present from her mother-in-law. The old worn-out seat fabric had been concealed using bright new seat covers with Indian ceremonial designs on them. The seatbacks had a majestic buffalo displayed with eagle feathers on either side. The seat covers were a gift from Jacody. She suspected Jacody's mother helped him pick them out even though Jacody had an artist's eye for composition and color. Wishing she could talk right now to her husband, she picked up her phone to see if there was any cell phone coverage. In doing so, the phone slipped out of her hand. One clumsy fumble for it and it was off her knee and on the floorboard. "Drats!"

Cupcake was holding a steady 40 MPH on the uphill grind when the motor home caught up and passed her. Marcy noticed the home on wheels sported Ohio license plates and was pulling a sick pea-green Fiat behind. She was amused by the bumper sticker on the back of the little car, "I Go Where I'm Towed".

Just over the crest of this incline was a sharp left-hand curve. On the inside of the curve, the mountainside had been excavated to make way for the road presenting a sheer rock wall on the left. The curve itself was banked to the inside to assist vehicles in negotiating the curve. In the winter it was especially important in case of snow or ice, any vehicle that lost traction would slide against the rock wall on the left and not over the drop-off to the right. On the right, just over the crest of the road and before starting a long downhill grade, there was a wide pullover where tourists often stopped to take pictures of the vista. Before the pullover and after the pullover, there were no guard rails on the right side of the road... just wide open space.

With the motor home now in front of her and no one behind her, Marcy started using her left boot heel to fish her phone to a place where she could safely pick it up. She knew there wasn't a "safe" way to do this unless she pulled over and stopped somewhere. There was no place to pull over here, and even if there was, Marcy didn't want to lose Cupcake's momentum on this uphill grade. But if there was a stray cell phone signal out here, along this grade might be the only place to find it.

Determined to have her cell phone if a signal became available, she continued to search for her phone. She had it corralled between the right seat support and her left heel. By quickly ducking down with her head below the dash, she might be able to retrieve the phone in mere seconds. Her first attempt demonstrated how far the seat sat up from the floorboards and how hard it was to swivel her head around the large steering wheel. She was trying to maintain even pressure on the gas pedal with her right foot to not lose momentum coming over the crest of the grade. But bending to the right without adjusting her right leg... was just too dangerous. She was going to have to wait. Well, what if she shoved the phone to the left side towards the door, she thought. She looked between her knees for her phone.

If asked, she would have to admit she was somewhat distracted as Cupcake followed the pea-green Fiat and motor home over the crest of the ridge and started gaining speed. When she did glance up from looking for her phone, instantly she saw nothing but bright red brake lights! Her knee-jerk reaction was to stand on the air brakes. Bracing against the steering wheel with her arms expecting to be thrown forward as the truck slowed up, to her horror, it felt as though it sped up. With all the truck transport tires locked up, it was like sliding out onto a frozen lake.

What happened in the next 8 seconds seemed an eternity to play out; the world had gone into slow motion. Immediately, her experiences, from playing in a snow-covered field sliding around in a pickup, to swerving to avoid road hazards in the Diamond Reo, all came into play. Marcy knew the truck was moving faster with the tires locked up and smoking than it would if she could keep the tires turning just enough not to slide. Easing up on the brakes ever so slightly, she felt control come back into the steering wheel. But the 25-some tons behind Cupcake weren't letting her slow down fast enough. The little Fiat would soon take a front-row seat inside the motor home, thanks to Cupcake. Right after that, if the binders broke, Marcy might have a cat in the cab with her... a Caterpillar dozer cat, that is!

Macy flashed a look to the right of the motor home. There was the vista pullover fully occupied by a long fifth-wheel travel trailer. It had its turn signal on indicating an intention to pull out onto the highway. To her dismay, the motor home from Ohio was coming to a complete stop with its right turn signal on indicating it was going to pull into the vista once there was room. To pass the motor home on the right and squeeze between it and the travel trailer would shoot Cupcake past the pullover out into thin air to the canyon floor far below. Mentally, she rewrote a Bible verse: "It would be easier for a camel to go through the eye of a needle than for Cupcake to squeeze between the motor home and travel trailer and live!"

The only route that had any chance of success was to steer into the oncoming lane. There wasn't any time left! There was no time to see if the lane was clear! Steering to the left, but still on the brakes as hard as possible without losing control of the tractor-trailer, Marcy could feel Cupcake's rear tandem skidding slowly to the right towards the motor home as the trailer tried to maintain momentum in a straight line. Steering gently a little to the right then, towards the motor home, got the trailer back in line behind the tractor.

A bright red pickup pulling a white horse trailer was in the oncoming lane. The pickup driver immediately focused on the huge Diamond Reo chrome grill that appeared to him to be as large as a CSX locomotive and coming at him fast. If the pickup swerved left it would crash head-on with the motor home. To go to the right shoulder he might get T-boned either in the side of the pickup or worse, in the side of the horse trailer carrying 4 horses. It seemed there was no decision space left for the pickup. Its last option, and the one the driver selected, was to continue stopping in the lane it was in and hope the diesel took to the shoulder. The cowboy driving the

38

pickup thought that would be the horses' best chance to survive even if it meant he wouldn't. But, at least, that option freed up the shoulder if the huge truck took it. With that decision and in a split second, the cowboy became a born again Christian! He put a death grip on the steering wheel and stiffened his legs. As he saw Cupcake move to her right slightly and line up with him, trying to keep her trailer behind her, he put no hope in the airbags to save him.

It appeared to Marcy the pickup and horse trailer were going to stay in the oncoming lane. The only option open to her now was to steer sharply left again and hope the lowboy transport trailer and dozer would follow without tipping over and sliding on its side into the smaller pickup truck. The pickup was a fairly new Ford F-350 Maga Raptor. Jacody would love to have a truck like that. It was pulling a four-horse trailer. Was the trailer loaded with four horses? Were the horses injured when the cowboy slammed on the brakes? Were they thrown forward? She wondered how it was when she was driving for her and Cupcake's lives, her brain would drift off and think about the horses, her husband, and what he would think about the pickup she was trying not to destroy! As time stood still Marcy flashed back to Ruby Mountain Equipment Rental and tried to recall if she double-checked the tightening of the rachet binders on each of the chains holding the dozer to the trailer. Would it have killed her if she had added 2 or 3 more binders? No. But it might... be that she didn't.

Calculating the space on the shoulder between the edge of the pavement and the sheer rock wall, she knew she had no room for error! A quick jerk on the wheel to the left started Cupcake towards the rock-cut wall. She could feel the weight behind her shift. The heavy dozer was lifting the left side of the transport trailer and leaning toward the pickup. As soon as the front tractor tires left the edge of the pavement where the grit on the shoulder was loose and soft, she lost the ability to steer. She had to let off the brakes to regain it. It felt like Cupcake sped up as she headed towards the stone wall. Just before impact, Marcy pulled Cupcake back to the right in the nick of time. That sudden shift back to the right stopped the trailer's tilt towards the pickup. The trailer's left side triple tandems slammed back down on the highway only to lift the right side. If the left side tandems hadn't started sliding once it got to the shoulder, the dozer may have caused the tractor-trailer to roll on its left side into the rock wall. As it was, it slid back in line with the tractor. It was a miracle that it didn't tip over.

The travel trailer remained motionless in the vista pullover. The motor home from Ohio got stopped but almost overshot the vista turn in. The red pickup stopped even with the sick pea-green Fiat. Cupcake came to a stop about 200 feet down the road from the horse trailer.

Sharp jagged rocks had come loose from the wall and the rubble lay where the wall and shoulder met. The outside tire on the trailer's rear tandem ground into a large irregular-shaped chunk of rock and ripped the sidewall open. Despite all this, Marcy was able to keep the tractor and trailer in a straight line and bring

40

it to a slow stop well past all the other vehicles. Only then did she feel the full gravity of what she had just taken Cupcake and monster dozer through.

She sat there and listened to the diesel idle. Cupcake gave no indication that she was alarmed at all from being jerked back and forth or that she may have injured 3 recap tires. Marcy set the brakes with trembling hands. Slowly, time sped back up until it reached real-world time. Feeling that there was no way she could have made that many split decisions by herself or maneuvered this big rig and its load through the danger without divine intervention, she gave thanks to God!

The truck's fenders, the side of the sleeper unit, and the transport trailer were sitting inches away from the sheer rock wall. She could open the driver's door a little, but even if she could get out the door, she wouldn't have been able to get to the ground. So she crawled over to the passenger's side and climbed out of the truck onto the pavement. Remembering her culprit cell phone, she crawled back up into the truck, laid across the seats, and retrieved her wayward phone from under the clutch pedal.

Back behind her was the pickup and horse trailer with four horses inside. The cowboy had pulled over onto the shoulder. Across from the pickup, the motor home from Ohio still sat stopped in the road waiting its turn to pull over and take a picture of rocks and sagebrush that would be too small to distinguish on a cell phone picture. A little girl inside wanted to know if they were there yet. The fifth-wheel RV was still waiting to pull out on the highway. They were being held up by an older woman with dyed blonde hair piled high on her head. She was wearing a lavender sequined blouse, bright yellow capris, 3-inch pink heels, and butterfly-shaped sunglasses. In her arms, she cradled a yipping little ankle-biter. She told her husband, "See, Chiffon just needs more time to do her business."

Marcy walked up to the horse trailer to where the cowboy was looking through the sides to make sure his horses were not injured. Marcy asked, "Are you alright? How are your horses?"

The cowboy replied, "I'm fine. The horses appear to be alright too. But I really won't know until I unload them and walk them around a bit. How about you? It looked like you have done all this before! Are you a pro?"

"Sure. Yeah, I'm alright. Almost lost my meatloaf from lunch but that would've been a good thing." Marcy said.

"I saw my life flash before my eyes... and then I saw that dozer almost in my lap go flying by! It was leaning so far over it looked like it was above my pickup's hood!" The cowboy said.

"I'm sure it was a bull ride on the trailer! I think God kept everything in place." Marcy said with a sober tone, then added, "Looks like I've got at least one tire to replace. I hadn't planned to stop in Lakeview, but I guess I will now. I don't know about you, but I'm counting my blessings!"

The cowboy felt like he should do something to help a lady who was out in the desert all by herself, but, with Marcy's reassurance that his chivalry wasn't needed or expected, he got back in his pickup and drove off. Marcy walked back to her rig. At the end of the transport trailer, she climbed up and sat down on the deck. The people with the fifth-wheel travel trailer entered the highway and drove slowly past Cupcake. Marcy saw someone take a picture of her and Cupcake as they drove by. The Ohio motor home pulled into the place vacated by the fifth wheel and its occupants poured out to take pictures of their own.

Marcy took stock of her situation. She pulled her cell phone out of her back pocket and woke it up. No cell phone coverage here. There might be in Denio. She could wait until another trucker came along and call them on her CB. She could have them call for roadside assistance in Winnemucca when they got in range. Chances are it would be late before they could then get back to where she was, and even then, she wouldn't make it to fire camp this evening. With 3 sets of tandem axels on the rear of the trailer, she still had 11 tires to spread and support the weight. With the distance to Lakeview, she would expect a flat tire to heat up and eventually shed the recap tread, leaving an alligator as a hazard for another vehicle on the highway. Be that as it may, to move on seemed to her to be the best alternative. Besides, this mountain pass was no place to change a tire.

For just a little while longer she sat on the transport with one foot dangling off the side and one foot on the deck. She leaned back on the track of the dozer and let her gaze wander off across the canyon. Closing her eyes, she concentrated on relaxing every muscle in her body. On her cheek, she could feel cold air drainage coming from a ravine higher up in the mountain. Just down the road came the squabbling of 3 Robber Jays discussing finder's rights over a small, flattened piece of roadkill. She could hear Cupcake idling about 40 feet ahead. There was a loud hiss as Cupcake's air tanks released excess pressure. That or, it was her way of saying, "We're burning daylight and diesel fuel here!"

"Was it worth it?" she pondered. She felt like she had been gone a week already and it was only this morning that she left. She had been insulted and almost propositioned at Ruby Mountain Equipment, came close to food poisoning at the Must Stop Truck Stop, and, just a bit ago, barely escaped a 4 vehicle crash - 5 vehicles if you count the horse trailer. The little Fiat was too small to count.

She thought of Jacody and the ranch.

"Yep! It's worth it!" she yelled out loud as she jumped off the transport trailer and headed for the cab with resolve.

Chapter Four
Take a Load Off

Close to Denio Junction, NV, Marcy picked up cell phone coverage and was able to get in touch with Big Bud. She told him briefly that she shredded a trailer tire on rocks and would need to get it fixed in Lakeview. He told her he would look up a tire dealer there and send her a text she could get when she got back into cell phone service in Lakeview. That way she wouldn't be held up there waiting for information. She thanked him and headed on towards Lakeview.

The rest of the trip to Lakeview was uneventful. At the eastern edge of town, her cell phone announced she had a text. It was Big Bud with tire shop information. As Big Bud had directed her, Marcy was happy to see Goose Lake Tire Shop right on the highway as she pulled into town. Jose and Arnold,

Goose Lake's finest, had Marcy pull the transport trailer's first set of rear tandem axle wheels on the left side up on wooden blocks. That was to take the pressure off the axel with the tire that needed to be replaced and, hopefully, unloading the dozer wouldn't be necessary.

Marcy climbed out of the cab and joined the two men examining the shredded tire on the transport trailer.

Jose said, "Whoa! Lady! What you did to this tire! It's no good! You off-roading with this thing – you can't do that! Hi! My name is Jose this is Arnold." Arnold grinned and nodded. With hardly slowing up for a breath of air, Jose continued. "We gonna fix you up. Gotta get you to the fire pronto! Arnold, get the jack out here, I'll get the impact wrench."

Jose turned abruptly and headed for the shop with Arnold close behind. "Hi! My name is Marcy." Marcy called after them – her voice trailing off as the distance between them grew.

She wandered along behind the men. Just inside the shop was a door to a small room where customers could wait for their new tires to be mounted. Towards the back and on a counter, she found what she was looking for. Coffee! Mr. Coffee's pot was half full of cold coffee. On pegs behind the coffee maker were several mugs and she selected one she hoped was clean. "Do What You Love" was in bright red letters on the side of the cup she had selected. "Why not?" she thought, "I do! Why shouldn't it be true for a tire technician too?" Pouring herself a cup, she put it in the microwave for a minute to heat it.

Marcy sat on a bench in front of the tire shop. She blew on her coffee to cool it a little and slurped in her first taste. "What week was this coffee made?" was her first thought. Although still bitter, her second taste didn't assault her tastebuds as harshly as the first... and, after all, it was coffee! While she was waiting, she shot Jacody a text letting him know she was delayed but not why. She would fill him in with details later when she called him if, that is, she was able. When she looked up, she noticed a motor home towing a pea-green Fiat glide slowly past. "Now, that can't be good. I hope they head for Klamath Falls and don't turn South!"

In no time, Jose and Arnold came into the shop with the damaged tire. Jose threw the wheel on the "tire-buster", the machine that assists in taking tires off and putting them on, and started prying the old tire off the rim. Meanwhile, Arnold came from the warehouse area rolling a new recap. Marcy got up and followed Arnold into the shop. Tires were stacked in a semi-circle around the tire-buster 3, 4, or 5 tires high. The shop was ill-lit with one bright light right over Jose's workspace. Marcy walked over in the shadows next to a tall stack of tires to watch Jose expertly strip the damaged tire off the rim.

Suddenly, Marcy felt hot breath on the back of her neck and before she could move, she felt something warm and wet wipe against her neck! It startled her so much that she let out a yelp and jumped forward turning around. Her heart was racing! Looking from the bright workspace into the dim shadows, she was just able to see two gleaming eyes staring at her atop a tall square body.

"What in the world....! Marcy stammered.

"Woohoo! Jose yelled, "Arnold, did you see that. Lugnut scared our guest." Arnold nodded and smiled. Jose continued, "Man, she really jumped! Bad Lugnut, bad. What did you do? You didn't lick her neck, did you? Did he lick your neck? Are you alright lady? Come here, you bad boy!"

To Marcy's surprise, a black and white Austrian Shepherd jumped from the top of the stack of tires that had at first appeared to be a square-shaped body, to a shorter stack, then to descending stacks until he was on the ground. He ran over to Jose wagging his tail. The phrase, "bad boy" held only encouragement for him.

"Yes, he did lick me on the neck and, please, call me Marcy." Said Marcy, "But you.... Dog... you are such a pretty flirt!"

"His name is Lugnut", said Jose. "And Lugnut is our junkyard dog. He's supposed to be mean but he's not so much mean as, well, our Walmart Greeter. Lugnut! Sit! Let's show the lady how smart you are!"

Jose held out a closed hand in front of Lugnut. When he opened his hand up, there were 3 valve caps in it. Lugnut barked 3 times. Jose repeated it with 1 valve cap and Lugnut barked once. With 2 caps, he barked twice. Jose could mix it up and Lugnut got it right every time. Jose dug in his overall pocket and gave Lugnut a chew bone.

"Tell me, lady, have you ever seen such a smart dog that lives in a tire shop?" Jose asked.

"No, certainly not that lives in a tire shop, and please call me Marcy," Marcy said.

"Kids come by here now and then just to try and mix Lugnut up, but they can't do it", said Jose. "I tell you, lady, this dog is a genius!"

"Jose, could you call me by my name? It's Marcy." Requested Marcy.

But Jose had already turned back to the tire-buster and was spinning the new tire on its rim.

By 2000, or 8 PM, the tire was on, and the lug nuts torqued to specification. Marcy said, "Guys, I want to thank you both. You did a great job getting me and Cupcake ready to go and back on the road!"

Jose smiled and said, "That's our job lady, we're happy to do it. Cupcake, huh? Yeah, I saw that on your truck. You got a real nice-looking paint job on that big truck. I like it. You see that sweet metallic green 1963 Impala Super Sport? That's my baby! She's the fastest car in Lakeview. Ask anybody. That's right, isn't it Arnold?" Arnold grinned and nodded. "You got a nice truck. I got a nice car. I got a 409 with a 4-barrel carb, 4 speed with a Hurst shifter, Cragar Mags, smooth glass packs. I got custom tuck and rolled interior. I got to get home for supper! Arnold. Let's go buddy! Goodbye lady."

"I'm so happy... for... you," Marcy said to Jose's back as he headed for his car. Marcy held out her hand to Arnold.

Arnold grinned at Marcy and shook her hand.

"Arnold, he's never going to call me Marcy, is he?", asked Marcy.

Arnold continued grinning, shook his head, and said, "No, probably not." He let go of Marcy's hand and followed Jose.

Marcy climbed up in Cupcake's cab and looked out the side window as Jose and Arnold drove by. Jose pushed the clutch in and revved the engine several times just to hear the mufflers roar. From Marcy's vantage, she was looking down on the car as it rolled by. When she saw the graphic on Jose's car's hood – *El Gallo Verde*, it made her smile. "Yes Jose, you are a rooster... a cocky little banty rooster!" Marcy said to Cupcake. "But you are my baby, aren't you Sugar?" Marcy patted Cupcake's dash and the diesel leaped to life.

Once again, she was on the road and headed South into the South Warner Mountains. Marcy was glad she had fortified herself with Goose Lake Tire coffee. Running as fast as she dared at night through the high desert and rock flats, she was always concerned about hitting animals on the road. A large mule deer could do major damage to the front of her truck. She was reminded of a trucker her father told her about who came over a rise in the road and on the other side in the dip of the road was a herd of antelope. There was no time to stop and no way to miss them. There must have been 8-10 animals that were packed under the truck. Air lines and fuel lines were ripped out from under the truck. All the driver could do is coast till momentum all but ended. Then he cranked the wheel to get the truck off the road as far as he could. With no brakes, rolling the truck into the ditch and hoping it would remain in place was the best he could hope for.

Marcy didn't want to hit a herd of anything. So she used Cupcake's secret weapon! Daniel had installed a locomotive horn on the Diamond Reo in an effort to avoid just such situations. It was safe to use the train horn when there was no other traffic, and no houses close by. Did it really clear the road ahead of animals? Marcy didn't know, but at least, she thought it gave them fair warning that something really big was on the way! Besides, it was fun to blow. The sound made you feel invincible – tearing through the night like a mighty locomotive! Another benefit is it can wake the dead if the driver is getting sleepy. She blew it now.

Around 2130 she pulled up to the entrance of the Incident Command Post, rolled her window down, and waited until the camp's security officer walked over to her truck. She asked for directions for equipment staging. The officer told her it was about a half-mile on down the road in Sworinger Meadows, just outside of Journey, CA.

Marcy was always impressed when she first got to any fire camp. Just like this one, Stutler Ridge Fire Camp, within 24 hours, everything needed was in place or ordered and soon would be. Journey, with a population of 238 would explode to 738 or more. There would be a caterer capable of serving however many meals that were needed. If necessary, they could provide as many as 2,000 breakfasts, sack lunches, and dinners a day. There will be a shower unit, a laundry unit, multiple handwash stations, an appropriate number of portable toilets, a fuel truck, vehicles with drivers, water trucks – both potable and non-potable, a medical unit, communications unit, air service management unit, supply unit, mechanic's shop, chain saw shop and multiple offices for all the disciplines. If only every government effort could be as efficient and capable as the Incident Command System employed by fire!

She drove on and, in a few minutes, floodlights in a meadow indicated she had reached the staging area. She was really tired. Her neck and shoulders were aching from being strained. She thought it was ironic as she pulled off the road that the radio was blasting "The Weight" by "The Band".

> I pulled into Nazareth, was feelin' about half past dead
> I just need some place where I can lay my head
> "Hey, mister, can you tell me where a man might find a bed?"
> He just grinned and shook my hand, "no" was all he said

Marcy saw several other transport trucks and pulled up beside one with Big Bud Fontaine Logging on the door. She let Cupcake idle for a few minutes to cool off and then shut her down. She opened the door and slowly climbed down to the ground. Once there she stretched and limbered up her legs. There was no sign of Big Bud's crew; they probably had tents set up over at the edge of the meadow under some old growth Ponderosa Pines. She was in no hurry to join them. Tomorrow would be soon enough...In the morning she would get Cupcake, the transport trailer, and the dozer inspected.

She knew the caterers would be closed for the night but, having been in this situation before when on a hotshot crew, she knew the caterers never like to think of a person going to bed hungry. Walking over to the Ground Support yurt, she asked the equipment manager if he had a driver who could take her to the caterers. He opened the yurt door and called over to 3 or 4 drivers sitting at a table underneath a blue canvas fly, "Who's up next?"

Jeremiah jumped up and said, "Watcha got boss?"

Marco, the equipment manager, said, "This is Marcy. Run her over to the caterers and wait for her to bring her back."

The caterer was located in the parking lot of the Journey Area School. Most of the Incident Command Post was located in the school building itself. Walking around to the end of the 40' semi-trailer van that served as the caterer's kitchen. She went up the steps and opened the screen door. No one was there. So she went to another van attached by a covered walkway. That van appeared to be a prep area. 5 or 6 caterer employees were packing brown paper sacks with lunch items for tomorrow.

"Excuse me!" Marcy yelled to get attention over the radio blasting out Lynyrd Skynyrd's Sweet Home Alabama, "I just got into camp. Do you have any leftovers I could have for supper?"

"Why sure! I'll fix you right up!" said a large, tattooed man wearing a Harley Davidson do-rag.

We've always got something tucked away", and he winked at her. "Just stay put." And he hustled off.

"Okay," Marcy slowly said, not sure how to take the big fellow.

She watched the remaining help passing brown paper bags around the table in assembly-line fashion. Each person put several food items in a bag and passed them on to the next. The last person folded the top of the bag down, taped it shut, and wrote tomorrow's date on it with a permanent marker. They had to have almost 500 lunches bagged before they could turn in for the night.

In short order, Amos, the Harley guy with the tattoos, returned with a Styrofoam clamshell and a paper sack. "I heated up a couple of pork chops, green beans, and mac-n-cheese in the microwave. In the sack are a salad, a brownie, a small box of milk, and eating utensils. Here's a napkin." Amos said.

"Oh my! Marcy exclaimed, "That's more than I expected. Pork, huh?"

Amos grinned big, "You know what they say – when forests burn, pigs die!"

"Yeah, they do say that. And with good reason I guess." Marcy grinned back.

She located Jeremiah and got in his truck. Back at Ground Support, not having any better place to eat, she joined the drivers who were waiting for an assignment. The day's heat was retreating, and the food tasted great. It was a very relaxing environment to unwind in after driving all day. The drivers were from the local area and knew each other. Their laughter, and the sound of a radio softly playing music from John Denver and Marty Robbins, made her feel very comfortable. It made her feel she was going to have a very good assignment on the Stutler Ridge Fire.

Since it was late, she only ate a small portion of the huge plate of food Amos gave her. She hated to throw it away, but there was never a shortage of food for any meal at fire camp. Once back at her truck she dug out her toiletry bag and went to the hand wash station. She brushed her teeth and washed her face.

Back at her truck, she noticed she had 3 bars on her cell phone. Crawling into Cupcakes sleeper, she turned off the cabs lights and turned on one dim light in the sleeper. Once in her sleepwear, she gave Jacody a call and checked in.

"Hello, Sweetie Pie" came the voice on the other end of the line.

"Who is this?", Marcy asked.

"Who do you want it to be?" Said Jacody.

"The man of my dreams!"

"Well, you got the right number then, because that is exactly who you got" Jacody responded, "I'm sitting out on the side porch looking up at that big full moon wishin' you were here! So, how's it going? It's late!"

"Yes, it is late. Things are going better now compared to a few hours ago!" Marcy went immediately to the big dark cloud that had been hanging over her since mid-afternoon. "But, oh my! I need to get to sleep sometime tonight. I don't know if I have time to tell you. About 125 miles out of Lakeview this icky pea-green Fiat tried to run Cupcake off a cliff, but she would have none of it." She began.

"What! Are you kidding me?" Jacody asked incredulously.

"No. But that's just the Reader's Digest short version of it," Marcy said in defense.

She then told Jacody about her trip and what could've been the result had one thing gone just a fraction of a bit different. She left nothing out.

"Jacody, I feel like it was an actual real-life verse that could have been added to that song, 'Jesus Take the Wheel'. Jesus must have been driving – not me, because all through that near-miss, I was thinking of you, I was thinking of our dreams... it was surreal! I was watching myself drive like I wasn't doing it! Time slowed up when I had no time. After everything stopped for me and I was alone, I took some time to talk with Jesus and to thank Him for watching over us; Cupcake, me, the cowboy, and all the other people. I don't know what it is, but I know God has a purpose for your life and mine. We're not here just to put in the time and die."

It was getting hard for Marcy to speak there was so much emotion building up inside her. When this happened to her, she was always reminded of when she was very young, and she would get hurt playing outside. Maybe skinned up her knee and it was bleeding. She wouldn't be crying or anything but when she went into the house and showed Grandma Nellie, when her grandmother hugged her, and asked her what happened, suddenly, the tears would flow, and she could hardly talk she would be crying so hard.

Marcy had taken the events on the mountain in Nevada and tucked them away where she wouldn't have to deal with them at the time. She was surprised how raw her nerves were once she opened the flood gates and told Jacody about it. Now that she was all talked out, she was drained. Sitting in the dark of Cupcake's sleeper unit looking through the cab with the moonlight illuminating Cupcake's hood, all she wanted was Jacody. Since she couldn't have him, his voice would have to do.

"Oh my gosh, Marcy!" Came Jacody's soft voice. "I want to hold you so bad right now! I want to cradle you in my arms and never let you go. I wasn't going to say anything about this... I thought it was just me... but around 6 this evening I was out feeding your old nag..."

"Her name is Avalanche. You can call her by her name." Marcy softly said between wiping her eyes and blowing her nose.

"Yes, well, I was in the barn feeding Avalanche around 6 and I got this overpowering urge to pray. I still had a lot to do, and I tried to ignore it, but I couldn't. I got down on my knees and Chuck and Chew jumped on me and started licking my neck like they always do when they get the chance. I didn't yell at them or try to push them away. I just said, in a normal voice, 'boys give me a minute. God wants me to talk to Him.' It was weird! They both just stepped back, sat down, and looked at me. Well, I didn't know exactly what to pray about, but I said my usual howdy's to Him and thanked Him for stuff. Then words just started coming out concerning you on the road. I begged for your safety and that things would go well for you. And I'll tell you this, reluctantly, I'll tell you this: I cried, and I cried hard. After a bit, I got myself together. I thanked Him for taking such good care of you and watching over you. I thanked Him for bringing us together. When I said amen and stood up, I was exhausted, but I felt strong. I felt kind of confused before and I felt clear after. I had concerns for you before, but I had no worries after. Whatever you were going through, I knew His guardian angel was right there with you. If God be for you, who could be against you? Right? Just like we always say, we can go through anything if we go through it with the Lord."

"Oh Jacody, thank you for listening to God; He is so good. Thank you so much for sharing this with me. I think it is important! I was so busy steering that truck, I might have been praying... I don't know. But now that I know you were, and right at that time, now I understand how that dozer and trailer remained upright even though I thought I steered too hard and they should have flipped. All logic tells me there should have been blood and metal parts strung for half a mile and over the side down into the canyon!"

They were both quiet for a bit. They had both been bruised by the same event, or so it seemed. Marcy, from the memory of the chaotic near-miss, and Jacody, from the memory of surrendering to an overpowering spiritual urge to cry out for something he had no real knowledge of. In the quiet, more was said to each other than if they had been talking.

"So," Jacody said at last, "Are you good? You've had an exhausting day and I know you will be up before anyone else. You had better get some sleep."

"I know. You're right." Marcy said, "I'm tired but I'm not sure I'm sleepy. Talking about the 'Mountain Top Experience', and not the kind you want to have has my adrenaline pumping again. I'd like to talk to you all night, but, I'll be up at 0500 so.... I guess it is goodbye for tonight. I love you."

"Goodnight, dear," came the reply. "You know I love you."

Miles apart but sharing the same moonlight. Miles apart but sharing the same confidence and comfort that love is not diminished by distance. Cupcake's sleeper was really going to feel great tonight! Jacody's bed was going to feel empty!

Chapter Five
The Check In

Five in the morning is too early to wake up! It makes no difference if it is 5:00 AM, 5 o'clock in the morning, or 0500. It's too early even when you are used to getting up at six. Marcy got dressed in Cupcake's sleeper using the dim light from a headlamp. Then she turned on the truck cab's interior lights. Fishing out her toiletries bag, she climbed out of the truck onto the ground.

Marcy had to watch her footing in the stark contrast of the black shadows and the brilliant illumination from the generator's floodlights. Looking to the right without shading her eyes, she was temporarily blinded by the light. Carefully, she made her way to the side of the staging area where there was a row of blue palaces, or port-a-johns, and a hand wash station. The hand wash station was a trailer with rows of sinks on each side and a mirror above each sink. Potable water was stored in a large bladder bag and there was another large bladder bag for the greywater. A portable generator provided energy to run the hand wash station lights and water pump while a propane water heater provided hot water. After a visit to both locations, she returned to Cupcake and stowed her toiletry tote bag.

Last night, Marcy had parked Cupcake next to another transport trailer that was loaded with a tracked tree-feller/buncher, a machine that comes up to a tree, clamps onto the bole, cuts the tree off low to the ground, and stacks or bunches it with other cut trees. The words, Big Bud Fontaine Logging above a picture of a logging truck hauling one huge log was on the tractor's door. A four-door three-quarter-ton red pickup with the same company logo on the side was parked facing the transport. The pickup's tailgate was down, and two men were sitting on it. Another man was standing facing the other two and they were engaged in casual conversation.

"Well, it is time to meet the crew." Marcy thought to herself as she walked over to where they were.

"Hey, Marcy! Big Bud said you were coming to the party." In the light provided by flood lamps on telescopic poles attached to a generator trailer, Marcy recognized Jock Sanders as the speaker. Jock was one of Big Bud's equipment operators. "Good to see you again!"

"Hey, Jock!" Marcy said, "Yeah, same here, and it's always good to see someone you know in fire camp!"

Jock said, "well now you're going to know two more! This is Larry Steuben, he's the other transport driver and he's mind'n the store while Big Bud isn't here."

Marcy nodded and simply said, "Larry," in acknowledgment.

Larry said, "Hell's bells, I'm glad y'all is a woman! Ever since I got up'n seen that gaudy-looking truck with Cupcake on it, thought y'all must be one'uh them queers from San Francisco. But them I-dee-ho plates didn't match up. Get it now."

Marcy stiffened and then forced herself to relax. She didn't want to pass judgment too fast. She'd worked with coarse people before who actually had a compassionate heart of gold. Larry could be one of those.

Jock finished the introductions, "And this is our new feller/buncher operator, Carlos Santana! He's a pretty good...' feller', I might add, even if he don't... ' bunch', much!"

"And I might add, you're full of it Jock!" said Carlos good-naturedly. "Carlos Santiago. Nice to meet you, Marcy."

Nice to meet you, Carlos." Marcy laughed, "Jock, it's nice to know you haven't changed. I learned early to only believe about half of what you say."

Jock feigned surprise, "Marcy! You cut me to the quick! When have I ever lied to you?"

"How about... 20 seconds ago?" Was Marcy's comeback.

"Load up!" Larry boomed, "Let's get sump'un to eat afore they throw it out to the hogs!"

Marcy got in the back seat of the pickup with Jock, Carlos drove and Larry rode shotgun. The parking lot at the Incident Command Post was filling up fast but Carlos found a place and parked. Already at 0530, this place was a beehive of activity, people in green, yellow, grey, or black Nomex pants with yellow Nomex shirts were walking in all directions. Over by the caterers was a refrigerated van and people were picking up drinks, bags of ice, and the lunches Marcy had seen the kitchen crew putting together the night before. The drinks came from skids of water and various flavors of Gatorade that sat between the refrigerated trailer and a large ice container. Some people from the planning shop were over on the platform taping huge maps on the 8' X 8' posting board at the back of the platform. Other people were hurrying to their pre-briefing meeting for the final tune-up of today's plan before the 0600 Morning Briefing.

Marcy and her compadres fell in line with a 20-person Hot Shot crew walking single file to the steps up to the kitchen's serving window on the side of a semi-trailer van. Plates full of food were handed out almost as fast as a person could walk by.

When Marcy got to the window she leaned down and spoke under the raised screen, "Two eggs over easy, please."

No sooner had the words left her lips, than a plate piled high with a chicken fried breakfast steak, 2 eggs over easy, a biscuit with gravy and hash browns was handed to her from a heavily tattooed arm.

"How was your supper last night?" Marcy leaned back down to look into the lighted kitchen again and saw Amos' large grin through a big black beard.

"Oh my! Thank you... it was much more than I could eat! Just like this breakfast. I'll never be able to eat all this." Marcy replied.

Amos laughed, "Just as you come up to the window, just call out real loud, 'Happy Meal!', and we will cut your meal by about half."

"Okay, good to know," said Marcy. "But do I have to yell?"

"No. You don't have to yell, but if you do, then everyone will know a lightweight is coming through, and... we will taunt you!... Eh?... Taunt you?... No? Okay, you're not a Monty Python fan. But do say Happy Meal and you'll not get as much. Now! You're holding up the line Lightweight! Get mov'n!"

"Thanks, Amos", Marcy yelled as she moved on, "Let's do supper sometime!"

Then it was down the steps and into the salad tent to get bacon, salsa, flapjacks, syrup, yogurt, toast, jellies, butter, fruit – fresh and canned -, several kinds of cereal and granola, milk-white and chocolate - juices, coffee, and lastly, napkins and eating utensils.

From there, people moved into a large, circus-type tent that was the dining area. Looking at over 400 some firefighters eating their breakfast, she finally spotted her crew who had gotten ahead of her at the kitchen window. Squeezing around between folding metal chairs jutting out into the narrow aisles she made her way to a vacant seat next to Larry.

It had been a few years since her Hot Shot days, but, so far, everything was much as she remembered. A wave of nostalgia swept over her as she began eating. The memory of four seasons working and

living with the same 20 people on a hotshot crew
certainly left a deep groove in her grey matter. The
odors in the dining tent, the murmur and the press of
firefighters, even the sound of a boom box pumping
the music of Fleetwood Mac's Rumours album into
the tent made her almost believe she just turned 21
again.

She glanced around at the people inside the tent.
Her crew members were different now; older, heavier,
softer in the middle, and more mature than her crew
of old. But the crew of old was here. It just wasn't her
crew anymore. They moved easily like athletes in top
physical shape as they made their way around the
narrow aisles balancing plates of food and drinks.
Scruffy faces, mustaches, or beards - some long, on
the men. Women with hair in a long braid in the
back. Throughout the dining room, there were groups
of people wearing T-shirts of the same design. The
group at the next table wore shirts with Homewood
Hotshots circling crossed Pulaski's on the back.
Sixteen men and four women... a habit Marcy
acquired back in the day... what's the ratio on a crew,
men to women? She always looked at the women.
Did they join in with the laughter and jokes, did they
look happy, were they downcast. Did the women flock
together, or did they seem content to be mixed
haphazardly among the group? She thought of Alantis
who was on the shots with her for almost a season.
Her favorite line to her male crewmembers was, "Men
are pigs. If they aren't pigs, they aren't men." She said
the fact that it didn't bother any of them when she
said it, proved her point. True. A woman on a crew

with a bunch of men has to have a strong self-image and thick skin, but, to her surprise, she found out the same is just as true for a man – they are just really good at hiding their feelings most of the time. She had always kicked against Grandpa Sam when he would say, "a man has a reputation to make and a woman had a reputation to keep." Begrudgingly, she had come to see that that inequity, like it or not, was true. She did, however, change it up a little in the fire environment: "a man had a reputation to make, and a woman had both a reputation to keep and she had a reputation to make." The old axiom still rings true; a woman has to be twice as good as a man to go half as far. She smiled to herself as she added, "fortunately that's not hard!"

One thing did seem to have changed a bit and that was the average age in the dining room had increased. More white-headed people seemed to be in the crowd than she remembered. And more women who didn't appear to be fire line qualified now, or ever. Grandmas and grandpas who could be home playing with their grandchildren were, instead, using their experience and skill to help the fire organization. She could see Grandpa Sam fitting in here, eating more than Grandma Nellie wanted him to, getting another cup of coffee, and carrying it out into the morning darkness to go to work. So, why not these 60-70-year-old kids? No matter the age, fires, and fire camps never slow up for anyone.

Breakfast in fire camp was never "casual". Firefighters were here to fuel up their bodies in preparation for a long, hot, calorie-burning day.

Everyone was shoveling food and anxious to get to the business part of their day. Even the caterer's employees in the dining room tended to their duties with a sense of urgency. When a place at a table became vacant, they were fast to wipe the area down and get it ready for the next person. As necessary, they picked up residue... coffee cups, empty butter pads, and the like, and took them to the trash. For the most part, these employees had an attitude of service that was attractive and contagious. Marcy wondered if they knew how much their attitude improved the attitude of everyone that they were around.

There wasn't much time to catch up on things at Big Bud Fontaine Logging or for idle chit-chat. At 0550 Marcy stood up and announced she was heading to Morning Briefing. Jock and Carlos got up too, and, like Marcy, collected their empty plates, milk cartons, plasticware, and paper cups to put in one of the large trash barrels spaced just outside the tent.

Larry said, "y'all go on, I'm still eat'n; I need ta make me a bacon sandwich ta tide me over til lunch. Sides, if three of us are thar, that should be enuff."

The three BBFL (Big Bud Fontaine Logging) employees headed across the parking lot. They hit the blue palaces and hand wash station. Then they joined the swelling crowd of crew leaders, squad bosses, overhead, and interested firefighters in front of the platform for Morning Briefing. It seemed almost everyone had papers in one hand and a cup of coffee in the other. From memory, she recalled handouts and coffee were usually available upfront at the make-shift stage. Trialing behind several other firefighters who were weaving their way through the crowd brought them to the platform. There, they picked up an IAP (Incident Action Plan) out of one box and a current fire map out of another box. At the end of the platform, from one of two 120 cup coffee urns, they each got a cup of strong black coffee. Carlos picked up two packets of sugar and a little cup of cream, added both to his coffee, and stirred it with a swizzle stick. What fire camp lacks in quality coffee they make up for in quantity! From there they worked their way back to the rear of the crowd trying not to spill hot coffee on themselves or others.

The sharp shadows and contrasting features of the people began to soften as the sky lightened and dawn won out over the generator's floodlights. At exactly 0600, a stout, determined-looking woman walked up the steps onto the platform with a microphone in her hand. Planning Chief Sheila Shelton asked for the crowd's attention, "Welcome to the Stutler Ridge Fire Morning Briefing, Wednesday, July 14th." Once everyone quieted down, she affirmed the Management Objectives hadn't changed since yesterday, but in spite of that, read each one:

> 1. Provide for firefighter and aviation safety by adhering to the 10 Standard Firefighting Orders and Lookouts, Communications, Escape Routes, and Safety Zones.
> 2. Provide for public safety by providing timely public fire and evacuation information.

3.   Confine fires to the West of Jessup Ridge, North of the Falling Water Wilderness boundary, East of Carmel Branch Road, South of Forest Road 283, and West of Hot Forge Road.

4.   Protect known archeological and historical sites along the fire perimeter.

5.   Communicate, cooperate, and coordinate with local public and local, county, state, and federal agencies.

6.   Provide a safe and efficient initial attack on any new fire starts within the current fire area or as requested by local units.

7.   Maintain fiscal accountability and keep costs commensurate with values at risk.

She updated the 3 standard metrics:

1.   From infrared flight last night: 10,900 acre.

2.   Cost: Finance shop is not at full strength yet and is unable to give a running cost estimate.

3.   Personnel: 537

Marcy noted that this information was in the first part of the IAP. The last page of the IAP was an ICS-214, a blank "Activity Log" for those required to keep a log of their daily activities that will be filed in the fire's records. Since Larry wasn't present, at least to her knowledge he wasn't present, she determined that she would make notes on this page to share with him.

One by one, Planning Chief Shelton called on team members to brief the audience on important fire information in their area of responsibility. Night Operations, Day Operations, the weather person from NOAA, the Safety Officer, the Liaison Officer, the Human Resource Specialist, the Medic Unit Leader, the Air Operations Chief, the Finance Chief, the Information Officer, the Communications Officer, the Agency Administrator, and finally, the Incident Commander stepped up on the stage and gave a "pep" talk. He paid the troops compliments on what had been accomplished so far and encouraged them to continue working as a team. His last words before leaving the stage were, "go forth and do great things, be safe and come back to camp in one piece."

All this time, Planning Chief Shelton had been busying herself by hurrying from one speaker to the next to make sure there were only seconds between speakers. Her goal was to keep the briefing under 15 minutes. It was close. Fortunately, everyone followed directions not to tell any jokes... everyone, that is, except for David D'Angelo, the Human Resource Specialist. Now Chief Shelton took the stage again and announced that this concluded the Morning Briefing. "Find yourself in the IAP and go to your respective breakout session with the appropriate Division Supervisor. Structure Protection Group listen up! Structure Protection Group, you will meet with Division Zulu. Any unassigned resources are to come to the platform to get an assignment." There were large letters A, K, and Z on bifold signs set around the outside of the briefing area.

Again the mass began to vibrate as people moved towards their respective meeting places. Marcy had found FLR/BNCH BB Fontaine Logging with Carlos Santiago as the operator on Division Zulu. So she directed Carlos over to the group forming at the Z sign. Meanwhile, she and Jock went up to the platform to talk with the Planning Chief, since they were unassigned.

Marcy introduced themselves to Sheila, the Planning Chief. She told Sheila she arrived late last night with a dozer and hadn't checked in yet. Her resource orders had her transport as E-3 and the Dozer as E-4.

"Oh great! I'm so glad you are here!" Sheila gushed, "We are looking everywhere trying to find some big iron to put on this fire! There are so many fires going on everyone is already out. So you haven't checked in yet, right?"

"No, Marcy said, "We are over in staging. Should I get an inspection first?"

Sheila said, "No, you're already up here so go get check-in started, then get inspected. You can come back by and drop your inspection form off on your way to the line. Do that right after you are finished with your Div Sup breakout. I'm pretty sure we will have you in Division Zulu."

Sheila turned to the next person waiting to talk with her and Marcy and Jock hurried over to join Carlos in the group that will be going up on Division Zulu.

Don Peterson, Division Zulu Supervisor had just finished detailing where he wanted people to be deployed along the division when Marcy and Jock arrived. He was giving specific safety precautions that applied directly to the area people were going to. Immediately after that, the engine captains, hotshot crew leaders, dozer bosses, several equipment operators... everyone going up to the division, turned to head up to the line or finish any preparations they still had to make.

Marcy introduced herself and Jock to Supervisor Peterson. Larry had located them and now, he and Carlos joined them.

"So you are dozer E-4 and you're the feller/buncher E-6! Great!" said Peterson. "Sorry you didn't catch me earlier; I would have introduced you to the other operators. But no biggie! We can do that later on. Dozer E-4. Jock, you're the operator, right? Who's your transport?"

"That's Marcy." Said Jock.

"And the operator and transport for E-6, the feller/buncher?" Div Sup Peterson asked.

"I be the transport and Carlos the operator," Larry said.

"And you are?" Peterson asked, checking off names on his copy of the IAP.

"Uh... Larry Steuben," Larry said.

"I need both E-6 and E-4 up on Drop Point #11," Peterson said. "Larry, what are you hauling the feller/buncher on?"

"I got a Kenworth T680 and uh HD Deckover trailer," said Larry.

"I've got a Diamond Reo C-119 Raider and a lowboy trailer," said Marcy.

72

"Yeah. You should be good, Larry," replied Peterson. "Uh, Marcy. That's a steep long haul up there. We've got one dozer up there already and its transport is back down here. Maybe we should have that transport take your dozer up for you."

"I'm not following your logic here Supervisor Peterson," Marcy replied in an even voice. "You want us to unload my dozer and then load it up on another transport...., and, why?"

"He most likely wants that dozer up thar on the line and not down in the canyon on its head!" Piped up Larry. "That's whut I got out'a that."

"Larry!" Marcy was trying hard not to come unraveled. "If I..."

"No!" Interrupted Peterson, "not at all! Marcy, I'm concerned about a normal highway trailer like you probably have. The road up there is little more than a timber skid trail with hairpin turns. A highway trailer wouldn't be able to make some of those turns and could bottom out on rocks and humps in the road. You can drive it for all I care but the other driver or owner of the truck would have something to say about that. I have no reason to doubt your ability to put that dozer on the ridge! But, I sure can't afford to have that road blocked by a disabled transport trailer!"

"Okay. Gottcha. I guess that makes sense," Marcy, still wanting to pounce on Larry and his smug grin.

"Good deal." Peterson said, "The other tractor is E-1 and should be over in staging. I'll leave it up to you and Jock to tie in with the driver and figure the switch out."

"Okay Carlos," said Peterson, "just as soon as you can, I want you up on Drop Point #11 as well. Check in with the crew leader running a chipper we have there. He'll line you out."

"So! Are we good here?" Seeing only affirmative nods, the supervisor turned and was gone.

"Larry, did you get here in time to hear any of the Morning Briefing?" Marcy asked.

"I got here soon enuff ta see y'all and Jock go'n to breakout," Larry said.

"Okay, I made a few notes if you want to hear them," Marcy said.

"Don't need'em!" Larry held up his hand, "I already knowed all about whut they said. Sump'un bout - it's hot, gonna get hotter and don't back up into nothing. I'd say that be the meat and taters of it all!"

Before Marcy could object, Jock broke in. "So Larry, this rope walks into a bar, and the..."

"Whut you talk'n bout? A rope walks inna a bar! That's wacky!" Larry spouted.

"No, listen! This rope walks into a bar and the bartender says, 'I'm sorry, we don't serve ropes here,'" Jock continued. "So the rope goes out and lays down in the street. He rubs himself up and down, back and forth. He gets all twisted up. Then he walks back into the bar. The bartender..."

"This better be good'un,Jocko," Larry remarked.

"The bartender says, 'Say! Aren't you the rope that was just in here?' and the rope said, 'No, I'm a frayed knot.' Get it?" Jock laughed, "a frayed knot?"

"Jock!" Larry said dryly, "y'all'd be uh better co-median if y'all didn't try ta be funny!"

74

"Well, it was funny when D'Angelo the HRSP told it at briefing just now," Jock said defensively.

"So! Y'all think'n y'all be a Human Resource Specialist AND a co-median at the same time!" Retorted Larry.

Marcy said, "Focus! We've got things to do! Jock, why don't you take Carlos and Larry back to staging so they can get headed out. Once they're set, you can come back to pick me up. Meanwhile, I'll go get us checked in."

"Hey!" Barked Larry, "let me ask y'all... who died un left y'all King 'O the Universe!"

"I think you did, Larry," Countered Marcy, "you did when you checked out at breakfast!"

"Well, news flash fer y'all Miss High Horse!" Snarled Larry, "I'm a far piece from dead! That there tractor and trailer may be yers, but the dozer... that's Big Bud's and Big Bud left yers truly in charge of all his stuff on this fire!"

"Very well boss!" Said Marcy. "What's your orders?"

Larry said, "So, here's whut we're agoin ta do! Marcy, whilst y'all go git checked in, Jock'll take me'n Carlos ta the stage'n area. Then, Jock can come back here'n pick y'all up."

"I can't argue with that," Marcy said, doing her best not to roll her eyes!

"Larry you're such a jerk," Jock said.

"I know," countered Larry. "That'd be one'a my better qualities! Let's go. We gotta find that other driver'n switch that dozer to his rig. Oh! Best swing by the lunch trailer'n pick up lunches, water'n ice fer the coolers. We'll git a lunch fer y'all Marcy; y'all want reg'lar or vegie?"

"I don't have a cooler," said Carlos.

"Hey! Hold on. Don't go off half-cocked." Marcy held them up short. "You know that dozer isn't checked in yet. To be unloaded it has to be inspected first. Larry, you and Carlos get your feller/buncher ready to go. I should be ready to be picked up by the time Jock drops you guys off and gets back to me. I'll get the dozer and Cupcake inspected as soon as I get back to the staging area."

"I knowed that!" Larry retorted, "I wus just trying ta get another rise out'o y'all!"

"Yeah. Right!" Marcy replied. "I want regular and, Carlos, you can sign out a cooler over at supply."

"See you in a bit. Thanks!" Carlos called over his shoulder as the three men headed for the red Big Bud Fontaine Logging pickup.

In less than 20 minutes, Jock was returning to the staging area with Marcy as his passenger. Marcy had him drive to the far end of the staging area where the mechanic had his yurt and service truck set up. There was a large red CalFire Model 34 fire engine parked next to the service truck. Its crew of 5 were standing around focused on their cell phones.

Marcy walked up, and, to no one in particular, asked, "Hey guys, is the mechanic around?"

No one looked up but a voice came from under the fire engine, "I'm under here! Who wants to know?"

"Marcy Portman." Replied Marcy, "I'd like to get an inspection on a transport and dozer when you're able.

"I'm just about done clamping this exhaust pipe back together and then, I can do your inspection." The mechanic replied. "Really, I don't know how you folks ripped this apart, as far as it is from the ground!"

"Yes." Came a monotoned reply from the crew member that had one bugle on his Nomex. "Just another unsolved mystery that will plague us all until our dying days no doubt. Are we ready to go or not?"

From under the truck came the hollow sound of a creeper rolling across a 4X8 piece of ¾ inch plywood. When the creeper emerged, a spry white-haired man with rust from the exhaust pipe on his face and safety glasses sat up and smiled at the engine crew's Lieutenant. "Hit the road, Jack! And don'tcha come back no more! Not unless you need to. I'm always here!"

As if directed by an orchestra conductor, the four men and one woman put their phones down and moved to get in the engine. The mechanic jumped up, bent over, and picked up one end of his sheet of plywood to pull it out from under the fire engine.

Turning to Marcy, he said, "They'd a run over it if'n I hadn't moved it! So you want an inspection, do you? Name's DeLaney McGraffic but you can call me Del."

"Thanks, Del, my name is Marcy, and you can call me Marcy," Marcy said with a slanted smile.

"Aha!" said Del, "a live one!"

Macy laughed, "and, yes I need an inspection. I'm sitting halfway up the staging area. Do you want me to pull it down here?"

"Naw! Just let me get my clipboard and paperwork," Del said, "I'll jump in the back of your truck and we're off!

"I don't think we should...." Marcy began but Del was already heading into his yurt.

Back at Cupcake, Marcy assisted Del when he asked her to. He checked all the lights, turn signals, and meticulously went down his checklist to make sure everything on the transport and the dozer was worthy to have Delaney McGraffic's signature on the form that said the equipment was in good condition and safe.

Marcy said, "Del, I'm impressed with how thorough you are. You looked at everything with such a critical eye, I'm confident our equipment is in top shape and ready to go to work!"

"Funny you should say that!" said Del. "Just this morning I got an email from a young lady who said something of the same thing. Here! I'll let you read it!" Del proceeded to pull out his cell phone and navigate to his email inbox, click on the email he wanted her to read, and hand it to Marcy.

Dear Equipment Inspector/Mechanic,

I'm writing this to first handedly apologize for my lack of patience yesterday as I checked into the Stutler Ridge Fire here in California.

I may have felt that your requests to check the steering (as you crawled under the pickup I am driving) as well as check the tires size, pressure, wear pattern, brakes...etc etc was a little extreme!

I indeed admit that I may have stood over you, slightly irritated and impatiently tapping my toe, as you checked my.... emergency brake, head lights, taillights, reverse lights, blinkers, high beams, low beams, horn, filters, and fluids!

You see, up until today.... when I was sent to what they call "Sprag Spike camp" with supplies, I did not realize just how underappreciated you are!

I will however confess that as I climbed the 20 mile, 4,000ft elevation gain... dirt trail.... with nothing but terrifying cliffs, narrow ledges, rough washboard ruts, hazard trees, switchback corners, and a road so incredibly steep that the only thing you see over your hood is the sky you're now praying you don't end up in....that you never actually crossed my mind.

It is crazy when you're faced with the fact that one wrong move could cost you your own life and even worse the life of someone else.... how quickly you forget to count your blessings and begin to focus on who will be getting what in your final will. (Don't judge me.)

However....

Once I had all 4 tires safely back on the pavement all I could think about was how badly I couldn't wait to get back to camp so I could shake your hand!!

That being said...I'd like to thank you for holding me up at check in and dealing with my annoyed and ungrateful demeanor. Thanks for taking the time to make sure that not only myself...but the safety of everyone out on the lines remains so important to you, that you patiently put up with people like me!

You and all of those like you deserve to be recognized for a job well done!!

Sincerely,
Pickup Driver E-87
*Important Side note: How much would it cost to have you install a new driver's seat in this pickup cause I'm pretty sure by the end if this fire.... this one is going to need to be replaced! ☺

"She called me Dear!" Del smiled, "I haven't been called that since I left home!"

"People seldom thank people who do a good job, but I can see you earned it here because you did an impressive job looking at my rig and, evidently this person thought you did on her's as well," Marcy told Del.

"I haven't looked at the fire map yet," thought Marcy. "But I bet Sprag Spike Camp is on the way to Drop Point #11. I think Cupcake could make the climb... but maybe the Div Sup's plan is for a good reason. It sounds like my transport trailer may be too low to the ground."

Del handed Marcy two copies of the inspections for Cupcake, the transport trailer, and the dozer. To make it easy to identify, Del took out a white shoe polish bottle with a dobber in the top and wrote E-3 on the upper outside of Cupcake's windshield on the passenger's side. Then he opened the door and traced on the inside of the glass what he had written on the outside. If he had only done the outside, washing dust and fire ash off the windshield would have erased it. If he only wrote it on the inside, he may have written it backward as viewed from the outside, so it was easiest to write on the outside and then trace it on the inside. In the same fashion, Del wrote E-4 on Big Bud's shiny, never-been-in-the-dirt-yet dozer's windshield.

This being done, Del started whistling as he strode off towards his service truck. Marcy called out a thank you to him. He waved his arm above his head but didn't look back or break his stride.

"What a good person." Marcy thought.

Marcy spotted Jock walking towards her and noticed an old tall International all-wheel-drive semi-tractor start its engine up; black smoke was blowing from its exhaust stacks.

"I been talking to Ned," Jock said. "He'll be taking our dozer up to Drop Point #11. I didn't mention you might want to drive his truck."

"Oh my gosh!" Marcy blurted, "I should hope not! Why would you ever think that?"

"Well, I don't know... I didn't say anything," Jock said sheepishly. "It's just what the Div Sup said this morning."

"Yeah. He said it, but he was just talking. What he was saying though, was he wanted the dozer up there and he didn't care who drove it up there. My gosh Jock! You know trucks are personal! I'd never let a stranger even start Cupcake up unless I had to!" Marcy said a little more forcefully than she intended. She didn't want to be that demanding.

"Alright already! I said I was sorry and if I didn't.... I'm sorry! Can we drop it?" Jock said.

"We can. I'm a little touchy, I guess. I think Larry got me a little keyed up this morning. I'm still fuming about things he said," Marcy confessed.

"I get that." Carlos ventured. "Larry isn't usually such a jerk. You weren't what he expected, and he hasn't reacted well."

"Was I what you expected?" Marcy asked

"I don't know. I expected someone to be pulling in with a dozer. I hadn't taken my expectation beyond that. If you were a little green person from Mars... now, that would have put me off my feed for sure!" Jock tried to lighten the mood. This was a "feelings" type of talk and he didn't do well talking about feelings. Outside of his wife who always seemed interested in feelings, he didn't know anyone who did.

Marcy didn't laugh at his little green person comment, but he went on trying to untangle himself from this topic. "You know Marcy, there was this old guy who lived up the canyon from us up on the Sawtooth. He said, 'If you don't have any expectations, you'll never be disappointed.' I always thought that was pretty good advice.

Marcy was ready to launch out about what kind of life would it be without expectations, but the old International had pulled past them and was now backing its transport trailer butt to butt against Cupcake's trailer. Brakes set with a loud "hiss", the International's driver came around from the front of the truck and approached them. Marcy wondered as he got closer if Jacody was going to age like this cowboy. She figured in his younger days this guy probably broke horses or rode bulls in the rodeo. The driver had this awkward gate that couldn't be attributed solely to his bowlegs. His face was tanned by the elements and wrinkled. A large white mustache drooped well below his chin at each end and he probably hadn't shaved for a week. A sweat-stained white felt cowboy hat sat on his head. In his prime, he may have been close to six feet tall but now, slightly stooped, he might be five foot nine.

"Hi", clear sky-blue eyes looked up at Marcy and he smiled, "Ned Carpenter, Miss."

"Nice to meet you, Ned." Marcy held her hand out. "Just call me Marcy."

When Ned took her hand to shake, Marcy could feel the years of hard labor common to cattlemen in his hand. She could also feel strength and confidence flowing from him to her. She resisted the urge to hug this man, Ned Carpenter. In him, she saw a younger Sam Portman. A wave of homesickness flowed over her for a moment. She was surprised, not that she was missing home, but that she was missing it so much, so soon... this was just day one!

"The pleasure is all mine young lady!" said Ned. "Now let's get this iron up the mountain!"

Chapter Six
The Track

"What to do, what to do?" Marcy queried to the great big blue sky up above.

She had just looked through the brown paper lunch sack the guys had picked up for her from the lunch trailer this morning before coming back to the staging area. The total calorie count, as near as she could tell, was well over 2,400. For a hardworking 20-year-old on the fire line, it was about right. For a twenty-something truck driver, it was enough for 2 to 3 days of lunches. She hated to throw anything away, so she put what she didn't eat back in the sack. She would ask around and see where a donation box for the local food pantry was located. In most of the fire camps she had been to, the donation box was kept in the Public Information Officer's yurt at the Incident Command Post.

Marcy was sitting on Cupcake's front bumper and leaning against the side of her radiator grill. As she ate a ham and cheese sandwich, she took in the staging area. The way she saw it, the fire camp is like a small mobile city. This side of town is the retail section. She gave each area a familiar name.

Entering on the one-way main street into the North end of Sworinger Meadow, the first shops on the left are Walmart (ballpoint pens, tents, sleeping bags, extension cords, etc.), Lowes (duct tape, plywood, 2x4s, light bulbs, etc.), Tractor Supply (pumps, hoses, couplings, water tanks, etc.), Old Navy (Personal Protective Equipment – Nomex shirts and pants, web gear, fire shelters, etc.), all combined in one large department store called Supply.

On the left is Manpower, or Camp Crew. The folks who work with the Camp Crew are often taken for granted but are just as important as any other unit. They do just about anything that needs to be done. They are the ones who count how many eat breakfast and supper so the vendor can accurately be paid, they record who gets lunches and hands the lunches out. They sweep, clean, and disinfect workspaces. They keep the camp area free of trash and empty the trash containers in the work areas. They manage recycling efforts, help put up yurts and take them down. These crews are often young people dispatched from reservations through BIA (Bureau of Indian Affairs), Crusade for Christ, or a locally organized group.

Continuing down Main Street, on the left is Enterprise Rental (loan out pickups as requested), Luxury Limousine Service (vehicles available with drivers), and Two Men and a Truck (hauling service). These businesses fall under the umbrella of Ground Support.

Still on the left side next to Ground Support is Tow Mater's Repair Shop. That's where the camp's master mechanic, Del McGraffic's work area is set up.

Most of the right side at this point in the meadow is where all the transports, water trucks, dozers, excavators, skidgins, skidders, and the pickups associated with them are parked when they aren't up on the fire line. Marcy named this area Stutler Ridge Equipment Center.

Remaining on the right side and past the Equipment Center is Timber Jack's Repair Shop. Marcy could see the proprietor working on a chainsaw; a big burly man with a long black beard wearing a red MAGA hat. A flag hung from each of the two tall teepee poles that supported the front of his shade screen. The one on the left flew the American flag and the one on the right had the MIA-POW flag.

At the end of the row of businesses on the right side is Sparkly Clean Car Wash, commonly referred to as the weed wash station. The purpose of the Car Wash is not to wash cars, but to remove any seeds that may be trying to hitchhike out of the area. It is an attempt to avoid introducing non-native plant species into other parts of the country.

Finally, on the left again and just before the exit, is Chuck Mansfield's Shell Station. He maintains a fuel truck for all the firefighters' vehicles. The support vehicles for heavy equipment generally have fuel cells

and they fuel up dozers and the like out of them
without depleting the fuel at Mansfield's station.

Groups of colorful individual tents belonging to
those who work out of the various shops, or yurts, are
pitched back behind the yurts. There are crew tents
crowded along the major irrigation ditch that feeds
into the West side of the meadow. Across the ditch, is
a barbed wire fence that keeps livestock and
firefighters alike from getting into the alfalfa field.
The shade from willows and Cottonwoods growing
along the fence line provide opportunities for a break
from the intense heat of mid-day.

Her survey of the area was completed, and she
didn't see anyone she could help or anything to get
involved in. "It's a lot like the Army," she supposed.
"Hurry up and wait! It must be a good time to walk
off that lunch."

Marcy got up in Cupcake's cab, reached around
into the sleeper, and came up with her CrossFit shoes.
Patting Cupcake's front bumper, she walked over and
got in the BBFL pickup. Moments later she was
parking in the school's parking lot. Behind the school
was the ¼ mile track.

Marcy walked through the gate and over to the
bleachers. She was just lasing up her shoes when
Planning Chief Sheila Shelton walked onto the track.
They waved at each other, and Sheila waited for
Marcy to join her.

"Hi, Sheila!" Marcy said, "you trying to get some
laps in?"

"Yep! Come join me." Sheila said. "Several of us
try to walk off some lunch right after our Command

and General Staff Meeting at 1200. We're usually done with the meeting by 1245 or 1300. The others that usually join me must have gotten pulled off with some task or another."

"Those big lunches weren't a problem for me when I was a shot," Marcy said. "But sitting around waiting for some action with a dozer is going to turn me into a slug if I don't walk it off!"

"Haha! How do you think most of the Incident Management Team members got to be the size we are?" Sheila laughed. "Most of the people on the team eat a meal and then snack until the next one! At least, if I'm not careful, that's what I do."

"So, tell me, I'd be interested to know. How did you get to the Planning Chief level?" Marcy asked.

"You know, sometimes I ask myself the same question! "Sheila said. "When I started with the Forest Service as a firefighter on an engine out of high school, it was just for kicks until I figured this whole 'rest of my life' thing out. We had a lot of fires and overtime, so I did pretty well. With no time or reason to spend any of it – no bills, little food to buy, no rent – I saved a lot of money, but then spent it all during the off-season. The next year I was more responsible and serious about the job. I worked harder and enjoyed it more. So, by the 3 rd. season, I was given my own engine. I was an engine boss for 3 years. That went well and I was promoted to an Engine Strike Team Leader. 2 years later I was working as a Division Supervisor. Then I worked as an Operations Section Chief Trainee for two years before being a full-fledged Operations Section Chief. A couple of years later and I'm a Planning Section Chief trainee. A few seasons later and I'm signed off as a fully qualified Planning Section Chief. That was a couple of years ago, but it seems like only yesterday my parents were saying, "you better go to college and make something of yourself!"

"Haha!" Laughed Marcy. "That sounds familiar. It's what my in-laws told my husband when he announced he was going to work on a hotshot crew when he got out of the Marines. What do your parents say now?"

"Oh, they brag about me now!" Sheila said. "My older sister took their advice and got a degree, met a guy her senior year, got married, and moved to Kansas City. Her degree is in Oceanography and hasn't been near an ocean since! I do envy her though. Maybe if I had gone to college as she did, I'd have met my soul mate and I'd have a family to go home to in-between fires. I have 2 nieces and a nephew that I think the world of. I think my life would feel complete if I had children like hers."

Marcy said, "It's not healthy to dwell on 'if's'. You seem to love this work or you wouldn't put up with all the inconveniences – pit toilets and sleeping in a tent on the ground. Hopefully, if you went to college, you would have a job you love, but it probably wouldn't be this job! You will never know what the outcome would be if your - 'if you'd gone to college'- came about and was the path you had chosen. But it is easy to think it would have been better when you focus on what you don't have. One thing you don't have is a mate wanting to know if you're going to come home or extend for another week with the team. You know it is hard for marriages to survive in your line of work."

"Oh, I know. And most of the time I remain positive. I still would like the opportunity to try. I'm tired of it being only me.... I want...." Sheila fell silent.

"Well, yes, having a family can be important," Marcy said. "And it is possible to do what you do and still have a successful home life. People do it. And for you, I believe it could still happen. Things often happen when you least suspect it."

"Easy for you to say! I believe I heard you mention a husband," Sheila said without malice. "And I gotta tell you, I've been 'least suspecting it' for such a long, long time to where I wonder if I'm suspecting in the right direction!"

"But you impressed me this morning at the briefing," Marcy said, choosing not to respond to what Sheila had just said but making a note to remember it for later perhaps. "You stood up in front of all those people and spoke just like you are speaking to me now... like there weren't 300 pairs of eyes on you carefully listening to you. You directed everyone when to speak, how long to speak, and then closed it out like it was nothing. Everyone, including the Incident Commander and the Agency Administrator, followed your direction. I don't know that I would ever be comfortable trying to do that."

"That's the easy part of my job!" Sheila laughed. "Pulling all the parts of the puzzle from the people who have them to make a workable plan is the hard part. And if things go to hell in a handbasket, you know who gets the blame! It's not the weatherman!"

"I can see that, for sure," Marcy commented, "that is world-class responsibility, I can't see myself doing that either! But having to talk to large groups of people like you do would be my demise. I think you are amazing!"

"Thank you. I know some people would rather take a beating than talk in public." Sheila went on, "but maybe because when I was in school, I realized that the only time people seemed to listen to me or even notice me was when I had the opportunity to get up in front of the class and talk – a book report, some assignment, an announcement, it didn't matter, I ate it up. People listened to me."

"That sure wasn't me," Marcy said. "You may not have noticed but I'm a little bit over average height."

"Gee! Now that you mentioned it...." Sheila's voice drifted off.

"In school, I'd do anything to avoid being noticed. I was hitting 6 feet tall in the 8th grade!" Marcy moaned. "I went to a Jr. High School dance with a boy who was 5'4". Can you imagine slow dancing and I'm looking over his head like he's not there?

"Well let me ask you this," Sheila said.

"Is it about being an Amazon?"

"Uh, no," said Sheila.

"Is it about how hard it was to get all that blue paint off my skin when they shot 'Avatar' the movie?"

"No! You're making me laugh! I'm trying to be serious here!"

"Ok," said Marcy. "But when it comes to my height, this is how I deal with serious. What's your question?"

"You went to a dance in the 8th grade with a boy. I bet you had a date to the prom. You probably had a date for all the school dances. You mentioned your husband. How much taller are you than him?" Sheila's voice kept getting quieter, "You found someone to love. As ungodly tall as you are, and I mean that in the best way possible, you found someone who would marry you."

"Oh, 'as ungodly tall as you are', Sheila," Marcy put an arm around Sheila's shoulder and squeezed her. "You and I are going to be such good friends!

"Well, you started it!"

"Look. I'm sorry. Here I am going on about poor me while you are the one feeling low. You know you can talk to me. Even though we just met, I hope you can trust me to be a friend."

"No. I'm sorry." Sheila said. "The truth is, I have been thinking about my well-educated-for-no-good-reason sister and her family. I thought that by now, I would have a family. I've always been able to imagine myself with two or three kids. I guess I'm having a harder time imagining I would have a husband, you know, a man that really loves me for me, and I would love him for him. I used to... but not so much anymore."

"Humm, that's sad.

"In school, all the girls acted like Barbie Dolls..."

"I know! All for stupid boys..." Marcy blurted.

"I didn't know how to do that, and I wasn't good at pretending. I was the one that people gave notes to, you know... to pass on to that cute guy or that cute girl. Sometimes I'd read them first and imagine they were about me."

"Oh, you're gonna have me in tears."

"It was just lame kid stuff, but I wanted some of that lame kid stuff too. You might have been taller than people in school, but I just happened to be stouter, stronger, and maybe more determined than most of the boys in my class growing up. I think they all had indelible memories of me beating them up in grade school. My guess is those memories lingered on into high school. That's not the kind of respect a girl wants from a guy – 'please don't hit me!'

"No, yeah, I get it!"

"But here I am now at 37 and at this age, I see the guys getting out of shape. I bet I can take them on at arm wrestling and still win! Just like in grade school! What a blessing, eh? Full circle!"

Marcy sucked her breath in, and said, "Well, it takes 11-13 years to get into Junior High and the rest of our lives to get out!"

Sheila went on, "again, I'm sorry. I guess I'm just really having a pity party for myself. I didn't mean to burden anybody with my pathetic life story."

"Mercy me, Sheila! Marcy said, "Here you are at fire camp. Who do you usually confide in here, or, at home for that matter?"

"Well, let me count them up.... None. No one. Here or there."

"Hmmm. Perhaps we should do a CISM, you know. Critical Incident Stress Management?" Marcy suggested.

"Oh my god no!" Sheila blurted out. "I'm shocked that I told you as much as I have. Trust me! This is not like me. I don't know why I opened up and told you these things so easily. I feel bad now."

"Oh, please don't feel bad."

"Well, I do. I've just been going on and on and on."

"Come on. You know, there's no condemnation coming from me. I can feel your pain."

"Thank you, but..."

"No, I'm not in your shoes, but listen - you mentioned your parents and it seems they care about you and want only good things for you. All my life, I have been envious of people who had both a mother and a father. My mother died physically when I was 3."

"Oh!"

"At that time, my father died mentally to me... not me to him, but him to me."

"You mean he just abandoned you?"

"No, he left me with wonderful grandparents, but I feel like I actually hungered for my parents. Maybe because I didn't know what having two functioning parents would be like and my imagination made the idea bigger than life. But I thought how wonderful it would be to have the very woman who gave birth to me wrap her arms around me and hold me close to her breast and say she was so happy I was her little girl....no matter how tall I got."

"Now your gonna bring me to tears! That's so beautifully sad."

"If only my father could have held on to me and reassured me that even though we both lost my mother, I would never lose him. How my heart longed for that."

"I can only imagine I would too. I talk to my mom on the phone all the time. Sometimes, when dad knows it's me mom is talking to, I hear him yelling 'I love you, Sheila!'"

"Awww. That's so sweet! My grandparents and I love each other dearly, but I have lived my life feeling incomplete. If one of my friends would say something horrible about their parents, even though I knew they didn't mean it, I would burst out in uncontrollable tears. I would never explain why, so no one ever knew how empty I was. They just thought I was an overly emotional girl."

"Yeah, I can understand that if you never told anybody. What else would they think?"

"As a grown woman – I don't expect to get any taller – I thought having a husband would fill that void. My husband is great. But he's not my mother. My father is back in my life, but he doesn't function as an emotional father. So, while I can't say I know exactly how you feel, I can tell you hurt, and I know what it is like to hurt over things you feel you have no power to change or to make better."

There, in the middle of lap 3 or 4– they lost count, they hugged each other and cried. Spent, they dried their eyes and walked on. There was an uneasy quiet between them now, they were strangers, but knew more about each other than many long-time friends know about each other.

The hot dry wind was blowing right in the faces. Marcy could feel it sucking what little moisture was left in her lips, right out. She reached in her pocket for her lip balm. "Should she offer some to Sheila? Ew! What was she thinking?" she thought. The silence was deafening. Three California scrub jays were making a racket under the bleachers as they walked by. The camp robbers had probably found something in the trash the camp crew had yet to pick up.

"Hello ladies, mind if I join you?" Nearing the entrance gate they were greeted by another team member.

"You're getting here late," Sheila said. "I've got time for maybe one more lap. Fall in and try to keep up! Marcy, this is David D'Angelo, our Human Resource Specialist. David, Marcy uh, Marcy, well! Good gravy! I don't remember your last name! How awful!"

"Hush!" Marcy said, "That's understandable. Nice to meet you David, Marcy Portman. Portman when I'm working and Jones when I'm not. I drive a transport and the truck is registered under Portman and the marriage license is under Jones."

"You just gotta keep throwing that husband thing in my face don't you!" Sheila joked.

"Oh, don't make me feel bad. I don't mean to make you uncomfortable!

"Come on, you know I'm only joking," Sheila came back. "So, David. What horrendous onslaught of unhealthy lack of mutual respect have you saved our firefighters from today? What tied you up; did you have to fill out a sniveler's report or a whiner's report? Somebody hear a discouraging word?

"Funny you should ask, Sheila. This is something I've been working on since we got here," David said confidentially. "I've been able to determine that Eric Clapton actually played on the original recording of the Beatles' song, 'While My Guitar Gently Weeps'. The only thing left to find out now is who played bass on the same recording. Do not share that information with anyone!"

Sheila said, "and you want me to keep that a secret?"

"Well, you do know what a secret is don't you?" David asked.

"Yes, I do, but I have a feeling you are going to tell me anyway! Sheila said.

"Of course I am," David replied. "A secret is something you tell... one person at a time."

Sheila said, "Marcy, can you believe this guy. This is who we trust to protect our moral high ground. He's the one who makes sure no one is offended or feels bullied, mistreated, marginalized, or insignificant. It's a wonder the whole camp isn't at each other's throat... or, at least, at his throat!"

Marcy laughed, "David that was a funny joke you told at the morning briefing. I hope people got your message."

"Had you ever heard that joke before? I've been using it for I don't know how long."

"No," Marcy said, "I hadn't. But some guys were talking behind me this morning at briefing, and I heard one tell the other that you used that same joke 2 years ago when he was on the same fire as you. The other guy said if they stick around long enough, they might get to hear you play your harmonica! What's that all about?"

"Oh yeah," David said. "I have to get special approval from the Incident Commander to play my harmonica. There are a few people who think I'm trying to be an entertainer, present company excluded, and I learned years ago you never want to blindside the IC. So I have my HRSP message in the IAP that has a picture of a harmonica and text that says: 'How you talk to others is like music coming from you. Make your talk a happy talk that people will want to hear again.' Then, at morning briefing, without saying good morning or anything, I walk out on the stage and slap a harmonica on the microphone and let go with a little 'Joyful, Joyful'. It shocks people awake and at first, they don't know what to make of it. But they do pay attention."

Sheila said, "I'll say! I know when he's going to do that and I use my phone to video the crowd. You can get the weirdest expressions!"

"When I finish, before they can start clapping, and if they do clap I think it is because they are glad I have finished... but before they can start to clap I tell them I didn't do that to entertain them. I did it to make a point. The point is, I had the option to choose any kind of song I wanted. I could have played a 'tears in my beer' song, a funeral dirge, or I could have just played a long boring single note."

Sheila said, "Kind of like our Finance people at morning briefing reminding us to get our time turned in – waaaaaaaaant yoooour tiiiiiiime!"

"Sheila! I want to see you in my yurt to watch a PowerPoint on remedial mutual respect!"

"Ha! You'll get no respect from me, Sir!"

"Quiet! Where was I!

"Something about choosing a song... a single note... maybe." Offered Marcy.

"Oh yeah. But I purposely chose a happy uplifting song, one that maybe you would like to hear again. How you talk to others is like a song coming from you and you can choose, just like I did here with my harmonica, what kind of song you want others to hear when you talk to them. You may have noticed there was a note or two that was off; that was just not right."

"You're not right. Not right in the head!" Joked Sheila.

"Hush!" David continued, "I hope you can overlook my errors in playing the harmonica. As you talk to people you may notice some of the things they might say are a little off; not quite right. I hope you can give them the same grace I'm asking you to give me. And that, Marcy, is my harmonica Human Resource Message."

"Wow! I've never thought that what I say to people could be compared to a song," Marcy said. "There are some kinds of music I can only listen to for so long and I have to turn it off. Then there are other kinds I can listen to all day. Like, I never go through the radio station trying to find elevator music. Music like that can lift you up one minute and let you down the next.

"Oh! Now that, that right there is good! Can I use that the next time I do my music message? Elevator music lifts you up one minute and down the next. Up and down, up and down. I know people who talk to you just like that! Why can't they always be up? They have the power to decide! People are uncertain about you if you are "Elevator' music!"

"Marcy, you are no help at all!" Sheila exclaimed. "I only allow each speaker a minute and a half... except for the Ops people, they always need a little more time... and when this guy plays his harmonica, he goes to about 3 minutes. You just gave him 15 seconds more that I have to compensate for somehow!"

At that moment, Marcy felt her cell phone vibrate and she heard her In-A-Gadda-Da-Vida ring tone. She pulled her phone out and saw the call was from Big Bud Fontaine.

"I've got to take this. You guys go on. I'm gonna bail on you for now."

Chapter Seven
Pinecone Assassins

It was Big Bud Fontaine on the phone. As usual, he was all business and in a hurry. He explained to Marcy that her low boy transport trailer did not meet the specifications of the equipment he had signed up with VIPR (Virtual Incident Procurement), the process the government uses to get the equipment they need on an incident. He would still pay her as agreed but since she wouldn't be able to move Jock's dozer from place to place on the fire with her trailer, he had located another trailer for her to use. Through his timber associates, he had found a high deck trailer that did meet the VIPR contract specifications, and he wanted her to go pick it up and use it.

Marcy was happy to have a mission. She was not one to sit idle waiting for something to do. This was a 70-mile trip to a timber sale and, with a trailer she could use over the rough, uneven dirt access roads around the fire, it meant she could be more useful. With any luck, this trailer pick-up should be a quick turn-around. She plugged the destination coordinates Big Bud had given her into Google maps and was off to find one Mr. Tim Hutchinson, her contact person with the high deck trailer.

She was watching her map app and clicking off some landmarks: there, rising out on the sagebrush-covered valley floor to her left was Rattlesnake Butte – a nice place for a picnic, she was sure. Then Kelly Hot Springs with steam rising into the air even with the air temperature in the high 90s. If she blinked, she would miss the small community of Canby. Now, turning to the North up Howard's Gulch towards Klamath Falls, OR., the grade leveled off on a huge plateau that dominated the landscape.

Once up out of the gulch, she turned right off the highway onto a gravel road. Big Bud had told her this was the Devil's Garden, called that because there was nothing for miles except juniper, stringers of Ponderosa Pine, White Fir, Incense Cedar, and rocks - rock flat after rock flat. No one made their home there in times gone by and no one lived out here now. The Indians said that, once you walked out in the devil's garden, the devil would rearrange the rocks, which were the landmarks, making it hard to find the way back out again. Seeing it firsthand, she could understand how a person could get turned around if they were not familiar with the roads. Traveling cross-country on foot would be a real challenge over the near pancake-flat high plains and only being able to see from one stringer of timber across a rock flat to the next. It did seem like an enchanted landscape that continued on and on without end.

Marcy paid extra attention to her GPS and eventually arrived at the coordinates Big Bud had given her just past the intersection of Hackamore and Boles Roads. Up ahead was the log landing she was looking for. At the far end of the landing, she saw the likely transport trailer, but it was hooked up to a tractor already. There were several pickups, a car, and a log loader next to a very tall deck of logs. She set the brake on Cupcake and climbed out to see if anyone was close. Marcy loved the earthy smell of the forest, but something very unearthly happens on a log landing when clay, pine needles, branches, and water get mixed like ingredients in a mortar and pestle by the constant churning of the ground by skidders. She knew of no words to accurately describe the abhorrent odor. "Baby poo" was the only thing she could think of. Getting past the offensive odor, she strained her ears to hear off in the distance one or two chainsaws and maybe a skidder. She walked past the loader and was just stepping around the log deck when she heard a gunshot just off her right shoulder. It startled her and she immediately dropped to one knee straining her eyes in the direction of the gunshot. Not seeing anyone and a little unsure of herself, she called out, "Hello!"

Ahead and to the right of her, A man stepped out from a grove of old-growth pumpkin pines. He looked around trying to locate the interloper. After a bit, he saw Marcy kneeling by the log deck. He smiled real big and waved. "It's okay! Friendly! Friendly!" he shouted as another man stepped out beside the first. "We're just shooting pinecones!"

Both men had hard hats on and wore identical grey "logger" zippered shirts. The man with the pistol was maybe 6 feet tall with shaggy blond hair and a beard. She thought he might be in his late thirties or early forties. The other was around 5 foot 9 inches tall and clean shaved. There was no hair sticking out from under his hard hat. Marcy imagined it was shaved or the man, in his late fifties, was bald. He was a stout, barrel-chested man with a round face.

Marcy sighed and stood up. The two men approached her as the blond-haired man holstered his pistol. It looked to her to be a 9mm Glock. "Hello, would either of you two be Tim Hutchinson?" she asked.

"No," the man with the Glock answered. "I'm Jimmie Lee, I run the loader and this is Omar Goodlord, the Forest Service Sale Administrator. Tim is out on the skidder bringing some logs in. I'm waiting for a log truck to come in to be loaded."

Omar said, "I'm waitin' to chew on Hutchinson's ear myself! You may have to get in line. What are you doin' running around out here in the woods all by yourself?"

Omar looked at Marcy in a way she liked to describe as "He gave me the stink eye!" Normally, standing out in the woods with two strange men with absolutely no one near who might hear her should she need to yell for help would cause her to be just a little cautious and nervous. To be standing out in the woods with two strange men, one of them armed and

104

the other asking if she is all alone and looking at her with one eye squinted and the other wide open, well, that should be enough to make her jump out of her skin. She didn't know about the younger man, but the older, gruff talking man struck her as having a guardian complex. He would do her no harm. She was willing to trust her gut on this.

"I'm Marcy Portman. Big Bud Fontaine Logging made arrangements with Mr. Hutchinson to use that transport trailer back there on the landing, at least, I think that might be the trailer. I'm here to pick it up."

"What you got to pull it with?" Omar wanted to know.

"I got a semi-tractor on the other side of this deck to pull it with," Marcy responded.

"Well, Tim just left on the skidder, and it'll be a bit before he gets back," said Jimmie Lee. Turning to his shooting partner, Jimmie said, "Omar, you've got 4 shots left and 5 cones on the log. If you quit now you owe me $4. If you go back and get a cone with each of the bullets you got left we break even cause I left one. Let's go before a truck or Tim gets here!" The pair turned to go back to their sport.

With nothing else to do, Marcy trailed along behind them. On the other side of the grove of huge Ponderosa Pines, the "Pumpkin Pines", and a thick dog hair patch of young pine seedlings, Marcy saw an old-growth pine that had blown over. Omar's 5 pinecones were set up waiting for him.

They were shooting from about 15 yards. Omar did pretty well but he missed twice and had to give Jimmie a dollar. Jimmie made a big deal out of it, but it was obvious it was all a part of a game they played often.

Jimmie turned to Marcy and said, "so, you got any money? I think I've taken all of Omar's lunch money his mother gave him!"

Omar replied, "I've still got ten dollars that say I leave with some of your money in my pocket!"

"Yeah, this looks like fun!" Marcy said.

"What! We've got a player here! Baby needs new shoes and I'm gonna buy 'em tonight!" Jimmie said excitedly.

"Naw. That just doesn't seem right." Omar said. "Don't let Jimmie take your money."

"Oh, we just met and now you want to be my daddy and tell me what not to do?" Marcy laughed.

There was that stink eye again, "Listen! I raised 3 kids meaner than you! I blistered their butts when they needed it and I'll blister yours too!"

Jimmie laughed, "don't you believe it. He might'a been tough on his boys but that daughter of his led him around by the nose! But he's right. You don't have to prove anything to us. So you drove a truck up here. You seem to know your way around. Maybe you are a better shot than me. Look, I'm not really that good. I only got this gun last week and Omar had to show me which end of the gun to point at the target."

"Now, you're just trying to get me to double the bet, aren't you?" Marcy asked. "But you should be careful who you bet with. I bet I could clean your clock on Call of Duty any day. Shooting pinecones can't be much different, can it? So if you think you can shoot better than me let's make it $3 for cones left standing!"

This time the stink eye was turned on Jimmie, but now it came with a sly smile.

"Okay big talker! So you're good on a video game." Jimmie said, "but this ain't no video game and this ain't my 8-year-old son's gun. You're on!"

"Good deal! Set the cones up and I'll be right back." Marcy said and turned to go back to her truck.

When she returned, Omar and Jimmie had 2 groups of 10 cones set up on the bole of the blown over old-growth pine.

"Uh-oh!" Grinned Omar when he saw the Smith & Wesson 45 strapped around Marcy's waist. "I think we may have been played, or, Jimmie, you have been played, to be more accurate! Hardy-har-har-har!"

"Hold on Omar, you old cuss!" Jimmie responded. "Give the Devil his due! I'm just getting warmed up. You wanna couple of practice shots before we get serious little lady?"

"I didn't need a couple of practice shots when that guy tried to break into my truck and I was in it and I don't think I need any now!" Marcy came back. "Go ahead.... Take your best shot!"

"Oh no, ladies first!" said Jimmie.

Marcy smiled and drew her pistol as she was turning to square her shoulders with the target. No sooner did her pistol come up in line with the pinecone on the extreme left did she squeeze the trigger. The cone exploded and the dust drifted off in the slight breeze!

Omar said, "Jimmie, just give her the $30 and save yourself any more embarrassment!"

After the last shot was fired, Jimmie gave Marcy a $10 bill and told her to keep the change.

"Omar, do you need any lunch money?" Marcy asked Omar.

"I don't take money from strange women!" Omar was smiling but he gave her the stink eye anyway.

"Aw, I haven't been called strange in a long time, how nice!" Marcy said.

Jimmie said, "Alright, alright! Enough of that! Let's see about that trailer."

The three of them went around the trailer looking at the fifth-wheel hitch, the air hoses, and checked the tires for wear. They chocked the wheels, dropped the landing gear, and unhooked the fifth-wheel. Agreeing all was in good shape, Jimmie started up the Freightliner and pulled the tractor over to the side. Marcy backed Cupcake up to the trailer and Jimmie hooked it up. Marcy attached the air hoses while Omar cranked up the landing gear. They threw the chocks and blocks onto the trailer.

Marcy became aware that what had been a faraway humming sound was now growing increasingly loud. Soon after, a skidder appeared from behind the high deck of logs. Even sitting still, skidders were the very image of a mechanical beast; a dozer blade for smoothing landings and skid trails on the front, four massive wide tires - each wearing thick heavy loose chains, and an arch on the back resembling a scorpion's tail where the winch lifted the near end of logs to keep them from plowing into the ground. The fat tires rose a foot or more above the floorboard of the cab giving it the look of a giant-sized child's toy. In action, it had no resemblance to a toy, however.

Coming into full view, Mr. Hutchinson's head bobbed around like he was a bull rider on a killer bull! The three observers held their ears to dull the sound of the screaming diesel engine and loudly clanking chains of the skidder as it made its entry onto the log landing. The skidder was clawing its way forward and, thanks to a full hitch of logs snugged up to the arch, was squatting on its back tires. The front tires were almost bouncing off the uneven ground at times. It came dancing across the landing like a grotesque belly dancer undulating back and forth with its shimmering silver chains excitedly vibrating and jiggling. When the logs were at the desired location the beast settled and rested. The engine idled down to a low hum, and the operator hit the release on the winch. The suspended ends of about 8 large logs thumped to the ground allowing the skidder's weight to shift evenly to the front.

Mr. Hutchinson jumped down between the silver adorned tires and quickly walked over to where the three were standing by the trailer.

"Tim, this is Marcy Portman – came to pick up this trailer," Jimmie said.

"What!" Tim yelled.

Jimmie pointed to his ears and yelled, "Take off your ear protection!" He waited for Tim to comply. "This is Marcy Portman – came to pick up this trailer."

"What!" Tim yelled.

Jimmie pointed to his ears.

Tim unsnapped the breast pocket on his western trimmed shirt and fished out two hearing aids and plugged them in his ears.

Jimmie yelled, "This is...." Tim held up his hand to stop him.

Tim reached up to each ear and snaped the hearing aids' off/on switch to on, "OK!" he said.

Jimmie yelled, "this is...."Tim held up his hand to stop him.

In a soft voice Tim said, "Jimmie, you don't need to yell. I can hear you just fine."

Jimmie turned his back to Tim for a couple of seconds in order to compose himself. Then he turned back around and in a normal tone, slowly said, "Tim, this is Marcy Portman. She has come to pick up this trailer.

"Yeah. Fine. Nice to meet you, Marcy. Are you set? It looks like you are all set." Tim said as he shook Marcy's hand.

"It is nice to meet you, Mr. Hutchinson." Marcy said, "and, yes, I think I'm all set."

"Well, you're smart to be armed around these two!" Tim winked, turned, and headed back towards the skidder taking his hearing aids out as he went.

Jimmie said, "and that's Tim. A man of few words – spoken or heard."

"Ahh, that's not nice" Marcy laughed, "I want to thank both of you for your help."

"The pleasure was all mine," Omar said, "just watching you school little Jimmie here in the art of shoot'n firearms weapontry was worth it all!"

"He's not going to get to tell anyone about it though! I know more stupid stuff he's done that I could tell people if I wanted to, so he won't dare talk about this!" Jimmie laughed.

They turned, took a few steps, and stopped.

Jimmie said, "Wait around until I get this load that Tim just brought in stacked on the deck and I'll give you a chance to win your lunch money back!"

Marcy heard Omar say, "Naw, I gotta get back to the Ranger Station, and besides, my hind leg is a hurt 'n me."

"Your hind leg!" Jimmie chortled, "I always knew there was something different about you Omar!"

Omar gave Jimmie the stink eye.

They continued talking and walked on out of earshot. Marcy could imagine the trash talking would continue until quitting time.

Chapter Eight
The Shower – A Reveal

Two hours later Marcy was backing the borrowed high deck trailer next to her lowboy in the staging area just outside of Journey, CA. Larry would still be up at Drop Point #11 with the company pickup and fuel cell. He would top off both the feller/buncher and the dozer with diesel fuel before bringing Jock and Carlos back to camp this evening.

Since she wasn't expecting the crew back for a while yet, this seemed like the perfect time to get a shower. Retrieving her towel, washcloth, toiletries bag, and change of clothes, she began the short quarter of a mile walk towards Journey to where the shower and laundry units were located.

Marcy was happy to find this was one of the nicer contract shower units. She walked under the shade screen that was stretched between two shower trailers parked parallel with each other and about 20 feet apart. She set her toiletries bag on one of the many chairs that sat on an outdoor carpet beneath the shade screen. Each trailer had 8 private showers with exterior doors that opened out to the seating area. Marcy stepped over to a box of large paper bath towels and ripped 2 from the roll for herself. From a tub of flip-flops, she picked up a size large thinking too big would be better than too small.

Leaving her boots by the chair and wearing the shower flip-flops, she picked up everything she brought and looked at the shower stall doors. She saw the green "vacant" sign on the door of stall number 3, went up the steps, and entered it. Once inside, she pushed the lock lever which not only locked the door but changed the outside green vacant sign to a red occupied sign. She hung her belongings on hooks along the wall. Her "not so fresh" clothes she put into a plastic bag. Stepping inside the shower itself, she pulled the shower curtain and enjoyed the hard spray. Having to duck her head a little to wash her hair, she wondered how a really tall person must have to bend to do the same.

Refreshed after her shower, Marcy went over to a bank of sinks attached perpendicularly to the end of the shower trailer. Behind each sink were mirrors and power outlets. Using her hairdryer she dried and combed out her hair. She didn't feel the need to put makeup on, just some facial lotion with a sunblock. Absently, she had been wondering how her horse, Avalanche, and Jacody were getting along. She smiled slightly at the irony. While her horse lived up to its name, Jacody's horse was suitable for a 3-year-old to ride despite its name... Piledriver. "Men!"

At the end of the row of sinks, she noticed someone taping up a poster. It was Mick Bainey, the Liaison Officer.

"Hey!" Mick smiled at her, "I'm letting people know there will be a non-denominational worship service over in the briefing area at 2000 Sunday evening!"

"Good to know," said Marcy. "I'll try to make it."

"Great! I'll look forward to seeing you there!" Said Mick enthusiastically. "I'm Mick Bainey."

"Nice to meet you! I'm Marcy Portman."

"Have you met Rick Barron?" Mick asked. "He will be leading the group."

"No, I don't know him, but his name sounds familiar," Marcy responded.

"Rick is one of our Safety Officers," Mick told her. "He is often the one who gives the safety messages at Morning Briefing."

"Say, didn't I see you at the Morning Briefing on stage?" Marcy asked. You're the Liaison Officer, right?"

"Yes, I am," replied Mick. "You must have been paying close attention!

"Oh! You don't think the little people would take the time to go to morning briefing and then not listen, do you?" Marcy joked.

Mick acted hurt, "Little people? That's kind of like they say to actors, 'there are no little parts, only little people. On fires, however, there are only big parts filled by big people. If you're not a big person, you wouldn't be here!"

Marcy liked this Mick guy. To herself, Marcy mused, "He goes by Mick, and he looks Irish... he must not care if some people consider Mick to be an ethnic slur." Red hair and a well-trimmed red beard, he carried himself with confidence. " The way he talks is like a song I would look forward to listening to," she smiled to herself thinking of the discussion with HRSP D'Angelo earlier today.

"Talking about no little parts," Marcy said, "you were talking at the briefing this morning about evacuations. Now, that is a very big part to have. It seems so scary and sad that people must decide what to take with them and what to leave, possibly to be destroyed."

"Well, it is difficult." Agreed Mick, "Personally, I've never had to do that. But I've grieved with a lot of people who have had to make those decisions and some who, when looking at the burned ashes of their homes and whatever was left that they couldn't take with them, are happy to have escaped in time to save their lives!"

"I would be too, I think," Marcy said in a distant voice.

"Right now, there are a few ranchers between the fire and the community of Fandango who are busy hauling equipment and livestock, horses, and goats, and the like, to other ranches far from the danger. They are also moving some household goods even though they haven't gotten the word to load up."

"You can tell people to load up or get ready to evacuate before they actually have to evacuate?" Marcy asked." How do you know when to tell people to do what?"

"Well, first of all, it is not just me," the Liaison Officer said. "In a perfect world, evacuation plans are completed with several people's input. I include people with our Incident Management Team and local offices as well. We consider how fast a fire is moving and what direction it is going. Then we establish points, we call them Management Action Points, on a map and we take action when and if the fire gets to that point. It's not as simple as it sounds, but that's how we know when to tell people to get ready or to leave."

"It just seems like an awesome task just to think about what to take with you, you know, the pre-evacuation work," Marcy said.

"Well, it is!" Said Mick. "We can warn people and they can decide not to act. They think, 'how bad can it really be?' Then they stay and maybe they survive and maybe they don't. Or they wait until all they escape with is the clothes on their backs."

"Ouch!" Marcy winched, "I hope they don't wait that long!"

"But try to think about it. Think about all you have." Mick went on, "Normally, you just 'have' it, you don't weigh it out as to how important things are to you. Now, consider you have just been informed you have 6 hours, at best, to remove yourself and whatever matters most to you to another location miles away from here. When you return there may be nothing left but ashes of the home you once had. It is a totally alien way of looking at your possessions."

"Wow! Yes. I have never considered that." Marcy said thoughtfully, "The iron skillet Grandma Nellie gave me, or the old 22 single shot lever action Grandpa Sam gave me. Which one? Both I guess!"

"Now, I know I just met you, but I would have never thought a skillet and a rifle would be the first two things to save that would pop into your mind!" Mick exclaimed!

"Well, to do it right I'd need several more hours and a couple more trucks!" Marcy assured him.

"See, if you hadn't given any thought to what, among all your possessions, was most important to you, you might just freeze up and start putting things in a truck. Things that take up room but may not be what you love the most or need the most. So we give people a list to at least make sure they get what they need first. We give them a guide we call the Six P's:

- People and Pets.
- Papers, phone numbers, and important documents.
- Prescriptions, vitamins, and eyeglasses.
- Pictures and irreplaceable memorabilia.
- Personal computer hard drives and disks.

How many is that? One more I think... uh... got it!

- Plastic (credit cards, ATM cards) and cash."

"I can see how that would help. Lists are something you can focus on. That's good!" Marcy said.

"We also have a pre-evacuation checklist that includes planning an evacuation route, an alternative evacuation route, designating points of contact, developing a rendezvous location in case family members get separated, and other things they can do before the evacuation order is given."

"I should probably make plans like that just in case," Marcy said. "Making arrangements for our livestock would be monumental!"

Mick answered, "I was on a fire in Nevada - it was mostly sagebrush - but I met this really nice ranch family who ended up losing everything but their house. The year before, there had been a 500,000-acre fire that burned up his BLM (Bureau of Land Management) grazing allotment and a large portion of his cattle herd. They were working so hard to get things back operational again when this fire started. The rancher and his wife, along with several friends and neighbors were working on their own, independent of our efforts, trying to stop the fire from reaching his home ranch. They almost died in the fire but turned and drove their vehicles through the flames and got to where the fire was sparse enough, they didn't perish. One from their group contacted me and said if we came over where they were with water drops from our helicopters, they could stop it.

We had crews and other resources depending on the plan we had and couldn't divert resources to something outside that plan. The result was the ranch couple lost the remainder of their cattle and a couple of barns. Fortunately, they did have their home plumbed for fire – they had sprinklers set up and all burnable material scraped away from around the house. "

"That sounds horrible! And the incident management team ignored their requests for help?" Marcy asked.

"Well, it was horrible!" Mick agreed, "and it sounds bad like the team was cold and uncaring. But that's not the way it was. The team's plan was formed without the help or knowledge of what this group was independently doing. All the fire's resources were obligated in that plan. It would have put the government's plan in jeopardy to peel resources away from it. The government had other homes in more immediate danger. Progress was being made and the team expected to hook the fire and stop it. Then, without forewarning, there was a rare wind shear event.

It was like you see in the movies; a wall of sand going across the desert. The other liaison officer and I were traveling on a highway up through the fire. There weren't even any smokes in that part of the fire, it had passed through days before. But we looked to the West and there was this wall of thick, black, ash hundreds of feet in the air! It is hard to describe! We could look to the South and see this wall of ashes rushing Eastward. It was crystal clear to the left and impenetrably black on the right as we looked at the approaching wall. We pulled over, sat in the truck, and held on. When it overtook us, the sun was blotted out – it was pitch black. The truck rocked back and forth and it felt like it was moving but you couldn't tell. After the initial front of the wall hit us, we were aware of a constant force pushing against us from the West towards the East."

"Oh my gosh... were you scared?"

"Probably. Maybe. Let's just say I was very apprehensive. I had never seen or experienced such a thing before or since. It was so surreal; it was hard to know to be afraid if that makes any sense! Almost as fast as it came, it left. We found out later that where it crossed the highway South of us, it snapped around 30 power poles along the highway."

"It was this unpredicted wind event that took the fire in a way that destroyed all of the rancher's remaining possessions save the ranch house. Even if we tried to comply with their request, the wind had grounded all our aircraft."

"My point is," Mick continued, "we can only do our best and not look back. This fire that wiped out the remaining half of the rancher's herd turned out to be 500,000 acres and the only thing that stopped it was it ran into the first 500,000-acre fire that took out the rancher's federal grazing land and the first half of his herd the year before. Now, isn't that one catastrophe putting an end to another one?"

"How terribly sad that is." Marcy said, "I worked on a hotshot crew for four years and I have seen homes burned down. I've also seen where structures were wrapped with reflective material and plumbed with sprinklers surviving some intense heat. But barns and herds of cattle… they are sitting ducks with a fast-moving intense fire."

"Right! Most people are so busy building their livelihood, they fail to protect what they have built to date," Mick said.

"That would be me and Jacody!" Marcy said with certainty. "It's all or nothing! We would not walk away if we thought we could save it. In 6 hours we could set up our irrigation systems around the buildings and disk up fire breaks.

"Yeah. That sounds familiar," Mick said. "Tell me, does your irrigation system pump water with electricity? Do you have alternative energy from a gas-powered generator?"

"When I get home, I think we will go over our fire preparedness plan. Well, first I guess we should make a fire preparedness plan." Marcy said reflectively.

"Well, if I have inspired you to write a fire preparedness plan, my work here is done!" Mick said puffing up his chest in jest. "But I'd better get back to putting up these posters or Rick will be all over me. Good talking to you and, if I don't see you before then, I'll see you Sunday night!"

"Yeah! I think I learned some things. Thanks for sharing with me." Marcy said.

Soot-covered firefighters had been coming into the shower area while Marcy and Mick had been talking. Now all the stalls had red "occupied" signs displayed on the outside of the doors. Beside the chairs between the two shower units stood unlaced leather boots with

Vibram soles and logger heels waiting patiently for their owners to return. To the unfamiliar eye, the boots pretty much looked the same, but to the fire veteran the various brands were easy to identify – White, Carolina, Redwing, Chippewa Wolverine, Georgia, etc.- one of the most important things a firefighter has are their boots. If you don't take care of your feet, you are out of work.

Marcy went over to the chair where her boots stood waiting. After donning her clean socks, she put them on. Dropping the flip-flops she used in a tub of disinfectant and her wet paper bath towels in a plastic trash barrel, she headed for the staging area. The hot shower had relaxed her shoulders and she felt reenergized.

Marcy made her way back to Cupcake and stowed her toiletries. She hung her towel over the steering wheel and draped her near dry washcloth over the gear shift. It was close to being dry from the low humidity there in the high mountains. The plastic bag with her dirty clothes got tossed in a corner to be added to later. She had just landed back on the ground when the BBFL pickup pulled up beside her.

"Jump in!" Larry yelled, "we're going fer supper!"

Back at the staging area, Marcy got ready for bed. She wasn't tired and didn't feel like she had worked all that hard today, but she was anxious to get in Cupcake's sleeper. She had thought off and on all day about Jacody, wondering what he was doing, how his day was going, and what was up with the Roberts Ranch irrigation system he was installing.

All things will come to pass eventually. The time to call her husband had arrived. One ringy-dingy. Two ringy-dingy.

"Hello, baby. You want some of this?" came a deep, mellow voice.

"Barry? Is this Barry White?" Marcy played along. "Where's my husband? What have you done with JJ?"

"I'm just a love machine, and I won't work for nobody but you (yeah baby). You don't need JJ when you got me." Jacody sang.

"You better not be working for anybody but me! I'd skin you alive!"

"I think you would too! The boys and I are missing you. We've been lonely since you left."

Marcy laughed, "you are talking about Chuck, Chew and you, right?

"Oh sure. That's who I meant. We're sitting out on the porch listening to The Best of Moody Blues. 'Nights in White Satin' isn't keeping me from missing you any though. I don't think anything could!"

"Maybe you should play some CCR then. Try 'Fortunate Son' because, after all, you ain't no senator's son!"

"No. I can't listen to that without hearing Huey or Blackhawk helicopters in the background and I don't need those thoughts!" Jacody said.

"Yeah... I should know that. So, how about 'Walking On Sunshine', that oughta cheer you up?"

Jacody laughed, "Yeah, that'll work! You are my sunshine, you know! So, tell me, how's it going?"

Marcy went through her day with him. She didn't share the feeling she was getting from Larry, that for some reason, he seemed to be kind of antagonistic. The emotion she felt talking to Sheila on the school track came back to her when she shared their discussion with Jacody.

She told him when she got home, one of the first things they would do would be to write a Fire Preparedness Plan. Jacody asked her where that came from so she told him all about her conversation with Mick the Liaison Officer. Jacody seldom interrupted her but listened closely to what she was sharing with him. If it was important to her, it was important to him.

"So, I think I'm all talked out. Tell me now, what's your day been like?"

"Well, you know I've been over at Robert's Ranch. I didn't do too much over there today. The well driller got there about mid-morning. He may finish up tomorrow, then we will know for sure if we will have a well that will produce enough water to justify putting in all the irrigation piping for a new system."

"Oh, and you might notice if you get on your laptop and check our Discover Card records... I got a job for an estate gate and I bought a few things to get that going."

"Wow! Great!" Said Marcy, "who are you building that gate for?"

"Uhhh... Lew... Jane Lew." Jacody said.

"Jane Lew. Jane Lew. Isn't she from West Virginia somewhere? Marcy asked.

"No. I don't think so. Remember. Back when Hiram was of clear mind, he had told us that she was a schoolteacher who came here from Indiana. She had never been married and Hiram had joked around that at one time he thought she might have been sweet on him. Then she up and married John Lew that worked over at the hardware store. This isn't the first time we talked about her, and you tried to connect her to West Virginia."

"Okay, yeah. I think I recall that now."

"Speaking of Hiram," Jacody went on. "Your grandpa and grandma were visiting Hiram at the nursing home today and he seemed to be having a really good day. He asked them if they would bring him out here to the ranch and they did."

"Oh? How did that work out?" Marcy wanted to know.

"Well... mostly... I guess it was good. He seemed confused by a few things - things we have changed from how he had them."

"That could be expected though, right? He so seldom remembers the recent here and now." Marcy said.

"Yeah, I know, "said Jacody, "and I know this really shouldn't have bothered me, but when we were in the house there were two times when he kind of stared at me as if he had never seen me before. Then he leaned over towards Grandpa Sam and in a low voice said, 'what's this black man doing in here.' I finally just went out in the barn until they got ready to leave. Grandpa Sam came out to talk with me and I told him I understood. But still..."

125

"Ah, honey. Please don't feel bad. What do you think is bothering you? That he didn't recognize you, or that he didn't recognize you and specifically called attention to you being black?" asked Marcy.

"I don't know. Maybe both. I have head knowledge of Alzheimer's Disease but maybe I just found out I don't have heart knowledge of it. There are several things I'm trying to sort out. The three of us lived here for a year and a half before Hiram needed more help than we could give him. In all that time I never once thought he had a racist bone in his body. But when he looked at me with no trace of recognition in his eyes and the way he said 'black' man, well, it just wasn't the Hiram that we know and care so much about."

"Take some time to think about it. Don't get all wrapped around the axel over it. Remember the old Hiram that had a clear mind. Think about when you two went fishing together. Remember how much he appreciated you taking him elk hunting even though you didn't shoot any. That is the Hiram who didn't see you as anything other than a Christian brother and a friend. He thought of you as a son. And you know, with him being in an altered state, he only has long-term memory. The last time he saw me he thought I was still a little girl. He may have just wondered why someone he didn't recognize was in his home and that is all. Did my grandparents have any trouble taking him back to the nursing home?"

"As I said, I went to the barn," Jacody replied. "I didn't ask Grandpa Sam and he didn't mention it. I knew Hiram could be cantankerous even when he was clear-minded, so I can only imagine what he might be like now. If he did object, I bet he won't get to come to visit again. That is really sad when you think about it."

"We should have flipped this whole conversation around. You should have told me about Hiram first, we could have been sad for a bit, and then talked about all the happier stuff and hung up feeling all right. So, how are you feeling right now?" Marcy asked.

"I suppose I'm feeling okay. I'll go to bed listening to 'Walking On Sunshine' and think of you."

"OK Mr. Barry White," Marcy teased. "I'll go to sleep tonight listening to you and Edie Bricknell singing 'Good Times'. You know I always think of us when I hear that song. 'Gimmie some of that'!"

"Yeah, we should add that to our list of official songs."

"Yes, we should. And we should also say goodnight if you are feeling all right." Marcy said.

"Yes, dear. I've overcome a whole lot worse. I'll be fine. I'd say you need to get your beauty sleep, but I don't want you getting any prettier while you are out there among the heathens." Real fast, Jacody added, "now I know you are going to object to me saying heathens, but that's any man you are near that isn't me. I know there are some good people there... somewhere... maybe one or two. I'm just looking for some reassurance here!"

"I do know you. There are some good people here and I know you know that. Remember, I told you there are a couple of guys preparing to hold a worship service on Sunday. So that counts as good, doesn't it?"

"Yes, you told me. But you are there, and I am here. There isn't much that is going to make me happy about that, but, yes, I know you and I know me. I try not to get jealous. It is a work in progress."

"So how long of a good night is this going to be? I love you and I have to get to sleep and so should you!" Marcy said. "Now I feel like we are just saying things to avoid saying good night!"

"Hey! It's your fault. You started up with that Barry White stuff. Now you got me going!" Jacody objected. "I'm fine. As soon as we hang up I'll start looking forward to your call tomorrow night. That's just me."

"Maybe it is my fault because I'd like to keep talking to you. But I can't. I will call you tomorrow. I love you JJ! Good night."

"I love you too Sweetie-pie. Pleasant dreams. Talk to you tomorrow. Good night."

The line went dead but both parties seemed unwilling to move. Marcy and Jacody both were feeling like this just wasn't right. When they said good night to each other they should still be in each other's arms or spooning.

Marcy clicked off the one light she had on in Cupcake's sleeper unit and rested her head on her pillow. She was hoping Jacody understood how much she loved him. It wasn't all that important to say when they were together. Apart, it seemed she couldn't be sure she was making it plain enough.

Jacody went inside the house and got ready for bed. Once under the covers, he picked up his smartphone and went to Youtube. Instead of typing in "Walking On Sunshine", he typed in "Good Times" by Edie Bricknell with Barry White because he thought that might be what Macy was listening to. He would like to have gone right to sleep but his mind would not shut down. He didn't like to deceive Marcy. He smiled when he thought of how she got Jane Lew mixed up with someone from West-by-gollies-Virginia.

Chapter Nine
Portman – Jones Story

Ground Hog Day. Marcy could already see how she might fall into a routine, and it would be like Ground Hog Day – the same day repeated over and over until she was released from the fire. Rushing here – rushing there. Breakfast, Morning Briefing, the morning breakout for specific directions, pick up drinks, ice, lunch, and then the day just rolled on like a silver ball in an old pinball machine.

By late morning, Jock and Carlos were up on the line operating their equipment. Larry had gone into town to fill up the fuel cell in the back of their BBFL pickup. Marcy's nose for coffee had located a bottomless pot of black gold in the Ground Support yurt. Unit Leader Jim Blanchard brought the special blend of coffee with him from a South Dakota Incident Management Team he had previously been on. The coffee was dubbed "Goodness Gracious Great

Beans of Fire" after an old Jerry Lee Lewis song "Great Balls of Fire".

There was no one in the Ground Support yurt but she filled her insulated thermos cup up and put a five-dollar bill in the donation jar sitting next to Mr. Coffee. Stepping out of the yurt, she noticed her driver from her first night in fire camp sitting under the driver's shade fly.

"Hi, Jeremiah!" She greeted him, "mind if I join you?"

"No, not at all!" said Jeremiah, "Marcy, right?"

"You got it."

"Hey. That's pretty good! We remembered each other's name!" Jeremiah said.

Marcy sat down in a folding chair at the table across from Jeremiah. "So, tell me, is Jeremiah a family name? It sounds like a grandfather or great grandfather's name.

Jeremiah laughed. "You could say that. It was passed down to me through my father's side. I go by Jeremiah, but my whole name is Peyton John Jeremiah. People seemed to always think my first name is Jeremiah, so I just go with that."

"I like Jeremiah, but you have some nice options there. John Jeremiah sounds good. And Peyton sounds distinguished. PJ could be fun." Marcy said.

"Eh! Too many John's, PJ is short for getting ready for bed – got your PJs on – and I haven't done anything distinguishing enough to be called Peyton. So, I'll just stick with Jeremiah. Who knows, once I figure out what I want to be and do, I might be a prophet like in the Bible!"

"Well," Marcy said, "today it appears you are a driver in Ground Support. How's that working for you?"

"Really well, actually! I'm not into money.... but it appears money is into me. I can't do much without money and this job is bringing some in. And it gives me time to think about what I'm going to do next. I think I have come to a fork in the road, and, since going in either direction requires finances, this job helps."

"A fork in the road, huh?" Marcy said, "You know what they say; when you come to a fork in the road...."

"...take it!" Jeremiah finished her sentence for her.

"Interesting! For a young guy, you seem to have put a lot of thought into this already. How old are you, 17? 18?" Marcy asked.

"You would be miserable at guessing ages in a carnival!" Jeremiah laughed. "I'm 25!"

"Wow! I'm usually a better age-guesser than that! You look so young. You should be so lucky to go through life with people thinking you are years younger than you are."

"Well, hey! Don't feel bad. I know I look a little younger than I am, but when you couple that with me sitting here as a hired pickup truck driver... well, that's not necessarily a career that can support a family kind of job. That alone would suggest I'm either a kid or retired. If you are going to error, you are wise to error on the too young side."

"Yeah, well, don't forget that cute boyish charm you've got going for you! That can be deceiving too! So, if you don't mind me asking, have you done anything else besides driving a pickup for the last 6 years?" Marcy asked.

"No, I don't mind at all. Right out of high school, I got a degree in Early American History with a minor in Spanish. After I graduated, I took a job in Spain teaching English." Jeremiah said. "I spent a year there."

"That sounds like you have done some stuff, you have had some experiences and now you are having more. Evidently, you can mark off teaching English in Spain or you would still be there! You said you feel you are at a fork in the road. Do you have two directions you could go in but have to choose one?" Marcy asked.

"There are two directions I'm considering. I haven't thought of a third that would be acceptable. But neither of the directions is easy to identify and describe. There are subtle differences between the two and one doesn't necessarily have to exclude the other." Jeremiah said, "can I ask you a question? Then you will see what I mean. I have asked a lot of people this."

"You've sure got my curiosity up. Of course, ask away!" Marcy replied.

"Okay. I've asked this so often I put it on my cell phone. Here it is. I'll just read it. It probably sounds lame, like a script or something, but here goes.

As we're going down serious and consequential roads in our lives, what matters the most to you in charting your course? Specifically, would you rather maximize your quality of life so that you have the most satisfying relationships, and you feel the best from day to day, or would you rather have an exceptionally purposeful life, where you feel like what you do is of incredible importance even though it may bring you personally considerable suffering and hardship? These obviously are not mutually exclusive, but which one is more important to you?"

"Uh... what? Important to me? No... I mean... that's a lot to think about and try to separate all at once. Can you clarify it just a little?" Marcy asked. She noticed her coffee had cooled enough to drink and thought she could buy some time concentrating on sipping a few swallows.

"Of course, it is a lot to take in all at once. Quality of life would be a regular but satisfying job with a family. You would move through life with predictability and stability. A purposeful life, on the other hand, would be of service to others. Going to a third-world country and helping a village get clean reliable water would be exceptionally purposeful. Something like the Peace Corps, Red Cross, or even Samaritan's Purse could be avenues to pursue. Going in this direction would be less predictable. Projects might be interrupted by a change in politics or hostile groups. The future would certainly be less secure."

"Wow! I think you need a crystal ball to see deep into the future. It sounds like you have thought of some options for a purpose-driven life, do you have anything in mind for a quality-focused life? Any jobs or professions, any candidates for a wife? Anything like that?" Marcy asked.

Jeremiah laughed, "I sure wish I had something more definitive. I do have maybe six possibilities that I feel strongly about, but I'm having a hard time separating them. I can't seem to rank them."

"Bummer! Maybe you have too many options. And can I assume you are talking about jobs or professions? Not candidates for a wife?"

"Yes, of course!" Jeremiah laughed. "No potential girlfriends at the moment. But I've talked about this with the HRSP guy, David D'Angelo, he's a good listener. He suggested since I couldn't put one option ahead of another, to write each one on a piece of paper. Then place each one in an envelope, put all of the envelopes in a box and mix them up. The one I draw out is the direction I will take."

"Just like that?" Marcy asked. "You'll forget about the other five and commit to whatever you pull out of the hat, or box?"

"Well, yes," Jeremiah said. "D'Angelo points out that if any one of them is just as good as any other one, then it doesn't matter, I just need to land on one. Now, there is a caveat. If, when I open the envelope, I'm disappointed, I'll know this isn't a good choice for me. Should that happen, I discard that one and draw another one. If I'm not disappointed with that one, I'll go with it. I'm to pursue it for the rest of my life or until I find some reason it isn't working for me. Then I'm to do the whole thing over again."

"My my!" said Marcy, "that sounds like a simple but good solution. Why don't you follow his advice and do that?"

"Oh. Well. Hmmm." Jeremiah said hesitantly. "I keep asking people so I get the best possible advice."

Marcy said, "Choosing a path is not a death sentence!"

"I just want to make as good a decision as possible! Jeremiah said.

"Of course you do," Marcy said, "but deciding to make no decision is making a decision. I believe we often make little decisions that don't seem to be very important, but lead us to a certain set of large, life-changing decisions and exclude us forever from being able to consider other sets of certain large, life-changing decisions. But, to me, it sounds like you don't want to make even those small decisions. Tell me! How did you ever decide to go to college or, even more remarkable, go to Spain?"

"Wow!" said Jeremiah. "You sound just like D'Angelo when I told him I did just what he told me to do and was disappointed with all six!"

"Jeremiah! Are you kidding me? You went through all six envelopes and were disappointed with each one?"

"Yeah, sad, isn't it?" Jeremiah said.

"No. I wouldn't say that." Said Marcy cautiously. "I'd say you just aren't ready to commit to anything yet."

"Again, it sounds like you and D'Angelo are in cahoots with each other!"

"Nooo..." Marcy exaggerated, "I'm just saying pick a spot and stand there... and stand there... until you have a reason to stand somewhere else. If you wait for all the answers to all your questions, you will still be waiting after life has passed you by."

"Yeah. I worry about that too." Jeremiah sounded somewhat depressed.

"I don't mean to sound all doom and gloom. Shouldn't you move on? Take your experiences and education and apply for different jobs. Ask girls out on dates. Find out what opportunities are waiting for you. Tell me you're not going backward trying to find the answer to happiness in other people's opinions."

"And what is your degree in?" Asked Jeremiah.

"That's fair!" Marcy said, "All I have is opinions... just like everyone else."

"Jeremiah!" Called Equipment Manager Vito Pellegrino. "You appear to be the only driver here so you're up! You're headed to Drop Point #10 for some haul-back. You should be able to get it all on your truck. Drop it off in the back of supply. Take your lunch. Make sure the batteries are fresh in your radio! Let me know when you get back. I'll sign you out now."

"It seems like you rarely get to the end of any good discussion on a fire." Marcy thought contemplatively. She drifted back over to Cupcake and got her lunch out of the cooler she kept on the passenger's side floorboard. "Let's see. I think I'll start with this bag of M&M's."

1400 calories later Marcy gathered up all the uneaten nonperishable food items from her lunches and put them in a paper lunch sack. Then she headed toward the ICP. She was going to walk the track so she thought she might as well start walking from staging. She would stop in at the Fire Information yurt and drop the food in the donation box there. The community was always happy to absorb any extra the fire camp generated.

The Command and General Staff Meeting must have ended early. When Marcy walked onto the track she saw Sheila, D'Angelo, Bainey, and one other person she knew was a member of the Incident Commander's staff but she hadn't met yet, finishing a lap.

"Hi, Marcy!" Sheila greeted her. "Glad you could make it."

"I ate lunch and now I have to pay for it!" Sheila laughed at Marcy's comment. "How are you all doing?"

"Hey, we're doing fine." Said Sheila.

"Marcy, this is Rick Barron, our Safety Officer." HRSP David D'Angelo said. "Rick, this is Marcy. She is planning on joining us Sunday at worship service."

"Great!" Said Rick, "I'm glad to meet you and happy you're going to join us. Maybe you can encourage Sheila to come with you."

"Nice to meet you, Rick," Marcy said. "But why do you want me to encourage Sheila? Isn't David here the one convincing everyone to come together?"

"Oh she's smooth David," came Rick's reply. "See how she just slid that right back in your court? Now, Marcy, I don't like to talk about David right here in front of him, but he hasn't been effective in getting

Sheila to come to any of the prayer meetings we've had, and I don't think he's doing any better getting her to commit to coming to worship either."

Sheila said, "you didn't say you didn't want to talk about me right in front of me like you did David, so that must not bother you at all!"

"Nope! Didn't bother me at all!" Rick grinned. "If I can't say something in front of you, I better never say it behind your back!"

"Yeah, well. You know I don't want any part of that hocus pocus, 'take me to church I'll worship like a dog', stuff. Sheila stated.

"Yes. We have discussed it and I know how you feel. I don't know how or why you feel that way but that is your decision and your right." Rick said, "just know that because of my belief, I only pester you about it because I care about you and your happiness. Oh, and that song you quoted from... it has the word church and worship in it but has nothing to do with church worship."

"I'm happy! I keep telling you that. You're just not listening. Why you wanna mess with that?" Was Sheila's response.

"Yes, dear. I'm sure you are." Rick added, "David, you want to jump in here?"

"I've heard you two talking about this before and I'm too smart to step in!" David D'Angelo said. "I know what would be good here, but I also know not to get mixed up in some things. It's like, knowledge is knowing that a tomato is a fruit. Wisdom is knowing not to put tomato in a fruit salad. I got wisdom!"

"Sheila, you know you are always welcome to come and find out what it's all about." Rick said, "for now, I've got to peel off and get ready for Bainey's cooperator's meeting. See you all later."

"Hold up Rick, I'll go with you." D'Angelo said, "There was a discouraging word I heard, and I have to go check it out! We'll see you ladies later."

"See you!" Sheila said, and then to Marcy, purposefully loud enough for the men to hear, "I thought they'd never leave!"

"Later." Marcy called after the men and then, laughingly to Sheila, "you do have a broad mean streak, don't you?"

"For a broad, I do," Sheila said. "D'Angelo and I have been carrying on this way for years. Rick and I have worked together a few times and he is catching on, but I'm not gonna cut him any slack either!"

A helicopter with a large red bucket suspended below it crossed high above them - the staccato rattling of its blades echoing off the surrounding steep slopes. As the women walked on, the mid-day sun bore down on them. Both were satisfied with a slow and casual pace due to the heat.

Finally, Sheila broke the silence. "So, our talk got interrupted yesterday, and I wanted to ask you how you got where you are?"

"I began life as a child..." Marcy began.

"Alright!" Sheila interrupted. "Could you maybe fast forward? First, more specifically and to the point, tell me about how you met your husband!"

"Okay, Jacody and I were rookies on the Fireline Hotshots at the same time. That's where I met him.

The first thing that attracted me to him was how tall he was. Finally, a man I didn't have to stoop so I wouldn't be taller than him!"

"Good god! Is he like, the Jolly Green Giant?" Sheila laughed.

"No, of course not. He's as normal as I am!"

"Oh quit! You don't need to make my point for me, Mrs. Jolly Green!" Sheila laughed.

"Wait! There are a lot of people who are as tall or taller than Jacody! He's only 6'-6"! Lots of people are taller than that... really, they are!" Marcy protested. "And I'm not all that tall!"

"Sorry, but you said, 'normal'. Like, we could expect to see NBA and WNBA basketball teams working during their off-season on fires as Hotshot crews or something." Sheila mocked. "Please. Continue. I'll keep quiet. If I can. So you guys started dating?"

"No. We didn't. I saw him as a possibility the first time I saw him, but then later, I didn't think he was into me like that. I was sure he liked me, but more like a sister. At least, that's what I thought at the time."

"What made you think that?

"We were on our first fire together and I was getting pushed around. Jacody stopped it and, after that, it just seemed like he thought I was his sister to take care of." Marcy said.

"Well, that sucks." Sheila said, "What was going on – the bullying I mean. How'd that make you brother and sister?"

"Okay. We had this guy on our crew, he was a squad boss, real mouthy, and thought he was god's gift to women. Now that I think about it, my crew member, Larry Steuben reminds me of him... but that's another story. So some of us were sitting in the crew buggy eating lunch. This guy, Jesse, was sitting across from me and Jacody was sitting a couple of rows behind us. A few other people were sitting closer to the front. Jesse was getting ready to eat his salad and had just ripped open his packet of ranch dressing. I had just peeled back a banana. Jesse said, 'Hold your banana out!' Like a great big dummy, I did. He squirted a dap of ranch dressing on the tip end of it. 'Now eat it!' Jesse said. He had this impish grin on his face. I thought, 'huh?', then I got what he was getting at. I snatched my arm back and broke the end of the banana off. I threw it at him hitting him in the face."

"Oh my gosh! What did he do then?" asked Sheila.

"His face turned red immediately! In a flash, he picked up the piece of banana and leaped out in the aisle towards me. With his left arm around my neck and his left hand holding my chin, I couldn't move away from him. His grip was so firm, that I remember feeling his bicep hard against the back of my head. He was trying to smash that banana tip in my mouth. I was struggling hard against him and had both my hands around his wrist to keep the banana off my face. When I tried to raise, he put his weight on my shoulders. When I tried to slip down, he put his knee in my stomach. All this happened in a split second, but it seemed much longer. My strength was leaving me. I was about to give out when Jesse was jerked up off his feet. I thought he was going to tear my head off! At first, I didn't know what was happening! Jacody had come up behind Jesse. With one hand on Jesse's Nomex shirt collar and the other on his belt at the back of his pants, Jacody reefed Jesse up and over the seatbacks across the aisle from me like a huge bale of hay! He threw Jesse two rows back!"

"Then what!" More of a demand than a question from Sheila.

"I was just sitting there trying to catch my breath. I mean, this all came out of nowhere. I trusted Jesse and never thought he would attack me like that. I knew he liked off-colored jokes and was always making sexual innuendos, but I never felt like he was a threat to me. Jacody looked down at me and, very calmly asked, 'You okay?' Still shaken up, I nodded that I was. Then he walked back to Jesse, leaned over with his face inches away from Jesse's, and, just as calmly, asked him if he was okay. I think Jesse's back was really hurting him and maybe his throat, but he quietly said, 'yes'. Then Jacody said, 'don't do that kind of shit to your crewmates.' He continued with his face in Jesse's until Jesse said, 'okay'. Jacody said, 'Okay what?' and Jesse said, 'Okay I won't do stuff like that to my crewmates.' Jacody said, 'I guess we're good here then,' and stood up straight. Still staring at Jesse he said, 'are we? Are we good here?' Jesse nodded his head and said, 'yes. We are good here.' I had never seen anyone go from a raging bull to a timid little weasel so fast!"

Sheila was beside herself, "Unbelievable! What a jerk! If some guy tried that with me, I'd have his nuts, scrotum, and all hanging from my rearview mirror!"

"Sheila! Really? I wanted nothing from that scum bag." Marcy said. "Certainly none of his body parts!"

"I see what you mean though," continued Sheila. "If Jacody was interested in you he would have given that Jesse guy a real whupp'n!"

"That is what I thought then, but since then, I've found that Jacody doesn't do things without a reason or in a fit of anger. First, he wanted to get Jesse off me. He did that. Second, he wanted to intimidate Jesse to the point he would never do anything like that to a crewmember again. He did that too. Anything beyond that, like smashing Jesse's face in, would have exceeded Jacody's intentions. There would have been questions to answer. Things would have gotten messy. Jacody's time in the Marine Corps trained him to keep his temper in check and keep his eye on the goal. As it was, by the time the crew went on the next fire, our crew boss had switched Jesse out with another squad boss from one of the other hotshot crews that Acme Fireline, Inc. has. After that, I lost track of him."

"All's well that ends well!" Sheila said.

"Well, I suppose it did end well for me. Now that I think about it, the crew had a new problem to deal with, so maybe it didn't end so well for them. The person we got in exchange for Jesse, was Alantis. Now, there was a scary woman! I think all the guys on the crew could have filed a complaint against her if they hadn't been too afraid of her to do so."

144

"So when, then, did you start dating?" Asked Sheila.

"Two years after that, Jacody left the shots. I didn't see him for a while but late that fall, he came to the "End of Season" party that Acme Fireline always throws for all their employees. The company operates with several hotshot crews, 4 or 5 engines with crews, a few overhead people, and 2 or 3 office services mobile units plus their own business office."

"Yeah," Sheila interjected. "I believe the mobile office unit we have here now is one of Acme Firelines' units. They do all the printing for us, things like the IAP, fire maps and transition plans, and the like."

"Exactly," Marcy went on, "this particular year it was in McCall, ID, and Jacody came to it. The affair was at the Shore Lodge right on Payette Lake. It was a beautiful night I'll never forget. I had stepped out on a balcony overlooking the lake. The moonlight was dancing on the water. Jacody found me out there. We talked about old times on the shots together, fires we were on, stunts that had been pulled on our friends and us, that kind of stuff. Then he got serious and said with him not being on the shots, he was afraid we might not ever see each other again. I hinted that it didn't have to be that way if we didn't want it to be that way. He told me he would be sad not to see me and he didn't want it to be that way. I told him I felt the same – I wanted to continue to be able to spend time with him."

When Marcy stopped and turned towards Sheila, Sheila stopped too and turned, wide-eyed and expectant, towards Marcy. As she took hold of Sheila's arms Marcy's voice became softer and quieter, "then, he took me in his muscular arms and leaned me back... he looked deep into my eyes and, ever so gently, kissed me sweetly. He was holding me so close; I could feel how badly he wanted me." Marcy stopped talking.

After a beat, Sheila sighed, "Oh! He kissed you! Just like that! And you could feel he wanted you!"

"No, silly!" Marcy laughed, pulling away from Sheila. "You're not the only one who has a mean streak! He just said, 'cool, I'll call you.' A couple of days later he called me, asked me out, we dated for 4 months, and then got married."

"You really had me going there!" Sheila punched Marcy in the arm with a force that almost knocked her over. "Real funny. I can't believe I was so into that fairy tale...Oh yeah! 'I could feel how badly he wanted me'." Sheila mocked Marcy.

"But didn't that sound romantic?" Marcy said as she rubbed her arm hoping it would stop throbbing soon. "Much more than, 'cool, I'll call you.'"

"It did, but it was all horse shit!" Sheila said and acted like she was going to punch Marcy again.

They both laughed.

From the entrance to the track at the end of the straightaway, Marcy heard someone calling her name. It appeared to be Larry Steuben.

"Oh great. I invoked his name just a bit ago and he appears!"

Sheila said, "This is the guy who reminds you of Jesse, the crew member that your husband took care of?"

146

"Yeah," replied Marcy. "He didn't remind me of Jesse until just now when I was telling you about him. Larry is a much bigger man than Jesse, physically and, I hope, morally! Now, what in the world could he want?"

"He's coming this way. I'm sure we'll find out." Said Sheila.

"Hey Marcy, I been looking fer y'all! Whut y'all do'n walk'n round in the sun?" Larry asked.

"I'm trying to have a heat stroke, Larry! What are you doing out here in the sun."

"Who's this?" Ignoring Marcy's question, Larry said, nodding in Sheila's direction.

"If you would get to Morning Briefing, you'd know!" Replied Marcy. "This is Sheila Shelton, the Planning Chief. Sheila, Larry Steuben, one of the truck drivers for Big Bud Fontaine Logging."

Shifting his weight to one foot and placing a fist on his hip, Larry did his best John Wayne impersonation and said, "Well now! Let me tell y'all whut! If y'all ain't just as cute as a bug's ear!"

Sheila took a step forward and nailed Larry's arm with a good hard punch. "I bet you say that to all the girls!"

 Larry did his best to hide the pain and not to flinch.

"Shut your mouth, Larry," Marcy said, "you're gonna swallow flies.

Again ignoring Marcy, Larry spoke enthusiastically, "Well, not all the girls... just the cute ones!'

"Larry. Larry?" Marcy asked, "were you just walking by, or did you want something?"

"Oh yeah," Larry said without shifting his eyes from Sheila. "Div sup's got a job fer us." Now turning his attention to Marcy, "I'll go git the pickup and swing by fer water, then pick y'all up. Y'all be ready in bout 15 minutes?"

"Yeah, I'll be ready. I'll meet you out by the main entrance to the ICP." Marcy replied.

The two women watched Larry walk away rubbing his arm where Sheila's punch had landed.

"Sheila, I remembered something from when we talked yesterday that I wanted to ask you about."

Sheila said, "Fine. What is it?"

"You said you were tired of... I think you said, 'least expecting', and that perhaps you might start... 'expecting in another direction'. What did you mean by that?"

"Oh, nothing really," Sheila said as they resumed their walk around the track. "It has just finally dawned on me. You know I've always thought that, someday, there would be a man, a man who loves me, who would come and sweep me off my feet! He would fill this vacancy we talked about in my soul. Maybe it doesn't have to be a man. I know several women whose partners are women. They seem happy. Maybe I'd be happy too."

"That's kind of what I thought you might mean. I know some women too who have a woman for a partner. I guess many of them do seem content with their situation. I think their moral compass points to a different True North than mine, however."

"Is that a bad thing... that their moral compass points to a different True North?" Sheila asked.

"This is a kind of a difficult topic for a believer of God to talk about with a non-believer," Marcy said. "I can't judge a non-believer. But I am to judge if what they are doing is what a Christian would call 'fruits of the Spirit'. If you ask a Lesbian if she had good moral values, she most likely would say she does. Because I have read and believed the Bible, I would have to say she does not, but I'm coming from a different set of standards. So, for me, it is a bad thing. If she becomes a believer and really digs into the Bible, she will adjust her moral compass to true North – it would be pointing to the 'fruits of the Spirit'; to the things Jesus would have us to do."

"Hold up there. First, why would you say I don't believe in God?" Sheila asked.

"Well, you told the guys earlier that you don't believe in that hocus-pocus stuff. Did I not hear you correctly?" asked Marcy.

"Oh, yeah. You heard me right. But I only say that so they won't bug me about going to their little worship ceremonies. I mean, really! Rick Barron is a Safety Officer who is a religious fanatic!" Sheila said.

"So you do believe in God but see no problem denying him; saying or acting like He doesn't exist." Replied Marcy.

"Like God is going to hit me with a lightning bolt for that!" Sheila laughed. "I believe in God. But why would he care what I say? I know a lesbian priest and she must believe in God to be a priest! Right?"

Marcy said, "Sheila. Satan believes in God! Look, let's get back on track here. You indicated you might want to have a same-sex experience to see if it is right for you. Let me ask you this, have you ever been quietly and peacefully going about your business, thinking about the task at hand, and then, out of the blue, an old memory smacks you right between the eyes? Something that you tried, or did that just didn't work out right and you have tried to put behind you, but it keeps ambushing you for no good reason?

"Well, I suppose so. Doesn't everyone?" Sheila asked.

"I think they do." Marcy continued, "I have several such things waiting in the bushes to assault me. I believe just experimenting with the same sex would become one of those things. You're well into your 30s, you haven't had any strong inclinations towards a sexual relationship with the same sex, you don't find yourself looking at same-sex porno... (do you?) but you want to get naked with another person of the same sex? This will come around and bite you in the butt and I'm not talking about foreplay! It will become a vivid memory you wish you didn't have."

"I'm not wanting to get naked with anyone! Sheila protested. "I'm not so naive to think love follows sex. Jeez! What's your degree in, anyway?

"Huh!" Marcy startled, "that's the second time today I've been asked that! I must have a complex of some kind. I told you this is a difficult conversation, and you are right. I am totally sticking my nose in where it doesn't belong. I have taken way too many liberties with our young friendship. I don't want to jeopardize that. I hope you can forgive me – I'm sorry! I'm concerned and I overreacted."

A heavy silence fell over the pair. As they walked along, they watched the helicopter with the bucket returning for another load of water. The bucket trailed off at more of an angle indicating it was empty. Its suspension line would be closer to vertical going back to the fire full of water. The sound of the rotor blades began sending out a deeper whoop, whoop, whoop as the ship slowed up and went into hover mode above the reservoir not far away. After dipping the bucket in the water, the sound changed its pitch again picking up the heavy load and looking to gain altitude.

After half a lap on the track, Sheila broke the silence. "You know, you are the only one I've talked to about this. I don't know why I've talked so openly with you."

"If I was guessing, it is because we don't have a history, you and I. We have shared some personal stuff so we have built some trust, and we may never work with each other again. That makes me kind of a safe harbor."

"Could be," Sheila said, "and I don't feel you are condemning me or judging me. Well, I feel like you are judging me a little. You think I'm stupid."

"Aww! When did I say you were stupid?"

"Well, maybe you didn't say I was stupid, but you said I'd regret trying a same-sex relationship and that I'd be a sinner rotting in hell even though I told you there were lesbian priests!" Sheila blurted.

"Humm. Huh? Okay. I think some of that was before you told me you believed in God. The fact that you do believe in God shifts the conversation slightly. As I mentioned, Satan believes in God!"

"Oh yeah... now you are saying I'm no better than Satan?

"No, of course not! That's not what I'm saying." Marcy was quick to say. "You believe in God. Fine. Now, what do you believe about God? Do you have a personal relationship with God?"

"Why, yes I do. We go bowling together every Friday night! You probably heard us and thought it was thunder! Nope! Me and God."

"Well," Marcy said, "I'm glad you are taking this conversation well, but really, Sheila... for each and every person on this earth, the way they... we... live our life is a reflection of what we know about God! God gave us His Word. He gave us the Bible which is His Word. He wants us to read it and learn from it. If we are distant from God, it is because we are distant from the Bible. If we don't know much about God we live distant from God."

"I'm like Calvin from Calvin and Hobbs. The more I know, the more I have to consider. Therefore, I'm good just like I am! Why would I want to mess that up?" Sheila said jokingly.

"What?" Marcy asked. "Calvin and who?"

"Yeah, well, never mind!" Sheila said, "I didn't mean to derail you."

"Okay, but see, I want you to know God on a real level." Marcy said earnestly, "I have problems with Him... it's about my parents like I told you... but I can talk to Him about the problems I have with Him because I have a personal relationship with Him. There is that saying: 'There are things we know that we know, and there are things that we know we don't know. But there are also things we don't know we don't know.' And this might apply to you... you know there is a God, but that seems to be about it. In the absence of biblical knowledge, we give God attributes based on what the world thinks would be a good God. It's like, a good God would never send me to Hell."

"Well, a good God wouldn't if He's good, would He?" Sheila asked.

"On that, you are correct, but not in the way you think. He sends no one to Hell. But he allows you to go to Hell if that's where you want to go. It's your choice!" Marcy paused hoping what she just said would gain traction with Sheila. "You know there is a lot more you could know about God if you tried to find out. The biggest thing, it seems, is that you don't know what you don't know, and one of the most important things is how important it is for you to find out all you can about God and how to respond to Him."

"Are we still talking about lesbians?" Asked Sheila

"No...! Yes...! Yes and no!" Replied Marcy. "Listen! What I'm trying to tell you is way more important than lesbians! If you come to know Jesus in a personal way, all your questions about lesbians, men, women, love, lust, family, right, and wrong will receive some kind of answer."

"Marcy, what you are indicating is that the government was wrong when it declared sexual orientation as a basis of discrimination. Do you think you are right and the rest of the world is wrong? And you side-stepped lesbian and gay priests completely!"

"Okay. The government is not where we are to get our moral compass! It may be the last place. Most news outlets are trying to get us to think a certain way. They are not just reporting the news. Do you really want Hollywood, the most artificial salespeople in the world, telling you what is normal and natural? It is the people who believe the Bible is the inspired Word of God that is right. As far as gay or lesbian priests, I have tried to figure out how that is appropriate according to the Word of God. I can't! People who add or interpret things in the Bible so it is more in alignment with the world's way of thinking are wrong. For example, where the Bible says a man is not to lay with another man as he would a woman, they add unless 'both are consenting adults'. It's not in there! That is not in God's Word and so, it is not His intent. It is not me saying what I think... it is me reading the Bible and believing what God put in there is how I am to live."

"The Bible is just an old book; a collection of what a bunch of old guys wrote based on what they thought," Sheila said as though done with the conversation.

"You're right! And that's all it will ever be to you if you don't pick it up and read it. The fact that there were over 40 authors who wrote the various books of the Bible over a period of 1500 years or more, and yet, not one author contradicted the other or put their personal 'spin' on the Word of God, is supernatural. For me, that validates it as the inspired Word of God.

For you and me, right here, right now... none of this is important. Not yet it isn't. Down the road, it will become important whether you want it to be or not. Right now, here is what is important. First, admit you are a sinner. Then understand that as a sinner, you deserve death. Believe Jesus Christ died on the <u>cross</u> to save you from <u>sin</u> and death. Repent by turning from your old life of sin to a <u>new life</u> in Christ. Receive, through faith in Jesus Christ, God's free offer of salvation."

"Geeze, do you have to make it so personal? Lighten up!" Sheila complained.

"This is what I believe about my life and death, and what I believe about your life and death. I could easily remain silent if I didn't care about me or you." Marcy said earnestly.

"Okay, but that still sounds like a bunch of hooey! I'm a good person. If there is a heaven, I'm going there." Remarked Sheila.

"Are you peaceful?"

"What are you talking about, am I peaceful?" Sheila asked.

"Just that. Do you consider yourself a peaceful person? Simple question."

"I doubt that it is a simple question, but I'll play along! Yes. I'm a peaceful person." Sheila said cautiously.

"Well, there's a quote, and I'm not sure who to attribute it to but it goes like this: 'You can't truly call yourself "peaceful" unless you're capable of great violence, if you're not capable of violence you're not peaceful, you're harmless'. I look at God and heaven the same way. The possibility of heaven can't exist unless there is the possibility of hell. We all know..."

155

"We all know what? Maybe I'm not peaceful, but I'm harmless. What's wrong with that?" Sheila interrupted.

"Haha! So you want to live like the song John Lennon wrote for the Beatles, Imagine:

>Imagine there's no heaven
>It's easy if you try
>No hell below us
>Above us only sky
>Imagine all the people
>Living for today.... Aha-ah...
>
>Imagine there's no countries
>It isn't hard to do
>Nothing to kill or die for
>And no religion, too
>Imagine all the people
>Living life in peace...

"Imagine being harmless. Sin entered the world and that ship sailed! Look! We would all like to be peaceful people – we would all like to be at peace. We can't find it trying to be harmless. And we can't find it through others. I believe we can only find it when we focus our eyes on the one who gave His life so that we can be free of all accusations one day. When that day comes, I will be found faultless. Not harmless or harmful. But pure and clean. I will be welcomed into heaven because I believe and understand what I believe. This world is not my home."

"You're a kook!" Sheila said with a wry smile.

"Well, I appreciate your frankness!" Marcy said. "With no more than you know, I don't expect anything more than that. But surely, you've seen people, families, who are Christians. There is a difference.

You may continue to turn Christ's offer down, but I would like you to know a little about what you are declining. A good place to start is Sunday evening at 2000 over at the briefing area."

"You've spent all this time just to do Rick Barron's bidding – get Sheila the Sinner to go to one of his meetings?"

"I just want you to find the happiness in Christ that I have found. I want you to find a refuge for your soul as I've found for mine. If you find this, all your other concerns will be addressed. God is pursuing you, Sheila. He wants you to be happy – to be fulfilled. There is a lot more in store for you than just punching people in the arm. I don't want you to miss out."

"What do you mean, 'miss out'? Sheila asked.

"Just remember that. It will come to you at the right time." Marcy said.

"Well, that's kind of cryptic!" replied Sheila.

"As Forrest Gump would say, that's all I'll say about that!" Marcy said, realizing she had reached the limit she could expect Sheila to tolerate.

"We can only hope!" was Sheila's response.

Leaving to meet Larry, Marcy called back to Sheila, "Do you think there is any chance there will be pork for supper?" They both laughed.

Over her shoulder, she heard Sheila calling, "forests are burning and pigs are dying!"

Chapter Ten
The Rock Hound

Larry seemed to be in a bit of a huff when Marcy jumped into the passenger's seat. She barely got her seatbelt clicked when the truck lurched forward. Larry began to steer the pickup to the right when Marcy said, "Stop! Go left. We have to go to staging. I have to get my fire shelter out of Cupcake."

Without slowing, Larry jerked the truck to the left. "Jesus H. Christ! Are we ever gonna get go'n? I been a'wait'n on y'all fer ten fucking minutes!"

"Whoa! Hold on! There is no reason for you to be vulgar! Do you even know the definition of 'fuck'?" Larry looked straight ahead, his face red but not with embarrassment as Marcy's had been at first, but with anger – as Marcy's had become. Since he remained silent, Marcy continued. 'Fuck' is sexual intercourse with all the love and compassion of two dogs in heat. Now, how does that have anything to do with how long you had to wait for me? It doesn't! It is just vulgar! Vulgar people say vulgar things! I'm even upset that I said something so vulgar just to tell you how vulgar the things you say are! Awwwgh! Now I'm upset with both of us! And to make matters worse, you used vulgarity right after saying the name of my Lord and Savior, who was as far from vulgar as..... as..... as far as the East is from the West!

"People who use the 'F' word show absolutely no respect for other people around them. I just think they don't care about anyone else except themselves. When I hear it, it jars my nerves so much, that every time I hear it, I have a very hard time hearing anything else they have to say. Do you understand the words coming out of my mouth?"

That was all Larry could take. He could no longer remain silent. "Y'all a real nut job, know it? This here's the very reason women ought'a stay out'a man's way! Y'all don't belong here! If y'all was a man..."

"If I were a man, what?"

"If y'all was a man, we wouldn't be hav'n no problem!"

"The only problem we are having is a problem you created in your narrow little mind!"

"Why don't y'all just go home, Marcy. Y'all got no business here! God done cut yer tree down and split yer stump! Go home now'n be a woman. Have a litter of kids or sompthun y'all can maybe do!"

"Larry! Tell me the truth! Did your mother drop you on your head when you were a baby? That thing! That thing you just said! You are about as smart as a three-pound pig! Oooh! The things I'd like to say to you.....!

"Well go 'head Sweetheart! Don't let me stop y'all!

"Haha! If you only knew! It's not you stopping me, believe me!"

"Y'all know whut? Y'all make my head hurt! Y'all don't make no sense even when yer try'n. Yre'a try'n ain't cha?"

"What is your problem, Larry?"

"Problem?"

"I'm serious. You hadn't even met me or said hello and you were bad-mouthing my truck!"

Larry laughed, "what'd y'all expect. Y'all take a great tractor like a Diamond Reo, put pink flames on it, paint 'Cupcake' on it'n think people going ta go 'Ohhhh, badass woman trucker'?"

"You wouldn't understand, and I didn't paint Cupcake like I did to make a statement. I painted it the way I did because that's the way I wanted it. You didn't even think 'badass woman trucker' when you saw it. You thought it said, 'lesbian trucker'."

"Well... could'a been that."

"Did it ever occur to you that not everybody thinks like you? Some people are considerate. Some people are polite. Some people even wait to get to know a person before they make up their minds about them. I've never met someone who took an immediate dislike to me as you have. Are you just rude to everyone when you first meet them? You don't seem to have a dislike for Carlos or Jock."

"Whut y'all talk'n bout? Why'd I have a problem with them?"

"Why would you have a problem with me? That's what I want to know."

"Just shut the f... face! Just shut yer face. Get out and get yer fire shelter. Grab yer radio too! Y'all gonna need it! We should'a been up thar by now!"

To Marcy's great relief, Larry was not in a talkative mood. She really wanted to ask him about where they were going and what they would be doing, but she didn't want to even look at Larry, much less talk to him. How could they start being civil to each other after the conversation she had just suffered through? She sat quietly and stared out the side window all the way to Journey.

At Journey, Larry wheeled into the only gas station/convenience store in town. Without a word, he got out of the truck and went into the store. In minutes, he reappeared. Once in the truck, he threw a tin of Copenhagen dipping tobacco and a pouch of Redman loose leaf chewing tobacco on the dash. She recalled seeing Larry build a "chew". He had offered to let Carlos and Jock build one for themselves, but they refused. With good reason, she supposed. Jock had told her that first, Larry doctored his Copenhagen with a healthy teaspoon of Peppermint Schnapps. To build his chew he would put Redman in the palm of his hand and make a hollowed-out place in it, like mashed potatoes for gravy. Then, a three-finger pinch of Copenhagen was placed into the "nest". All that was left to do was to fold the loose leaf into a ball, sealing the Copenhagen in the center. Jock had told her that he had tried one once and when the juices started flowing from the center, he actually got a major buzz on! Marcy worked at suppressing an involuntary gag reaction as she recalled her adolescent attempts at chewing tobacco!

Just outside of Journey, they turned East on Hot Forge Road. When Marcy was in the 'dumps' like she was after the confrontational conversation with Larry, she liked to look for something to make her smile. She believed there would be something if she only looked for it. This was no different. Her reason to smile came compliments of the California Department of Transportation. There are two tiny communities East of Journey. One is named Maybe, and the other is Fandango. The department's mileage signs gave the distance to each of these communities:

| Fandango | 4 |
| Maybe | 6 |

"How far is it to Fandango, really? By now, one might have thought they could be more precise, is it 4, 6, or something in between?" Marcy pretended to wonder.

During their non-conversational trip, Marcy thought about the man driving the pickup. Larry's unusual method of preparing tobacco to be chewed wasn't the only thing that Jock told her about their coworker. That was just an interesting sidelight of the real conversation. Jock has known Larry for several years. Driving a truck is all Jock has ever heard of him doing. "Back home, Larry went to work, to

Rusty's Last Chance bar, and home. That's about all."
Jock had told her. He lives with his mother and his
mom packs him his lunch every day – just like when
he was a kid. As near as Jock could recall, years ago
there were several women that he went out with – to
Rusty's Last Chance – of course. There may have
been a couple of those women that he went out with
twice, but never a third time, One-eyed Jack, the
bartender had told him. Jock says Larry had a couple
of friends that he drank with and that seemed to be
about all there was to know about Larry Steuben.
Marcy's follow-up questions drew blanks from Jock.

Marcy had filed the conversation with Jock about
Larry in a mental file folder and wrote "Larry" on it.
As she contemplated whether to put it in a bin, "Sad
and Lonely People", or just thumbtack it on a message
board, a whimsical mental sticky note got stuck on the
mental file. She never questioned why when this
happened, she just went with it. She read this one,
"Contrary to the popular belief held by the non-
tobacco chewing public, chewing tobacco is not to be
chewed."

In a couple of miles, they turned right onto Jessup
Ridge Road and crossed the Dancing Branch Bridge.
Just before the road took a sharp turn and started up
the mountainside they turned into a wide pullover.
Marcy and Larry walked over to where 3 guys were
looking at a map rolled out on the hood of a green
Forest Service truck.

A short, clean-shaven man with his Nomex shirt
sleeves rolled up past his elbows stepped back and

asked, "Are you the two drivers that are managing traffic for us this afternoon?"

"Ayup." Answered Larry.

"Hi, thanks for volunteering! I'm Cliff Singleton, Div Whiskey Supervisor."

"Hello, I'm Marcy Portman."

"Hey. I'm Larry Steuben."

"Okay, let's get this show on the road! Cliff said, "This is Thadd Dungston, grader operator, and Stew Forbes. Stew'll be keep'n the road watered. Look here," pointing at the map on the hood. "I want one of you to station here at Drop Point #13 and the other stay right here at Drop Point #12. We have 'GRADING AHEAD' signs at each end of the work area. "

"Great! We done this a'fore. We'll radio one another, keep things safe'n traffic moving." Larry said.

Thadd said, "I'm just cutting the washboards out of the road, and Stew there will keep it wet so it rolls good and we don't lose a lot of fine material such as dust. I figure 5, maybe 6 passes at the most. Those washboards can cause a person to lose control and go off the side. We need you to control traffic because on this narrow canyon road we can't risk having big rigs trying to pass me."

"I'm good," Marcy said, "I think I know what you need from us."

Larry said, "Yep. I got 'er." Then he turned to Marcy, "I got the truck. I'll go up." Marcy nodded and went to get a couple of bottles of water out of the truck.

Larry followed Cliff up the mountainside and pulled over at Drop Point #13. Marcy held up her hand to stop Stew from pulling out on Jessup Ridge Road until a pickup got past. Then she motioned him out and he hit the spray hoses to wet, but not flood, the roadway. Behind him, Thadd set the blade on the road grader and started rolling the left side of the gravel surface to the center of the road.

So the afternoon went by. Marcy moved to the shade of the cottonwoods along Stone Creek when the equipment went uphill. When she got the radio call from Larry that the grader was headed downhill, she moved back to the road to stop any traffic from going up. At last, she got the radio commo that Thadd was cutting the outside, or canyon side of the road out and it would be the last pass. Larry would be following the grader down.

Stew pulled into Drop Point #12 where Marcy was and hooked up a draft hose to fill his water truck up from Stone Creek. Thadd pulled the road grader over to the side of DP12 and shut it down. After he climbed down to the ground he still had the door open. He reached up and rolled a large rock across the floorboard and out of the grader's cab and into his arms. He pivoted and set the rock on the ground next to the road grader.

Marcy walked up to Thadd and said, "what'cha got there Thadd?"

"I flipped this bad boy up just down off the slope when I was cutting the canyon side of the berm. It almost spun the grader around. Have you ever seen such a large nigger head?" Marcy shows her disapproval for a moment, then the clouds faded away. "Oh! Sorry, my bad. Have you ever seen such a large geode?"

"Whut! That bother y'all Marcy? It was Larry. Ain't like y'all is married to a nigger, is ya?"

Marcy turned to face Larry. He was standing there with a stem of Johnson grass idly dangling from his mouth. The clouds reappeared around Marcy with a vengeance... her ire was so apparent, that even a 40-watt bulb like Larry could see it. Marcy locked eyes with him and the world slowed up its spin. For a moment all that was heard was the bubbling sound of nearby Stone Creek, a raven calling high in the cottonwoods, and the insects buzzing in the weeds along the roadside... there was the rhythmic click, click, click of the grader's engine as it cooled. Unnoticed was the oily smell from a leaky hydraulic hose. The hot sun bore down relentlessly while the deep, dark shade under the trees along the creek waited to offer tempting relief from the heat. "I should have stayed over in the shade! Why now? Why ever?" If the world slowed down, inside Marcy's head, wheels were turning at hyperbolic speed! She was resisting an overpowering urge to lash out at every insult, every racial slur, every sexist remark that has tried to keep her "in her place" and "in her lane". She thought, "if he will just keep his mouth shut, I can get past this! Please! Not another word!" Silence for a beat..., the raven flew away, then another beat... she was vaguely aware of Thadd awkwardly shifting his weight from one foot to the other.

Marcy saw the seed head of the Johnson grass quiver ever so slightly at the end of its stem. Then, clear as a country church bell piercing a quiet Sunday morning clear blue sky... "Y'all is... isn't ya? Y'all is married to a nigger!"

Stew was walking over to the three and heard what Larry had just said. Turning on his heel, he walked rapidly back towards his water truck. Thadd left his geode on the ground and eased behind Larry and circled around to follow Stew.

To herself, and God, she said, "Please let me see this for what it is. Give me the words, give me the calm I need to understand what I need to, to forgive this man." Then to Larry, "how can you live with the hate that must be in your heart? You can't be happy with yourself. I believe you are a very, very sad man and I feel sorry for you."

"I look sad to y'all I don't feel sad to me," Larry said indifferently.

"Well, that might be the problem." Marcy continued in a soft voice that was not what Larry expected. "You don't have a clue. Who do you think you are hurting when you say racist things? Do you hear what comes out of your mouth? That is what is in your heart! No caring. No compassion. Not even a trace of human respect. Your heart is cold, empty, and lonely! Tell me Larry, was there no love where you were raised? Did you grow up with no one who cared for you? Is there anyone who cares about you?"

Larry's mouth opened, but nothing came out. He felt exposed, like, his reoccurring nightmare where he is out in public and trying to act normal, but he is completely naked. Unlike his nightmare where he tries to appear like it is normal to be naked in public

167

and bluff his way to someplace private, he can remove himself from this situation. And that is what he did. He turned and headed for the pickup. There were no words; he was out of there.

Marcy walked over to Thadd and Stew. "So Stew, do you have room for one more in your truck?"

Chapter Eleven
I Shall be Released

It seemed like it was taking a long time for the sun to drop below the Western horizon. Marcy knew that Mt. Shasta's snow-covered cap could be seen over 100 miles across the vast expanse from the ridgeline above Journey. She wished she was there now. What a disaster this day had turned into!

Marcy was sitting in her folding lawn chair next to Cupcake. She had set her cooler out on the ground and was using it as a footrest. Her mind would not stop hashing over the conversations with Larry. As tired of it as she was, she could not help thinking about what she could have said, what she would like to have said, and she was trying to find some happy way forward. In her mind, she often circled back to something the Christian author, Max Lucado said: "Man's two greatest fears are the fear of death and the fear of insignificance." With a smile she thought she was not afraid of death – just the "getting dead" part. It was the fear of insignificance that she was often troubled with. Larry's words had struck her hard in the "significance" department. She had such good head knowledge of where she professed to draw her significance; it comes from the Lord. Why then, did she seem to stumble when put to the test like it was today? Her heart knowledge must be so very weak to crumble so easily. Her head was being an enthusiastic cheerleader, yet her heart, so far, was having none of it. The wisdom found in the Bible has proved to be true over and over: "The heart is deceitful above all things and beyond cure. Who can understand it?" Jeremiah 17:9

"This is all on Larry," she thought to herself. "I should not be affected adversely! What part of his racist, misogynistic, egotistical, attitudes did she have responsibility for? None! But he is such a jerk!"

Her heart was screaming at her loudly. "Pack it in and go home! Unhook the high deck trailer, hook up your own transport, and hit the road! Big Bud can have Larry take the borrowed one back! Big Bud can find a man to replace her and he can deal with the trailer and Larry! This isn't worth the money no matter how much they are paying!"

The voice of reason in her head was calmly plodding along with its usual logic. "Yes, you could leave. How would you feel then? Would the words sting any less in Idaho than they do in California? When have you ever backed down from a bully or adversity? Never. You know this is not about you

170

unless you take it on and let it be about you. Up there. Up there on the mountainside. The last things you said to Larry. Where did that come from? Did something just click that made you turn from 'it's all about me', to, 'this poor man's heart is a dark and lonely place'? Stay. Plant some seeds. God is giving you an opportunity. Pray for Larry. Preach a sermon of love and respect to him by your actions."

Marcy prayed, "Oh God! You alone are almighty; you alone are my God. I praise your great and mighty name. Please come close and comfort me now. Holy Spirit, council me and set my footsteps. Quiet my hurting heart. Remind me of who and what is important. I desire to be of service to you in this time of discord. Please help me to make myself available to Your will. Help me to empty my undeserved hurt and redeem my responsibilities to serve You. Guide me as I wait upon you. Amen.

As if on cue, Marcy's phone vibrated and sounded the notice that someone had just sent her a text. It was David D'Angelo, the HRSP. "Hey Marcy, as soon as you're not busy, please come by my yurt!"

"Oh great! Now what?" was Marcy's initial reaction. "Sure." She texted, "Be there in about 15."

Fire camp was benefitting from some cold air drainage coming down from the ridges above. The 15-minute walk to the HRSP's yurt in the cooler air refreshed Marcy's spirits somewhat.

"Hi, Marcy! Good to see you. Take a seat." D'Angelo motioned to a folding metal chair across the table from him. "We missed you at supper tonight – pork chops!"

171

"Thanks. Yeah, I skipped supper tonight. I've been eating way too much. The problem with not eating supper is I graze through uneaten lunches and wind up eating more calories than if I just ate supper!" Marcy said as she sat down.

"I hear you... same here. I just wanted to check in with you – see how you are doing."

"I'm doing alright. Why do you ask?" Marcy said.

"Would you believe this is just what I do? I text each of the... what are we up to now... 680 firefighters and have them drop in so I can ask them how they are doing."

"Did someone tell you that I'm extra gullible or something?" Marcy quipped.

D'Angelo said, "no, but someone did tell me some things that made me think you may have had a particularly trying day."

"What is this? Are we back in Jr High again? Someone pass you a note?"

"Haha... but, no. You must know fire camp is like a commune with no walls or privacy. If you don't want anyone to know something, don't do or say that something! Everyone has two eyes, two ears, and one mouth. You can bet they are going to use 'em. I'm not sure I've got it all as it happened and I'm sure I don't have it right. My information started over at the lunch van when Larry was picking up ice and water. He got into it with a young lady on the camp crew who was giving out ice."

"Good grief! It would seem I'm not the only one having a bad day." Marcy exclaimed.

172

"Larry pulled up and ask for ice and water without getting out of his truck. That's not unusual, but when the girl handed him the ice, it slipped and fell into the dirt. You know there's a couple of inches of silty dust from all the vehicle traffic out there. So, naturally, the plastic bag was wet on the outside and it got all muddy. She picked it up and handed it back to him through his truck window. It slipped again and this time, it slimed mud down Larry's shirt to his lap. He was not happy about that! Larry picked the bag up and threw it at the girl and said a few things he shouldn't have to her."

"Yikes!"

"Fortunately, the bag missed her, but she was all freaked out. The young guy working with her got a clean bag of ice, and some paper towels and gave that to Larry. When he left, Larry spun his tires spraying dirt and gravel on the kids sitting at the lunch van."

Marcy remained silent so D'Angelo went on. "I wanted to talk to you before I talked to Larry since I understand you left camp with him and, of course, because you two work together. I thought maybe you had something you would like to add."

"Okay. Let's see. That's bad. Larry should be more polite to people. I wasn't there so I really don't know what went on at the lunch van."

D'Angelo sat there in contemplation. He was tapping the eraser end of a pencil on the table. He didn't want to pump Marcy for information, but it was evident that she wasn't going to throw Larry under the bus. "So, here's what's going on. As the HRSP, I'm supposed to take care of problems that come up that don't have anything directly to do with putting the fire out. These problems just make it harder to put the fire out or may lead to unsafe situations. In the rest of the world, we have time to go through a lengthy complaint process if someone is being bullied, for example. We don't have the luxury of time here. People and resources are easily put in jeopardy in a matter of hours. We can't let a liability linger while we make sure we have all the information we need to be fair to everyone. So when I get wind of something that might be lack of mutual respect, I have to get on it immediately before it turns into an unsafe situation."

Marcy asked, "tell me how this is unsafe... except for spinning dirt on people, that's unsafe. But how is Larry being rude or crude or just being Larry makes things unsafe?"

"Okay, I understand you were on a shot crew, right?"

"Yes. For four years," Marcy replied.

"On your crew, or another one, did you know of a crew member being harassed or to feel like they weren't respected?" D'Angelo asked.

"Well, yes." You're talking to one who was, Marcy thought.

"Now, if that person felt discounted, not valued by his or her crewmembers, and was just plain fed up because the harassment and bullying had gone on too long – would you assign that person the job of the lookout for the crew on a hot, windy, red flag day? Would you put the lives of your crew members in the hands of someone who was looking to even the score?"

"No, I'm sure I wouldn't do that. But how is the girl handing out ice wanting to settle a score with Larry rising to that level?"

"Fair question," D'Angelo replied. "For all the different resources we have on a fire and the sharp boundaries that define each one, there is not one that can tolerate lack of mutual respect within or without their resource and not affect, to some degree, the entire fire organization on a fire.

"Picture this scenario. So Larry continues to be disrespectful to the little lunch van girl. When she's had it with him it's time for payback. Now, she is dealing with a little camp crud. At the time, she wants to be real close to the blue palaces because nature is calling unexpectantly and often. This is something she would only want to share with her enemies. So, she carefully opens up a lunch sack. Then the baggie that has the lunch meat in it. She separates the two slices of meat and blows snot from one nostril on the meat. Then she closes it all up so no one can tell it's been tampered with. She makes sure Larry gets the infected lunch sack. Larry eats the lunch, gets camp crud, sneezes all over the pickup steering wheel, you get in the truck to go somewhere and get crud spray from the steering wheel on your hands, rub your eye... now both you and Larry become super spreaders and the effectiveness of the camp takes a nosedive."

"I've got more examples. Want me to go on with the helitack group?" D'Angelo asked.

"No. You've been more than convincing. I think you may have given me camp crud!"

"Haha! So, tell me about the geode incident."

"Oh geez! I'd really rather you asked Larry about that."

"You want to trust your side of the story with your friend Larry?"

"Point taken. So tell me what you know," suggested Marcy.

"No, it doesn't work like that. I want your words without you gauging how much I already know. But first. Tell me what's going on with you. Why are you being such a hard nut to crack? I can go to the IC this evening and say, 'here's what I know, and based on that I recommend we cut Larry lose right now.' So, see? You are not going to help him any by keeping things in the dark. Before demobbing him, I will talk with him and let him talk it out. He will most likely downplay the whole disrespecting the young lady and throwing dirt from the tires. I'm guessing there is something there that needs to be changed. Something like an attitude adjustment. Every one here is fully qualified and has a right to be here. Not everyone has a right to stay here if their work or attitude does not qualify them." D'Angelo said.

"Look, David. I don't want to be difficult, and I respect what you are trying to do. I don't know what you heard about... the geode. But I'm not going to say I was bullied if I don't feel I was. Larry said some things I can only hope that, sometime in the future, he'll smack himself in the head and wonder how he could have been so stupid. I can stand up for myself.

I don't need the government to shield me from some insensitive fool who is trying to hurt my feelings. I do plan on talking to Larry about our 'conversation' today. He may come to you looking for protection from me... but I plan on arriving at an understanding with him."

D'Angelo said, "So you are not being bullied. Got it. But, really Marcy, if he causes problems for you, I can help. You may well be able to stand up and look a bully in the eye. There are a lot of people who don't seem to be able to do that. Look. There was a young girl on the camp crew a few years ago that reminds me of the girl on the lunch van here. She was running out of clean clothes because she didn't want to take them to the laundry. She wouldn't come to talk to me, but one of the guys on the crew found out, and he came and talked to me about her situation. Then I talked with her together with another young girl on the crew to find out just what the problem was. It seems this young guy working at the laundry had said some suggestive things to her as she walked by. Things like, 'Is that as good as it looks?' and 'Yeah baby, gimmie some of that'. So, I pulled the one guy in and talked with him. He denied any such thing. Before he could get back to the laundry, I separated him from the other guy that worked there with him. After a heart-to-heart talk, this guy gave me all I needed to approach the vendor and advise him that he could swap out his employees or we would swap out our laundry service. By that afternoon we had fresh employees running the laundry. I did not stipulate the gender, but I was glad the new people were female. I can imagine the young woman not wanting the mouthy guy anywhere near her clothes, personal clothing especially. Figuratively speaking, I don't want anyone having to walk around in smelly sweat-stained clothing because they don't want to make waves or stand up to bullies or perverts, no matter the situation. And that is why, Miss Marcy, I will follow up with the ice bag incident. One of my guiding principles is 'what you permit, you promote'! And I sure don't want to promote that kind of disregard for other people."

"Well, I'm glad you are here," Marcy said. "I'm glad you seem so sincere about doing your job. I guess I never realized the HRSP did much at all except being a cheerleader for mutual respect, posting things on bulletin boards, and sticking an HRSP message in the IAP! Oh! Now I also know you tell jokes and play the harmonica!"

"I hope you know I don't 'seem' to do my job, I 'do' my job. My job, doing all I can so that people don't have to ever feel bad about being at work, that job... to me, is as serious as a heart attack. I'm committed to it. Most people on a fire will never know what the HRSP is doing or has done. That's how we have to work to be effective."

"Well thank you. I'll let you know if I get in over my head," Marcy said.

D'Angelo said, "sure. Just remember, the hardest thing about being at work should be the work! Humm! I should get a T-shirt with that on it!

"Fine. Okay." D'Angelo continued. "On another subject. Cupcake. I'm curious. How did you wind up with that huge truck? And how did you come up with the name Cupcake for it? Newsflash: that beast is not a gentle little cupcake!"

Marcy told D'Angelo about Grandpa Sam buying the Diamond Reo in 1974 and how she had been driving it since she was 13 or 14. She told him about after her mother died, how her dad had driven the truck cross country and painted the name Desperado on it. She shared how her father joined the Army and then, when he got out, tried to go back to driving. Her father, Daniel, suffered from PTSD. When he tried to drive, he often had flashbacks and became disoriented.

Marcy explained, "so, the truck kind of fell to me. I had to..."

"Wait! Hold on." D'Angelo interrupted. "I've had so many veterans working on fires that are dealing with PTSD. The demons they face are seldom noticeable by most people. I'm interested to hear more about your father becoming disoriented if you don't mind. I don't want to pry where I'm not wanted. But what happened that caused your dad to give the truck up?

"No. I don't mind you asking. At first, he would just come in later than he should have. When we asked him what the hold-up was, he was real evasive. He usually smelled like a brewery. Once, he left to pick up a load and just didn't show up. He was supposed to pick up a load from the Champion sawmill. The dispatcher knows my grandpa and called him to find out what happened. Grandpa went looking for him and, on the way to the sawmill, he noticed Desperado sitting behind the Oodle Inn, a bar located about half a mile before the sawmill. Grandpa said he found him sitting in the back booth just staring straight ahead with a warm beer he hadn't touched sitting in front of him. Dad said he just stopped in for a quick drink and time just got away from him. The last run he ever made with Desperado was over in Washington state. He had been driving through timberland for a couple of hours and then the highway went up a canyon out of the forest. When Desperado cleared the canyon, as far as the eye could see were sand-colored freshly harvested wheat fields. To dad, he had just come out of a wormhole into Afghanistan! He was shocked 5 to 6 years back in time. His reality became Taliban and roadside bombs. The state police were called and they found dad sitting in the truck where he stopped, right in the middle of the highway. They had a hard time getting dad out of the truck because he was suspicious of everything. State Police and Afghanistan Police looked different, but dad couldn't tell if he was in Afghanistan with American police or if he was with American police in America. Now I know that sounds the same to us, but to dad, it was a mental battle he was trying to win, rational or not. Grandpa and I had to drive over and pick him and the truck up. Grandpa Sam didn't trust him in the pickup with me so he drove the pickup with dad in it home and I finished dad's haul in the Diamond Reo. The guys at the unloading dock looked at me funny, but I was tall for my age and I stayed in the cab."

"Wow!" said D'Angelo, "that's quite a story... quite an introduction into the realities of life for you!"

"What? Are you saying not everyone starts as a long-haul trucker? If you knew my life before this, you'd be thinking this was when things started looking more normal."

"So how's your dad doing now?" D'Angelo asked.

"Well, he still has his 'vacant' times. But we try to make sure he stays busy and away from alcohol. He works on the ranch doing whatever needs to be done and he builds guitars and sells them. Can you imagine he works on each piece, meticulously sanding and shaping them until he can get them to ring out with a C# tone? He says that's why his guitars have such vibrant clarity! Too bad he's not a better guitar picker! We could be liv'n on Easy Street!"

"Is he working with any professionals to deal with his PTSD?"

"Yeah, almost every Thursday evening he goes to a program called 'Recovery'. It's through Faith Baptist there in McCall. We think it helps. We can't tell if dad is making progress but at least he's not losing ground. We don't hear him having night terrors as often... maybe fewer nightmares too."

"Marcy, I gotta say. I have the deepest respect for people like your dad and his service to our country. You must be proud of him."

"Yeah. Well. All I ever wanted from him was a dad and I can't seem to get that." Marcy said and immediately rebuked herself. Like the loosed arrow and the spoken word...

"I think there are support groups for people who live with those having PTSD, alcoholism, gambling, and the like," D'Angelo said. "Have you gone to any such meetings?"

"Yes, I've thought about that." What Marcy was saying to D'Angelo in her mind was, "Zip it, Zippy!" His help wasn't helping.

"Hey! I'm probably not helping. But, here is something that helped this one guy." David D'Angelo flipped through some files from his briefcase. He handed Marcy 4 typed pages of paper. Several years ago I met an EMT on a fire who had bad experiences in Viet Nam. In his efforts to rejoin the 'real' world, he wrote this. He said his therapist told him it would help."

"This guy doesn't care if other people see what he wrote?" Marcy asked.

"No. He assured me, I could do whatever I wanted to with it. It seemed to comfort him to think others would read about what he's going through with his PTSD. So, take it, share it. If I knew how to contact him, I'd let him know that what he wrote might be giving someone else a little comfort. It might reassure your dad. Although I know he knows it, he is not alone. Lots of people are dealing with similar demons. I don't know if it will ever get better, but it sounds like he is letting the sunshine in at least a little."

"I agree, David. Thanks. Listen, it's getting late. I'm gonna head for my sleeper."

"Late! Are you kidding me? I'm on the clock til 2200! I do some of my best networking about this time!"

"Haha! You just network away. You can do that without me. About Larry, I've got something in mind for him. He's not gonna skate free. If you demob him, release him from the fire, he'll be beyond my ability to 'reach out and touch him.' I hope you don't do anything rash."

"Me! Do anything rash! What about you? You're planning on reaching out and touching him. With what – a 2X4? Maybe I should demob him to save him from bodily harm at the hands of his 'friends'!"

"Naw. C'mon. Trust me. I can't speak for Cupcake, but I'm not gonna break his body. I haven't worked it out yet. I don't have the answer I'm looking for, but I'm waiting."

D'Angelo leaned back in his chair and locked his fingers behind his head. "Okay! I think I see where you are going here! A little, 'practice what you preach' maybe?"

"Yeah. I guess you could say that. Not what I wanted at first. You ship him out of here and he just gets harder, and he learns nothing. I'm betting God has a better plan."

Marcy sat in Cupcake's passenger seat. She was ready for bed but had to settle a few things in her mind. She didn't think it would be wise to share the geode stone incident with Jacody. She wasn't ready for him to know of the conflict between her and Larry yet. If her husband got even a sniff of the hostile work environment she was in, she would have a 6'-6" man permanently attached to her hip! She wasn't going to lie about it; just not going to mention it.

Her eyes came to rest on the driver's seat. How many hours, how many miles had she been privileged to pilot this mighty Diamond Reo? Is it unhealthy to attribute human emotion to an inanimate machine? It had provided food, clothing, and shelter for her, her father, and her grandfather. It had made utility payments, bought livestock feed, transported things to the ranch, and hauled things away from the ranch. As "Cupcake" it had served as a confessional for Marcy. All of her deepest personal thoughts had been shared out loud here when there was no one else in the world she could tell. As "Desperado", had it also been a confessional? Desperado had certainly been a witness to some of Daniel's most conflicted times. "If this truck could talk... If Daniel could talk..." Marcy said out loud.

"Humm. If dad could talk about 'it'... maybe, we would know what 'it' is." Marcy thought of the Viet Nam vet David D'Angelo told her about and decided to read what the vet had written.

Forty-three years ago, a long way from home, I remember asking myself what I am doing here. I recalled that moment just yesterday. The Stream Lake Fire at Red Mt. Ranch started three days ago and as an EMT with Mineral Cunty I was on standby while two crews of twenty hotshot firefighters were working the fire in a very steep rugged terrain. Fifty yards in front of me was a Bell 205 plus, plus helicopter with a four-hundred-gallon bucket being filled with water to dump on a hot spot up the mountain. The ship was very much like the Army Huey choppers in the Vietnam era only much faster. The sound it made was eerily the same and it caused me to recall, what I am doing here. Our infantry unit was doing recon missions from a firebase. A Chinook helicopter came in and blew a soldier off balance against a steel engineering stake taking all the skin completely off his forearm so I could see his veins and muscle tissue as though I was looking through a window. No blood, just the window. What am I doing here, I thought and I quickly remembered when the soldier came up to me. Life on a firebase was busy. The sound of the helicopter was constant, I remembered, as the bird in front of me took off with his maximum load and came back again for another every four or five minutes constantly for several hours, constantly reminding me, constantly taking me back, over and over. The laboring sound of it taking off and the heavy sound of it coming in, it was so close the ground shook and the force of the wind from the blades was still strong as it hovered some forty feet above the lake while the bucket filled. It went up the mountain sometime high above a half-mile away and the faraway sound was just as familiar, just as haunting.

Recollections are pouring in as I witness this operation all around me. Earlier that morning a hotshot crew prepared to "move out". They had checked their gear and had been briefed and were prepared to go. They left in a single file very close together. I recalled doing the same many times forty-three years ago, only yesterday all of a sudden. We would leave the base for a recon mission in exactly the same way. We even looked the same, determined, ready for action, eager to do our job, wanting to do our best, and hoping that we can. Our weapons were cleaned and ready. Our knives were sharp. Our packs were full of food and water and a landing zone had been established or, at least, plotted on a map in case it was needed. Are they as brave as we were, were they as scared? They headed into the unknown carrying chain saws and gallons of gasoline into a burn area. That seems brave and scary. They are soldiers for sure. We walked into the unknown perhaps more cautiously much further apart, five or six paces. If I missed a step or stumbled or slowed down at all, Tennessee would poke me in the butt with the barrel of his M-60 he carried. "Come on Doc, don't make me have to stop". We were excited at first, scared but excited. Combined with the uncertainty and very little, if any knowledge of the situation or mission, scary

took on a new meaning. The soldiers I'm
watching were only two steps apart, sure-
footed, and no evidence of any possibility of a
missed step or stumble. I was impressed. Do
they stop for smoke breaks, do they build a fire
at night, and do they write to their girlfriends
and think of their families back home? There
are women soldiers as well. Small and frail-
looking but tough and rugged too, they do not
miss a step and through the gear and tools they
carry and through the black soot on their faces
when they return, still beautiful as women
usually are.

Soon it became common, ordinary, a way of
life. Many times while in the mountain jungles
you would welcome the sound of an incoming
bird and hate to see it go. This depended, of
course, on its mission. Was it bringing mail,
food and water, or supplies? Was it coming to
take us back to the rear or to another location?
Would it be a hot LZ, (landing zone) with
enemy in the area or just another hilltop? Not
too far away we hoped as we usually had to
walk back. Each specific reason for its'
sometimes heavy and sometimes light as a
feather decent had a different sound somehow,
although some would say it was always the
same, it was not to me.

The chopper returns coming in light and
taking off again heavy with its' 12-hundred-
pound load. Its near sounds and far sounds
constantly coming and going bringing in

buckets of memories and taking them back out
again. That's the way it has been for forty-
three years. They come and they go. They
sometimes cause reactions that I do not like,
nor do the people around me who do not
understand and who are not allowed in to find
out. Apologies are nearly impossible as they
would require explanations that are impossible.
As I am not certain how to even spell PTSD - I
certainly cannot explain it. Once you are told
you have it for about 30 seconds it feels good to
know what has been wrong all this time,
decades of stress and distress. Then comes
anger and there is no denial. I finally asked for
help with sleeplessness and depression. Now,
it seems, I've been asleep for a long, long time.
Help is coming painfully slow. But I'm no
longer looking for a rope and bridge as they say
and at times I'm feeling much better, thank you
very very much. I hope to feel alive real soon.

So now you are in or, have a foot in the door
as I've spilled my guts and found it necessary to
express these thoughts. I'm told it helps to talk
and in a way it does and in a way it doesn't.
There are definitely pros and cons. For sure
and especially if you care for others, they will
care for you. Thank you soldiers for all you've
done, for all you did and all you do and will do.
Shaking hands and being thanked for your
service feels good forty-three years later. I
wonder what it would have felt like back in the

day. Thank you soldiers for making that a popular response these days.

Why am I here? I guess I'm here to be inspired. Inspired to tell someone, inspired to thank someone, inspired by helping someone, inspired to be someone, inspired to feel like someone, inspired to know I was and am someone. This experience could have been a nightmare. Perhaps it has awakened me from one. Sounds of firefights in the distance or bombing runs by the B-52s remind you of where you are as you dream of home. The sound of chainsaws in the distance reminds me of that and where I am.

The soldiers return walking down the mountain as they went up, in line, very close as if they were marching down the street with no gear, chain saws, packs, or weapons of war. They look as though they would turn right around and go back if asked though I'm sure they look forward to the downtime. They take care of their equipment and tools first before gathering for food and conversation and enjoy a comradery they will never forget or lose. Yes, they are soldiers. We returned not nearly so sure we had accomplished something or nearly as much. They are black with soot and have a more experienced look about them, maybe a look of victory, maybe worry or concern - certainly not defeat. If they had prayed for rain, they have received. If they had prayed for health and safety, they have all returned. As the skies grow dark with clouds the thunder roars and the lightning strikes all around, I'm reminded of our National Anthem as our flag still waves which is posted on the hood of the flight crew maintenance truck.

Cupcake's cab and sleeper became a private, secluded, secure sanctuary. All the hustle and bustle that continued in the staging area fell away. It became silent. Marcy closed her eyes and went to her safe place in her mind.

"Ohhh... ," an involuntary moan escaped Marcy's throat from deep inside. Tears flowed down her cheeks. Tears for the Nam vet she had never met... tears for Daniel, the father she wanted to meet. "Why? Why! Why should it be so? It seems like it should be so simple. Just... throw off the cloak! Look! You're here! You are not there! I'm here! I'm your little girl! Daddy! Daddy! Oh Daddy I love you! Where are you?" Marcy pleaded.

Turning, Marcy slid off the seat to her knees on the floorboard. With her face in her hands on the seat, she prayed. "God. God? Abba Father. I have no words. Please, please listen to my heart... speak to my soul. These men and women, - my father - these people are not damaged goods to be set aside. They have families who need them. Give them the stability of mind and thought to cast off this mantle of destruction, violence, and carnage. You are The Great I Am, The Creator of All Things. To me, you are All Things! Are You not greater than the horrific circumstances that consume and control my father and others? Can you not overshadow and overpower these forces of evil that deceive them? Please Lord, will you not pull them to Yourself and set them free? Break the chains that bind, restrict, hinder and deceive! Release them from their prison Lord! I am pouring myself out to You! I want my father to come out of his shell and be who you intended him to be."

Marcy was quiet for a bit. She found a handkerchief and mopped her face dry. She considered her conversation with God. Had she said all that was weighing on her? "Lord, one more thing if I may. I feel a burden for Larry. I see him as a lonely man with a cold, empty heart. Please help me to tolerate him. Help me to find some good in him. Let us not give up on him, but show him the way to salvation. May he find peace and love through You."

"So, Lord. I've begged. I've cried. I'm weary. I'm finished. My trust and my faith remain in you, Lord. Thank you, Jesus! Amen."

Marcy felt like she was just coming out of anesthesia, even though she had never experienced it. She felt groggy. She wanted to lay down in Cupcake's sleeper, pull her other pillow to her chest, curl up in a fetal position, and numbly drift off for the night. But she couldn't. She had a phone call to make.

She gave herself another 15-20 minutes to adjust her attitude. She played a few hands of solitaire on her laptop. On Youtube she found a Bob Dylan song performed by the Jerry Garcia band; I Shall be Released.

They say everything can be replaced
Yet every distance is not near
So I remember every face
Of every man who put me here.
I see my light come shining
From the west unto the east
Any day now, Any day now
I shall be released.

It seemed all her news of the day had a tone of sadness that she didn't want to pass on to Jacody. Since she wasn't ready to talk about Larry, she had the Nam vet and his description of his PTSD to talk about. Jacody would easily understand how Marcy would want to relate that to her father.

"One ringy-dingy. Eh." She didn't feel like being goofy tonight. The phone rang two more times.

"Hello, Baby!" Jacody recognized Marcy's ring tone.

"Oh JJ. I've been wanting to hear your voice. I knew it would be good, but it's better than I thought it'd be!"

"Hey, hey! What's going on. I know you are happy to hear me and I'm happy to hear you. But something is bothering you!"

"No... it's alright, but yes. Something is bothering me. I'm so very sad and forlorn." Marcy said.

"Forlorn! That sounds... dramatic and very serious. What's up?"

"I didn't mean to start our call off with me whining," Marcy said.

"You never whine when you are talking to me. I never hear you that way. But you do concern me, and

I want to jump up and slay the dragons that dare to cloud your eyes."

"Oh JJ! I love you so much! You say I'm being dramatic and then you come up with slaying dragons! What would I ever do without you?"

"You'll never know, Love! But tell me, what's got you down this evening?" Jacody said.

"Well, some of the same old stuff! Poor me. My dad's here but he's not!"

"Yeah. I know that song. What got that started?"

"It's that HRSP David D'Angelo's fault. He..."

"So! It is he I shall slay!" Said Jacody.

"No, silly. He asked me how I came by Cupcake."

"Ah... poor guy! He had no idea the can of worms he was opening, did he?"

"Not a clue! So I went through the whole thing or was going through it, but when I mentioned my dad's PTSD, he got really interested. He said he worked with lots of guys who suffer from that.He gave me this Viet Nam vet's write-up that was to help him deal with his own PTSD and suggested my dad might want to do the same."

"Surely, that's not something new that hasn't been suggested to Daniel before, is it?" Jacody asked.

"I'm sure it's not. But I plan to share this with dad. Even if it doesn't move him to do the same... it is just one more person who has to deal with the demons of war as he does. I tell you, JJ, this... this syndrome is so despicable... it robs people of people. And tonight, the theft of my father is just really laying heavy on my heart!"

"Sweetheart. I want to dry your tears. I want your head on my chest and I want to go to sleep tonight holding you close. I want to wake up with you in the morning and fix apple slices fried in pancake batter for your breakfast. Most of all, I don't want you to ever have another sad moment if I can help it... "

"Stop! I think I just heard Cupcake's glow plugs click on. You keep talking like that and she will start up and head home regardless of what I want."

"You don't want to come home?" Asked Jacody.

"Of course I do... but at the right time. Eyes on the prize! Remember?"

"Yes, dear. I remember. You're right. But the heart wants what the heart wants. Since when did the heart use logic and reason?" Asked Jacody.

"I know. Just don't tempt me. So I'm blue. We talked about that. What about you, Chuck and Chew?"

"Aw, the boys and I are fine. Roberts well came in strong. I started to dig a 500-foot ditch from where the pump head will be to the center pivot. I should finish that up tomorrow and start putting pipe in the ditch. So, that is on target and moving on."

"How about Jane Lew?" Marcy asked.

"Whaaat?.. oh yeah! The estate gate for Jane Lew."

"You forget?"

"No, no. I didn't forget. I've got a layout and a form made for it down in the shop. I'm still tinkering with the computer design for the plasma welder. But it's coming along... I just hope Jane likes it."

194

"Well, if she doesn't, you can put it on our driveway. I can't get you to do one for us so I'll be content with hers!"

"Eh! You wouldn't like hers." Said Jacody.

"Why not?"

"Because it's not yours." Said Jacody.

"Then make one that's mine!"

"All in good time dear, all in good time."

"Sigh. Speaking of time. You've calmed me down and I think I'll be able to dream of you tonight. It's time for me to go nighty-night. Said Marcy.

"Alright! I'll let you go to bed. I plan on dreaming of you tonight also. Love you dear, sleep tight!"

"I love you too. Pleasant dreams! Good night, JJ."

"Hey! Wait!" Said Jacody.

"What?"

"Tonight, get on Youtube, and let's go to sleep together listening to Fox and Fossil's cover of Neil Young's 'Harvest Moon'. I'll pretend you've got a cold and so you're sleeping far over on your side of the bed so I don't get sick!"

"Oh my gosh! You are such a romantic sap! Are all ditch diggers like you?"

"The really good ditch diggers are! Now, come on, you know you want to!" Said Jacody.

"Yeah. I want to sweetie pie. But why do I have to be the one with a cold?" Asked Marcy.

"Alright. It was my idea. I'll be the one with a cold and I don't want you to get it. That is the only reason I'm staying on my side of the bed tonight!"

"Yes, dear. Thank you. You are so considerate. Now, good night!" Said Marcy.

"Good night, Love!" Said Jacody.

To Marcy's surprise, in no time at all, she felt the welcoming waves of sleep washing over her.

> Come a <u>little</u> bit closer
> Hear what I have to say
> Just like <u>children</u> sleepin'
> We <u>could</u> dream this <u>night</u> away
>
> But there's a full moon risin'
> Let's go dancin' in the light
> We know <u>where</u> the music's playin'
> Let's go out and feel the night
>
> Because I'm <u>still</u> in love with you
> I want to see you <u>dance</u> again
> Because I'm <u>still</u> in love with you
> On this <u>harvest</u> moon

With music faintly drifting from Cupcake's open sleeper-unit window, the shadowy figure that had been listening quickly slipped deeper into the night and away.

Chapter Twelve
Home Alone

Jacody was taking a break. Work on the Triple Rocking R Ranch was at a halt. He was sitting on the shady side of the truck, leaning against the back tire of his one-ton flatbed dually. This was the next to last bottle of water in his cooler. He had shared it with Chuck and Chew who were sprawled out under the truck dozing. It was a force of habit, he supposed, sharing whatever he had with the two dogs. All morning they had made trips over to the creek to drink or lay in the water. They certainly didn't need his water.

At each end of the alfalfa field where Jacody was working, groundhogs had taken up residence. Chuck and Chew had spent most of their energy going from one side to the other attempting to herd the two groundhogs to one place. With no concept of the "herd" mentality, the shy animals always ran into their holes in the ground when the dogs approached. Once, Chuck and Chew were able to get between one of the groundhogs and its hole. The groundhog did a 180 turn and ran to another hole. The two dogs just stood there looking at each other for a moment in disbelief, "should'da known – he has a back door!"

A cool 87° in the shade and hot 95° in the open sun, there would be sweat streaming down Jacody's face if it weren't for the low humidity in the high desert. Jacody was thankful for the cool water, but it was hard to really appreciate things like a cooler with bottles of water in it when you were missing really big important things. Well, only one big important thing, but that thing was Jacody's whole world. He and Marcy had worked together on everything since before they were married and now, here he was by himself. It wasn't the extra hands helping on a job that he was bemoaning... it was his other half, his spiritual mate, his physical mate that he was pining for. Oh, the luxury of sitting in the shade like he was doing right now and having her beside him. They'd talk about anything - simple things, philosophical deep talks, immediate day-to-day talks, her needs, his needs, their needs, family, friends, opportunities, whatever - how they might be most productive when that dump truck load of crushed stone shows up! How's that plasma welder going to pay for itself if they don't get more orders for estate gates? How are they going to find the time to rack that 6-gallon carboy of wine fermenting in the basement? Where would they put the stuff stored in the small bedroom if they ever decided they might need a nursery.

Jacody's thoughts hung up on that last idea, as it always did. Marcy didn't seem to have much energy to talk about a nursery and the reason they would need a nursery. She said there would be plenty of time to figure that out if they ever needed to. She would tell him to be happy, he already had two babies that he treated like his little kids. Then she would jab him in the ribs right where it made him jump when he'd say something like, "dogs are fine but babies don't shed as much!" Ahh. He was home, but he was homesick never-the-less.

His melancholy ruminations were suspended when he got a call on his cell phone. It was from Stone Mountain Stone. Bad news. They reported to him that one of their trucks had broken through a rancher's bridge with their only other truck trapped on the ranch side. They were just letting him know that they weren't going to be delivering crushed stone to the Robert's ranch today, but they would try to get it delivered within the next few days. He would get a call from them to confirm when.

Jacody was both disappointed and relieved. Disappointed because he was at a stand-still here until he got the crushed stone to use as a bed for the underground water pipes he was ready to place. Relieved because he would be able to go home and work on the estate gate that he was planning for Marcy. So, with a new direction for the day, he picked up all of his tools and locked up his backhoe. With all secured, he got in his truck and headed for home. He didn't need to look to see if the dogs were in the back of the truck; that was a foregone conclusion.

As soon as they got home, he emptied the contents of his cooler into the refrigerator and fixed himself a sandwich. Then he called Grandpa Sam and Daniel to let them know he was home and working on the estate gate if they wanted to come join him. Daniel said they would be there in 20 minutes.

Jacody had shared the surprise he planned for Marcy with Daniel and Grandpa Sam. Since he wanted to get it done before Marcy got home, Grandpa Sam and Daniel had offered to help out. They came over in the evenings and fed the animals and helped with the gate. The two of them had already created an area 32 feet wide and 20 feet deep where Moon Ranch Road and Weiser River Road meet. Independent of Jacody, they worked on the stonework approach that would form a wall around the pull-in area in front of the gate. Being able to rely on Marcy's Grandpa and dad to manage big jobs like this was the only way Jacody could hope to get the gate done before Marcy returned to Moon Ranch.

Jecody was making good progress with his forms for the two 8-foot gate halves, and he had his computer design done for each side. When closed, the top rail of the 16-foot-wide gate would resemble a low bell-shaped curve; starting at 5 feet high at the outside ends and gracefully rising to 8 feet at the center. Vertical bars were designed to go from the bottom rail through the top rail and extend to a pointed end 6 inches above the top rail

Daniel and Grandpa Sam were pulling into the barnyard as Jacody took his last swig of iced tea to wash down his second sandwich. They wasted no time getting busy. Jacody had the mainframe of the left gate in the form on his large welding worktable. He measured the lengths of the vertical bars for the gate and Daniel and Grandpa Sam cut them to length. Each one was different to fit the graceful upward sweep of the top rail.

Once all the vertical pieces were cut, Grandpa Sam went to feed the animals while Daniel continued to work with Jacody. Each vertical rod had to be clamped and welded one piece at a time. Jacody took special care to ensure each rod was positioned exactly right so it took a while to complete one side of the gate.

By the time they were done, Grandpa Sam came back to the shop. He said he had just got a call from Grandma Nellie and supper would be ready in about 45 minutes. "She also said if Daniel and I expected to eat any of it, we'd better make sure young Jacody here comes with us!"

"Humm! I don't even have to know what she's fixed to know I won't turn that invitation down!" Jacody responded.

"Yeah, it don't matter what mom's fixed... but did she say what she fixed?" Daniel wanted to know.

"Navy beans and ham hocks have been simmering all day. I know that for a fact," Grandpa Sam said. "She told me she had vinegar coleslaw, American fried potatoes with onions, cornbread, and rhubarb-strawberry pie. She had a big jug of sun tea sitting out in the front yard when we left."

"Well, that seals it! You guys head out, I'll put these tools up and be on your bumper in no time!" Jacody said enthusiastically.

Jacody was sitting on the Portman's front porch polishing off the second piece of pie with a big mug of strong black coffee. Obviously it was Grandma Nellie who had made the coffee and it was good. "Too thick to drink and too thin to plow!" was how Grandpa Sam's coffee was described. The Western sky was all ablaze; the sunset made more intense due to the many forest fires burning in that part of the country. Jacody felt comfortable and at ease with these people – his in-laws. Being here with Grandpa Sam and Grandma Nellie sitting in the porch swing, Daniel on the front steps trying to work out a song on the last guitar he had built, Chuck and Chew sprawled out in the middle of the porch with their cousin Bojangles, Bo for short, and Bo's adopted brother, a rottweiler named Quigley, gave him a strong sense of belonging. What he was experiencing only made him miss Marcy more – things felt good, but just not right.

"I talked with Marcy again today," Grandma Nellie interrupted Jacody's thoughts. "She usually calls me around 2 every afternoon."

"I won't get to talk with her until tonight just before she turns in," Jacody said.

Grandpa Sam said, "I don't get to talk with her none at all! I have to be content hearing everything 2nd hand from Nellie here."

"This is a big change for you, isn't it?" Nellie asked Jacody, choosing not to respond to Sam.

"Well, yes, it is. A bigger change than I thought it would be."

"Seems you two have been inseparable, doing everything together for going on three years now," Nellie said.

"It is odd. We always make the bed together every morning. She makes her side and I make mine. It's how we start the day off. Together. Doing what needs to be done, doing what we want to do but doing it together." Jacody gave a sad smile. "Then she makes breakfast and I watch her. I eat breakfast and then she watches me!" He laughed, "no, I'm just kidding. But we work together really well. She is a good organizer and a good hand. Kinda funny. I'm putting in that irrigation system for the Robert's and I turn to ask her a question or I'll be on the backhoe and wonder why she isn't doing what she usually does when I need her. I get really lonely."

"I could maybe give you a hand if you want." Jacody didn't realize Daniel was listening. With a guitar in his hands, he usually drifts off in his own world.

"Hey thanks, you helping with the gate and all is a'plenty!" Jacody said. "I'm doing fine on that job, except for getting the crushed stone I need. It's just that I got used to always being able to rely on Marcy, and, now it's different. Not that she isn't doing her part, she is doing way more than that. I'm just being selfish."

"Did Marcy say anything to you about some guy on the fire that works for that logging company too?" Nellie asked.

"No. What about some guy?" The fork clicked on the near-empty plate as Jacody dropped it and his eyes narrowed on Grandma Nellie. There was no mistaking a change in Jacody's easy-going voice to one as serious as a heart attack. "What's going on?"

Nellie could hear Marcy scolding her already. "Loose lips sink ships!"

"Oh... nothing really," Nellie recovered a little from the shock of Jacody's sudden change in attitude. "She just told me this guy that works for the same guy she is working for is a little disgusting in the way he talks. Then this other guy, and I don't know what he has to do with anything, was going to kick him out of a job but Marcy told him she would handle it. Then this woman hit him and her on the arm real hard, and.... Well, it just sounds really complicated. Aren't they supposed to be putting a fire out? How can they be walking around a track and digging up rocks? You worked on fires. I thought maybe you could tell me. I usually just say yes like I know what she means but I'm lost most of the time."

Jacody relaxed and smiled his usual friendly smile. "Yes, it can be confusing. You know Marcy. She wouldn't let anyone do something for her if she can do it herself. If someone is being crude around her, she will tolerate it only so long before she puts the hammer down... then Katy bar the door! She did tell me she walks off some of all the extra calories from the meals they give them. I even made the mistake of asking her if she was being forced to eat everything. She found no humor in that. I think most of what she is doing is like firemen at a firehouse. They keep as busy as they can when there is nothing burning, but their purpose is to be available at a moment's notice when they are needed. So, she and others do have time to walk around the track while not needed to do other things. I don't know about digging up rocks."

Nellie said, "I don't know where the rocks came in so I wouldn't concern myself about that. I'm just happy she isn't out facing the fires like you and she used to do on that shot hot crew. She is safe and far away from danger."

Jacody chuckled a little. "You mean the hotshot crew, I think."

"That was some time ago and I'm lucky to have the right words. Do I really need to put them in the right order?" Nellie laughed.

"Woman you don't need to worry," her husband said, patting her knee. "We all knew what you meant!"

Twilight was beginning to settle across the land. The oppressive heat of the day was gone. Jacody stood up. Like they were shot out of a canon, Chuck and Chew were off the porch standing in the yard looking for a sign; house, truck, or are you just going to stand there? Jacody reached to gather up empty cups, saucers, and forks.

Grandma Nellie said, "Oh my! Jacody! Leave all that. I'll get those when we go in. Don't you worry about them!"

"If you insist," Jacody said. "And thank you for a very good meal and nice evening. I am anxious to start cutting some designs out."

Nellie said, "What?"

"For the gate!" Jacody laughed, "designs for the estate gate we are making!"

"Well of course," Nellie said, "for the gate!"

Jacody bent over low and gave Grandma Nellie a hug and a kiss on the cheek. He gave Grandpa Sam a strong handshake and, as he went down the steps, a fist bump to Daniel. "See you guys tomorrow?"

"You betcha!" Sam said.

"I'll be up first thing, but you guys show up when you're ready. See you tomorrow then. Good evening and thanks again," said Jacody.

Moon Ranch was dark and gloomy. There were no lights on in the house. The two security lights, one in front of the barn and the other illuminating the implement yard, did nothing to lift Jacody's gloominess. He parked his dually in its stall under the shed roof on the side of the barn. Once in the house he turned a few lights on in the kitchen and made a pot of coffee. Filling a thermos with the black gold, he took it out to the workshop. He had his earbuds in and had Pandora playing the best of Santana.

Setting up his computer projector, he pointed it at the sheet of steel he had carefully set up on edge exactly perpendicular to the projector's light, he traced the first design on the steel with a Sharpie. Then the second, and so on until there was no room left on the sheet of steel. Jacody continued cutting designs out until Motown's Martha and the Vandellas

206

singing "Nowhere to Run" was interrupted by Marcy's 10 PM phone call.

"You have reached the number in which you have dialed. If you intended to reach a wrong..."

"JJ!" Marcy said, "knock it off you goofball!"

"Hello love! It is so good to hear your voice tonight."

Marcy said, "you sound happy. Have you had a good day?"

"Oh, I don't know. I guess it has been as good a day as I can expect. Things have slowed up over at Triple Rocking R Ranch, but that has given me time to work on other things."

"What else have you been working on?" Marcy asked.

"I'll tell you the best thing I worked on!" Jacody said. "It was the rhubarb-strawberry pie your grandmother made! I went to your grandparents for supper tonight. Man, was it good!"

"So, you liked it a lot, did you? Best you ever had, was it?"

Recognizing a trap when he hears it, Jacody answered, "it was really, really good! Almost as good as the meals you fix Honey Bunny."

"Good save, you turkey!"

"So how was your day, dear? What's new with the fire?"

"The fire is fine and healthy! It grew 7,000 acres yesterday. The outlook weather conditions aren't looking too good," Marcy said.

"What have you been doing? What's keeping you busy?" Jacody wanted to know.

"Today I moved Jock's dozer around a steep canyon. He worked up to the rim and then back to a Forest Service road where he loaded up and Cupcake and I took him down the mountain on one side of the canyon and then back up on the other side. It was slow, slow work. I was either standing on the brakes with my jake brakes on a steep downhill or I was jamming lower gears to keep moving on steep uphills."

"So how are you and Jock getting along?"

"You know I've worked with Jock for several years. I think he's great – real easy to work with. And he's good at his job."

"Who else do you work with?" Persisted Jacody.

"Hey! What's going on? I feel like you are asking direct questions looking for something. Tell me what you want to know. Don't just ask me open-ended questions. I feel like eventually, you'll ask me a question and when I answer it you'll go, 'ah-ha! Got you!' Just ask me!"

"Good golly Miss Molly! One of us is not very subtle!" Cried Jacody.

"Well it sure isn't you and I don't intend for it to be me! Now spill the beans!"

"Yeah. Well. I was talking to your grandmother..."

"Okay, what did Grandma Nellie tell you?" Marcy snapped.

"I'm afraid she was a little confused about specifics, but she had some generalities that caused me concern. I understood her to say you are working with a Big Bud employee who is not a very nice guy."

"Well, she got that part right!" Marcy continued, "I work with Jock, who we talked about, Carlos, who operates a feller/buncher, and Larry, who transports the feller/buncher. Larry was raised by animals and lacks certain... no, that's not right... lacks any social skills."

"So, what about some guy sending him down the road?"

"That would be the Human Resource Specialist. You see, Larry mouthed off to a young kid on the camp crew and the HRSP was looking to see if a case should be built against Larry. Since I work with Larry he wanted to know if I would throw him under the bus, so to speak. I told him Larry was somewhat vulgar, but I didn't want to see him sent home. You see, the HRSP is a Christian brother so, when I ask him who was going to witness to him if we don't, he agreed that, if the camp crew kid was satisfied with Larry being warned, he would wait and see if there was another instance of disrespecting people. If there was, Larry would be history."

"That sounds like you... but listen! Do not put your safety in jeopardy! I don't care about the money you are earning if you get hurt in any way... mentally or physically. Not my monkeys, not my circus! I'll come and get you and clean house while I'm there!"

"Okay, okay! Quit beating on your chest. I will be careful," Marcy said.

"Grandma Nellie said you were digging up rocks. What was that about?" Jacody asked.

"What? Rocks? What did she say about rocks?"

"I don't know that she said anything about rocks. She just said digging rocks and some woman hitting some guy and maybe you. You know how your Grandma Nellie just says a bunch of words and then expects you to put them in the right order. I thought maybe you could do that. You are her granddaughter."

"I am. And that's a good thing!"

"Yes dear, I know it is," affirmed Jacody.

"So, do you have any other questions to ask me, Sherlock Holmes?"

"No, I guess not. I just had to get that burr out from under my saddle," Jacody confessed.

"Well, say! I've got a question for you! Listen! Can you hear that buzzing sound?" Marcy asked.

"No. Is your air conditioner acting up?"

"No, no... be real quiet. I'll hold my phone out the window. Did you hear it? Oh! Wait! Do you hear the bullfrog croaks?" She asked after waiting a bit.

"Hold your phone out the window again, Marcy"

After a moment or two, "How about this time? Did you hear it?" Marcy asked.

"I may have heard the buzzing sound, but I definitely heard the bullfrog sound," said Jacody.

"So do you know what makes those sounds?" Marcy asked.

"Yes, I do," responded Jacody. "It is croaking bats and that buzzing sound was them sucking the blood out of jackrabbits. Make sure you keep your truck windows rolled up! Are you next to a wet meadow?"

"Are you serious? Why haven't I ever heard about blood-sucking bats?"

"Are you next to a wet meadow?" Repeated Jacody.

"Yes I am, but I don't believe you... not just for a minute!

"What do I hear? Are you cranking the windows up in Cupcake so the bats don't get you?" Accused Jacody.

"Yes I am, but I don't believe you... tell me the truth... did you even hear the sounds?"

"Yeah... I did," admitted Jacody. "And I do know what it is. Nighthawks make that sound and..."

"I bet they peck your eyes out while you sleep, right? Nighthawks. Do you know or not?" asked Marcy.

"No, I'm telling you. Their call is the buzzing sound you hear. And, now this is really interesting, the croaking sound you hear is a part of their mating ritual."

"Jacody, stop. Their call is a buzz and they croak to attract a mate?"

"Yes, but they don't croak. The Common Nighthawk's mating ritual requires the male to gain some altitude and then go into a steep dive. At about 3 feet above the ground, the bird pulls up out of its dive and the wind going between its feathers causes the feathers to vibrate making the bullfrog sound."

"No way. You may be smart, but this doesn't even sound like something you would even know!" Marcy said.

"Ha-ha!" laughed Jacody. "Busted! I didn't know... but I do now! While I was spoofing you about blood-sucking bats, I was on my laptop looking up buzzing and croaking sounds on google. Then, viola! Common Nighthawks popped up!"

"For true? That is so bizarre! I think I'll keep my windows up tonight anyway!" Marcy said.

"I'm sorry. You'll be alright. I shouldn't have messed with your mind. Nothing is going to come through your window. I want you to be able to sleep well tonight!"

"Eh. I'll be alright. But. Speaking of sleep, I'd better get to it. What have you got for me tonight?"

"What do you mean... have for you tonight?" Asked Jacoby.

"Song. What song are we going to go to sleep with tonight?"

"Oh! How about our song?" Suggested Jacody.

"You mean Van Morrison's 'Have I Told You Lately'?"

"That's the one! I can't hear that song without wanting to hold you in my arms and dance real slow," said Jacody.

"Humm, that would be nice. But, right now, I'm going to sleepy town. Good night JJ, I love you and I miss you."

"Good night, dear, I love you and can't wait to talk to you tomorrow. Bye."

"Bye."

Jacody sat on the shop bench for a moment. Then he picked up his plasma cutter and started cutting out designs again. "What was God thinking when he created Nighthawks," he mused. "Does that loud burping sound really attract a mate? Almost as odd as some human mating rituals I suppose!"

Jacody felt good imagining Marcy drifting off to sleep thinking she and he was both listening to "Have I Told You Lately". He stopped cutting and scrolled through his phone until he found and started Morrison's song. It would be several hours before his head hit the pillow for the night. He would listen to it again then.

> Have I told you lately that I love you?
> Have I told you there's no one else above you?
> Fill my heart with gladness, take away all my sadness
> Ease my troubles, that's what you do
> For the morning sun in all its glory
> Meets the day with hope and comfort too
> You fill my life with laughter, somehow you make it better
> Ease my troubles, that's what you do

Chapter Thirteen
Cold Trailing

Saturday morning. Cartoons and silver dollars. Marcy was leaning back in Cupcake's sleeper unit thinking back to what Saturday mornings were like when she was a kid. Roadrunner and Wiley E. Coyote cartoons were the best. Grampa Sam was in his glory dipping cored apple slices in pancake batter fixing what he called silver dollars for breakfast. Sometimes he would go off on a tangent and experiment. Shredded sharp cheddar cheese in the bottom of a muffin pan with an egg, chopped ham, and more cheese on top baked in the oven was one of his favorites. "Time, oh good, good time. Where did you go?"

The plan this morning was to move Jock's dozer once he finished up the dozer fire line he was working on. While she waited up on the mountain, she read her book. A pleasant pine-scented breeze blew through the truck's cab. Far off in the distance, she could faintly hear the rise and fall Jock's bulldozer's diesel engine almost a mile away pushing a double-wide line of bare mineral soil. This is the line where the firefighters plan to take their stand against the forward progress of a very determined army of wind-driven flames.

The place Marcy was waiting was a wide area at the end of West Hot Forge Road. It was at the entrance of Hatters Branch Ranch. All the livestock and the occupants had been evacuated days ago when it was evident the fire lines on Jessup Ridge were going to be overrun by the fire. All of the ranch's buildings had been wrapped with reflective material to reduce the likelihood of the building catching on fire. So far, the flanking lines had prevented the fire from continuing to the North, but the wind was determined to keep it moving East and widening to the South.

While Jock was constructing a line in front of the fire, Marcy's location was back along the fire's northern flank. Last night, while the humidity was relatively high and the wind moderated, the night shift had burned out the fuels between the fire line and the active fire in this area. This greatly reduced the hazard that, as the day progresses and burning conditions become more volatile, the fire could cross the dozer line and begin a new, unrestricted run across the landscape.

Marcy knew only too well that in any burned area there are often fuels that escape the initial fire as it passes through; a single tall tree here, a stringer of trees, or a grove there. There are often pockets of brush, protected by rock outcrops that the fire rushed by and did not consume on the first pass. That left them capable and ready to burn later. From her hotshot days, she also knew that roots can continue to burn, or charcoal, underground, and hours – even days later, emerge to the surface with flames. So, unless these "hot spots" are mopped up, conditions may occur that reignite an area that firefighters thought was out. This remaining "heat" must be dealt with to secure a fire line. If crews aren't cutting fire lines, they are often mopping up using rubber bladder bags full of water or a hose line from an engine, to mix small amounts of water into hot spots with tools such as a shovel, Mcleod, or Pulaski. Once there are no smokes seen 25 or 50 feet in towards the fire, the Division Supervisor might ask the crew to "cold trail" the line. This requires a crewmember to remove a glove and feel with their fingers all along the burnt edge of a fire line. It is a slow and dangerous job as is all of the mop-up work. Stump holes, falling snags, snap-off treetops, rolling rocks, and hot coals are among the many hazards facing firefighters engaged in mop-up. These are all reasons that call for high "Situational Awareness" – look up, look down, look around.

In the same wide area where Cupcake was sitting, now known as Drop Point #14, were also parked 2 hotshot crew buggies and several pickup trucks belonging to the division safety officer, a line medic, a fire behavior specialist, the local district archaeologist, and a resource advisor. By now, Marcy had become

216

familiar with who did what on the fire and recognized them from the Morning Briefing Breakouts. Everyone was out along the fire line tending to their particular area of responsibility.

Just arriving at the Drop Point was Hot Sprocket Engine E-146. The engine captain had decided they would stop under a group of old-growth Ponderosa Pine trees where there was some shade and eat lunch before driving down the dozer line to where they would begin their mop-up assignment. Marcy could hear their music and, occasionally, loud voices and laughter. It was the usual noise that came from crews that work together in close reliance on each other. It didn't bother her reading any.

She was, however, disturbed after a bit when she became aware of two voices just below her sleeper unit's high window engaged in a serious discussion.

A male voice demanded, "You can't just pull out on us like that! We will be short one person and the fire will demob us. Greybeard Contracting doesn't have anyone to replace you with!"

Marcy heard a pleading female voice reply, "What am I supposed to do? I'm afraid something bad is going to happen!"

"Naw...naw! Nothing is going to happen! You're overreacting!"

"How can you say that?"

"Look. I've been going on fires for years. Guys are guys. This is nothing! Just keep your head down and do your job. We need this assignment. You'll be alright!"

"You know I don't want to be the reason the engine gets dropped, but I don't think you're taking this seriously enough!"

"So tell me! What do you want me to do? I go up to him and lay this out like you're saying, and he gets all up in my face and says it's ridiculous! Then we get all the shit jobs he can find for us and, eventually, he will find a reason to send us down the road. That's a black mark on Greybeard Contracting and we don't get dispatched to any more fires! Is that something you can live with?"

"I hoped..."

"You hoped what? I just told you what your hope would be. This will all be on you! It will all be on you!"

Macy waited a bit before stretching out of the sleeper unit to look in the passenger's side mirror. The male was walking past the end of the transport trailer and the female was leaning against Cupcake's rear tandem tractor tire with her head down staring at the ground. Marcy was just ready to climb over onto the passenger seat and get out of the truck when she saw the female straighten up, take a deep breath and, reluctantly, follow the male.

"Good enough," she thought while she relaxed back into the sleeper. It seemed to her she had been wading into too many people's private lives already. She didn't need to crash this party too. Besides, the engine crew loaded up and headed West down the dozer line.

Marcy noticed that the far-off rising and falling sound of the dozer's diesel engine had become a constant hum that was growing louder. Soon Jock would be here, and they would load his beast up to move it over to the West side of Hawkenfoot Ridge. From there, Jock would start working a dozer line back to the West to tie in with the hotshots who were extending the line he just left. Because of environmental concerns, he couldn't continue through the Hatters Branch floodplain, so it was handline only through there.

Loading, move, unloading, wait, loading, move, unloading, wait... repeat. That was the meat and potatoes of Marcy's job. Always be ready. The trip down the mountainside, across the Hatters Branch Drainage, and back up the mountain along Hawkenfoot Ridge was uneventful. Uneventful because of Marcy's close attention to every curve, slope, and hazard along the way.

Jock was already pushing brush, following the blue plastic flag line that directed him back towards Hatters Branch when Larry arrived in the pickup. He and Marcy talked briefly. At the end of the shift, he would top off the dozer's fuel tank and bring Jock back to camp. He had already topped off the feller/buncher but he would still go back to Drop Point #14 and pick up Carlos. That freed up Marcy to head back to camp by herself. It didn't matter a whole lot to her; she figured she could sit up on the mountain and do nothing or sit back at camp and do nothing – the pay was the same.

On her way, she stopped in at the gas station/convenience store in Journey, parking in the vacant gravel lot across the street. This was Marcy's first time going into the store, but she had heard it had a half-decent coffee shop. More than a gas station convenience store with a coffee shop, it also served as the community's post office, Fed Ex drop off/pick up point, Sharing Library – take a book leave a book - and beer distributor.

At the back of the building in one corner was the Busy Bean Coffee Café. Marcy placed her order for a Cinnamon Dolce Latte Grande. Kind of upscale sounding for an outpost in the wilderness, she thought. Obviously, someone from Journey had traveled outside these mountains to where the people lived and brought back a taste of refinement! Immediately she chided herself for having such snobbish thoughts – as she lived in a place almost as isolated as Journey. At times, she even felt a little like Bilbo Baggins, a very tall hobbit away from the shire.

In short order, her latte was handed to her. She took her drink and selected a plastic Walmart chair at one of the three round tables. If she was going to be loitering the afternoon away, she may as well start by loitering here. She had her radio with her in case someone needed her. As she nursed her drink, she thought about her short conversation with Larry. He was business-like – well, as business-like as Marcy could imagine he could be! "I'll be a'waitin rat chair til Jock gits threw." Larry didn't swear and he seemed to avoid eye contact. He kept his head down most of the time. "Something is up," she thought. "I bet D'Angelo has talked to him. I wonder what he said."

Later on, back at the Incident Command Post, Marcy stopped by the Planning yurt to see when

Sheila was going to supper and if she wanted any company. Planning Chief Sheila Shelton had her serious game face on, and it looked like she had several gators nipping at her heels. She finally saw Marcy standing behind the group gathered around the large table map of the fire. During a lull in the conversation, she stepped over to Marcy long enough to tell her she might not have time to go to supper with her.

Marcy wandered out of the Planning yurt and walked to the edge of the ICP where the HRSP yurt was located. Nobody home there. Back to the center of the ICP, she looked into the Incident Commander's yurt where Bainey's Liaison Officer's work area was. The yurt was deserted. The same story in the next yurt where the Safety Officers' workspace was located. No Rick Barron. "Perhaps it's time to find some more friends who don't have to work all the time!" she thought.

So, she went to supper by herself. She sat with a Hotshot crew from the Mendocino National Forest, and it was fun... but not what she expected. She could identify with the crew, for four years she had been where these firefighters are now. But it was obvious they didn't identify with her. They seemed so locked into their opinions that any opposing ideas weren't worthy of consideration. During the meal, Marcy gleaned the crew's sentiment towards politics, federal agency administrators, morality, religion, and race relations. "Was I so entrenched in my judgment of ... of everything when I was that young?" She questioned herself as she headed back to the staging area. In her mind, lines from "My Back Pages" written by the prophet Bob Dylan seemed to say it all for her:

> Half-wracked prejudice leaped forth
> "Rip down all hate", I screamed
> Lies that life is black and white
> Spoke from my skull, I dreamed
> Romantic flanks of musketeers
> Foundationed deep, somehow
> Ah, but I was so much older then
> I'm younger than that now

"It sure would be nice to be that cock-sure of who is right and who is wrong now. A lie becomes truth if it is said often enough. I was so much older then and I am younger than that now!"

Since she wasn't expecting the crew back for a while yet, this seemed like the perfect time to get a shower. Retrieving her shower essentials and change of clothes from Cupcake's sleeper, she began the short quarter of a mile walk towards Journey to the shower. Near the entrance of Sworinger Meadow where the crew parking and the tent camping was, Marcy nearly collided with a young firefighter rushing out from between two fire engines.

"Hey!" Marcy said jokingly, "where's the fire? Besides up on the ridge I mean."

"Oh jeez! I'm sorry. I guess I was off in my own little world," the young woman said.

"Ha-ha! No problem," said Marcy. Pointing at the woman's towel on her shoulder and what looked like a toiletry travel bag. "It looks like we are headed to the same place."

"We are if you are going to the shower," the young woman replied.

"Let's walk together... if you've got time, that is. My name is Marcy." Marcy smiled.

"Yes. Well. Sure! My name is Linda." Linda said. "I'm really not in that big a hurry... I'm just... I don't know. Preoccupied might be the word for it I guess."

"You certainly did look a little... 'other world' when you came flying out from between the trucks," Marcy said. "What's up?"

"Oh. Just stuff. You know. Everyday stuff."

Marcy smiled. "What's your job here on the fire?"

"I'm a crew member on Hot Sprocket Engine E-146. It's a Greybeard Contracting engine," said Linda.

"What has your engine been doing on the fire?" Marcy asked.

"We've been on Division Zulu mopping up into the black and then cold-trailing along the fire line," Linda said. Then today we were moved to Division Whiskey doing the same thing.

"I was on a shot crew for four years. I've lots of experience doing the same thing. Real important work with little recognition or thanks for doing it." Marcy said. "But now, things must be different. When I used to do it, I got filthy dirty – soot and ashes from head to toe and you look clean as a whistle!"

"Uh. Yeah." Linda acted as though she had just gotten caught with her hand in the cookie jar. "Well.

223

See." There was an awkward pause. It appeared Linda had just gone through all the logical ways to deflect Marcy's question and came up empty.

They stopped moving and Linda cocked her head to one side and considered Marcy closely. She was on an all-male crew. She wanted to talk to someone who she could trust but even more importantly, she wanted to talk to someone who would understand and not shrug her off.

"Well, see," Linda began. "I took a shower when we first got in from our shift. Just a bit ago, I got back from supper to our sleeping area. I just, I don't know... I just felt like I needed another shower. That's all."

Marcy considered Linda right back. She noticed Linda's eyes were getting all watery. "That's all?" Marcy said. "How long have you been a firefighter?"

Linda lifted her head, "This is my first season and second fire."

"And you always take two showers a day?" Marcy asked.

"No," said Linda softly.

"You don't have to tell me, but you're not practicing situational awareness as witnessed by our near-miss between the trucks just now. Maybe you aren't peacefully sleeping after working hard all day, and now you feel you need another shower? What's up?" Marcy probed. "Sometimes it is good to talk to a near stranger that doesn't have a dog in the fight."

"It's going to be okay. I'm... I'm alright." Linda said unconvincingly.

Linda's face belied everything she had just said. A tear rolled down her cheek but she tried to ignore it.

"There it is!" Marcy thought. "The child can keep it all bottled up until the confession begins."

"Linda, life on an engine, life on a hotshot crew, on any job on a fire is difficult to manage even when everything runs smoothly. But this is life in hyper-drive. We all rely on each other to be real. If something is going on that is troubling you, it is troubling for everyone even if no one else knows about it. When trouble comes, if it is environmental or mechanical, we all work to figure it out and overcome it. If it is personal, the fire will not stop while we slowly unpack it and figure it out. We can't afford to have a personal problem become a fire problem. You seem to have a problem. If it is going to resolve itself before your next shift and not be a problem, then good. It is done. But let me ask you this, if it is not, where will things end up?"

They walked along quietly for a while.

"Hey," Marcy said. "I'm sorry. I was a crew leader on a Hotshot Crew and old habits are hard to break. What I just said to you.... I had no right. I was right! Don't get me wrong! But I had no right. If something is bugging you, I suggest you talk to David D'Angelo, he's the HRSP (Human Resource Specialist) on the fire. I've talked to him and he seems like a good guy. If you need help, he will do what is right for you."

Linda stopped and searched Marcy's face. "Can you and I talk?"

"Sure," Marcy said and led the way off the path between the shower/laundry and the staging area to a secluded spot under a large orange old-growth Ponderosa Pine.

Linda took her time, measuring out how much she wanted to say and just how to couch it in case she was being overly emotional or unreasonable. She just didn't know since this was new to her and she was inexperienced.

"Look... maybe you can help me figure this out." Linda stared off in the distance. "So, every day since we have been here, we have been doing mop-up. Every day, this guy – I think he is some kind of line supervisor – comes by when I'm away from the engine by myself working with the hose. It is like he is waiting until the guy working with me goes back up over the crest of the ridge to the engine. He seems like a nice guy. He jokes around and tells me helpful things about working on an engine and how I might move up in the fire organization. He says he can put in a good word for me after I get a little more experience. The first day, just before he left, he asked me if I knew the 10 Standard Firefighting Orders. I told him I did and had them memorized. I asked him if he wanted to hear me say them. He kind of gave me a twisted grin and said he would be more interested in me doing the special 11th Standard Female Firefighter's Order than hearing me recite the 10 Standard Orders. Now, I know I'm naive about some things, but I don't believe there is such a thing. He made the hair on the back of my neck stand up and a shiver went through me. I was shocked and I said, 'I have never heard of such a thing.' He said, 'Sure you have... think about it. I'll check back with you later.

We can figure it out together.' And then he left. I kept expecting him to step out from behind a tree or a bush or a big boulder! I didn't see him again that day."

"That was it?" Marcy asked, "You hadn't met him before?"

"No, that was the very first time I had ever seen him! Linda replied.

"You are right... there are no Standard Firefighting Orders specifically for females. I agree, you are dealing with a true creep! So, you said, 'that day'. Has he approached you since then?" Marcy asked.

"That was 3 days ago." Linda continued, "Every day since then, he has shown up and it has been the same thing: being nice and joking around. But again, each time just before he leaves, he asks me, 'have you figured out what number 11 is?' Each time I've told him, 'No. I have no idea.' He just says, 'Think about it. I'll ask you again tomorrow.' Then he just looks at me, smiles, and walks off."

"Humm. That would certainly cause me concern too!" Marcy said.

"The same thing happened this afternoon even after we moved from Division Zulu to Division Whiskey! It's like he knew they were moving us and followed me over there!"

"Okay, now that is just weird," Marcy said.

"What about tomorrow!" Linda cried. "What does he want from me? What is he going to say – what is he going to do? Am I being silly? Is he just joking? What if he gets the engine fired and it's my fault? I'm standing at the end of 300 feet of fire hose all by myself. I can't see the engine, and no one can see me.

I could scream and no one would hear me because the pump on the engine is running!"

"No... no. It is not your fault, and you aren't going to get fired!" Marcy assured her. "It's going to be alright."

"How can you be so sure?" Linda asked, on the verge of a complete breakdown. "My crew needs this job! I need this job!"

"You don't have to do anything except your job," Marcy said. "Your visitor needs to do his job and he isn't doing it. We need to put an end to this right now!"

"How are we going to do that? As I said, I think he is some kind of a boss." Linda said, "he checks on everyone, I think, everyone on the line. He walks around with a shovel, but he never uses it."

"It wouldn't matter what position he has! At the very least, he's playing a very unhealthy mind game with you, and at the worst, he is trying to set you up for some compromising situation." Marcy was very adamant, "you need to take this to the HRSP."

"I really don't want to cause trouble," Linda said quietly.

"That means you'd rather be the target of trouble." Marcy replied, "Nothing stays the same, it gets better, or it gets worse. You can direct which way it goes. Look. This guy, no matter what his intentions are, is nothing but trouble. Trouble for you, trouble for the fire. You could ride it out and hope nothing else happens, but that's like not putting a fire line around a fire and hoping the fire stays right where it is. Nope.

You need the guts to do the right thing and do it now. What do you say?"

"But my engine captain said if anything goes sideways and the engine gets demobed, we all lose out! He said it would be on me... it would all be my fault!"

"Okay. I have a confession to make," Marcy reluctantly said. "Today, up there on the mountain in Division Whiskey. Your engine stopped under those big pines for lunch. Do you remember that blue semi-tractor transport with the pink ghost flames coming back on the hood?"

"No," Linda said uncertainly.

"It has 'CUPCAKE' on the side of the hood. You don't remember that?" Marcy asked a little defensively.

"Big trucks all look the same to me," Linda said.

"Well, I guess it's not important that you don't recall that," Marcy said, realizing once again that not all women have an affection for semi-trucks. "But I was in the sleeper on that truck. You and your supervisor, I guess, were standing almost right under the truck's sleeper unit's window, which was open. I heard your conversation. If it had lasted 30 seconds more I would have been out there and smacked that weasel around some!"

"Why did you act like you didn't know what was going on?" Linda wanted to know.

"For one thing, I was an unwilling eavesdropper. I didn't mean to hear what was said, but I felt a little guilty anyway. For another, I didn't hear enough to really know what was going on, I just knew your engine captain was trying to put a guilt trip on you so he wouldn't have to do the right thing!" Marcy defended herself. "So, what's it going to be?"

"I... I don't know." Linda said quietly.

"Look! I have talked with the HRSP before and here's what I think. He will iron out the wrinkles in this guy, and you won't have to be looking over your shoulder all the time. As an added benefit, your engine captain and perhaps the whole crew will get a free lesson on teamwork and how to support each other."

"Will you come with me?" Linda asked.

Cupcake's passenger door made a loud squeaking sound when Marcy closed it. She kept forgetting to put a dap of grease on it. Sitting in the passenger's seat for a bit before climbing back into the sleeper, she felt the last bit of tension drain from her body. The day was over.

David D'Angelo took up more time than she had expected, and she had stopped for a shower on the way back to staging. After all, that's where she was headed before she ran into Linda and got derailed. Camp had grown in personnel and there was a waiting line. But it was all her time now. This had become her favorite time of the day. Anticipation usually started building a little after supper. It was time to call her soul mate.

"One ringy-dingy, Two.... Stop it!" she chided herself!

"You have reached the number in which you have dialed" came a flat monotoned voice.

"Jacody! Do you know how corny that sounds?" Marcy said, "but I'm so very happy to hear it anyway."

"Yeah, I know. And that coming from a person that says, 'one ringy-dingy, two ringy-dingy' as her phone rings whoever she is calling!" Jacody teased. "I think you may be the pot calling the kettle black!"

"Eh! Who cares? I am trying to quit anyway! I miss you and I love you. Is that corny?"

"I don't think so. That is my sentiment towards you and that's pretty serious. So. No, it is not corny!" Jacody replied.

"Tell me the news, JJ. How are things at home."

"Well, pretty much business as usual. I did get stone for the irrigation water line over at the Roberts 'place. I finished burying it this afternoon. If it wasn't Sunday tomorrow, I'd have the system up and running. But, I should finish it up Monday." Jacody reported.

"Fantastic! I hope it all goes well for you. How's the gate coming along? Marcy wanted to know.

"With the time off from working on Roberts Ranch due to no crushed stone, I've made really good progress on fabricating the gate itself. It looks like the mechanical and electrical components are going to take some time to get here but the gate should be installed and operable manually by early next week.

Marcy asked, "So have you figured your profit on this gate?"

"Funny you should ask that. I was so excited to do another estate gate I didn't even figure a profit margin." Jacody admitted.

"What? You can't be losing money here! This isn't like you," Marcy declared.

"Now, you know I'm not going to do anything stupid so don't be worrying yourself about it. Once you get home, we'll count the costs and I'm betting I can show a large profit!" Jacody said.

"Jane Lew must have given you a blank check then."

"Jane Lew and I have an understanding, don't you worry!" Jacody reassured her. "Now. What's been keeping you out of trouble... or in trouble?

"Oh my!" Marcy began, "I think I have just become aware of how socially isolated you and I have been for the last 3 years or so. It seems the few friends we have time to hang out with are Christians. Your parents are Christians. Grandpa Sam and Grandma Nellie are Christians. We get the opinion that the whole world is Christian. These last few days have been a reminder it ain't so!"

"Is it dragon-slaying time? Is that what you're telling me? Cause I'll get on Piledriver the mighty steed and we'll...."

"Yeah, yeah, yeah! I know. Why you seem to delight in me being a damsel in distress I'll never know!" laughed Marcy. "But all kidding aside, there is some serious stuff going on every day all around us."

"Serious huh? You mean like maybe the national elections next year might not be legit?" Jacody asked.

232

"No! Who in their right mind would think the 2020 elections would not be legitimate? No. I'm talking about people who look alright but are struggling with things fiction writers can't even conceive of! Just like most people don't know my dad is constantly backing away from the edge of a nightmare. He looks fine... but looks can be deceiving."

"Okay. This is getting deep. I'll be serious. Tell me what's on your mind. I'll listen."

Marcy told Jacody all about the events of the day, from accidentally overhearing Linda and the engine captain to Linda confiding in her on their way to the shower to Marcy and Linda relating the whole "me doing the special 11th Standard Female Firefighter's Order" story to HRSP D'Angelo. Jacody listened without interrupting.

"Wow! That is twisted! That is sick! I don't even know this Linda person and I'm concerned for her safety. And Linda doesn't have the name or job title of this guy? Does he even work for the fire? I can think of lots of questions! Too bad HRSP guy isn't Sherlock Holmes!" Jacody had a lot to say after being quiet for so long.

"No, Linda just says he comes walking through the burned area with his shovel. Except for his boots and his lower pants legs, he is squeaky clean. He's very neat, clean-shaven every day like he always wants to look his best."

"Creeeepy! I'd say putting the fire out is NOT what this psycho has on his mind! Does HRSP guy have a plan to figure this out?"

"There are a couple of things D'Angelo plans to do. First, he is meeting with Linda's engine captain before breakfast. He plans to find out what is making the captain afraid to stand up and support his crew. Next, he wants the engine captain and Linda to be with him after Morning Briefing. Linda's engine takes directions from an engine strike team leader so instead of going to briefing and breakouts, her engine is getting ready to leave for the line. Neither Linda nor her engine captain has ever had to go to the breakout so if the shovel man was there, they would still not be able to identify him. But in the morning, the 3 of them will look at the various division breakouts to see if our shovel packing friend is in attendance. See, the way D'Angelo figures, this all started on Division Zulu. When Linda's engine was moved to the adjoining Division Whiskey, they started working right at the division break between the two, and the guy walked over from the direction of Division Zulu. So the breakout for Div Z is where they will start their search."

Jacody said, "so all this is going to come down tomorrow morning... and I'm gonna have to wait until late tomorrow night to find out what happened?"

"Well, you could wait for the movie to come out... but... yeah. Most likely," teased Marcy.

"Well, you stand back in the shadows. I don't want you to attract this guy's attention your way," Jacody stated.

"I don't think we have anything to worry about. But we don't know who this guy is. It wouldn't be the first time someone got a set of Nomex clothes and

234

impersonated a firefighter. You remember the murder/suicide from a few years ago just outside of Counsel, Idaho? I mention that because David D'Angelo was the HRSP on that fire when it happened, and he brought that up this evening."

"Really? I'm surprised! I bet that freaked Linda out!" Jacody said.

"I think D'Angelo got a little caught up in himself. The way it came out, it was a little like when my dad says things he normally keeps locked away, but it just slips out. He's shocked when that happens. David recovered quickly and reassured Linda there was no reason to believe that this incident and that one had any resemblance to each other," Marcy said.

"Yeah, well. I think it was bad form," Jacody insisted.

"Come on. D'Angelo is like the rest of us: human."

"I got you. I'll be anxious to hear about how this works out."

Marcy said, "well, me too! I'm anxious to see how both deals work out."

"What do you mean both deals? What else is going on?" Jacody asked.

"Yep! I got another iron in the fire that I don't want to lose track of. Tomorrow is Sunday and the Safety Officer is leading a worship service after the evening meal. I think I've strained a new friendship to the max trying to convince Sheila to attend it with me. I don't know if she will or not. Her job is so demanding, that it would be easy for her to beg off and say she was too busy. She has been negative about going but she has never plain shut me down."

"A person always feels like they might be on thin ice when they share the gospel and it gets a cold reception," Jacody said.

"I said what I felt I should and now I'm trying to be content with that. But there's more." Marcy said.

"More?"

"Yeah, more. Somehow, I feel I need to witness in a very strong way to my crew members, Jock, Carlos, and, especially, Larry. I haven't figured out how to get that done yet."

Jacody said, "We've talked about things like this before you know. God doesn't expect you to be the one who kicks down their door. He will make a way. One person plants a seed, another person waters it, someone else pulls the weeds and then another person brings the harvest in. None of the people may ever know, in this lifetime, if their efforts had any influence on the person."

"I know. Pray for me. Pray that I'll have patience. I just want so much for these people that I hurt. Oh! Don't forget to pray for Linda as well. So now you have a lot to pray about," Marcy said.

"It's my privilege. I know God is with you and He is with me. I know we will do our part."

"JJ, this has been a long call and it is getting late. We both need to get some shut-eye. I love you dear, but let's say good-night."

"Okay. Give me a second here." Jacody tried to blank his mind as his subconscious went through his mental music library. In a couple of beats, his brain coughed up the answer. "Here it is... I'll be going to sleep to Van Morrison's 'Crazy Love'. What have you got?"

"I knew what you were doing so I'm ready. I'm doing a deep dive into the archives, not that 'Crazy Love' isn't, but I came up with Mary Well's 'My Guy'. That's because no one could ever drag me away from you!"

"I really like that!" said Jacody.

"Alright then. I love you, sweetie, good night. I'll call you tomorrow," sighed Marcy.

"Love you too dear. I'll be sitting right here on the side porch with my phone in my hand like I am right now waiting for your call. Good night."

"JJ you are a goofball. I can't let that be the last thing I say to you. You are such a caring beautiful person. Now bye!" Marcy laughed.

"You're a complicated woman! I wouldn't have you any other way! Goodbye yourself. Love you, dear," responded Jacody.

As the lights went out for the night at both Stutler Ridge Fire Camp and Moon Ranch, the worries and concerns of the day melted away for the two lovers. Their two song selections intertwined, confirming their commitment to each other and carrying them off to dreamland. In sleep, they are together.

Crazy Love	My Guy

I can hear her heart beat for a thousand miles
>Nothing you could say could
>tear me away from my guy

And the heaven's open every time she smiles
>Nothing you could do 'cause
>I'm stuck like glue to my guy

And when I come to her that's where I belong
     I'm sticking to my guy like a
     stamp to a letter
Yet I'm running to her like a river's song
     Like birds of the feather, we
     stick together
She give me love, love, love, crazy love
     I'm tellin' you from the start I
     can't be torn apart from my guy
She give me love, love, love, crazy love

Chapter Fourteen
Who Is That Guy?

Long before the sun would be shining, the fire camp was all abuzz with activity. The night shift Planning Crew was posting large, updated fire maps on the large plywood backdrop of the raw lumber stage. Office services was busy delivering the Incident Action Plan (IAP) and the small fire map handouts to the Planning yurt. The caterer was busy feeding around 700 firefighters; lunches, water, Gatorade, and ice were being handed out.

Linda was waiting beside Cupcake when Marcy came back from the handwash station. "Good morning, Marcy."

"Good morning Sunshine," Marcy replied.

"Oh please! I haven't even had my coffee this morning! You would do better to call me Cloudy... no, better yet, call me Stormy based on what we have to do this morning." Linda said. "Stormy with a chance of blizzards."

"Hey, believe me here. The hard part is over for you. Don't you think D'Angelo is going to see this through?" Marcy asked.

"No, I think he will, but Adam, my engine captain, really put me through the wringer last night when I told him he had to meet with us this morning. I've been able to avoid him ever since. I saw him leave for the Incident Command Post about 5 minutes ago."

Marcy said, "good! You and I need to get going then. We should get to the HRSP yurt right on time."

When the two women knocked and gained entrance to the HRSP yurt, they found David D'Angelo sitting on a metal folding chair with his elbows on the metal folding table that served as his desk. His fingertips were touching each other, and his thumbs were supporting his chin. He was looking across the table earnestly at Adam Sawyer, Hot Sprocket Engine E-146's captain. Linda thought Adam looked like a deflated balloon compared to all his blustering and loud talk last night.

Still looking at Adam, D'Angelo motioned for the two to take a seat. "Something comes to mind from Harry Potter that I'd like to direct to young Mr. Sawyer here. 'Dark times lie ahead of us and there will be a time when we must choose between what is easy... and what is right.' -Albus Dumbledore.' I say that time is now. How can you expect to be supported by your crew if you don't support them? It appears to me you have already tried to do what came easy for you. Do you understand one of your crew members

240

was being manipulated – slowly being maneuvered into a precarious position?"

Adam said, "Well, it seemed like this guy was all authoritative, like, he knew all about what was going on. I saw him talking to other people and he just fit in I guess."

"So, where do your crewmembers fit in... in your picture of the world we operate in?" D'Angelo asked.

"They're important." Came the reply.

"Words, Mr. Sawyer! Words! What counts is action. Your actions are speaking so loudly, I can't hear what you are saying! Can you put yourself in Linda's position? Maybe not."

"What do you want from me?" Adam said, "look! I just want to go to work. I don't have time to be sitting here listening to this."

"Hmmm. I see." Said D'Angelo, as though he was finally getting the rise out of Adam he was looking for. "You still want to take the 'easy' route. Linda tells me you told her that if she causes problems – I read that to mean if she brings light on the guy pestering her – and the engine gets fired, it will be her fault. Is that right; did you say that?"

Adam paused before answering, "yes."

D'Angelo continued forward, "I see things a little differently. I see you on your high horse, holding yourself above it all. You are looking down at the riffraff that obeys your bidding. Their concerns are beneath you to consider. Your failure to care about them makes you unapproachable, unavailable, and, in effect, a danger to them. You are no help."

"Wow!" Adam said, "That's harsh! I do care about them."

"I don't see how that will show up in the performance rating that goes back to Greybeard Contracting. For all the good work you and your engine crew have done, the one thing that will stand out is how you were rated as a leader." D'Angelo had Adam's full attention now. "Of course, that performance rating hasn't been written... yet. Your engine's services have not been terminated... yet.

"'What is easy and what is right,'" D'Angelo repeated for effect. "You see, I could do what is easy right now. I could stand up, thank you all for coming in. I could tell Linda you will take care of things. Go get a good breakfast. I could go have fun joking around with people that don't have problems. I could have a good day! Or... I can do what is right. I wonder... Adam... Can you help me do what is right? Can you figure out what is right here and do it?"

It appeared Adam was taking things to heart. "Of course I want to do what is right! Why wouldn't I?"

"It's just that, regarding this situation, I haven't seen you do anything but duck your responsibilities. How about we start from right here, right now. What do you propose we do? What are you going to do?" D'Angelo asked.

"What do you mean, 'what am I going to do?' Do you mean right now? Right now, I'd like to get going to work. I'll keep an eye on things and make sure Linda is never alone out there." Adam said a little unsure of himself.

D'Angelo sighed. "How long have you been a supervisor? How long have you been working with a crew?"

"I got on the engine last year about halfway through the season and then they promoted me to captain at the start of this year." Quietly Adam added, "I think they had some people quit and the result was, I got a better paying job as captain. But I got extra training too."

"So this is the only crew experience you've had?" D'Angelo asked.

"Oh no! I've got lots of experience on a crew," Adam replied. "Out of high school, I worked for McDonald's for two years. I ran the fryers."

"Okay." D'Angelo's tone seemed to soften. "As far as I know, you and your engine have been doing a good job. But the personnel side of things is not yet as good as they need to be. Let me help you get started with what to do 'here and now'."

"Fine! I'm all ears," Adam said.

"You have lost the confidence and support of Linda because you blew off some serious stuff she was trying to tell you about. She went to you for relief and all you did was try to guilt her if things became a problem. You left her in a position that was beginning to terrify her. If Linda no longer trusts you, that other crew member sitting in the engine waiting for the two of you must be having his doubts about you too. So let's start with Linda. She's sitting right here. Is there anything you might say to her to build some trust back?"

"Yeah," Adam said, turning to Linda. "Sorry."

Linda said, "that's okay."

D'Angelo said, "I guess that's a start... but, Linda! 'That's okay?' Really? No. That is not okay. And you Adam, 'sorry'? Yes, you are sorry! This is where you crack open the door and make her believe you acknowledge that she has a real problem. She believes she is between a rock and a hard place, and she is! Convince her that you are here and, as her supervisor, you are going to help her out of that place! Take a moment and think about how you might feel if some big brute of a guy took a shine to you. What if he was acting like he would like to spend some time alone with you. What would that mean to you personally? Suppose this guy might get you and your crew fired unless you became a willing participant. Do you get the personal impact that I am implying?"

"Yes," Adam said very quietly and uncomfortably. He kept his eyes on the floor.

"Good. Now imagine you told your supervisor and he or she... let's say she just to keep it interesting, just told you not to mess up and get the engine demobed. You are thinking because your supervisor is a woman, she doesn't know or understand this is a compromising position you are being forced into. After you've thought about it for a moment or two, try it again but this time convince her, me, and Marcy. We all need to know you get it."

Marcy leaned in D'Angelo's direction and quietly asked, "why do I need to know he gets it?"

"Shush!" D'Angelo hissed back at her without taking his eyes from Adam.

Adam took a little time to compose his thoughts and turned once again to Linda. "I can see why you were disappointed in my reaction to your situation." Pause. "I guess it is true, I didn't know what to do so I hoped it would just go away if I did nothing. I've been holding onto that as our best course of action. I am sorry if that made you feel unimportant." Pause. "Now that I've thought about it," he nervously looked over in D'Angelo's direction, "and we have talked about it, I understand why you might be very concerned about what this guy is up to. I promise to do all I can to support you and to make you feel safe when we are out working and here at camp. I will listen carefully to any concerns you have and do the best I can to resolve any issues."

Looking at Linda expectantly, D'Angelo said, "Linda?"

A single tear rolled down Linda's cheek, "that would make me feel so, so good."

D'Angelo said, "now then! There is the concerned, caring supervisor we knew was locked up in there Mr. Sawyer! Thank you for coming to the dance."

Adam's face reddened and he grinned a little sheepishly. He seemed much more at ease now that his lack of confidence in himself had been addressed at least to some degree. He didn't have to pretend that he had it all together anymore. Help was on the way.

"Okay folks!" D'Angelo began, "breakfast will have to wait. We can just get over to the Morning Briefing before it starts. Linda and Adam. Be on the lookout for the person in question. I expect him to be at a breakout group after the briefing. For your information, we most likely will be joined by the Deputy Incident Commander, Forrest Oliver. I briefed both him and the Incident Commander about this, so they are on board. Now, let's go!"

Marcy was happy to notice Linda and Adam earnestly talking as they fell a little behind her and D'Angelo. Linda seemed to be doing most of the talking and Adam most of the listening.

Perhaps more to himself as to Marcy, D'Angelo did a quick synopsis of what he knew and prepared himself for what he might find out. "Linda's story seems to check out, and Adam, in as much as is possible, has backed that up. This guy... this guy just seems to appear out of nowhere, looking and acting like a boss. Linda tried to tell Adam what was going on, but Adam didn't listen. All that speaks to the same thing. It is support for Linda's story, albeit thin support.

Talking more directly now to Marcy, D'Angelo went on, "We will locate this dude and hear what he has to say. He will have his side of the story and we can only imagine what it might be, but let's have nothing but respect for it when he tells it. As I recall, in Proverbs, don't ask me the chapter and verse, it says something like, 'The first to plead his case seems just....' and it goes on to say, then you hear the other side of the story which also sounds right. There is a strong urge to believe Linda and condemn this mystery man."

Marcy said, "I probably needed to hear that. I may have already convicted him, hung him, and not worried about a trial. This guy who is acting so suspicious around Linda can make other people nervous as well. How do we know his dark intentions, if he does have dark intentions, are focused solely on Linda? Now, this may mean nothing and I'm telling you this, not because I want you to do anything, so please don't, but I'd like to share it with someone."

"Zowies! You sure have my curiosity up! But I can't promise you anything until you tell me what it is. Are you planning a bank heist? See, in all good conscience, I couldn't keep that a secret. That's just me!"

"Now see! That's the kind of corny dumb stuff my husband says when I'm trying to be serious. You two are like peas in a pod!" Marcy responded.

"Okay. Serious. If I can keep it quiet, I will. But I can't violate my job or my principles." D'Angelo said.

"Good enough! The last two nights... I believe it has been the last 2 nights, maybe more, it seems like I've been here for months... I got this eerie feeling that someone was hanging out just below Cupcake's sleeper window. Because of that, I keep the truck doors locked and I roll the cab windows up except for maybe an inch. The sleeper unit windows are too high for me to worry about anyone getting in, so I leave them open. I've thought about Linda in her tent and what if this person follows her there. But really, the crew's tents are all close together. No one can get away with messing with someone without the whole neighborhood of 'tenters' knowing about it. Then I thought about myself. I am out in the staging area by myself in a sleeper unit. Roll the windows up and

only someone within 20 feet of the truck could hear
me scream!"

"Humm. I get you. Is it just a gut feeling or is
there more?" D'Angelo wanted to know.

"It is mainly a tingly feeling that someone is out
there. The first night I sensed it, it was right after I
hung up from talking with Jacody. Like an electric
shock, I remembered both my cab windows were all
the way down and the doors were unlocked. Very
slowly and as quietly as I could, I eased into the
passenger's seat. I thought if anyone was out there,
they would try to get in from that side. Staying at
arm's length from the door so no one could reach
through the window and grab me, I put my hand on
the window crank. As soon as I slammed the door lock
button down, I started cranking the window up as fast
as I could. When the window got a couple of inches
from the top, I threw myself over into the driver's
seat, locked that door, and cranked as fast as I could
on that window crank. I could visualize someone
running from the passenger side around the front of
the truck and jumping up on the second step on that
side to get at me before it was completely rolled up! I
probably looked silly! I just sat there gasping for air.
I told myself I had just let my imagination get away
from myself."

"So did you see or hear anyone at all?"

"Not that night," Marcy said.

"But you have since them?" D'Angelo asked.

"As I said, that was the first night. The second
night, just shortly after I finished talking to Jacody
and was lying there listening for Nighthawks, I was

248

sure I heard someone walk away from the side of the truck. The sound was like pea gravel crunching under a person's boots. It wasn't like I heard footsteps coming, you know, quiet and getting louder as they got near, and then quieter as they moved away like someone just walking past the truck. Not that they were ever loud, you know what I mean? I guess I should say they started kind of quiet and then got quieter as they got further away. But, again, it could all be my mind playing tricks on me. Especially after talking with Linda and thinking we might have a predator in camp! What do you think? Am I crazy?"

She thought it best not to mention how the bullet hole just above the door frame on Cupcake's passenger side got there. That was a little memento from a night she spent trying to sleep at the Reno stockyards waiting to get loaded about five years ago. A would-be attacker had broken the side window and was trying to unlock the door when Marcy fired just a little above his head. He lost a lot of blood jerking his arm back through the broken glass and, she supposed, had a ringing in his ears that lasted a long time. She also thought D'Angelo didn't need to know that she still slept with her Smith & Wesson 45 handy.

"When we talk with our... 'person of interest' in the Linda situation, we can see if he also hangs out around the transports at night. Regardless, what say we go ahead and tune our camp Law Enforcement Captain in on things. She will make sure night patrol spends some time in the staging area off and on through the night," D'Angelo suggested.

"Okay. But make sure whoever it is doesn't think standing around Cupcake would be a good thing. I don't want to mistake L.E. for a stalker!" It would be a real mistake if they climbed up on the truck steps to look in the truck window, Marcy thought.

"Deal! Now let's go up to the stage and get an IAP and cup of coffee." D'Angelo suggested. "Besides, I have to let Sheila know I want to speak this morning."

Sheila was checking off names so she knew who was speaking at the briefing. As usual, she was reminding those that could, to keep their message to the troops under a minute and a half. She frowned and started wagging her finger at HRSP D'Angelo when he asked her to plug his name into her list. He smiled and nodded his head that he understood.

D'Angelo stepped back over to Marcy and suggested she go back into the crowd and find Linda and Adam. He said he would join them right after he spoke. They would meet up over where Division Zulu holds their breakout in case they don't locate each other before then. The current evidence points to Division Zulu as where the guy they were looking for may be assigned, so that is where the search should start.

Just as Sheila started the briefing with the fire's objectives, Marcy spotted Linda and Adam among the several hundred people in attendance. They were standing close to the back in the center of the briefing area. As she was weaving her way to get to them, she fortunately passed by Carlos and Jock. She made sure they would be at the breakout for Division Whiskey since she most likely would not be there. They needed their marching orders for the day.

Marcy, Linda, and Adam listened along with the large audience to the Morning Briefing. They were distracted by looking at the dark silhouettes of which any one of them could be the supposed stalker.

The briefing droned on with statistics: 83,323 acres, $2.8 million, 35% contained, 735 personnel. aircraft currently available: 1 SEAT, 3 heavies, 1 medium, 1 light. Available for initial attack on any new fire starts and medivac.

Night Ops reported some unburned pockets of fuel kicked up and sent fire up drainages out of Stone Creek. Burn-out operations went well in Division Whiskey.

I-Met predicted high wind warning today with a potential of 60-70 mph winds. Hatters Branch drainage will be most affected. At 10,000 feet, relative humidity will go up to 60% while temperatures will be down. There will be no air support available due to high wind. Red Flag high fire danger warnings are predicted for tomorrow beginning around 1300.

Fire Behavior reported the fire will wake up today. Expect it to be most active between 1100 and 2300 hours.

Communications reported all the radios will need to be cloned before going to the field today.

From the stage, HRSP D'Angelo asked everyone to turn to page 21 in the IAP to reference his HRSP message. He drew attention to the picture of a herd of zebras. The message below the picture read, "When people are free to be whatever they want, they usually imitate each other." D'Angelo read it and then added, "So be careful to pick someone worthy of imitating... and make sure you, yourself, are worthy of being imitated." As usual, he ended with the comment, "Try not to offend anyone today; try harder not to be offended!"

"Nice!" Marcy thought. "Less than a minute and a half and a good message for all of us!"

After all the other people had chipped in and the Incident Commander had given his pep talk, people were dismissed to go to their preassigned breakout groups for specific instructions for the day.

At the Division Zulu breakout, D'Angelo joined Marcy, Linda, and Adam. "Spotted our guy yet?" He wanted to know.

"Not yet," Adam replied.

The Division Supervisor for Div Z was talking to about 25 people who would oversee carrying out his orders. They were standing in a circle around the Div Sup next to the parking area lined with engines and crew buggies.

"It's still a little dark yet but look around carefully and see if our man is here." David D'Angelo said. Linda and Marcy went around the circle one way and D'Angelo and Adam went around counterclockwise.

Not seeing the person they were looking for, they repeated the process at the other breakout groups: Div A, K, W, and Structure Protection. Still not finding the person they were looking for they found themselves back where they started, at Div Z.

The breakout groups had begun to disperse, and people were heading out to their rigs when Linda gasped, "Is that him? I think it is!"

The sun had just appeared over Hawkenfoot Ridge to the East, and, in the light, a man stepped out of what had been shadows. From between two large engines, the man they were looking for walked up to the Div Z Sup and began talking to him.

D'Angelo said, "Are you sure? You sure that is the guy?"

Linda said, "Oh I'm sure alright! He must have been in the shadow of that engine facing the breakout group when we looked the first time. I must have walked right in front of him as I went around the group!"

Adam said, "That's the guy all right."

D'Angelo said, "Okay. Linda and Adam. I want you to go to the HRSP yurt and wait. Marcy, I want you to..."

Linda interrupted, "I want Marcy to come with me too!"

"Just hold on, I know you want your support person with you. She will be." D'Angelo was quick to add. He pointed across the field towards the Morning Briefing stage. "Marcy, do you see that guy over at the stage talking to Sheila? That's Forrest Oliver, the Deputy Incident Commander. You go tell him that I'm over here with the person I told him about last night. Tell him I would like him to join me here as soon as he is able. Got that?"

Marcy nodded her head affirmative.

"Okay, after you talk with him, go and join Linda and Adam at the HRSP yurt," D'Angelo said.

Marcy thought it must have seemed like an eternity to Linda before D'Angelo stepped in through the yurt's door. Linda leaned to see who, if anyone, was following him. Relief visibly washed over Linda when she saw no one else was coming.

"What happened? Did you talk with him? Am I in trouble?" Linda blurted out.

"Now, what did I tell you?" D'Angelo began. "How could you be in trouble? You did absolutely nothing wrong... as we have been telling you. The Deputy IC and I talked to the guy in private. In his own way, he confessed. Well, he didn't confess as much as backed up what you, Linda, told me. The Deputy IC came to a conclusion, made a decision, and sent the guy home. I just have a few things to follow through on. You and Adam can get back to mop up and Marcy can get back to moving dozers around, and we will all get back to putting this fire out!"

Marcy said, "If Linda isn't going to ask you, I will! What all happened? Tell us more!"

"Of course. I should get right to it – I know you all are anxious to know exactly what happened." D'Angelo sat down and opened a bottle of Blue Ice Gatorade. "First of all, the guy's name is Bruno Mitty. He is the Division Zulu Supervisor. The reason we didn't pick up on him when we first looked for him at Div Z breakout is that the breakout was being led by

Ty Weston, Division Supervisor trainee. Ty has been doing Mitty's work and Mitty has just been mentoring him. Ty is as good as having his task book for Div Sup all signed off on and is ready to be confirmed as fully qualified. Anyway, that has given Bruno Mitty a lot of time to just walk around and "talk" to people. People such as you, Linda."

"Are you saying that this guy has been doing the same thing to other people?" Linda asked.

"Eh! We can't be sure, but I think not." D'Angelo said. "You seemed to be working in an environment that he felt comfortable with. I don't know if we have any other females working in the same kind of semi-isolated conditions as you have been. There may be, but if so, no one has come forward to let us know. We also have to keep in mind that Mr. Mitty has not broken any laws. We cannot lock people up for being creepy."

"Go on. Tell us more." Marcy urged.

"Well, I waited until I saw Bruno start to leave. There were still a few other guys there waiting to talk with Ty. I stopped Bruno and told him I wanted to talk with him and Ty when Ty was finished. He, of course, said sure and wanted to know what I wanted to talk about. I put him off. I told him I didn't want to have to repeat myself half a dozen times. The Deputy IC, Forrest Oliver, joined me just as Ty did. Oliver didn't want an audience when we talked with Mitty so he suggested we go to his office area in the IC's yurt. I agreed with him."

"Once we were in the yurt, I asked Mr. Mitty if he had been making regular contacts with people along the fireline on the division. He answered in the affirmative. I ask him if he spent time talking to each of the engine crews as they did mop up. He said he thought he talked to all of them. He may have missed one now and then – 'it's a long division and there are a lot of engines', I believe is what he said. I asked him if there was any particular engine crew he made sure he talked to. He said, 'no'. I asked if he sought out Hot Sprocket Engine E-146 to talk to daily. He replied that he often talked with them, but he couldn't recall if it was daily or not. I asked if he knew the crew on that engine. He said, 'not personally'. I asked him if he knew the crewperson whose name is Linda. He said, 'OK, I think I know now what this is all about. She's that little black-haired girl that keeps coming on to me.'"

"What!" Linda blurted out. "He actually said I was trying to pick him up? He said I was coming on to him! I'm going to be sick!"

"Hey, I'm just repeating what the guy said," D'Angelo continued. "He said, 'I told her this was a fire and not a bar where you pick up men. I think she got her back up. You've obviously been talking to her and she's trying to get back at me for turning her down. She is one good-looking little honey and used to getting her way with guys. I'm sorry if I hurt her feelings but I know better than to get involved with someone on a fire... especially some little no-body on the end of a hose line!'"

"Okay! That did it for me! I won't feel sorry for that Mitty guy even if he gets fired! This 'little honey' is ready to take him all the way down now!" Engine

Captain Adam Sawyer looked at Linda like it was the first time he had ever met his crewmember!

D'Angelo proceeded with his description of his conversation with Mitty, "I asked him what the 11th Standard Firefighting Order was that only pertained to females. He said, 'oh that! Yeah, I was joking around with her. I joke around with everyone.' I asked him if he talked to others in his division; if he joked around like that with them and, if so, would they back up his statement. He said he didn't know. That people might not remember him. I asked him, didn't he think people would remember the Division Supervisor? Especially, if they were told to expect him back the next day and be ready with an answer? Then that same Div Sup keeps coming back every day asking the same question? Wouldn't that leave an impression on the crew's mind?'

"At that point, DIC Oliver ran out of patience and didn't wait for him to respond to my questions. He challenged Mitty by asking what he was doing completely out of his division tracking this young lady down to ask her the same question. Mitty said he just lost track of where he was and, at the time, didn't realize he had walked into Division Whiskey. So, long story short... Oliver directed me to walk Mitty over to Demob and start the process of removing him from camp. I scratched out an emergency demob message on a 213 form and Oliver signed it. That authorized the Demob section to fast forward the paperwork to remove Mitty from camp. At this very moment, he is going through the demob process and should be headed back to his home unit within the hour. I will be writing up an explanation letter for the Incident Commander to sign that will be sent to Mr. Mitty's home unit. The letter will explain why Mitty's fire assignment was cut short. We will have to rely on his home unit to take any other actions they think will be appropriate. As we discussed earlier, Bruno Mitty has not broken any laws, he has just creeped some of us out. His actions have been deemed inappropriate and his explanations seemed evasive. The IC and DIC did not want to wait and see if his actions would eventually end up breaking the law. So he is history."

"So it is over?" Linda wanted to know.

"Yes, it is. You can rest easy." D'Angelo reassured her. "Adam, I expect you to stay nearer to your crewmembers than usual for a while just to get things on an even keel again. You may discuss all this with your other crew member if you wish. I might add, however, don't blow this thing up. We really don't know where it was headed, we only know that Mitty's action was a form of bullying and inappropriate. Let's just let it die a peaceful death as far as here at the fire goes. So! If you don't have any questions... let's get back at it."

Linda and Adam filed out of the HRSP yurt, but Marcy held back. "What do you think, David? Was this Mitty guy hanging out by my truck at night?"

"I can't answer that. That creep could have been up to anything!" D'Angelo said. "The way he was sidestepping our questions, I didn't think there was any way he would honestly answer a direct question about the possibility he was stalking you too. If he was, he is out of camp now. I will give our security his description and if they see him again after he leaves this morning, they will detain him. He no longer can come and go as he pleases here in camp. In my 20-some years as an HRSP, I know about only one semi-successful physical sexual assault. And that one was pretty lame: 'I was on my way back from the toilet in the middle of the night and opened her tent flap by mistake. I didn't mean to fall on top of her!' Still, I'd prefer that nothing ever happened even as lame as that was. We won't let our guard down."

Marcy said, "I guess that is as good as I could hope for. Still, I'm going to stay on alert. I'll make sure I'm in my sleeper each night before the generator lights go out at 2230."

"I hate to say it, but please do that. Of course, you would be nervous. I don't know what else to tell you. Both the IC and the Deputy IC know of your concern and they are concerned as well. I expect something along the lines of personal security and awareness will be a topic at the noon Command and General Staff meeting today. Your name and circumstances will not be mentioned. The fact that the Division Supervisor for Div Zulu will now be handled solely by the Div Sup trainee and a vague discussion about the reasons why Mitty is gone will also be on the agenda."

"Well, thanks for taking this seriously," Marcy said.

"Geeze Louise," D'Angelo quipped. "What am I doing here if I don't take things like this seriously? Of course, I, and every other HRSP on a fire, are going to listen and do what is right anytime someone comes to us with things like Linda did, and like you did. Please,

please don't think you caused me any problems! Rest assured; this will be resolved. I want you to sleep easy tonight."

Chapter Fifteen
Is You Is, Or Is You Isn't?

Back at the staging area, Marcy made her way over to the shade screen stretched over the table next to Ground Support. There, besides getting a place to sit down out of the oppressive sun, she expected to get a sack lunch from the large box of lunches Jeremiah or one of the other drivers picked up for Ground Support. She found Jeremiah and a few other Ground Support drivers eating lunch and waiting for Ground Support Unit Leader Vito Pellegrino, or one of his equipment managers, to give them an assignment. As was often the case, fellow transport driver Ned Carpenter had also shown up to eat lunch and kill some time hanging out with them.

Drivers were always coming back, waiting to go, or going. You could almost feel the pulse of the fire by what the drivers were doing. What they took up to the line and where on the line they went, what they brought back from the line, who did they pick up and where did they take them- it all went into a logbook by which a fire could be tracked.

Marcy could tell this "coffee klatch" had become very comfortable being together from their cajoling and laughter. Mostly young kids, well, younger than herself, but not by much. One of the drivers spoke up, "So Ned, what story are you going to tell us today?" This was HaRin Bell. She was a forestry student at the College of the Redwoods in Eureka.

"Well now," Ned began in his cowboy philosopher storyteller voice. "Why don't you narrow that down from the entire universe to something a little more specific?"

"Are there any topics that come to mind that you would like to share with us?" HaRin asked.

"I don't know," said Ned as he pulled on one side of his long drooping mustache. "Snake dens, firewood, freak ranch accidents, motorcycles, rodeoing, Basque Sheepherders, fishing... interrupt me when I hit on something you want to hear about..."

"Fishing is fine", Jeremiah said.

"Fresh or salt?"

"Fresh!" Marcy said.

"Lake or stream?"

"Stream!" Jeremiah said.

"Fly, crankbait, live bait, or feel?"

"Ooooh! I've got this one!" HaRin exclaimed. I've gotta hear about feel. Unless, of course, you're going to talk about how you "feel" about fishing. It's not like you told us the other day about how Roy Rogers felt about his new cowboy boots is it? That was lame, I gotta tell you."

Some of them laughed recalling that story – "cat that chewed your new shoes up!" sang Tom Stevens, a young driver from over around Likely, CA. To those who didn't laugh, he said, "I guess you had to be there."

"Okay! Feel it is, but no guarantees!" Ned said. He leaned forward with his elbows on the table. His clear blue eyes were twinkling with amusement. Marcy could tell he was in his element.

"It was fall of 1975... or was it 76? Let's see. Oh, the year don't matter. I traveled back to the midwest to visit my cousin Dawson Alley. Oh! It was the year Jimmie Carter was running for president. He was stump'n up through Little Egypt... now there's another story I could tell ya!"

"Feel fishing?" Jeremiah inquired.

"Sure! I'm getting to it. You got someplace to be, Jeremiah? I didn't hear Vito come out and give you a run to make! So I'm back there, and Cousin Dawson invites me to go feel fishing with him on the Big Muddy River, it runs down along La Rue Pine Hills into the Mississippi River. Feel fishing! What do I know? I probably thought the same thing you did when you first heard it! But I said, 'Sure! What do I need to go feel fish'n?' Dawson said, 'hold up your arms.' So, I held up my arms. He said, 'everything you need to feel fish, is right there at the ends of your arms. When you feel something touch your hand, you clamp down on it real fast and throw whatever you've got in the boat.' So I asked him, 'are you serious? You just grab a fish? They're gonna let me just reach out and grab'em?' 'Well now,' he says, 'hold on. It's not as crazy as you think. I've caught lots of stuff feel fish'n. Some of'em have been fish!' Whoo... I thought about that, I don't know!

"So, anyway, we load up Dawson's 16-foot johnboat and head for the river. When we get there, we stand on the bank right above the river and look down at it. I tell ya, that water was as brown as muddy water can be. You could see 2, maybe 3 inches below the surface. Right where the sunlight made it through the big sycamore trees you could see several alligator gars sunning themselves at the top of the water. I had never seen anything like that. They looked pretty ferocious; all long and barracuda-like. They were 6 to 8 feet long with 18 inch snouts lined with sharp pointy teeth. I said, 'I ain't putting my hand in the water just so's one of them things can bite it off!' Of course, Dawson, he started making chicken sounds at me. He told me those rows of needle-sharp teeth weren't for biting off things – just for holding things. They wouldn't bite nothing they couldn't swallow, so I didn't need to be afraid of them.

"While we were standing there look'n at the gars, he told me LaRue Pine Hills was an ecological wonder. It had the Northernmost range of naturally occurring bald cypress, you know, those trees with the roots, or "knees" that stick up out of the ground. That place has a lot of other plants only found much further South. Plants from the far North can be found there too. Some from as far away as Alaska. The seed source supposedly was carried down by glaciers. So here you have the extreme South meeting the extreme North.

"Because this is such an ecologically diverse area, there are a lot of different snakes here, he tells me. That's why, when you are feel fishing you want to keep an eye on the water all the time. Snakes don't always come up from under the boat, but if they do, just pull your arm up slowly and roll away from the side. If you close your hand on something that feels like a snake, let go real fast. He told me that when he fishes there by himself, he brings one or two cats in the boat with him so he'll know if a snake sneaks in while he's busy look'n at his bobber.

"Well, we got the boat down to the water and started loading it. Dawson says, 'one more thing I should probably tell you. There could be snappers in the water.' 'Snappers?' I says. 'Snappers.' Dawson says back. 'They'd have no trouble clamping down on a man's hand or wrist and they won't let go until it thunders.' 'For real?' I asked him. 'I think so,' he says. 'That's what my grandpap always told me and he don't lie. Don't worry though. You can see the hump of their shell get close to the surface before they are close enough to grab hold of you.' Let me tell you, that didn't make me feel none better. By now, I'm wondering who the bigger idiot is, Cousin Dawson, or me!

"Well, we just pushed off the bank real gentle like and let the slow current take us along. I ask Cousin Dawson again, 'you sure you done this before?' He says, 'Oh yeah! Plenty of times. We'll get us some Bluegill, some Google Eye, maybe some Crappie...

we'll have a good fish fry tonight!' So, Cousin Dawson laid face down with his head to the back of the boat and hung his right arm over the side in the water. What could I do? So I laid face down with my head to the front of the boat and my right arm over the side as far as I could stretch. After a bit, we hadn't felt nothing, so I scootched over to the side a little farther to where my short sleeve shirt started soaking up water. You really couldn't see much in the water it was so muddy... maybe only 2 inches. I didn't figure anything would get close and, to be honest, I didn't want anything to get close. To keep'em away, I started wiggling all my fingers, thinking that would scare 'em off.

"By now, I'm really uncomfortable, laying face down and all, so, with great effort, I twist my head around to look at Dawson. He's laying there with both arms under his head asleep! I start to pull my arm out of the water and, wham! Something grabs me up by the elbow and slams me against the side of the boat nearly turning it over. It pulled so hard and so fast, it flipped Cousin Dawson up and over the side of the boat in the water. I grabbed the side of the boat with my left hand to keep me from being drug off. The boat spun around with the front starting to take in water. The back end was high in the air and went right over the top of Dawson's head, him still trying to figure out how he got in the water. Meanwhile, I'm staring at two beady eyes about a foot and a half apart and my arm has disappeared into a big greenish smile. Well, I gotta tell ya, my life started passing right in front of me. It was a huge monster's green face I was look'n

266

at! It was like the time we were climbing this glacier... well, that's another story. I was never so glad as when that thing let go of me and the boat laid flat on the water again. I helped Dawson back in the boat and we just sat there for a bit shaking. Finally, Dawson said, 'did I tell you about the really big catfish in here? Yeah, they usually will just bump you first to see if you're a tree limb or dinner. Then you can figure out if you want to try and grab'em or not. That's what they do, unless, of course, you're wiggling your fingers.'"

Like the rest of them, Marcy enjoyed Ned's story. Unlike the rest of them, she had difficulty keeping her mind on his story, outrageous as it was. All the events of this morning kept crowding in, taking over her conscious thoughts. She felt Linda was in the clear now. She just wasn't convinced that her own concerns went down the road with Mr. Mitty.

Lunch was over and several of the drivers left on assignments. Ned busied himself elsewhere. Marcy gathered up nonperishable food items and put them in the cardboard box that the lunches had been delivered in. She planned to take the box to the Information yurt to make the excess available for the local food pantry.

As she turned to leave, she saw Jeremiah coming out of the Ground Support yurt. Calling to him, she said, "Hey, how about giving me and this box a lift up to the main camp. I've got to drop this food off at the Fire Information yurt."

"Bummer," Jeremiah said. "I just got orders to take my pickup over to supply. But, if you can wait a few, I can do it after I get my truck loaded."

"Sure," Marcy said. "I can do that."

On Jeremiah's way to DP#13 on Division Whiskey with a load of hose and 2 Mark-3 pumps, he dropped Marcy off at the Incident Command Post's main entrance. As she passed by the large double yurt used as a meeting room, she was joined by Sheila. The Command and General Staff meeting had just ended. "Walking the track?" Sheila asked Marcy.

"You betcha!" Marcy answered. "I just have to drop this box of goodies off at Info first."

Having made their delivery, they headed over to the track behind the school buildings. "So what important stuff did the important people have to talk about at the C&G Staff meeting?" Marcy asked.

"Oh, let's see. What might interest you?" Sheila began. "Well, everyone was admonished not to take I-Met's warning about tomorrow's Red Flag alert lightly. We are all to make sure our units are very aware of where everyone is, that they have safety zones located and prepared by early afternoon. As you probably heard at this morning's Morning Briefing, we are to get dry lightning and we'll need to respond to Initial Attack on any new fires that start outside of our box that the Stutler Ridge Fire is in."

"Yeah, I heard all the specialists talking about extreme fire conditions for tomorrow afternoon. They were calling for heightened awareness. How about here in camp?" Marcy asked.

"Fire starts here in camp?" Sheila asked.

"Well, maybe not fires, but general heightened awareness in general," Marcy said.

"Heightened awareness in general. What are you talking about?" Sheila asked.

"I don't know. I just thought we should all be careful."

Sheila took hold of Marcy's arm and stopped walking. "Hey! This isn't my first rodeo. I can tell when the conversation starts going off the rails. I don't think you are talking about fire anymore. What gives?"

"Why nothing! I'm just feeling..., I don't know, I'm just nervous for some reason," Marcy stammered out.

"Okay. The big tough girl is nervous! Do you know something I don't? Do you know what D'Angelo was talking about in the C&G Meeting?"

"I wasn't there... how could I possibly know what he said?"

"C'mon Marcy! It's just you and me talking. D'Angelo said there was a disturbance in the firefighter's universe, but the problem was handled and sent packing. I thought it was maybe just one of his 'discouraging word' mutterers that he felt was going to ruin the peaceful process of overcoming a natural disaster. Now I'm thinking I should have listened closer. Why are you nervous?"

Marcy looked down at Sheila, a full head and half shorter than her. After a pause, she said, "If D'Angelo didn't spell it out, I don't know if I should or not."

"Ah-ha!" Sheila said exuberantly. "You do know what he was talking about! You're not sure whether you should share that information or not... but you're gonna... aren't you? How are you involved?" she asked, but now, without all the bluster. She sounded truly concerned about what she might hear and what Marcy may be feeling.

"D'Angelo said he preferred we not talk about it or make a big deal out of it. He didn't forbid us from talking about it." Without further coaxing, Marcy brought Sheila up to speed on all that had happened with Linda and how she became involved.

"Crim...in...nently!" Sheila said after Marcy finished Linda's story. "You know I'll soon be hearing about this shortly anyway. I'll have to replace that peckerwood Mitty as Div Sup Zulu on the plans. That guy was just too good looking for his own good! And vain! I'm sure he was his own biggest fan. You'll have to point out Linda to me sometime. I'd like to let her know how important I think it was that she came forward and we got that scum bag out of here. She's a hero!"

"Yeah. I will. I think she would like that," Marcy said.

"Okay. The guy is gone. So why are you still nervous?" Sheila asked.

Trapped! There was no other way to put it. She wasn't good at lying or being evasive when a direct question was pointed at her. So she gave Sheila the rest of the story and her misgivings that her concern had left camp with Linda's stalker.

"Well, Annie get yer gun!" Sheila blurted out when once again, Marcy ended her story.

Marcy smiled inwardly. If Sheila only knew how spot on she was! Annie already had her gun! "I'm just out there in that big parking lot! Once they shut the generators down, with no moon, it is pitch black! I'm

270

not sure if I'm better off out there protected by Cupcake's cab and sleeper, or... would I be better off in a tent surrounded by other people in their tents."

Sheila was quiet for a bit. "So tell me. Why you? How many women are out here sleeping in tents, sleeping in RVs, the back of SUVs, some are sleeping in their work yurts. I'm not being judgmental or anything, I just want to understand. Why do you feel you are a target and none of the rest of us are?"

"Would you buy: I feel what I feel, and I own my feelings?" Marcy asked.

"No," Sheila said flatly.

"Okay. I'm not gonna go down this rabbit hole with you, but I'll tell you this. Two things. One, Linda's story resonated with me. I could easily put myself in her position. It was almost like it was me instead of her, even though I knew it wasn't me. Second, and don't ask me any questions about this, I had a guy break into my truck one night. I was able to drive him off. I drove to another part of Reno and got a motel room for the night. I didn't feel safe that night nor for several nights after that. It was a long while before I stayed in Cupcake's sleeper after that. It may be irrational, but I'm having to beat back those feelings now to keep them from ruling my life."

"Oh geez! Marcy, I'm so sorry. How'd you..."

Marcy's hand flew up to stop her. "You can ask a question but only if it is not about me or what I just shared with you!"

The two, on the track now and had been for a while, walked on in silence. Each one seemed to be flipping through their least favorite memories of their lives. Marcy was thinking of all the things she wanted to push down and not be reminded of. A twinge of guilt passed through her. "What about Sheila?" She thought. "I've got things in my history that can upset me even today if I dwell on them. I have no idea what Sheila has in her past that could be just as hurtful or destructive if she was to focus on them. I bet both of us would benefit from a CISM, a Critical Incident Stress Management, meeting."

Sheila and Marcy were jarred from their private thoughts when they picked up three more walkers: Deputy Incident Commander Forrest Oliver, Liaison Officer Mick Bainey, and the seemingly ever-present HRSP David D'Angelo.

"Hey gals! What's up?" Mick hailed them.

"It's about time you slugs got off your duffs and burned some calories," Sheila replied.

Marcy brightened and replied, "D²S²!"

Forrest said, "That's 'Different Day, Same Stuff!' Right?"

"Close enough!" Marcy laughed.

"I expect you two to be at the worship service Rick Barron is holding tonight," Mick said.

"I am planning to be there," Marcy said.

Sheila said, "To borrow a worn-out phrase from our esteemed HRSP here, 'conflict is nothing more than unrealized expectations!' So expect away if you must – just don't be surprised if we end up in conflict! But seriously, I might be there, just don't hold me to that."

Marcy gave Sheila a sideways glance. "Good. I'd really like the company. I'd like you to go with me."

"As I said, don't hold me to that. I have to see where the planning shop is at that time. I can't just walk off and leave it on its own, you know," Sheila said.

"Make it if you can. We all have responsibilities we have to tend to. But we'd all be happy to see you there," Mick said.

The three guys, engrossed in discussing the upcoming cooperator's meeting that Bainey was responsible for, began pulling ahead of the two women.

"Marcy, I have been wondering about something," Sheila said.

"So what's that you are wondering about?" Marcy said.

"It seems to me that we've made a lot of laps around this track together. We have had some rather deep conversations, haven't we?" Sheila asked.

"Yes. You could say that," Marcy replied.

"So you told me all about how you and your husband met; all about the ruckus with that banana incident he broke up. But you never mentioned that your husband was black. I wondered why you didn't mention that," Sheila asked.

"I don't recall ever telling you Jacody was black. How did you come by that and why does it matter to you?" Marcy asked.

"I don't know the exact grapevine, but probably something like water truck driver to safety officer to engine captain to division sup to day ops to personnel time recorder to medic to I-Met to me. That's the 'how'. Why does it matter? I don't know that 'it' matters, but why I found out through the grapevine instead of in casual conversation between you and I might. Just maybe... it hurt my feelings to know you, to have spent this time with you, but not know that... if that makes sense."

"I suppose I should have known that the stand-off between Larry and me would be a topic of casual conversation. It was a big deal, evidently, to Larry, and it was a big deal to me that it was a big deal to Larry... if that makes sense!" said Marcy. "Now I'm wondering if it is a big deal to you too!"

"Me? No! Why would you think it is a big deal to me?" Sheila protested.

"Because it sounds like you are making it a big deal. I've had to face racism before. As you said, we've spent some time talking some deep stuff. I'm thinking we are pretty good friends even though we haven't known each other all that long. I would be very disappointed if I found out who I chose to marry was a problem for you based merrily on the color of his skin," Marcy stated.

"Ha!" Sheila snorted! "I was trying to figure out how you could be a racist, and yet, be married to a black man. I was just thinking how we could be good friends and I know so little about who you married. If you didn't want to say you married a black man, I'd have to think you had a problem with that fact. Now I'm thinking you two probably have adopted an Asian and a Hispanic child and you don't want to tell anybody about that either!"

"Look. I'm sorry if you interpreted me not telling you the race of my husband as something I'd like to keep secret – it's not. I'm sorry if you feel like we are less friends because you heard it through the grapevine. Would you feel the same if my husband was a white guy and I hadn't told you he had blond hair? What if you found out through the grapevine that his eyes were blue?" Marcy asked.

Sheila thought about this for a bit before she answered. A helicopter working bucket drops rattled overhead. The cinders under their feet crunched as they walked on. "That's kind of tough to answer, but I don't think so. I guess it would be, 'normal'. We just expect white people to marry white people and there would be the 'normal' variations in hair and eyes and the like. To be surprised or taken off guard because of a mixed-race marriage doesn't make me a racist."

"Maybe not," Marcy said. "But how surprised would you have been if, before you met him, you heard Mick's hair was not brown, but was in fact, red? Would you have wondered why you thought his hair would be brown? Most likely you would have been open to any of the possible colors his hair could have been. Once you met him and saw that he had red hair, would you have thought to ask why no one told you first?"

"Well. I'm not a racist," Sheila answered.

"Again, maybe not. But I wonder about your expectations. You seem to be in conflict with yourself. Didn't you say to the guys just minutes ago, 'Conflict is nothing more than unrealized expectations.' You seem to have expectations that people will stay in their lanes – a person is outside their lane if they hook up with someone who is not of their race. That's prejudice in action; that's racist," Marcy affirmed.

"Geez." Sheila sighed. "No! I think you are being way too sensitive about this and you are missing the point!"

"Well enlighten me then! I'm trying to understand you," Marcy said.

"I don't know how I get myself in these discussions. I've never been good with social skills. I don't seem to be able to read body language or something. I thought I was just asking an innocent question. I'm ahead of the game in planning strategies for combating fire... but I get blindsided when I try to talk about personal stuff with people! Now I suppose you think I'm awful."

"Look. I don't think you are awful," Marcy said. "Actually, I'd much rather you talked honestly about how you are feeling and thinking than not talk about it at all. I think we all have a smidge of racism in us if we are completely honest with ourselves."

"So we should pat each other on the back for not being racist?" Sheila asked.

"No... that's not exactly what I'm saying. What I'm saying is let's just be aware everyone has their share of prejudice to different degrees about everything. You do, I do, Jacody understands he does... but none of that matters! It's not a problem unless we decide to make it a problem," Marcy said.

"So it could be hair color," Sheila said.

"What?" Marcy asked.

"Yeah. I'm a brunette but I'm prejudiced against brunettes with no blonde highlights or streaks. So I add that color to my hair."

Marcy laughed. "Yes, I guess you could look at it that way. Some people don't like licorice, the traditional licorice. But they really like red licorice. Oh! Hey! Before you hear it through the grapevine, I like both black and red licorice."

"Haha," Sheila said, "big deal!"

"No, someone could make it a big deal! You see, Jacody came from a mixed marriage himself. His father is black... but his mother is Native American... she's red! Black and red licorice! I didn't want you to hear Jacody's mother is red through the grapevine!"

"Well now I think you are just making fun of me!" said Sheila.

"Maybe I am. I'm just glad that you're not really a racist. You may be right. I may be too sensitive. I tend to jump on anything that I think might have racism at its core."

"Told you so!" quipped Sheila.

"Just understand that I didn't mention it because I try to make it less important." Marcy continued, "to me, what is more important than what race you are, is have you accepted Jesus as your Lord and Savior!"

Sheila said, "God!"

Marcy said, "Yes, God!"

Sheila said, "No... I mean... golly! Are you always going to turn everything back to religion?"

Marcy said, "Religion... no. Jesus and salvation... yes!"

"What's the difference?" Sheila asked.

"There is a difference. A big difference," Marcy assured her. "It can be summed up with the saying, 'He who has religion as his god has no god for his religion.' In effect, that means if you pay more attention to what men are thinking and expecting rather than what God is telling us through His Word, you are worshiping a religion and not the One True God."

Sheila just looked at Marcy for a bit. "Good grief," she said. "Have you ever considered running for public office? That was nothing but gibberish!"

"Yeah," Marcy agreed. "If you are not familiar with religion or Jesus it would be difficult to make sense of it. Ask me this again after we go to the worship meeting tonight. It will mean more to you then."

"Geez! As much as I hate to, I need to get over to the planning yurt. Are we good? Should I be concerned?" Sheila said.

"Yeah, we are good – no concerns!" Marcy said. "I need to get a move-on myself. I need to find my little buddy Larry. We need to get up to Division Whiskey and haul our dozer and feller/buncher back to camp. In the morning they want us to pre-position them on Drop Point #7 on Division Charley... but why am I telling you this? You probably are the one who made the plans for us to do this."

"Ha-ha," Sheila laughed. "There are planners in planning that plan things out. I know the plans in general, but I don't always know the specifics, like the names of the exact dozer and operator that is going to go to one place or another. So let me tell you this. The road up to DP#7 is little more than a jeep trail and very steep. We haven't worked on any dozer or hand lines in Div C yet. You've got to be careful and make sure you are back down off the mountain before the red flag warnings take effect."

"Don't worry, I'll put fresh batteries in our radios. See you around supper time?" Marcy asked.

"Sure. If I can. Take care," Sheila replied.

Chapter Sixteen
Close Your Eyes

Rick Barron stood on the ground in front of the stage used for the Morning Briefing, a guitar in one hand and a Bible in the other. Right at 2000 hours, he calmed the group standing out in front of him. "Good evening. I'm encouraged by how many of you were able to attend this worship service tonight! Praise God! I'd like to welcome you if you are a long-time Christian or if you came tonight just to see what we are about. We are glad you are here. If you would like a New Testament Bible, I have a box of them up here on the stage. Come forward and get one if you want, they have some inserts that should be of particular interest to firefighters, and I encourage you to get your copy – they are free. Also, up here on the stage, I have the words to a couple of songs I'd like us to sing. We'll get started as soon as everyone gets their handouts."

Marcy and Sheila filed up to the stage with 15 to 20 other attendees and picked up a New Testament as well as the words to the music. Marcy was fighting off her conflicted thoughts about the three men who remained standing like statues in the back fringe of the group. She refused to let their failure to participate discourage her. She picked up a New Testament and handouts for each of them. Larry was flanked on each side by Jock and Carlos. Obviously, they came just to see what this service was about – not to participate in it. She got no thanks when she distributed the reading material to them.

She moved a distance away from the 3 and joined Sheila but continued ruminating over their motivations for being here. Expectations, she reminded herself. What did she expect? It was certainly better than she expected. She had hoped Sheila would join her and had been somewhat confident that she would. That Larry would attend was beyond her imagination, but she told herself no matter how he reacted, it would, in some way, be for the better in the long run. Carlos and Jock? She had kind of overlooked them. She had let them know about the worship service and invited them, but she hadn't felt the same urgency to get them here as she had for Sheila. The only thing she could reason out was when Jock and Carlos found out about Larry's intention to attend, they thought, "Now, this is going to be interesting! Larry in church! We can't miss this!" It had nothing to do with worshiping the Lord. Be that as it may, they are here and will hear the Word preached; the seeds of faith will be scattered, and, who knows, those seeds may take root and grow. But Larry! What spurred him to join this group tonight? "We can make our plans, but the Lord determines our steps." paraphrasing Proverbs 16:9. God's hand is in this tonight!" Marcy was convinced.

When the group was once again standing in front of Rick, he got their attention. "Let's begin praising God with the first song on your handout, 'Chain Breaker' by Zach Williams:"

> If you've been walking the same old road
> For miles and miles
> If you've been hearing the same old voice
> Tell the same old lies
> If you're trying to fill the same old holes inside
> There's a better life, there's a better life
>
> If you've got pain, He's a pain taker
> If you feel lost, He's a way maker
> If you need freedom or saving
> He's a prison-shaking Saviour
> If you got chains
> He's a chain breaker
>
> We've all searched for the light of day
> In the dead of night
> We've all found ourselves worn out
> From the same old fight

We've all run to things we know just ain't right
When there's a better life, there's a better life

If you've got pain, He's a pain taker
If you feel lost, He's a way maker
If you need freedom or saving
He's a prison-shaking Saviour
If you got chains
Oh, He's a chain breaker…

As the song ended and the last chord from Rick's guitar faded, Rick said, "Let us bow and pray. Our Heavenly Father, we praise your name! You are the Almighty One, The Great I Am, the Creator of everything. You spread your grace over us so generously! We know that each of us has a void in our soul that can only be filled by You. Help us to remember You when we are in need, when we are lonely, when we are uncertain, or when we need a friend. We thank You for caring enough about us to provide a plan for us to join You in Your heavenly home when we leave this earth. Be with us in this place as we worship You. May any who need encouragement, any who might need to be awakened to Your presence, any who need reassurance that You are ready and able to touch lives with Your goodness and grace, receive the message that You have for them right now! We ask these things in the name of our savior, Jesus Christ. Amen."

"I'm very pleased to see you all here this evening. I don't want to assume that you all sang or listened to our opening song just now with the knowledge and confidence that Christ is a chain-breaker; that God is, in fact, a way maker. If you don't know our Lord, we must start with something much more basic. Dr. Francis Schaeffer said, 'The first argument of the gospel is not, as we often think, that Jesus died for our sins. Nor is it, as we are sometimes told, God loves us, and has a wonderful plan for our lives. The first argument of the gospel is, God is there. There is a God, and he is in control of life.' It is hard to go forward in the faith if that basic belief is not affirmed. That God exists and is real in our lives is the foundation that every Christian operates from. Tonight, I want us to look at the actions of five men who firmly believed that God is real and they based their actions upon that belief.

"I hope you all picked up a New Testament," holding up his bible. "Let's turn to Mark, the 2nd chapter. We are going to look at the first twelve verses." Rick read the verses about the crowd of people outside and inside of the house where Jesus was staying. There was a paralyzed man on a cot, or a mat, being carried by four men intent on getting him next to Jesus so he could be healed. The press of people was so great, that they were unable to get into the house. So the men carried their burden up on the roof, dug a hole in it, and lowered the mat with the man on it down in front of Jesus.

Rick said, "Now there is a lot to talk about just in these first few verses. Let's think about it. There are 4 guys carrying another guy. I'm thinking all 5 men are good friends, all 5 men have enough information about Jesus to be absolutely certain He can heal their friend, and all 5 men are wildland firefighters!" Laughter rippled through the group at Rick's assumption that the men were wildland firefighters.

"To fight fires, it is necessary to have a vision of what you want to accomplish. You take that vision and develop a plan that will accomplish that vision, or goal. Using that plan, you attack the fire. That is how victory over the fire is achieved. These guys have a vision: get their friend to Jesus. They have a plan: load their friend up on a mat and carry him. They attack the obstacles: dig a hole in the roof and lower the man down. They are victorious: Jesus heals their friend. I see these guys with rappelling ropes around their shoulders. They have a hold on the mat with one hand and in the other, they are carrying a Pulaski. They are wearing T-shirts with Bethlehem Hotshots on the back.

"This is unthinkable! Can you imagine the faith it would take to climb up on a roof and use your Pulaskis, or axes, to chop a hole through someone's roof? A hole large enough to lower a mat with a man on it through to the floor at ground level! Think about the commotion below in the house. People down below yelling at the men to stop! There is debris falling on those below as the ceiling is torn away! Talk about breaking and entering! This was no minor amount of damage! How would you explain this to your insurance company? Yet, these men did it! It was that important to them that they get their friend in front of Jesus.

"Some of you may be here because you have friends whose belief in Jesus is so unshakable, they are willing to chop a hole through a stranger's roof just so you can meet Jesus. If so, you are truly blessed. Even if you have just one such friend you are blessed. If you don't know Jesus as your Savior and you don't have a friend who believes in God to the point they would lower you on a rope through a roof to meet Jesus... friend, you need to find one who has just such a belief!"

Rick talked about the benefits of being well-grounded in the Word. He said it is the foundation that a truly happy, contented, satisfied life is built on. Rick talked about how we have all sinned and come short of the glory of God. He said, "We will be held accountable for our lives here on earth. Non-Christians will be judged by God on their merits, keeping in mind none of us are worthy. Those who have accepted Christ as their savior will be judged as if they were Christ and they will be found blameless. All of those will be welcomed into Paradise, God's own home. God knocks on the door of our hearts; He is knocking on your heart right now. He paid the penalty for your sin and is willing to bring you home to live with Him! But only if you are willing to stretch out your hand to take His!"

Then he said, "I'd like to do something a little different tonight. Please bear with me. There are not that many of us, so this should be easy. Let's move into a circle. Good! Set your Bibles and handouts on the ground in front of you. Now, I want you, as we all get in a circle here, to hold the hand of the person on each side of you."

Marcy and Sheila both noticed that Larry, Jock, and Carlos didn't move away fast enough and ended up next to several big burley-looking men that appeared to be lumberjacks or sawyers. They clasped hands before the 3 men could melt away from the circle as they no doubt intended to do. Trapped, they offered no resistance. Marcy turned and winked at Sheila who grinned back at her.

"Look around the circle... smile at everyone." Rick began. "In Ecclesiastes, we read, 'Two people are better off than one, for they can help each other succeed. If one person falls, the other can reach out and help. But someone who falls alone is in real trouble. Likewise, two people lying close together can keep each other warm. But how can one be warm alone? A person standing alone can be attacked and defeated, but two can stand back-to-back and conquer.' We are not meant to walk through this world alone. Just like steel sharpens steel, Christians improve Christians."

"You can let go of each other's hands now. Christians should meet and spend time together. We become more like the people we spend the most time with so we should be aware of that. Spend time with people who love the Lord as you do."

"Now, I just said it is good to spend time with others and it is okay to depend on others, but here is a truth: you will meet Jesus by yourself. I want you to go with me on this... probably for most of you, this will just be an exercise... for one or more of you... it may be much more."

"Please close your eyes... clear your mind... blot out this Stutler Ridge Fire... this camp... the people in this area... the people in this circle. Blot out the person on your left... the person on your right. You are standing here alone." As he spoke, his voice softened and grew quieter.

Rick paused for dramatic effect – then he continued.

"In your mind's eye, I want you to go to a special place. Someplace quiet. Someplace you feel safe and at ease. Think about a cool, crisp fall afternoon.

Rick gave them time to form the picture in their mind.

"You see a mountain valley full of greenery and fall colors."

He was quiet again for a few moments.

"See the mountain ridgeline beyond the beaver pond. It may be the Sawtooth Mountains, it may be the Grand Tetons, it may be a mountain range you have seen before or have never seen before."

Rich remained quiet for several seconds letting the group form the picture in their own mind.

"Feel the sun, warm against your cheek."

He paused.

"Hear the light breeze making the golden aspen leaves rustle and shiver."

He paused again.

"You breathe in the crisp air and it is like a drink of cool spring water from a tin cup. You smell the earthy aroma of the meadow."

Audibly, Rick drew a deep breath in his nose and exhaled it so people could hear him. Several other people mimicked what Rick did. It was evident people were tuned in to what he was saying and doing.

"Soak it all in... Relax... Relax."

Rick paused and then paused again for another beat or two.

"Slowly, still with your eyes closed, turn a little to your left. In your mind's eye, you see a man in brilliant white clothing walking up to you."

Rick lets a little time pass.

"You have never seen Him before, but you know it is The Son. It is Jesus. You know Him... and He... knows you."

Rick gives this just a short pause.

He embraces you. You embrace Him. His right hand is holding you firmly at the small of your back. With His left hand, He pulls the side of your face to His chest. It is the touch of a Father holding His dear child."

Rick lets this visual soak in deep before going on.

"You don't speak. There is no need to speak. He knows everything you have to say. He knows your trials, your triumphs, and your failures. Radiating from Him you feel love. Love and acceptance. There is no criticism, no censorship. You are simply a child of God."

Rick maintains a steady tempo between visualization and rest.

"This is the one who loves you so much, that He offered himself up as a sacrifice to pay... for your sins. You feel the assurance that when you cross over to the other side, and when you stand in front of the judgment throne, God will only see the pure life of Jesus, not your imperfect life. When God passes judgment on you, it will be like passing judgment on His Son. You know that. All the unholy, unworthy acts, and thoughts that would make you ineligible to enter God's kingdom, Jesus paid for them all at the cross."

Rick pauses.

"Before Jesus leaves you, He puts a hand on your shoulder. When it is time for you to join Him, He will be waiting for you. He wants you to make sure you will be ready to meet Him at that time!"

After saying that, Rick went right into praying.

"Our Heavenly Father, we thank you so much that You devised a plan that brings all who believe in You... and follow Your commandments... to spend eternity there with you in Your Heavenly Halls. We cannot conceive of a love so great that You would send Your Son, Jesus, to be sacrificed so that we might live.'

"We ask that You watch over each and every firefighter here engaged in this effort. Some may need special protection as they go about their jobs. We never know whose life may be required of them and at what time. Please spread Your grace over us Lord."

"Amen."

"You may open your eyes... but let's finish this evening as we are; standing in this circle."

"If you have a full understanding of what Christ has done for you, you have been changed... and are continuing to change. You want to study His Word and learn all you can about this wonderful plan that He has for your life. Do you all have Bibles? One last reminder, I have Firefighter's Bibles free for any who wants one. Even if you have one at home, take another one so you will have one here. Please don't let society tell you what Jesus would have you believe.

Don't let the government tell you. Don't let some preacher tell you... don't let me tell you. Confirm everything with the Bible. This world is not to be trusted – God's Word is!"

"Okay, if you will, turn to the last page in your handout, and we will sing a closing song. You're dismissed after the song, but if anyone would like us to pray with you or if you have any questions, Mick Bainey and I will hang around for a while after the service."

As Rick reached for his guitar on the stage, he said, "This is an old, old, hymn written by Francis Crosby. Pass Me Not, Oh Gentle Savior."

> Pass me not, o gentle Savior
> Hear my humble cry;
> While on others Thou art calling,
> Do not pass me by.
>> Savior, Savior,
>> Hear my humble cry,
>> While on others Thou are calling,
>> Do not pass me by...

A few people hung back to talk with Rick Barron and Mick Bainey after the song was over. Marcy and Sheila walked over towards the Planning yurt through the parking area. They were passing the BBFL pickup right as Larry, Jock, and Carlos got there.

Marcy was the first to speak, "I was really glad to see you guys there! I wasn't expecting that."

Carlos said, "We weren't expecting to be there either. Jock and I went to see if they would do an exorcism on Larry. We just know he's demon-possessed!

"There ain't no demons in me!" Larry said.

"I don't know about that," Jock said! "The jury may still be out."

Larry said, "Yeah, well, you guys don't know nothing!"

"Okay, stop," Marcy said. "I was proud of all three of you when we got in a circle. I thought maybe you would all bolt."

"Oh yeah!" Jock said. But we stood there for a bit too long looking at that preacher man after he said hold hands. The next thing I knew, these guys stepped up next to us and snagged our hands. So. There we were. A part of the circle of life! Like it or not!"

Sheila said, "Are you saying you didn't like it?"

"Oh, I didn't mind it," Jock said. "It was like church camp when I was a kid. I thought we should have sung Kum ba yah though."

"I, for one, kind of liked the whole service," Sheila said. "It gave me a lot to think about."

"Yeah! That's whut I was thinking too!" said Larry enthusiastically.

Sheila slugged Larry on the arm real hard and said, "yeah, we sure do think alike, don't we!" Sheila laughed and actually rubbed Larry's arm where she hit him.

Larry looked a little confused by Sheila's attention, but said, "I will say that closing your eyes part gimmie the hebie-geebies. I was peek'n round. I got this chill like someone was maybe sneaking up behind me. I don't think I like closing my eyes with a bunch of people I don't know."

"Carlos, what did you think of the service?" Marcy asked.

"Oh, I don't know," Carlos said. "I still don't know what this guy Jesus has to do with me."

"Was this the first time you have ever heard about Jesus?" Marcy asked.

"I think my grandmother used to pray to Jesus and sometimes he gets mentioned on TV when there's a movie or something. But I never paid any attention to it." Carlos answered.

"I gave you one of Rick Barron's New Testaments, do you plan to read it? Marcy asked Carlos.

"Well, yeah, I might," Carlos answered. "Everybody else seemed to think it was a good thing to have so, I'll see what's in it."

"The New Testament is full of good information. It is the inspired word of God. I do hope you read it. Also, I think it would be great if you talked with Rick Barron tomorrow. It would be helpful if he put it in the proper context for you." Marcy said.

"Well, that's for tomorrow to decide. Tonight, I just want to get to my tent!" Carlos said.

"What about you, Marcy," Sheila asked, "What did you think about this meeting?"

"It spoke to me, but any church service that worships God and speaks His truths speaks to me," Marcy replied. "The God I worship is a living influence on my life. One of my many favorite verses is from 2nd Timothy: 'for I know whom I have believed, and am persuaded that he is able to keep that which I have committed unto him against that day.' In short, that means I trust God with my life now and when I leave this earth."

"Whut kind of nut memorizes all this stuff?" Larry scoffed.

"People remember things that they like or mean something to them," Marcy said. "Anyone remember a line from Dirty Harry?"

"Go ahead punk! Make my day." Carlos was quick to answer.

"How about Cool Hand Luke?" Marcy asked.

"What we have here is a failure to communicate," Jock replied.

"See? If something resonates with a person, they remember it," Marcy said.

"If verses are important to us, we will go out of our way to memorize them. The verses I've memorized are available instantly to bring me reassurance and comfort. I love and rely on the Word of God!"

"Marcy," Larry said mustering up his best authoritarian voice, "people like y'all need a crutch ta git by on! Me myself, I rely on my wits alone!"

The others just looked at Larry with a mixture of disbelief and amusement.

"Whut?" Larry muttered.

After a moment, Sheila said, "yeah... and I've got to get over to Planning. We've still got a fire to put out."

Larry said, "yep! Let's load up. Time to git going."

Marcy said, "you guys go ahead. I'm going to walk."

"Suit yer self!" Larry responded.

One ringy-dingy... two ringy-dingy... three...

"Hello Marcy! I've been waiting for your call." Jacody said.

"Hi Sweetheart! I miss you!" Marcy said.

"Chuck, Chew, and I are sure missing you too! It was 7 days ago when we watched your taillights go towards the highway. I don't think we have ever been apart this long since we got married."

"I think you are right. It's funny. I don't seem to do much of anything here, but the days just click right along. I climb out of Cupcake before daylight and climb back in after dark. With little variation in what I do; what I did yesterday, I did today and will do tomorrow. I'll just keep doing this until my prison sentence is up and I'm released. Then I'll come home to you!"

"Well," Jacody said, we are halfway there!"

"No, not until after tomorrow. The 14 days start with the first full shift day. Travel to and from the fire don't count in the 14."

"Drat! You're right! Now I have to wait another day before I can get excited about you being halfway through your assignment."

"So. What did you do today?" Marcy wanted to know.

"I slept in a little late this morning. I gotta say, it's a lot more fun sleeping in when you're here! Then I had to hustle around and get the morning chores done and get cleaned up to go to church."

"How was church? Was the family all there?"

"Church was good. Pastor Namon's sermon was based on, 'how can you show me your faith if you don't have good deeds? I will show you my faith by my good deeds.' He started with that old saying, 'If you were brought up on charges of being a Christian, would there be enough evidence to convict you?' He got a lot of 'amens' this morning!"

"And the family?"

"Oh yeah. We were all there in 'our' pew! Afterward, Grandpa Sam insisted on taking us to Li's Kitchen."

"How'd you do?"

"Oh, I did alright. I didn't say anything. It doesn't do any good to bellyache. You know, I will never get used to eating Chinese food on Sunday. It's more of a Saturday night meal."

"Haha! As I always say to you – tell that to the Chinese on Sunday! They live there and they must eat. Right?"

"Yeah, yeah. I know what you always say. Later on, your dad, Grandpa Sam and I went fishing in that second big hole up from the small alfalfa field and caught some trout. We went back to their place and Grandma Nellie fixed us a fine supper. Then I mostly loafed around this evening until you called. That's my day!"

"Sounds like it was very relaxing yet, very full!"

"Yes it twas, it twas. How was your day? Tell me all about it." Jacody asked.

Marcy told Jacody all about Division Sup Mitty getting sent home. She purposely left out her own concerns about being stalked. Then she shared some of the stories she heard at lunch from Ned Carpenter and the drivers. She talked a little about her walk with Sheila and the talk they had about racism. Marcy admitted that she may have pulled out her guns to shoot racist ideas down that really weren't there. Jacody warned her, again, that she seemed more sensitive to racism than he was. Marcy shared that, to her, it seemed Sheila is very insecure about what holds a friendship together. Then she told him about their evening worship service with Carlos and Jock thinking they might get to see an exorcism performed on Larry.

"What was Sheila's reaction to the worship service?" Jacody asked.

"It is hard to tell, but I think pretty well for what might have been her first experience at a true worship service. After the service, we kind of got tied up with "Larry, his brother Darryl and his other brother Darryl", if you recall them from the old reruns of the Bob Newhart Show."

"You mean Larry, Jock, and Carlos, right?"

"You got it." Marcy said, "Sheila reminded me that, earlier, I told her she would have a better understanding of 'he who has religion as a god has no god for his religion,' after she attended the worship service. Well, she said she had no better understanding than before. I told her that, if she noticed, Barron talked about our relationship with God – not our relationship with religion. That's the difference. It counts for nothing if you are considered a Baptist, a Catholic, a Methodist, an Assembly of God, a Nazarene... and I could go on naming "brands" of organized religions... if you are not focused on God."

"Did that help her understand?" Jacody wanted to know.

"When I asked her that, she gave me an unconvincing nod yes. I told her she experienced a worship service focused on God. I hoped she would go to a church when she got back home and, when she did, be mindful of where the church puts its emphasis. If it is not on the God of the Bible, go to another church and keep looking for a church that is focused on God. I wish she could go to Council Community Church with us."

Jacody said, "Well, you can't be a mother hen and cover everyone with your wings! I have to think she will find her way. Who knows who else God will send her way to encourage her to grow her faith."

"I know. So. That was my day.... It is getting late. I don't know how long we've been talking. I'm up early as usual. I'm hauling Jock's dozer up along the Southside of the fire first thing. Larry will be bringing Carlos' feller/buncher up. The plan is to hold the fire from spreading to the South now."

"I know it is getting late... but I have one more thing I want to tell you."

"Oh. Sure. What is it?" Marcy asked.

"It may have to do with what you just mentioned, taking the dozer up the mountain in the morning. I was out in the barn with the horses just after sundown and I started feeling this almost irresistible urge to get down on my knees and pray. I put my elbows on a straw bale and bowed my head. As always, I went through my usual method of acknowledging how great God is and then, thanking him for all He has blessed us with; how amazing His grace is upon us. I kind of let my mind go blank then. It was a bit of time before it started coming to me. It was all about you, but not only you! I was filled with concern for people I don't know but I'm sure you know. I prayed for everyone's safety against a powerful force. Tomorrow, you are to let your instincts guide you. I don't know what tomorrow is going to bring... but don't be swayed by what other people are telling you if you feel you should do something different. I've prayed the Holy Spirit will be with you and guide you. Don't be afraid but be bold."

"My gosh JJ! Are you trying to encourage me or scare the bejabbers out of me!

"Humm. I worry about you all the time to some degree. And maybe this evening that little worry got the best of me. I always trust God when I think about it. It is when I'm not thinking about God that I want to take that worry out and stroke it into something too big for God to manage, you know, like He needs my help. But then, when I become aware of what I'm doing, I put it back in its box and let God have it again. This is different. There may be something on the horizon we don't know about. However, it still isn't too big for God, and I am, once again, at ease. But I did need to tell you about it so you can pray about it too. It is a warning. Take extra care out there. You can also look out for those around you and maybe that's why I prayed that way. It was to tell you to look out for opportunities to help someone around you."

"Okay. We both know that God does not send out a word for no good reason. I'm forewarned. Again, I thank God that you are such a spiritual person and I believe God uses you as a conduit to reach other people."

"I don't want to assume anything," Jacody said. "I just want 'to be'. And if He places things in my mind, then I'm humbled. Do you recall that little book we read, 'Mere Shadows'? It was about a woman who often had directions from God."

"Yes, I remember that book."

"Well, this is a little bit like that. When I first read it, I was a little skeptical. Too much has happened in my life to doubt it now."

"God is so good to us!" Marcy said.

"That's for sure!" Jacody responded.

"I'll keep everything you told me in mind, and I'll pray about it too. But right now... we need to get to sleep. Before I called you, I was thinking about everything that has been going on here and all the lack of mutual respect..."

"Mutual respect... that's a different term for you to use, isn't it?" Jacody asked.

"Yes, I guess it is. The HRSP guy is preaching it all the time. It has become easy for me to use now. So, like I was saying, before I called you, I was thinking of a song for us to go to sleep by tonight. Keeping mutual respect in mind... and thank you Grandpa Sam for pumping hours and hours of 1960's music blasting in my head... I'm thinking we should listen to 'Get Together' by The Youngbloods. I'd like to go to sleep tonight thinking that, not only you and I being together, but everyone else coming together in peace and love. Let's all be hippies! Good song, yes... no?"

Jacody said, "Yeah, I'm in. Sweet dreams Sugar Pie. I love you, I'll be thinking and praying for you tomorrow and every day!"

"Goodnight JJ, you are so precious to me! I love you too. You and the rest of the family are in my prayers as well. Goodnight."

Marcy slipped into her bedroll. The generators had shut down about a half-hour ago and the only sounds were those made by nature. She could hear an owl up in the top of the 200-year-old Ponderosa Pine, "whooo coooooks for yoooou - whooo cooks for yoooualll". The Nighthawks were buzzing and burping as Nighthawks do. A little way off, Marcy thought she heard a truck door shut. Refusing to dwell on that particular sound, she hit play on her cell phone.

Get Together

Love is but a song we sing
Fear's the way we die
You can make the mountains ring
Or make the angels cry
Though the bird is on the wing
And you may not know why
     Come on, people now
     Smile on your brother
     Everybody get together
     Try to love one another right
     now

Chapter Seventeen
Lightning In the Air

The sun had been shining up over the Warner's ridgeline long enough to get a breeze blowing to the East and clear out the smoke that had the Westside socked in. And so Monday morning began much the same as all the previous mornings on the Stutler Ridge Fire. The IAP, Incident Action Plan, for the day had Jock, Marcy, and their D-6 dozer, Carlos, Larry, and their feller/buncher assigned to Division Charlie. Marcy and crew had attended the morning briefings as usual and now, were listening to Division Charlie Supervisor Jared Hornsby at division breakout. Safety as an emphasis item was being hammered on over and over.

Div Sup Hornsby declared, "Yes, late afternoon lightning is expected today, so we will be on high alert. Even so, we will go into Division Charlie and establish a safety zone and start a dozer control line South to tie in with the line extending North in Division Bravo. If we can't get all of this done by early afternoon, be prepared to pull back to Drop Point #8 in Division Alpha no matter what we have accomplished."

"We scouted out the wilderness trailhead parking lot yesterday," Hornsby continued, "and I gotta tell you, there's not much room up there. This is identified on your maps as Drop Point #7. Here's what we came up with as far as moving in and moving out up there. We will stage at Drop Point #8. I want Dozer Boss John Helmsley to go up with me to limit the number of vehicles. Next, to get things going, I want the feller/buncher with the operator to follow. Everyone else holds until the feller/buncher transport unloads and returns to Drop Point #8. Then bring up the dozer with the operator. You shots and everyone else can follow the dozer up after 30 -40 minutes. Give the transport time enough to get up there and get turned around before coming into the parking area. If there are no questions, get ready for the day and I'll see you at Drop Point #8. I'll go over the traveling orders again there."

It was the same, but different. Marcy felt an uneasiness about this morning. She had been with the scouting party yesterday and agreed with Hornsby's plans, but she felt a cloud hanging over fire camp that wasn't smoke. "Monday, Monday. Can't trust that day..." the old Mamas and Papas song kept going through her mind.

High in the Warner Mountains at 0800 and the tiny parking lot for the trailhead of the Falling Waters Wilderness Trail started receiving fire vehicles. As planned, the dozer boss and Div Charlie Sup Jared Hornsby got there first. The two checked the fire map and Div Sup went over the general location where he wanted a safety zone pushed by the dozer. Then they went over the approximate location of where the fire dozer line was to be located. The plan was to work to the West in the direction of the dozer line in Division Bravo.

No sooner had the dozer boss walked off to start tying plastic flagging to bushes and tree branches as a guide for the heavy equipment to follow, than the sound of a large diesel engine running at maximum RPMs was heard. The last 300 yards of Forest Road 810 was a steep grade, so it was several minutes before the grill of Larry Steuben's bright red Kenworth slowly emerged up on the flat plateau just before the wilderness trailhead parking area. With Carlos Santiago spotting the back of the trailer as it backed up, Larry was able to turn the tractor and transport trailer carrying the feller/buncher around. It took a lot of backing up and pulling forward with several small trees getting trampled by the transport's rear tandem tires in the process.

Now that the safety zone was being identified and Carlos was removing all the trees from it he could, Larry in his transport was headed back down the mountain. Div Sup Hornsby tried to do a communication check with Stutler Ridge Fire Dispatch. Repeated attempts failed. Three days ago, the communications shop had set up a radio repeater to facilitate radio traffic up the canyon on that side of the fire. However, Murphy's law that states, "if something can go wrong, it will" appeared to be in effect. An inability to communicate with the ICP, Incident Command Post, put everyone on Division Charlie in jeopardy. They could communicate via their portable radios there on the fire line, but not with the outside world.

Hornsby gauged the immediate situation. By now, Larry was out of radio range, as was everyone at DP#8. The dozer would be on top here at DP#7 soon and everyone else would be coming along shortly after that. Chances are, if they headed back down the mountain now, they would meet Marcy and her transport with the dozer, and, on this skinny road, they would have to back up all the way to the trailhead parking area because the transport wouldn't be able to back up. Hornsby decided it was best to wait until Marcy got to the top. The Bushrod Hotshots would be right behind her and one of the crewmembers could be snagged to try and set up a human repeater to restore communications with the ICP. Red Flag weather conditions weren't predicted until the afternoon. Well before then, the safety zone would be pushed in and the equipment and personnel would have a safety zone if, in fact, one was needed.

Marcy had 2 challenges. The first one was keeping Cupcake's front tires on the road. Once she neared the top of the long steep grade, she no longer had the road in her windshield... just green trees in the distance above the radiator and, above the trees, blue sky. She hugged the cut bank on her left as close as she could to make sure she didn't go over the drop-off to her right. Jock, who was never comfortable when someone else was driving, was "helping" her by hanging out the passenger side window looking ahead so he could tell her if the front wheels started getting too close to the edge. Marcy ignored most of his nervous attempts at helping her steer.

Her other challenge was to make sure her tandem drivers maintained traction. With Cupcake's transmission transfer case in low range and the transmission in first gear, the semi could drag the Titanic up the mountain. The only hitch would be if it lost traction. Cupcake's dual tandem drivers provided 8 tires on the ground pulling the load. If Cupcake's tires started slipping and the truck lost momentum, this would be a precarious location to unload the dozer and get the transport moving again. On almost any other road, traction wouldn't be a concern. But on this narrow jeep trail with grass growing between two tracks, all Marcy could do is try to balance the RPMs. She needed to keep them high for maximum pulling power but ease up to avoid spinning out and stalling. So, Marcy's attention was divided; stay close to the cut bank on her left, be super sensitive to any rear tire slippage, and avoid being distracted by Jock.

Around 0950, the high-pitched sound of another diesel engine joined Carlos' feller/buncher's ringing sound coming from both its rotary cutting head and diesel engine. The air was filled with a cacophony of industrial equipment alien to the quiet of the wilderness. Two plumes of black diesel smoke became visible just before Cupcake's pink ghost flames and deep royal blue hood appeared up the steep grade onto the plateau.

Once Cupcake leveled off on top of the small plateau, Marcy started breathing easier. She had to will the muscles in her shoulders to relax. Once her truck and trailer were completely on top, she stopped so Jock could jump out and guide her as she backed up a little, pulled forward, backed up a little, and pulled forward over and over until she was turned around. She was situated where the ones who followed her up could get past her and she could go back down the road.

Marcy set the brakes and climbed out of the cab. The first thing she did was to go over to Jared Hornsby, Div Sup, and let him know she lost radio contact shortly after she left DP #8. Hornsby acknowledged he was aware of the situation and was going to ask Liam Johnson, Bushrod Hotshot Crew Boss to send one of his crewmembers out to be a human repeater when they got there.

She and Jock got busy getting the binders off the dozer. Once free, Jock negotiated the dozer down the trailer ramps and out of the way. Marcy collected all the chains and binders and hung them up on the back of the truck's sleeper unit.

Cupcake was sitting off to the right of the road and headed down. Once the dozer was unloaded, she could steer sharp left and then sharp right. Pulling forward, she would immediately feel her seat belt tightened as it kept her from sliding under the steering wheel on the steep descent. Coming uphill with full power always felt better than a steep downhill with the jake brakes on and standing heavy on the air brakes. The engine sounds so much different at high RPMs with no fuel as it works against the push of an empty trailer compared to high RPMs with the accelerator down pulling the weight of a loaded trailer.

Yesterday, they had been up on DP #7 to plan out how all the vehicles would occupy the limited parking area. Marcy had done a little exploring while the others were talking and planning. Walking through the manzanita and trees she had found a vista. Sanding on the rimrock, she had a clear view of Mt. Shasta, standing proud and tall with its snowy cap 110 miles to the West. She remembered what a Modoc Indian from Ft. Bidwell had told her about the sleepy volcano. Mt. Shasta is home to the matah kagmi, the Modoc word for Bigfoot. The Indian said that the matah kagmi are known as "keepers of the woods" and have been in existence as long as the Modoc people have existed. When she had looked at all that sparsely populated land it was not hard to think Bigfoot might exist hidden away somewhere.

At the base of the rimrock she was standing on, she had been able to look down on Forest Road 810 as it ribboned through the trees and made its way up the final long steep grade to the wilderness parking area. Yesterday, she heard ravens calling to each other from the rimrock across the canyon. Their raucous call bounced from one side of the canyon to the other. She had resisted the urge to add her voice to the ravens to hear it echo. She didn't want those back at the parking area to think she was being immature! What a mysterious, beautiful part of the state this was!

Such were her thoughts as she sought out the vista today. Upon gaining the edge of the rimrock, she saw the roofs of several vehicles climbing the slope up to the parking lot. Shifting her gaze towards Mt. Shasta, something caught her attention that made her blood run cold!

She was looking at a large cell of low-hanging cumulonimbus, clouds. These anvil-shaped clouds are called hammerheads or thunderstorm clouds. They are capable of hundreds of lightning strikes and, even if accompanied by rain, the moisture is seldom enough to dowse any fire that might have been started. Right before her eyes, thunderheads were building fast and speeding towards her location. From her hotshot days, SA, or Situational Awareness had been preached from day one. That training was kicking in now, LCES! Lookouts. Check, she was looking. Communication. Check, ummh... maybe. She would find out when she reported this to Hornsby. Escape Routes. Check. There was only one and it may be plugged up. Safety Zone. Check. As soon as one could be cleared by Carlos and pushed by Jock!

She was sure this was the Red Flag conditions I-Met was calling for but it was arriving hours early! Wasting no time, she hurried back to where Div Sup Hornsby and Safety Officer Barron were talking. The last pickup she had seen from the rock outcrop popped up on the plateau and made its way over to stop next to the two men she was going to talk with. It was Planning Chief Sheila and the Operations Chief.

They got out of their truck and was joining the two men as Marcy got there.

"Hey, I just looked out over the valley! We've got big problems headed our way!" she almost gasped. She was a little winded from running to get to them and she thought, "oh great! They'll think I'm panicking."

"What are you talking about?" Hornsby asked.

"From the rimrock over there I saw hammerheads drifting this way."

Sheila stepped into the group and said, "what? I haven't heard anything on the radio about that! Now that I think about it, I haven't heard anything at all on the radio!"

"The repeater they put up Saturday for us must be down. I had the shot's crew leader send a crewmember around on the Southside of the canyon to the rimrock over there to try and find a place where we can use him or her as a human repeater. But, what the hey! Thunderheads are not due until later on today!" Hornsby declared.

"Tell it to the clouds!" Marcy said. To emphasize her comment, a peel of thunder resounded up the canyon.

To everyone's wonder, their portable radios started crackling with the same information at the same time!

"Alturas Dispatch, Blue Mountain," Blue Mountain Fire Lookout was contacting the Modoc National Forest dispatch office in Alturas.

Silence. Each person strained their ears as they waited.

> "Alturas Dispatch, Blue Mountain," the call came again.

Silence.

"Liam, radio your crewmember to stop and stay where he is for right now. This repeater is acting temperamental. It may work from here on or it may quit again any second. We could need him then. Unfortunately, he won't be able to position himself until the repeater goes out again. If it does, we will deal with it then," said Hornsby.

> "Blue Mountain, Alturas Dispatch," Alturas Dispatch answered Blue Mountain Fire Lookout's call to them.

> "Alturas Dispatch, I have a smoke building. Azimuth 134.27°, over."

Instantly, Marcy recalled from her Hotshot training days that an azimuth is a line from a given point. Straight up North is 0 or 360 degrees. East is 90°, South is 180°, and West is 270°. So, Blue Mountain is looking at a smoke South and a little East (between 180° and 90°) of its location. If another fire lookout sees the same smoke and records an azimuth reading from their location, where the two lines, or azimuths intersect is the approximate location of the fire. If a third fire lookout calls in an azimuth from their location on the same smoke, an exact location is confirmed.

> "Copy Blue Mountain. Smoke. Azimuth 134.27°, over."

"Alturas Dispatch, Roger," Blue Mountain confirmed and ended the radio call.

Silence.

Operation Chief Hank Buzzard said, "What the hell! There wasn't supposed to be a build-up until after 1400! Where did those hammerheads come from?"

Jock joined the group. "What did I just hear on the radio?"

Every person became reverently silent. Each one understood how precarious their situation might become depending on the next thing that came from the radio's speaker. Eyes flashed furtively from face to face, their owners looking to see where strength might be found should additional strength be needed.

"Alturas Dispatch, Happy Camp," Happy Camp Fire Lookout was radioing Alturas Dispatch.

"OH SHIT!" Sheila and Hornsby said at the same time.

"Happy Camp, Alturas Dispatch," Alturas Dispatch answered Happy Camp's call.

"Alturas Dispatch, several lightning strikes on the West side of the Warner's. One smoke may be what Blue Mountain Lookout is reporting at azimuth 96.59°, over."

"Happy Camp, copy smoke at azimuth 96.59°."

Sheila laid out the forest map and pulled a clear plastic ruler from her vest pocket. She drew an approximate line 134.27° from Blue Mountain located North and a little West. Then she drew another line

313

approximately 96.57° from Happy Camp located West and a little North. The two lines crossed a short distance West of Drop Point #7 – the parking area they were standing in!

By now, everyone that was on Division Charlie except the Dozer Boss, Carlos, and the human repeater, had formed a silent half-circle around the front of Hornsby's pickup. They faced the narrow gap in the trees formed by the road and stared at the distant blue spot where low-hanging thunderclouds were building. Every so often there was a flash of lightning. In the distance was the constant sound of the feller/buncher rising and falling, punctuated with the far-off sound of rolling thunder.

"Alturas Dispatch, Hawkinfoot," now Hawkinfoot Fire Lookout was reporting to Alturas Dispatch.

"Here we go!" said Operations Chief Hank Buzzard.

"Hawkinfoot, Alturas Dispatch"

"Alturas Dispatch I'm seeing smoke, but it looks like it is deep in the canyon. I'm close but I don't see any fire. Azimuth 351.0°. That's to the center of the smoke, over."

"Hawkinfoot, copy light smoke, azimuth 351.0°, over."

"We're screwed!" said Sheila, drawing a line 351.0° from Hawkingfoot Lookout located South and a little East of their exact location. "Hawkinfoot is laying that line right over the top of us! They are looking at a smoke down in the canyon below the road we just came in on!"

"Alturas Dispatch, Happy Camp."

"Happy Camp, Alturas Dispatch."

"Yeah, dispatch. I'm looking right up the canyon where that strike landed. Smoke is black and it appears we already have some torching. It's getting wide fast. The smoke is laying low but heading towards FR810. This looks like it will blow right into the Stutler Ridge Fire"

"Happy Camp, copy. Possible torching, wind blowing fire towards Stutler Ridge Fire. Break. Stutler Ridge Dispatch, Alturas Dispatch, over."

"Alturas Dispatch, Stutler Ridge Dispatch."

"Stutler Ridge Dispatch, have you been following Blue Mountain, Happy Camp, and Hawkinfoot's transmissions? Over."

"Alturas Dispatch, copy, we're on top of it. Thanks for your help. We will head Initial Attack that way. It may be too windy for bucket drops. Over."

"Roger that, let us know if you need anything. Alturas Dispatch out."

Div Sup Hornsby asked, "Jock, how long will it take you to... wait..." Keying his radio microphone, "Dozer Boss Helmsley, Division Charlie." Then back to Jock, "...how long will it take you to..."

Division Charlie, Helmsley," radioed Dozer Boss Helmsley.

"Helmsley, return to the parking area now," radioed back Div Sup Hornsby.

"Jock, how long will it take you to..." the radio interrupted Hornsby.

"Division Charlie, I was listening to the radio, I'm almost there now." Helmsley interrupted on the radio.

"Copy Helmsley," said Hornby.

"How long would it take me to push a big enough safety zone?" Jock said. "I don't know... 30-45 minutes maybe. Those big ole pines Carlos had to leave will slow it down a lot!"

"Division Charlie, Stutler Ridge Dispatch." Dispatch radioed Hornsby.

"Jock, you've got 5 minutes to push an area for your dozer and the feller/buncher. Radio Carlos and have him be ready to park his machine as soon as you get an area for him. Then both of you get back over here. I've got a feeling both machines are gonna have to ride the fire out right where they are!" Hornsby said.

Already smoke was visible through the gap in the trees. Even if Jock could clear a large safety zone in time, it wouldn't guarantee everyone would be safe. The window of opportunity was closing fast!

"Division Charlie, Stutler Ridge Dispatch." Dispatch radioed Hornsby again.

"Okay! Choices people! Prepare to deploy our fire shelters and ride it out or run for it?" Hornsby guessed Stutler Ridge Dispatch was going to ask what their plans were, and he wanted to be ready with an answer. "Hank, what's your thoughts? As Ops Chief have you been in this predicament before?"

316

"Stutler Ridge Dispatch, Division Charlie."
Hornsby started the radio call.

"No, I haven't. Only in practice," Ops Chief Hank
Buzzard replied. "But look around. We got fuels
right up to this narrow road and beyond! The wind
blowing over this ridge is going to be violent! We have
the start of a safety zone, but it doesn't look very safe
even if we had 25 minutes of prep time with the dozer.
We are spending valuable time talking about it! I say
we run for it before it reaches FR810."

"Division Charlie, what is your situation?
Have you heard the radio transmissions?
Over." Crackled the radio.

"Sheila?" Hornsby asked.

Sheila could smell the wind-driven smoke.
Already it was apparent it was torching groups of trees
and the wind was spotting fire out ahead of the main
body. The wind was strong and keeping the smoke
low. She turned her eyes back to Hornsby. "Let's
roll!" was her quick reply.

"That's where I'm at too!" said Safety Officer
Barron.

"Good!" said Hornsby.

"Stutler Ridge Dispatch, Things are too
tight up here. The repeater has been sketchy
and we don't know if it will go down again or
not. We are making an orderly departure back
to Drop Point #8. We will regroup there and
once all are accounted for will return to the
ICP, over." Hornsby reported.

"Division Charlie, Stutler Ridge Dispatch
copies, stand by," replied Dispatch.

"Division Charlie, standing by." Radioed Hornsby.

"Shots! Liam call your man in!" Directed Hornsby, "Load up, count your people, then head out and radio if you have problems. Hank and Sheila! Get to your vehicles! Leave, now! John..."

"Division Charlie, this is Pat, all of you are professionals, keep your cool, be decisive, and don't doubt yourselves. We are all praying for you. Be safe. See you at the bottom. Over."

"Stutler Ridge Dispatch, Division Charlie, copy, see you at the bottom." Division Hornsby replied.

"See?" Hornsby said, "it's gonna be fine because the Incident Commander Pat Thompson just said so! Now let's get going! John! Get in with Rick and follow the chiefs. Go! Now!"

Hank Buzzard and Sheila Shelton's pickup truck went out of sight down the grade. It was getting smoky but still, visibility was decent.

Moments later, Rick Barron and John Helmsley followed the chiefs. Close behind them was the Bushrod Hotshot's crew buggy.

Marcy was rolling up maps that were left weighted down with rocks on Hornsby's pickup hood when Hornsby came over to her and said, "Hurry up! Get in the truck and let's go!"

"Marcy shook her head and said, "no! You go ahead. We will be right behind you."

"What are you talking about? Get in my truck! You can't run down this mountain in that semi! Wait! Did

Carlos and Jock not get in one of the other pickups? Where are they?"

"I sent them over to drop the landing gear on the trailer and chock it up. It's sitting in about as bare an area as we are going to find and since we are making a run for it, I don't want that transport trailer pushing me." Marcy said.

"No! The 3 of you get in my truck with me and let's go! We don't have time to fool with that transport. The road runs towards this new fire for a while and the fire is running towards the road! We don't have time for that! You don't have time for that! Let's go!" Hornsby said.

Marcy looked at him for a moment. Her first impulse was to follow the Division Supervisor's direct order. But what had Jacody told her just last night... "Tomorrow, I want you to be led by your instincts... don't be swayed by what other people are telling you if you feel you should do something different."

"This is it!" Marcy thought, "I am in whatever God was telling Jacody about! God, I am placing all my trust in You! Lead me, Holy Spirit"

"You don't know what you are asking me to do! I am not leaving my truck! Besides, four of us in your little Ford Ranger can't be a good situation!" Marcy turned and jogged back to the transport.

Hornsby went over and got in his truck. He drove past Marcy to where Jock and Carlos were feverously putting chocks in front and behind the trailer's tandems, putting blocks under the landing gear, and lowering it.

He was going to speak to them when Rick Barron broke in on the radio. Rick reported that the fire was almost to the road where they were, but they were continuing and making good time. His report served to add urgency to those behind them.

"Hornsby yelled through the passenger window at the two men working on the trailer. "Did you hear Rick? Everyone else is headed down. It is just the four of us now. Leave the truck and get in here with me. We gotta go now! Do you want to die up here?"

"You got a little 2-seater Ranger. 4 of us can't ride in that!" called back Carlos.

Marcy jumped up on the tractor deck and unhooked the airlines. As soon as the truck was free to move out from under the trailer, Marcy swung up into the driver's seat.

"What are you doing!" Hornsby almost screamed at them.

Marcy yelled back, "I'll explain it all to you some time. Right now you need to get moving or I'll run over you! Carlos, Jock, get in with Hornsby!"

Right then the passenger side door on the big Diamond Reo opened and Jock proclaimed, "If you can drive 'er, I can ride 'er! Let's go!" Carlos climbed over the passenger's seat to the sleeper unit and Jock swung up into the cab and closed the door.

Hornsby was laying across the seat and started to yell something else at them through his passenger's window again, but Marcy laid on the air horn and could only see his mouth moving. Cupcake started shuddering as Marcy slowly let out on the clutch and the trailer slid off the 5th wheel. Hornsby, feeling control of the desperate situation slip from his grasp, sat up in the seat, and headed down the grade on Forest Road 810 in front of Cupcake by himself.

"Man you are one stubborn bitch!" said Carlos.

"Watch it!" Marcy snarled! "Use that term in my direction again and I'll teach you something your mother should have!"

"Uh... yeah. I just kind of got caught up in the excitement. Let's just watch the road and get us out of here!"

The bug killed Ponderosa Pine and Lodgepole Pine was tinder dry and the wind-driven fire, although deep down in the canyon, was spotting up to a mile from the original start. The fire low on the slope preheated the trees and manzanita higher up on the slope. They burst into flames even before the main body of the fire below could get to them. Before the caravan got halfway down the mountain, the fire was burning on both sides of the road.

Soon Cupcake too entered the heavy smoke. Occasionally, flames were licking up out of the steep canyon walls and over the road. Over the radio, they heard Ops Chief Hank Buzzard report that there was an abandoned pickup on the side of the road. There was no one present as far as Hank could tell. He assured people that pickups and the crew buggy could get by the stalled truck. He didn't mention the Diamond Reo – most likely because he didn't expect it to be coming down in the convoy.

That had been the last sound the radio made. Jock repeatedly tried to contact the others, but no sound came back to them on their radio. Marcy told Jock and Carlos the only reason they had been able to have communications up on top where they were was because of the portable repeater that had been installed on the other side of the canyon. Now, she guessed, this new fire was raging up that side of the canyon as well and that the repeater was toast. The only human contact they had now was the occasional visual contact with the little Ford Ranger pickup Hornsby was driving in front of them. They could see no one in front of him.

Marcy knew that radiant heat coming through a window in a structure could be so intense that the interior of the structure would catch on fire before the fire could burn through an outside wall. With the wind rolling the fire up and over the road, she could feel the left side of her face getting extremely hot. She asked Jock to pull out his fire shelter and she pulled her sun visor around to her side window. She draped the shelter over the sun visor to protect her from the heat. Carlos was in the sleeper and she asked him to take his fire shelter and hold it up over the sleeper's side window.

Now the smoke was making it hard to see the little pickup's taillights. Every once in a while, the smoke would swirl up behind the truck and reveal the tailgate and roadway. Up ahead something was burning bright off to the side of the road. When Cupcake got to it, Marcy could make out what appeared to be a pickup with its front wheels hanging over the edge of the road. Someone had tried to turn around and, in the smoke, pulled too far forward, going over the edge with its front tires. The passenger's compartment was fully engulfed in fire. Marcy gathered that if anyone was inside, they were surely dead.

"Lord, I pray for the safety of whoever was driving that pickup! May they be with the people ahead of us!" Marcy prayed out loud.

The pickups and the hotshot's crew buggy were narrow enough to drive around the burning pickup, but not so the big Diamond Reo. Marcy had been traveling as fast as she dared, but now, she pressed down on the accelerator and slammed into the rear of the truck spinning it over to the side. There was a flash of light and Marcy concluded that the fuel cell in the bed of the pickup had ruptured and diesel fuel was adding to the flames. As smokey as it was, in her large side mirror, she saw the pickup slide off the roadside down into the hungry flames below.

Proverbs Chapter 30, the last half of verses 15 and all of 16 popped into Marcy's mind: "There are three things that are never satisfied- no, four that never say, 'Enough!': the grave, the barren womb, the thirsty desert, the blazing fire."

Perhaps a quarter of a mile past the burning pickup, the smoke behind the Div Sup's truck swirled up exposing the roadway clearly for a brief second. "Did you see that?" Marcy asked her passengers as she hit the brakes hard almost throwing Carlos up into the cab.

"What are you doing?" yelled Jock. "Go! Go!"

"I thought I saw a body lying in the ditch right back there!" Marcy said.

"How could you see anything? Keep going we can't even see any taillights now! How in the world do you think you saw the ditch – much less a body!" Jock protested, but Marcy had stopped and was already backing up slowly.

"Have you lost your mind?" Carlos yelled. "You don't stop when you're going through hell! You keep going!"

"There!" Marcy exclaimed. "The truck is blocking a lot of heat. Jump out and see what's in the ditch!"

"No! This is stupid! Get going!" Jock said. "Marcy... I swear..."

"The faster you get out there and check for me the faster we get moving out of here!" Marcy's cut Jock off.

"Arrrgh! Stubborn! Stubborn! Stubborn!" was what Marcy heard as Jock jumped down out of the truck.

The temperature outside the truck was like a blast furnace. The hot air was thick with ash and firebrands burning the back of Jock's neck. It felt like his windpipe was sucking in hot firebrands with the super-heated air. In a flash, he was along the ditch. Sure enough! He found a body lying face down in the ditch. There were patches of hair burned off the person's head. Jock grabbed the person's far arm and pulled the body towards himself, rolling it on its back.

"My god! It's Larry!" Jock yelled. "Quick! Carlos, give me a hand! I need help!"

Now, Larry was not a small man, but with the adrenaline rush, they were able to lift Larry, turn him around, and set him on Cupcake's first step. Marcy had climbed over to the passenger's seat and was pulling under Larry's arms while Jock and Carlos on either side of Larry pulled up on his belt. With effort, they got his butt up on the floorboard of the cab, then on the passenger's seat. Carlos climbed over him and got back in the sleeper and Jock stood on the step. From behind, Carlos wrapped his arms under Larry's arms and around his chest. Carlos straighten his legs as he fell backward, pulling Larry up, back, and on top of him onto the sleeper's mattress.

With Larry loaded and the door closed, they started out once more. Marcy was going as fast as she could with the poor visibility, but she was worried about Larry. Somewhere, she had read that most people could survive external temperatures of 140 °F for 10 minutes. It surely had been much cooler than that in the ditch, so what had happened to Larry? She was so thankful that she had that air conditioner unit installed.

Carlos had gotten Larry's bulk from off the top of him and Jock felt Larry's neck for a pulse. He thought he may have felt a weak one, but he wasn't sure, the truck was jostling him about so. "Man oh, man! It sure is a good thing you are one stubborn chick!"

Marcy asked Carlos and Jock if either of them knew how to do CPR. "You mean, put my lips on his and blow into his mouth?" Carlos asked.

"No," replied Marcy. "You don't have to do it that way. Do you know how to give chest compressions?"

"You better tell me. I'm not sure," said Carlos.

"Find the bottom of Larry's breastbone down towards his stomach. Put your left middle finger right on the end. Now put your index finger next to it. Do it! Got it?"

"Yeah, I think so." Came Carlos' uncertain response.

"Good! Now, put the heel of your right hand on his breastbone next to where you have your two fingers. Put your left hand on top of your right and interlock your fingers. Get on your knees and lock your elbows. Then with your weight, press fairly hard – not hard enough to break ribs, but fairly hard, 100 times, or beats, a minute," Marcy said.

"Okay, I got the hand part but how do I know what 100 beats a minute is? Jock, are you going to count and time me? What if I do it wrong?" Carlos asked.

"Do you know the BeeGee's song 'Staying Alive'"? Marcy asked.

"No!" Both men responded.

"No. I don't suppose you would. Let's see... Oh! How about Johnny Cash and 'Walk the Line'? I keep my eyes wide open all the time.... You know that one?"

"Yes," Carlos answered. "But how does that help?"

"It's 100 beats a minute! I'll get you started. I'll sing the song and slap the side of my seat until you can do it by yourself. You press on Larry's chest every time I slap the seat. And don't worry, you won't do it wrong!" Carlos mastered the art in no time. Marcy thought it might be that Carlos had to be coordinated to operate a complicated machine like a feller/buncher.

It was difficult to see the road through the smoke and Marcy was concerned she might drive right off the gravel road into the deep furnace below. The outside of the truck body was getting really hot. She could feel the heat starting to radiate off the plastic components on the door panels. If they didn't clear the burning area soon, they would die from toxic air inside the cab. What if Cupcake became disabled... tires overheat and blow out, saddle tanks full of diesel expand from the heat and rupture catching the fuel on fire? There were lots of possibilities and they all spelled disaster!

She put her hand down by the air conditioning output vent. There was nothing coming out. No wonder it was getting hotter inside the cab. It wasn't just because the wind was blowing heat and flames out onto the road, the ash had plugged up the filter on the air conditioning unit. It no longer worked. "Oh no!" She cried out involuntarily.

"What!" Jock said, "What's wrong?"

"Oh!" Marcy said, not wanting to increase the anxiety of her passengers. "Nothing. I think I just hit a rock in the road, but we are alright!" But Marcy knew what was starting to go wrong. If the filter for the air conditioner no longer allowed air into the unit, it was just a matter of time before the air filter for Cupcake's engine would also plug up. Anticipating the worst, Marcy pressed down on the accelerator just a little. With all her senses tuned to the truck's response, she couldn't be sure, but it seemed a bit sluggish. Maybe she was over-reacting, she thought. But it did respond – so far, so good!

Jock had been trying to contact Division Supervisor Hornsby on the radio without any success. He could raise no one and he still couldn't hear any traffic on the radio either. They were in thick smoke, and they were headed down a canyon where radio reception had been sketchy to begin with. They felt deserted and alone. Jock continued trying, desperate to reach the outside world. Not that he thought anyone was hearing him – he just needed to feel like he was doing something. He couldn't sit there and do nothing.

Suddenly, the truck seemed to buck! The windshield was showered with burning small branches. The bole of a large snag had just fallen on the back of Cupcake's sleeper unit. The noise inside the cab became deafening! The butt of the tree was dragging on the edge of the road sending a loud vibrating rattling sound into the cab. The bole slid down the back of the sleeper and became locked between the fifth wheel and the sleeper cab. The large end of the snag dug into the roadbed crowbarring the front of the truck to the left towards the drop-off and the rear tandem of the truck to the right into the ditch.

Just before the truck fishtailed sideways off the road into the great abyss, the snag snapped at the rear tires, and the end dragging on the road was left behind. Even though the truck wasn't going all that fast, Marcy had been fighting the log with the steering wheel cranked to the right, and, with the log no longer trying to direct the truck, it wanted to spin back the other way. Marcy cranked the big truck's steering wheel back to the left. Everyone was tossed from one side to the other, but Marcy regained control of the truck.

"I don't think we are going to make it out of here!" Jock said. "What's next!"

"Oh ye of little faith! I have good news for you guys!" Marcy said.

"Well great!" Said Carlos, as he resumed compressions on Larry after being thrown clear to the opposite side of the sleeper unit. "But the only good news I want to hear is we are in the clear and safe!"

"Better than that! Jacody knew we were going to be in a dangerous situation today. He told me, when it happened, not to listen to anyone else, but do exactly what I thought was right!"

"Oh Marcy! That's just too far-fetched for me to buy into!" Jock said. "Is this because I called you stubborn? And now I bet you're gonna say you're not stubborn – just doing what God tells you to do!"

"No. And yes!" Marcy said, "it's not because of what you said – but because if I hadn't done what Jacody told me God told him to tell me to do... Larry would still be in the ditch. Who would have picked him up? There was no one else! We were the last possible chance he would get out of there!"

"Maybe we were just lucky! Ever think of that?" Jock said.

"Luck! You think this was luck?"

"Maybe," Jock's response was barely audible.

"No! Think about it. Hornsby wanted us to get in his rig with him. We might have done that, and maybe we would have been in the clear by now. Don't you think that's right?" Marcy asked.

"Probably" Carlos answered.

"But would we have seen Larry laying along the road close to death?"

"Maybe," Carlos said.

"Maybe. But Hornsby didn't see Larry. And if we had been with him and saw Larry, what would we have done with him? Throw him in the bed of the pickup like a sack of potatoes?" Marcy asked.

"Well... that would have been a problem," Carlos said, and then with conviction added, "but instead of God talking to your husband, wouldn't you think things just worked out that way! You wouldn't leave your truck for anything and Larry... well that Larry is one lucky guy!"

"A lucky guy that lives with his mother!" Jock pitched in.

"As it was, we could just make out Hornsby's taillights. But at the right time, just like parting the Red Sea, the smoke cleared so I could see Larry!"

"The Red Sea?" Carlos asked.

"But it's not luck." Marcy insisted, ignoring Carlos' question. "God told Jacody to tell me to stay true to what I believe regardless of what others told me. Hornsby telling me to leave Cupcake. You guys telling me I didn't see Larry along the road when I knew I saw... something. You guys screamed at me to keep going! You called me stubborn! I ignored both of you guys because of what Jacody told me."

"So God told Jacody to tell you not to leave... Cupcake up on the mountain and keep an eye out for Larry along the road? Is that what you are saying?" Asked Carlos.

330

"God let Jacody know to tell me to stay true to my instincts. Then He, God, had the rest fall in place. It is that simple. A person just has to be open to hearing His word."

Jock said, "Carlos, I think maybe Larry is breathing on his own. His pulse feels stronger. Hold up. Let's see."

The euphoria Marcy felt after hearing the report on Larry was short-lived. Forest Road 810 was primarily all downhill. But now, the few times Marcy had to ask Cupcake to speed up, it felt like she slowed down. Marcy's concern about Cupcake's engine's air filter was starting to become a reality. Even with a much larger surface area than the air filter in the conditioning unit, the truck's air filter was starting to plug up. When Marcy asked Cupcake for more power now, the truck seemed reluctant. Marcy knew the fuel entering the engine's cylinders had to be within certain parameters for proper combustion. If the mix had too little oxygen, or air, it would be too rich with diesel fuel. That meant the fuel in the cylinders wouldn't explode with much force and, therefore, the truck would lose power or stop altogether! Fortunately, the road ahead of them was mainly downhill grades. She was, however, troubled thinking of one uphill stretch that they had to get over before they got to the last long downhill grade to Drop Point #8.

One thing was plain, Larry still needed medical attention as soon as possible. Hopefully, there would be assistance waiting for them when they cleared the flames. Had she seen an ambulance standing by at

Drop Point #8 when she had come up the mountain? What if the drop point is also being overrun by fire? What if they give up on Cupcake making it out at all? What if they leave before we get there... if we get there. What if.... What if.... What if we could contact them somehow and let them know we were still on the way? The radio still was not working.

"Cupcake's secret weapon!" she thought. "Not a sure thing, but at least... something!"

At Drop Point #8, Div Sup Hornsby, Planning Chief Shelton, and Operations Chief Buzzard stood at the back of the ambulance looking back up Forest Road 810 where the wind had just swept the fire over the entire landscape. They were North of the Eastward running fire, but it was spreading out in their direction. The drop point was along the edge of a large, long sagebrush flat. Airborne ash was starting to fall out in the open flat. So far, no firebrands capable of igniting the brush had fallen.

"Where is that damned truck!" Sheila said.

"I was seeing them behind me off and on through the smoke," Hornsby replied. "I thought maybe they couldn't get around that pickup that was burning, but then I saw them after we passed that. I thought maybe because the smoke was so thick, they were holding back so they didn't run into me."

"They should have just piled in our two trucks even though they'd have been sitting on one another!" Exclaimed Shiela. "You know what I was thinking about? Seatbelts! If we had an accident going down

332

the mountain, I wanted everyone to have a seatbelt! What's wrong with me?"

"Operations Chief Buzzard said, "Don't do that to yourself. Right now, we have to decide how much longer we are going to wait. That wind is going to eventually spot a fire in the sagebrush in front of us or in the dead timber behind us. We may not be able to outrun it a second time. We have to think of the medics and our own lives as well."

One of the medics joined the group and said, "You know, I was down at Paradise when the whole town got burned over. I've seen this situation before. It doesn't end well. I know you don't want to leave without those other people, but let's be realistic – they should have been here by now. They were close behind you, and now you've been here for over 10 minutes. Something has stopped them. It's very doubtful that they could get going again. They wouldn't have stopped on their own. The smoke is so thick they could have run off the road and crashed down in the canyon or a snag could have blown over and stopped them. I say it is time to load up and get out of here while we can."

"No! You can't mean that!" cried Shiela. "They have to make it!"

Ignoring Sheila, Hornsby said, "yeah. I'm afraid you are right. Let's get real. There is a fire front coming up the valley towards the road. If they were coming, they should have been here by now. I don't think they are coming. Let's go."

Hank put his hands on Sheila's shoulders turning her away from the vacant uphill grade and they all moved towards their vehicles.

Suddenly, Sheila stopped and turned around. Staining in the direction of the fire, she said, "Did you hear that?"

"Hear what?" Buzzard said. "Come on Sheila, get in the truck. We have to leave! Now!"

"Be still! Listen!" Sheila said, "is there a train track in these mountains? I know there isn't! But I swear! I heard a train blowing its horn!"

"A train? No, maybe it was just the wind in the pines, you think?" Said Hornsby.

"No! There it is again! Louder this time!" said Shiela

"Yes! I hear it too! What the hey!" exclaimed Hornsby.

Wooawwwwwwww!!!WooawwwwwwwwWooooo o...!!!

With one hand on the wheel and the other hand blowing the locomotive horn, Cupcake's secret weapon, Marcy was determined to get them all to safety even if she had to drive Cupcake out on her bare rims!

Does anyone know where the love of God goes
When the blaze turns minutes to hours....

"Not now Gordon Lightfoot, I've no time to think of the 'Wreck of the Edmund Fitzgerald. And it's waves, not blaze. However, the minutes sure have seemed like hours." Marcy had an almost irrepressible urge to roll the windows down to get fresh air. She guessed the temperature inside the cab was reaching 120°F. "How long can we tolerate this heat before we collapse from hyperthermia?"

The smoke thinned out some and Marcy could see more of the road ahead. With the improved visibility, she had to risk increasing their speed on the last downhill slope to gain momentum before attacking this last hill. She was only able to nurse maybe fifty percent of Cupcake's power as they started up the climb. As the RPMs dropped, Marcy had to shift from one lower gear to the next. Low range first gear was as low as the transmission went. Creeping along at 4- 5 mph, a brisk walk, the riders in the Diamond Reo were afraid to speak what each one was thinking; if the truck stopped, their run was over. Not just their run to get off the mountain, not just their run to get out of the fire, but their run here on this earth – it would all be over. But for now, they gave thanks for every turn of the wheels on that old truck that carried them closer to safety.

As they crested the uphill grade, the smoke cleared out a little more and, about 2,000 feet down the straight downhill slope, they could see 3 vehicles. Instantly, a cheer went up from everyone who was conscious in Cupcake's cab! Marcy quit blowing the locomotive horn and, even though Cupcake had no extra power to give, she shifted to a couple of higher gears to coax as much speed out of her as possible. Jock rolled a window down and 102° air never felt so cool before.

Marcy locked up the brakes close to the back of the ambulance and yelled, "Medic!" through her open window. The door handle was still hot when she swung Cupcake's door open and jumped down to the ground.

The two medics helped Carlos and Jock lower Larry to the ground. One medic started checking vitals and the other got oxygen and put a mask on Larry. Then they put him on the stretcher and strapped him down.

While the medics tended to Larry, Marcy opened Cupcake's air filter canister and pulled the filter out. She banged the filter on the truck step to knock the bulk of ash dust off. Then she slapped the filter back in the canister and locked the lid. She was swinging up into the driver's seat by the time they had Larry loaded in the ambulance and was closing the back doors.

With the lights flashing the ambulance headed for the Carmel Branch Road helispot, having already radioed ahead for a medivac. Cupcake, breathing much better now, was able to keep up with the ambulance. Jock was with Marcy in Cupcake and, falling in behind Cupcake was Carlos in Larry's Kenworth. The 2 pickups followed the semi-tractors bound for the helispot.

Once at the helispot, Larry was loaded in short order and the bird left for the hospital in Kamath Falls, OR. Having gotten Larry out of their care, the

EMTs turned their attention to Marcy, Carlos, and Jock. Red, irritated eyes, wheezing breath, runny nose, and coughing; all three were fitted with oxygen masks and taken straight to Journey's clinic to be checked out. Marcy felt Cupcake would be safe there at one side of the helispot next to the Kenworth. She would figure out how to deal with the Diamond Reo tomorrow. Right now, she was through thinking and through struggling. She willingly turned herself over into the care of others.

Chapter Eighteen
Father and Child Reunion

Done... Drained... And now, time to recover. Marcy sat in the HRSP yurt reflecting on this morning's near-disastrous events. All the air was out of her balloon. All she wanted to do was get Cupcake back on her feet, or tires as it were, and get back to Moon Ranch. She, Jock, and Carlos had spent around 2 hours getting checked out at the Journey clinic and were released with a clean bill of health.

It seemed like it was years ago now when she was enticed by a seemingly innocent phone call and she had easily fallen victim to temptation. Yielding to the lure of money almost wrecked her life and many others as well. She hadn't asked for time to think about it. She hadn't taken it to the Lord in prayer. She didn't even wait to talk with her husband about it. She immediately said "Yes!" to the lure of money and was hooked. Day after day she was slowly being reeled

338

in like a fish. This morning, close to the boat – the fiery landing net swooped down to claim her forever. She knew only full well, this was not "catch and release"! As happens sometimes, when the angler attempts to net its victim, the hook gets knocked free and the fortunate fish escapes into the depths of the water. Clearing that last rise in the road with Cupcake was the miss of the landing net. The lure no longer held any attraction for her. All Macy wanted to do now was to settle into the deep and recover.

She had thanked God over and over for everyone's safety going through the fire. What were the odds? Big Bud Fontaine Logging lost a pickup service truck and Marcy Portman's semi sustained damage from a large snag falling on the back of it. A 20-person hotshot crew, 2 heavy equipment operators, 2 truck drivers, a dozer boss, a Safety Officer, the Planning Chief, the Operations Chief, and a Division Supervisor had all made a run for their lives through the flames, but, so far, all had survived. All in all, a pretty good day!

Reports from the hospital in Klamath Falls indicated that Larry was still in critical condition. His Nomex had protected most of his body from falling embers, but his hard hat had either come off or, most likely, he wasn't wearing one, so he lost some hair and received burns to his scalp. His fire shelter was probably burned up in the pickup truck. Larry was prone to be casual with personal protective equipment. What may have caused the most damage was prolonged heat exhaustion that evolved into heatstroke. Being a little overweight and trying to run down the mountain with flames starting to boil over the road surely did him in. Who knows how hot he got as far from the pickup as he did! His internal core temperature could have risen to 104°F before his organs started being damaged. Falling into the ditch protected him from the main thrust of high heat for at least a while.

When Marcy and her crew found him, his blood pressure had bottomed out. The temperature inside Cupcakes' cab was much cooler than the ditch Larry had been laying in. It stayed that way until the air conditioner quit conditioning. Carlos' CPR forced Larry's blood pressure to stop dropping, if not increased it some. Regardless, without professional medical help, Larry would have passed over to the other side within the hour. Now, even if his organs survive undamaged, he will still have a lengthy recovery period. Time will tell if he regains his health.

Waiting in the HRSP yurt now, the song "Happytown" kept drifting through her mind. She couldn't remember all of Dave Carter and Tracy Grammer's words, but the ones she did remember spoke to her of how weary she was and her desire to be in a happier place:

> Beat down, misdirected, cropped short and sized to fit
> Honey if we're still connected, I could really use a hit
> I am not lookin' for a key to open every door
> Just a pillow on your floor where we can sit
> Here in the shinin city, here in the endless summer

Here in the cave of wonder number ninety-
two
The sky of never was was never quite this
blue
But it's all right, it's all right with me if it's all
right with you

The yurt door opened, and David D'Angelo walked in. "Sorry to keep you waiting Marcy. I was in a meeting with the Incident Commander and some of the staff about what happened this morning. Of course, in the big picture, there is going to be an after-action review to capture what happened that led up to this near-tragic incident. You know: what did we expect to happen, what actually happened, what did we do well that we don't want to lose track of, and what did we do wrong that we don't want to repeat. We knew red flag conditions were predicted, but how did we miss the time it would occur. On a more focused picture, the one concerning you, we decided to provide a Critical Incident Stress Management meeting for tomorrow for the 29 people that drove through the flames. Well, 28 since we can't include Larry, whose still in the hospital. I'm to set it up. We need to give the CISM team time to get here, so I'm hoping it will start around mid-morning."

Marcy said, "I suppose I'm okay with it. What're the others saying?"

"Often, no one wants to admit that they have been overly distressed when things like this happen. It's like admitting to a weakness. In some cases, if someone says they are not going to attend, and we just say, 'okay', they are really disappointed. They don't want to admit it, but they are looking for anything that will smooth out what's going on in their minds. So, although I would never insist people attend, I don't stop encouraging them. That way, they can say they didn't need the meeting, but was forced to attend. Our good friend Jock, for example, has said many times now, that all he needs is a football game and a 6-pack. He has said it too often – proof he really needs it. With a little help from his friends, I'm sure we can get him there!"

"David, here's where I'm at. Cupcake is damaged. I don't know yet how bad. There's some body damage to the sleeper from that snag. There may be some mechanical damage to hoses and the like. The air filter needs to be replaced. So that is one thing and that alone keeps me from wanting to continue on this fire. Here is the other thing... and I don't want anyone to think I'm a wimp... but I'm ready to go home. It hurts my head to think I must stay a full 2 weeks!"

"Now, you could have led with wanting to go home, and, no, no one will think ill of you for being ready to go home. Please listen here." D'Angelo continued, "Just the way that you told me you are ready to leave tells me you are suffering under a misconception. I believe you are thinking that you shouldn't want to go home. I'm thinking you might believe you should be fighting to stay. You feel you should be looking for a tractor to lease so you can stay, but the thought of trying to figure out anything almost makes you nauseous. Tell me, how am I doing?" D'Angelo said.

"I... uh. I think I agree with you. True, I'm not feeling too good... like I'm really confused. You are right. I've been going back and forth in my head. I have been trying to focus on how to continue here but every time I try, I don't know. My mind just shuts down. Even right now, I feel I don't have a good reason, but I'm emotional!"

"That's not only okay, but it is also very normal," D'Angelo said. "You are having a hard time comprehending the gravity of the incident that you just went through this morning. Think about the stresses your senses have just gone through... they are tired, your senses are weary, they don't need to come back to work right now. I suggest you give in to going home. You are far from being defeated but you do need to take care of yourself. What did your husband say when you told him about your ordeal?"

"I haven't told him yet," Marcy said. "That is one thing that is making me nauseous. I don't want to call him until I know for sure what I'm going to do. He will be here at the drop of a hat unless I can give him a good reason not to come. And, as I said, when I try to come up with a concrete plan to stay, it seems my mind just shuts down."

"I think your mind has it figured out. Come on Marcy. Give it up. We aren't looking for Super Woman here," D'Angelo urged. "Call your husband. Tell him to come and get you. Let him figure out how to deal with your truck. When do you think he could get here?"

"That sure sounds nice. It would be comforting to have Jacody here. It's about a 6 and a half-hour drive."

"Call him. Do it soon so he can figure some things out." D'Angelo said. "We are putting everyone who came off Div Charley this morning in a motel in Alturas tonight. The CISM will be at the Forest Service Supervisor's Office conference room in Alturas. You can let him know about that and the schedule when you call him.

"Oh, one other thing. We called Big Bud to let him know about what happened. He is looking around to find replacements and he said he would take care of the high deck transport trailer he had you go pick up. If you have any complications getting your truck and trailer home let me know and I'll see if there is anything the fire can do to help," D'Angelo continued.

"Thanks. I talked with Big Bud too just before you got here. He wanted to know about Larry and the whole situation with his equipment. He said he had also talked with Jock and Carlos. Big Bud offered to cover any expenses I had that the fire didn't cover. I need to turn in repair costs to him and he will work with the fire's cost/claim people... so, yeah. I think I'm good there. Thanks."

"Hi, Marcy! I was just thinking about you! Well, actually, you've been on my mind all day."

"Oh, Jacody, I..." Marcy was surprised by that old childhood "skinned knee" phenomenon where

344

everything is under control until you try to tell the comforter about the owie! She choked up and couldn't talk for a moment.

"Hey, hey, hey! What's going on Sweetheart?"

Marcy knew the phone call to Jacody was going to be a ticklish one at first. She didn't intend to blurt out that she had come near to death just this morning. He might call up a crop duster he knows and pay whatever to be flown to her side. No, she wanted to ease him into her reality softly. "Well, that didn't work!" she thought.

"No, don't worry! I'm alright! Everyone is alright." Marcy reassured him, once she got her voice back.

She began by reminding him of how great God is to take such good care of them. She told him that the prayers he prayed yesterday did not go unheard. Yes, she did need them. Thank you for listening to God and praying on her behalf. Feeling that she had talked enough to reassure Jacody that she was uninjured in any way, she dove into the morning's encounter with the run-away lightning fire. At first, Jacody admonished her for not jumping into one of the pickup trucks and getting off the mountain as fast as possible. Then, after some discussion, agreed with Marcy that it was his very words that may well have saved Larry's life. She did what he told her to do and Larry was alive. So, what could be wrong with that?

Marcy told him the condition Cupcake was in and she was having trouble trying to think of how she could continue at the Stutler Ridge Fire. She smiled inwardly at how hard Jacody tried to demand that she submit to him coming to pick her up without demanding that she allow him to come to pick her up. After she told him she was ready to let him handle everything and she would be content with being catered to, she felt a weight start to lift. Marcy told Jacody she and the others would be at the Rim Rock Motel in Alturas. Her only obligation was to attend a CISM at 1300 tomorrow and then she was released. Jacody said he would be there as soon as possible and would see about Cupcake in the morning.

As they ended the call, Marcy said to Jacody, "JJ, I am going to be so happy to see you tonight, but there is only one thing I want you to do tomorrow."

"What's that, Sweetheart?" Jacody asked.

"Drive me to the Moon!"

At 10 PM, Rhonda answered the buzzer at the entrance to the Rim Rock Motel. Three very tall weary-looking cowpokes walked up to the counter and asked for a room.

"You're lucky," Rhonda said. "I only have one room left for tonight! I can move a roll-away in so not all three of you have to sleep in one bed."

The older man with a weather-wrinkled bearded face who signed the register as Sam Portman said, "I don't think that will be necessary."

Rhonda tried not to show her mild amusement thinking of three broad-shouldered men, all of them well over 6 feet tall, trying to sleep in a queen-sized bed. She thought, "In this business, you see all kinds of things," then said, "Okay," as the next man signed the register as Daniel Portman.

When the younger man signed in as Jacody Jones, Rhonda dropped her inn-keeper persona and ran around the counter. "Oh, Jacody! I know you! Let me give you a big hug! I know someone who has been on pins and needles all afternoon just waiting for you to get here! She has told me all about you!"

Jacody was very uncomfortable with the hug. For one thing, the height difference made the hug awkward. For another, she caught him completely off guard. "Yes, mam," was all he said.

Rhonda said, "Your wife and I have had a great afternoon talking. I can't tell you how much I admire the courage of all those firefighters who nearly got trapped by the fire this morning! Now, I'm sure you are anxious to be reunited with Marcy. She is in room one-fourteen at the end of the parking lot. You other gentlemen are in room one-o-two, at this end of the parking lot."

They thanked Rhonda, took the passcards she held out to them, and all three went to the far end of the parking lot and knocked on the door of room one-fourteen.

The door opened and Marcy stood there beaming at them for a moment. Then she flew into Jacody's arms. Soon, she also embraced her father and grandfather. Although they were all tired, Marcy gave them a thumbnail sketch of what went on this morning up in Division Charlie. It seemed each time she told the story, she remembered new details. Things like the name Carlos called her when she started pressing the Div Sup's truck with Cupcake. Little things seemed to start clearing the fog in her memory.

"You know," Jacody said solemnly, "from what you've told us, it is not uncommon that people die in cases like this."

"Yes, but we were forewarned, and we prayed," Marcy reminded him.

Uncharacteristically, Daniel spoke up with real concern in his voice. "Marcy... when Jacody called us and told us what happened, I started to panic. it was like, for the first time, I realized that... just like your mother... you could be here one minute, and the next... I'd never see your beautiful face. Or hear your lovely voice. I could lose you just like I lost your mother."

"But you didn't lose me. No one did. Cupcake and I were able to run through the flames." Marcy responded as she wondered if this was really her father talking.

"You are the only little girl I have. I keep thinking I'm going to make all the lonely years up to you somehow. I just never have figured out the how. I've never been able to say how I feel about you. You were so small then, when your mother passed... and then you sprung up so fast and looked so much like your mother... it has made it hard for me to sort things out. But it hit me today. It was like twenty years of cobwebs just blew out of my mind. You could have left to be with your mother, and I would have lost any chance to say or do... anything..." Daniel began choking up.

Tears were coming down Grandpa Sam's cheeks. Oh, how he and his wife had ached to see a light like this beaming from their son. They spent years on their knees praying that their son would physically show up at their door. After that happened, they began praying for their son to mentally appear. Now it seemed to be unfolding right in front of him. Will it be complete? Will it last? He was missing his Nellie to share this with!

Her father tried to go on, "I need you to know, I love you! I love you as your mother loved you -the same way! I don't see how you can understand that... because I never did. I think I might now. And I am so sorry for all the wasted time I was not your father."

There, just inside of Marcy's room, father and daughter embraced as they hadn't done since Marcy's mother passed away. Grandpa Sam embraced the two on one side and Jacody stepped in and hugged them from the other side. All four of them were crying shamelessly. Sobs racked Daniel's body and it may have been Sam and Jacody that were all that kept him on his feet.

"Oh Daddy, all I ever, ever wanted to be... was your little girl!" Marcy said in between sobs.

"You've always been my little girl... I just watched you from afar. I felt like if I got too close to you... you'd be gone. Now, it seems like you could be gone no matter how far away I am or how close I get. Desperado, the military, booze... the war... they kept me from fighting to get back to you. Now, that truck almost took you away from all of us. That truck needs to be parked forever!"

"All these years, that truck has been the closest I have ever been able to get to you. When I drive the Diamond Reo, I'm going down the highway with my dad and with my granddad. How can I give it up?" Marcy cried.

"What about that son?" Grandpa Sam softly spoke up. "Can you do for your daughter what that truck can't? Can you show her the affection a daughter deserves?"

"I want to try. I need to try." Daniel said looking into Marcy's eyes. "Will you let me try?"

"Oh yes! I would like nothing more!" Was Marcy's answer.

"Then it is settled!" sighed Grandpa Sam as he slumped into a side chair. "I just have to sit down. I feel as wrung out as a wet washrag!"

With that, the tension in the room was broken. It seemed everyone breathed a sigh of relief. The men had been traveling since mid-afternoon and Marcy, well, Marcy had been under incredible pressure and this strange apparition her father just presented her with was almost enough to make her crumble!

Marcy sat on the edge of the bed. Daniel leaned against the door of the small room. Jacody sat down next to Marcy and put his arm around her. She leaned in against him, laying her head on his shoulder. All of a sudden, Marcy and her dad seemed a little shy. Two people who had known each other all these years were acting as if they had just met.

Jacody, the only one in the room who wasn't a Portman, looked around the room. No doubt, a miracle had taken place. Daniel reminded him of

John the Baptist's father who couldn't speak from the time the angel told him he and his elderly wife would have a son until the baby was dedicated and named. Then his tongue was "loosened". Daniel's tongue had certainly been loosened. Jacody didn't know about the likelihood Marcy could part her beloved Cupcake. Sometimes, he felt like she took better care of Cupcake than she did him. Be that as it may, if there ever was a pinnacle in a family's life, or where a pivot point was reached, this was it! The wind of change had just altered the future!

"It's late," Jacody said. "Let's go eat breakfast in the morning and we can figure out what we are going to do about getting Cupcake home. One thing is sure, right after Marcy's 1 PM meeting, she and I are headed home!"

"I like that!" said Marcy. The parent and the grandparent gave Marcy hugs and kisses and fist bumps to Jacody. Then they went to their room. Finally, it was just Marcy and Jacody. It was just the way she wanted it.

Lights out and under the covers, Jacody said, "Would you like to hear a song to go to sleep by?"

"No, not tonight."

"Good," Jacody said, "That would remind me of all the nights when all we had to hold on to was a song. I did have a song all picked out for the next time we slept apart. It was, 'Me and Mrs. Jones', cuz, we got a thing go'n on!"

"Why, Mr. Jones! You are a romantic, aren't you?"

"You know it!" he said.

"But dear, tonight, I just want to hear the sound of us breathing," she said. "I would be glad to be together any time, but after this morning's events, I'd hate to think what tonight would have been like without you here."

"Believe me, there is no place else I'd rather be than with you," he said.

They held each other and melted into intimacy. Not physical intimacy, but the intimacy of a higher personal level. An intimacy of mutual respect and admiration that speaks of a deeper love than physical intimacy could ever provide.

"Sometimes I wish God would take my brain out and scrub all the unpleasantness from it! Scrub out any dark grime hiding in the creases. Remove all memory of being almost petrified with fear and anxiety – the years of having a father who wasn't being my father. Even what happened this morning when I knew God had us protected in the palm of His hand, we saw what could have destroyed us. I never want to think of those things again."

"That would be nice, wouldn't it?" Jacody said. "But would you love me if you had never felt loneliness, never been blue, never felt that anything was missing in your life?"

"Okay, not all that stuff. Just the really scary stuff, like burning up... like the marshmallows you try to brown when you make s'mores." In the dark, they both could feel the other smiling. "God does know what He is doing!" Marcy added.

She was bone-tired! She told Jacody that her mind would not shut off. But it did shut off and although she had some troubling dreams – she desperately tried to run but her legs just wouldn't move – she slept.

When Marcy and Jacody stepped outside their rooms into the bright sunlight, the first thing they saw was Grandpa Sam and Daniel across the parking area leaning on a split rail corral fence. It appears the Rim Rock catered to horsemen and had facilities for horses.

Following morning greetings, Marcy said, "Rhonda tells me the Niles Hotel in town has a pretty good breakfast spread. Should we check it out?"

"I'm hungry enough to eat a horse!" Grandpa Sam said.

"Rhonda says they have a breakfast burrito called 'The Kitchen Sink' that should suit you just fine. We won't tell Grandma Nellie on you either!" Marcy said.

They made their plans while sitting around the table drinking coffee after the breakfast dishes were cleared. They decided to go out to the helispot on Carmel Branch Road where Cupcake waited. Grandpa Sam and Daniel would go over Cupcake and decide how safe it was to drive and what, besides filters, they needed. Marcy and Jacody would clean out the sleeper and cab of all of Marcy's gear and store it in Jacody's pickup.

Back at the Rim Rock, Grandpa Sam and Daniel dropped off Marcy and Jacody. Then they went on to Lakeview where they hoped to buy the filters and replacement air hoses they thought necessary to make Cupcake roadworthy.

The CISM team had divided the meeting up into 2 smaller groups. One group was the Bushrod Hotshots and the other group was the remaining 8 people. It would have been 9 but Larry was unavailable. All the participants of the CISM stayed at the Rim Rock Motel. Around noon, the shots, having completed their time together with the CISM team, pulled into the motel parking area. Marcy and Jacody had been hanging out at the picnic table under the shade tree and now they wandered over to talk to some of the crew. Safety Officer Rick Barron came out of his room and joined them.

Marcy and Rick wanted to know what the shots thought of the CISM. Of course, the answers varied. Several said it was good because it helped cope with having just been in a life-threatening situation. One or two said it was not helpful to them personally because it was unnecessary – they were ready to go back up the mountain this afternoon. Marcy believed it was the macho guys who didn't want to show that they, also, could be helped by talking through the event. Then others said they were in a better frame of mind and believed the CISM was appropriate, if not even very necessary. They felt better prepared to go on and deal with any backlash that might appear. No one had a negative comment to make.

There was the feeling of kindred spirits among everyone who had been up on Division Charlie yesterday morning. 29 people had snatched victory from the jaws of defeat. If the vehicle at the head of the escaping convoy had stalled, blocked, or even significantly slowed the group's progress, all could have been lost. Marcy found out that their understanding of the Big Bud Fontaine Logging pickup and what happened to the driver had been full of conjectures. The CISM had cleared that up for them, but they had questions for Marcy about how she found the driver and got him out to the ambulance.

The shot crew packed up and left for their home unit. Marcy asked Rick if he knew where the others in their group were.

"They said they were going to the Brass Rail, a Basque restaurant and bar over at the edge of town. They asked me to go with them, but I can only drink so much coffee or Pepsi. I had a feeling they were interested in getting really relaxed."

"Probably a good decision on your part," Marcy laughed.

"Hey, you want to ride over to the meeting with me?" Rick asked.

"That would be great! Marcy said, "Grandpa Sam and my dad have Jacody's dually, so, Jacody and I are on foot here."

"Yeah, that will be fine," chipped in Jacody. "I'll just hang out here and wait for the guys to get back from Lakeview."

Chapter Nineteen
You See It Your Way

Marcy and Safety Officer Rick Barron came to a stop at the only stoplight in Modoc County.

"Looks like we might have hit the midday rush hour in Alturas," Rick said.

"What do you mean?" asked Marcy. "There aren't any other vehicles here!"

"Yeah, there is! Look down there. Here comes a car... oh! Wait. No, it turned off on a side street."

"Modoc County's stoplight. 60 air miles by 70 air miles and less than 10,000 people in it. Maybe it's a pride thing that if you are going to be the county seat, you ought to have a stoplight!" Marcy mused. "When you say, 'California', most people think of Hollywood, traffic jams, or the Golden Gate Bridge. Older people hear the Beach Boys' music in their heads. In this part of California, it is open range, high desert, juniper, wild horses, and one stoplight!"

Rick pulled into an open space in the employee parking lot of the Modoc National Forest Supervisor's office. After shutting the vehicle off, neither seemed eager to open their door and get out, so they sat there.

"Do you know what you are going to do? Are you going home or stay on for the rest of your assignment?" Marcy asked Rick.

"I wait all winter to come on fires. I feel like I have a special purpose to be on any fire I'm called to, and it isn't just to be a Safety Officer, although I do take this job seriously. What do we have here... 900 to 1,000 people now? When we had to run for our lives through the fire, it didn't just affect us. To some degree, everyone on the fire was affected. They know it could be them tomorrow. So, they have questions about it – questions about themselves and... eternity. I need to be here for whoever might want to talk about it. It would be more troubling for me to leave than it ever could be for me to stay."

"That's exactly what I thought you might say," Marcy said. "Poor Cupcake needs to recuperate. Without her, and I hope I'm not just using her as an excuse, I have no reason to be here any longer."

"So," Rick asked, "shall we go in and face the music?"

Walking into the conference room, Macy noticed people were making their way to chairs set in a circle, but what attracted her attention most was the rich aroma of fresh coffee. Both she and Rick made their way over to a side table that held coffee, hot water for tea, some pastries, apples, and bananas. Then they took the last two available chairs. Sheila would have liked to have sat next to Marcy but hadn't thought to save her a seat. Everyone seemed a bit nervous. They all knew what a CISM was and why they were there, but somehow, going through it themselves seemed alien. They risked exposing their insecurities and talking too much may open them up to ridicule.

"I'd like to welcome you all here this afternoon and commend you for being willing to help each other work through what might be a confusing time," began the facilitator. Let me get who I am out of the way right now. My name is Clint Malloy. I'm a deputy with the Siskiyou County Sherriff's Department. Not only am I a deputy, but I also serve as the department's chaplain. In that capacity, I have been trained to facilitate CISM and CISD meetings. Notice, we dropped the M from CISM and replaced it with a D. That's because one tool of management, the "M", is debriefing, the "D". So that is what we are going to do this afternoon – debrief. To keep it simple, and since you all know each other, why not just tell me your name the first time you speak. Is everyone okay with that? Could I see nods yes or shakes no all around? Good.

"First off, I want to make sure each of you volunteered to attend and no one feels that they were coerced. If anyone doesn't want to be in this meeting, please, feel free to leave now."

Jock spoke up. "I'm here, but not because I need to be. Like I told our HRSP, gimme a football game and a 6-pack and I'll forget all about how we got run off the mountain. But he said it would help the others if I came. So, I'm just here to support these other guys. I don't intend to say anything."

"Thank you," said the facilitator. "I believe we all appreciate you being here even if you have nothing to say. Please tell me, what is your name?"

"Oh, yeah... it's Jock."

"Just so I know, what is your job here on the Stutler Ridge Fire?"

"Ummm, I run a dozer."

"Thank you, Jock. Is there anyone else who feels obligated to be here, not for yourself, but for others?" Pausing, Clint took time to look around and catch the eye of each of the other attendees. "No one? Then I trust we are all here because we want to be, and we hope to get something from this meeting.

"The experience you folks and the Hotshot crew that I met with earlier today went through will be just a little different for each individual. It holds serious consequences for some, while for others, it may have been no more impactful than almost getting hit in a game of dodgeball. And that's alright. That is normal. Normal for anyone who has been through an event such as you have. Just the same, it is possible that any one of you is likely to experience a menagerie of long-term and short-term emotions, symptoms, and reactions. This meeting is one way of getting out ahead of what may come and preparing you to cope with whatever it is. Recognizing the need for help and accepting that help following a traumatic event can lead to healing and restored hope – hope that this event won't interfere with any of your future endeavors. Stress debriefing also allows you to reflect on the incident's impact and put it in proper perspective.

"So, that's a little of the 'what' and 'why' we are here. What I would like to do now is for each one of you - each of you who are so inclined - to tell us, in your words, what you experienced yesterday. Please feel free to start from wherever you want. I believe it is important that you tell us how you felt as well. These meetings may have a bit of a stigma as a 'touchy-feelie' type of meeting, and I don't want to add to that. But let's be honest! When we feel threatened, we have emotions. The emotions we have are our own. No one can tell you that you are wrong to feel how you feel. They can only say they felt the same event differently. Often, hearing those differences gives us insight and perspective. It can clarify our own experience. Now then, when everyone has shared their thoughts, we will open it up to general discussion. You will be encouraged to ask each other questions and respond. You noticed on your chair before you sat down, that there was a pad of paper and a pen. Those are for you to write any thoughts you want to remember or share with us. So, I am asking you to not interrupt anyone during our opening comments but write down anything you would like to ask about or talk about later.

"When you are ready, whoever wants to start us off, tell us about yesterday from your perspective." Facilitator Clint kept his eyes on the floor in the middle of the circle and paused. From experience, Clint knew he had talked long enough. What he had to do now was wait out the deafening silence until someone felt they could not tolerate it any longer. Once the first person talked about how they viewed their shared experience the rest would be more eager to talk about how it was for them.

"Nice to meet you, Clint. Thanks for coming to meet with us. My name is Rick Barron. I'm the Safety Officer." Rick paused for a moment to compose his thoughts a bit more. "I have to laugh a little now... not at what we have been through... that wasn't funny. But I have to laugh at myself. I don't know how many times I have said, 'Max Lucado, the Christian author writes: Man's two greatest fears are the fear of death and the fear of insignificance.' Right after I would say that I always added, 'I'm not afraid of death, it's just the getting dead part that scares me!' It seemed like a fun thing to say, and people found it humorous. Now, the 'getting dead part' keeps coming back to me. It is no longer humorous... it is as serious as a heart attack! None of us know how we're going to die – just that we will. John and I ran into smoke right after we left the top. The further we went the thicker the smoke got but the wind was mixing it up pretty good. Then we started seeing flames. After we got to the pickup Larry was driving and saw the front of it on fire, I started thinking of the 'getting dead part'. I started wondering just how this was going to work. Would we die from asphyxiation? Would we burn up first? So the getting dead part suddenly became a very real thing instead of a cleaver line I liked to repeat. I think I put the humorous side behind me up there just past the pickup.

"A person better be ready to die, no matter how or when death takes them, and it is very, very, serious. I am ready, if not even willing to die... I could say the same thing that Paul said in Philippians 1, verse 21: 'For to me, to live is Christ and to die is gain.' I know I am ready to lay this earthly tent down, but I'm not sure about my friends. I was praying for everyone coming off the mountain yesterday morning. To be completely honest, for me to know each one of you on a professional level, and to not have done everything possible to lead you to the saving grace found in my Jesus before you die, would be heartbreaking for me! With your permission, I wish to speak with each one of you in the time to come about where you are with your eternal destiny! I can't leave this earth until my work here on earth is done. I hope you all can respect that. To me, nothing is more important!

"When John and I made it to safety I thought my heart was going to explode! God is so good! But I was still apprehensive. Hank and Sheila were there with us at Drop Point #8, but we still had the shots, Jared, Marcy, Jock, and Carlos up there on the mountain.

We assumed it was Larry who had driven the pickup that was abandoned. And I wasn't sure at that time if Larry was up there or down here somewhere! In just a few minutes, the shot crew rolled in. In another 10 minutes, Jared showed up. He told us the last 3 were behind him in the semi truck. We were surprised and concerned. 'What about getting past the burning truck?' we asked. We still didn't feel much better after Jared said he saw the semi's lights after they were all past the disabled truck.

"That's what has been foremost on my mind." Rick paused and idly started tapping on his pad of paper with his pen.

"Good afternoon Clint. I'm John Helmsley, Dozer Boss. I came down the mountain with Rick here. I've been stringing plastic flag lines out for dozers to follow for years now. My job often takes me close to active fire that has no control lines in front of it. My job is to indicate where those control lines will go. Dozers and crews create at least some kind of buffer behind them in the way of bare ground. A slow-moving ground fire will come up to their line and stop. Me? What have I got? A line of plastic flagging isn't going to do me any good! Don't get me wrong, I'm not supposed to put myself out there close to a windblown firestorm and hold up my ribbon to ward it off. But I'm kind of used to feeling a little exposed to fire without immediate shelter. That is why leaving the top in the face of the on-coming fire didn't rattle me. It wasn't until we got to that pickup that was starting to burn that I got pulled up short. That told me things could, and were, getting out of hand. Rick and I had lots of questions. So who was driving the pickup? How long ago did the driver try to turn around? Why did he try to turn around? Did he hear about the fire on his radio and tried to turn around

362

then? Did he see smoke? Was the repeater working when he dropped off the road and got hung up? Maybe he radioed someone, and they came up and got him. We planned to pick the driver up if he was trying to walk out but we didn't see anyone. Rick was praying hard that God would protect whoever it was, I sure remember that. Concerns about the pickup driver were the one thing that kind of rattled me. I knew we just had to keep driving without running off the road until we got out of it. But, overall, I'm a little like Jock, I don't expect this experience to affect me."

When John fell silent, Sheila gave her perspective, "Clint, my name is Sheila Shelton, Planning Section Chief. I rode down with Hank. I guess I was a little like John at first. We are all 'fire-breathers'! For most of our adult lives, fire has been our focus. Like any other day, I was going through the motions –but with more purpose and urgency when this happened. We deal with whatever comes our way, and, sometimes it is dangerous. We try to keep dangerous things at a distance. When we got to the pickup off the road – we were the first ones coming down - it was still cool enough that Hank could jump out and, shielding his face from the heat, was able to run over and make sure no one was in it. We were unable to read what was on the side of the door, if it even had a logo on it, so I had no idea who might have been driving it. We were hoping the driver was back at Drop Point #8 and out of danger, but we were constantly straining to see through the smoke in case they were on foot trying to make it out.

"Hank and I talked about our responsibility in this. Jared, we agreed as the Div Sup, it was your call, and we trust you. But when we couldn't see the road, and trees start torching around us, I'll admit we started second-guessing our combined decision. We asked ourselves how did we get into this situation; what could we have done differently? Could we have gotten a safety zone constructed soon enough and large enough that we could have remained in place on top? None of that doubting changed anything but it gave us a distraction and that helped. I think I almost flipped out. I had to tell myself to take shallow breaths, shallow breaths!" Sheila gestured with both arms out in front of her. "I believe I was starting to hyperventilate. Finally, we decided what we needed to do was put those questions and doubts in a box and set them aside. So I tried to forget the what if's and focus on what can I do now. I just tried to remain positive. I kept repeating to myself, 'we are going to make it!' or 'there's no place like home!' over and over. Rick, I was so glad I went to the meeting you had Sunday night. Without it, I might have been saying, 'oh god', but not because I thought much about a God who cared. Hearing about Jesus kind of kept me afloat... kept me from thinking it was hopeless!"

When Sheila fell silent, Hank spoke up. "I'm Hank Buzzard, Operations Section Chief. I think all of us were going along with a 'matter of fact' attitude, not thinking this was a life-or-death situation. At least, I was. That all changed when we saw that pickup as the first casualty. Finding a body in that truck was my first fear. I looked quick, but I looked good too. I found no one. After that, I began fearing for the rest of us. I was hoping it wasn't a preview of what was ahead. Right after that, we plowed into thicker and darker smoke. We slowed up to a painful crawl, or so it seemed. We had to slow up! We just had to. Move too far to the right and you hit the cut bank. Big rocks that you couldn't see might stop you. Move too far to the left and you go out in mid-air, that would be death

for sure. Go too slow and we would get cooked! I had
a vise-grip on the steering wheel. Having Sheila with
me was a great help. I needed someone to talk with
and keep me calm. As we talked, it was like I was
carrying on two separate conversations. One with
Sheila out loud, and one with myself inside my head.

"I thought a lot about whoever was driving the
pickup truck that was burning up behind us now. Do
they have an 11-year-old boy playing Little League as I
do? Is there a wife and daughter out delivering Girl
Scout cookies like mine? What if that driver is out
here breathing in the super-heated air from this
massive furnace? Is he dead or will he soon be? Oh
God, I thought, I want to see my son play ball! I don't
care if he doesn't catch fly balls that land right in front
of him and I don't care if he strikes out without
swinging. He's going to know I'm his biggest fan. I
want to work with my daughter so she can earn all the
badges she wants in Girl Scouts. I don't care how
tired I am when I get home from work, I'll feed her the
basketball until she says enough. What were the last
things I said to my wife? Probably something like,
'yeah, when I get around to it.' That can't be it, I
thought! I never want her to doubt that she is my
whole world and I love her dearly! I couldn't be sure
I'd be able to tell her though... would this road be the
last place I ever draw a breath? I had to drive fast.
But I had to drive slowly. I so didn't want to be there!
I think you could have heard me shout HALLILUYA
when the smoke cleared and I saw the drop point on
down the road! As soon as I found a place with bars
on my cell phone, I called my wife and made sure she
understood how important she and the kids are to me.
I couldn't tell her enough that I love her.

"I've talked with Incident Commander Thompson,
and I think I need time at home with my wife and

kids. I'm not thinking about anything but family right now. Perhaps this bothered me more than the rest of you – I don't know – but I'm not going to be of any value here. Thanks, Clint for coming and helping us process this... this incident. I yield my time to whoever wants to talk now."

"I guess I'll go next. I'm Division Supervisor Jared Hornsby." Hornsby said, nodding at Hank. "I'm gonna be honest here. Starting down the mountain, I was mad as hell. I take my job seriously. If somebody on my division gets hurt- worse if someone dies -it is on me! It's my fault! Division Charlie is my responsibility. I asked others for advice, but I make the decision. We talked about staying or going, and it sounded like everyone... everyone I asked... agreed. We needed to move off the hill as safely and as rapidly as we could. Now, I made one mistake. In the scramble, I miscounted how many were left after the first two pickups left. Then the crew buggy left and, I don't know, Marcy had been the only one still standing there - I thought she and I were all that was left! She could get in the truck with me, and we would all be headed down the mountain. Then it hit me! We still had 2 equipment operators somewhere that we needed to get down as well. Sorry, Jock and Carlos," nodding in their direction. "I wondered; did they jump in with the first two pickups? I didn't know. So I asked Marcy and she told me she had sent them off on what I thought was a fool's errand. To me, it was a foregone conclusion that the semi truck and transport trailer was going to sit right where they were. And there she had them getting the trailer ready to drop! I told her it was staying here, and they all were to crowd in with me. Yes, it would be uncomfortable, but we could make it. Actually, I saw no other option. Well, Marcy just said no! Then she turned and headed for her truck at a run. I'm not used to people who are under my authority defying me, so I was kind of shocked. What was I to do? I got in my truck and pulled up next to her semi to try and convince her to do it my way. I felt like all three of them turned against me because none of them would get in with me. Once she got up in her truck, she laid on her horn and drowned out what I was trying to say. Her truck started jiggling forward as she let the clutch out. I thought she was out of control and was going to plow right into me! I had no choice, I had to move forward - still, I felt like I was abandoning them. I had to drive on and leave them to follow me. I couldn't turn around or just pull over. The way her semi was parked, all I could do was drive forward and down the road. I drove slow at first thinking I needed to see the front of her truck. Then I had to speed up to keep her from ramming into me! This just felt so stupid and uncalled for. I was furious! No one has died on my watch and now, it looked like it might happen! How could I live with that? I wasn't thinking about what the fire was doing on down the road – I was thinking the first thing I was going to do once I got to fire camp is march Miss Portman down the road and out of here. If we live through this, that is. I was thinking we waited too long to evacuate.

"Well, the smoke got worse, the fire got up to the road, and, just like the rest of you, things got really serious for me when I got to the stalled pickup and saw it fully engulfed in fire. I knew it was a very tight squeeze for the shot's crew buggy to get by. I slowed way up after I got passed it and looked back for the semi. I knew Marcy's truck couldn't get around it. That was a big concern for me right there! Was I going to see 3 people die trying to get into their fire shelters? I was horrified! Then, suddenly, there was an explosion of flames where I thought the burning pickup was! The next instant, I saw headlights and the clearance lights on top of Marcy's truck coming through the smoke right at me like a bat out of hell! I punched the accelerator and almost shot out into the canyon! We both slowed down and, for a bit, I saw her truck lights peering through the smoke on occasion. Then Marcy seemed to slow up and after a while, I realized I didn't see her anymore. The smoke had gotten even thicker. I was afraid to stop again, I might not be so lucky a second time – she would push me off into the deep canyon before she saw me.

"So, I went slowly on. I wasn't mad anymore, I just wanted us all to survive this. I thought about that disabled pickup. In our early morning plan, no one was to be headed downhill for several hours. So that driver wouldn't have expected to meet anyone headed down. If they had not run off the road but tried to make it to the top, in the smoke, there could have been a head-on collision and blocked the way out for all of us. We all would have died! All of us! A person could say it was an act of God that put that pickup off the side of the road!

"Well, I couldn't see anyone ahead of me, no one behind me – they may have gone off the edge - no radio contact... I have never felt so all alone! I wanted us all safe back in fire camp. I think I was seeking help from above as well. No human could help us now!"

Jared rested.

"Let me say this!" Jock blurted out. "I know I said I wasn't going to say anything, but here's the thing. Think about what we just went through. Pretty scary, right? We went through some scary stuff. First of all, Jared told us to get in his little truck, and Carlos and I acted like we didn't hear him. But really, how much do you weigh, Jared? No, don't answer that – but you're sitting in that little Ford Ranger, a 2-seater. Carlos could sit on my lap, but where were you going to put Marcy? Marcy could be a power forward or a center on UConn's women's basketball team. Did you think you could wad her up in that truck? Maybe she could have sat on your lap, Jared, and put her feet on the passenger door window frame. Her knees would have been pressing against the ceiling. We would have been packed in there like sardines, heat-sealed, and everything. Jared, you wouldn't have been able to see to drive! Well, we got past that, didn't we?

"Next, if you know me, you know I get nervous any time someone else is driving anything I'm riding in. So that's scary for me. We got past that, right? We drive down into the smoke and it gets scarier. We can't see the ditch or the canyon most of the time but, somehow, Marcy manages to stay in between them! I'm like a cat in a room full of rocking chairs. We almost run into the back of Jared's little truck. Scary, but got past that.

"Next, we have a pickup on fire and Marcy plows into it like Lee Marvin driving that Nazi half-track in the movie 'The Dirty Dozen'. And there's Jared again like he wants us to ram him off the road like we did the burning pickup! Jared takes off and disappears. Still scary but we are all okay.

"Then Marcy stops... stops in the middle of hell I tell you... and backs up in the dark smoke. She forces me out of the truck, and we find a body. The heat and the body are freaking me out! I don't want to touch a dead body. But I roll him over and it's Larry. I think he's dead and I think I'm gonna die out there with him. My lungs are burning, and hot sparks are landing on me. We load him up and get him laying partly between the seats and mostly on the sleeper's mattress. Marcy gets Carlos pounding on Larry's

369

chest. So here we are, in the middle of a blazing forest fire, smoke so thick you can only see 5 feet in front of the truck, I'm trying to raise anybody and everybody on the radio, Carlos is bouncing up and down on Larry's chest while Marcy is singing I Walk the Line. In the middle of all this, a freak'n snag falls on the truck and makes it sound like we are riding in the rotating drum of a concrete mixer truck! Isn't that enough? I ask you, isn't that enough to make a person lose it?

"Well no! There's more! I saw Marcy reach down and feel the air conditioner vent. Then she yelps when she feels nothing coming out of it and blames it on a rock that only she felt the truck hit. I knew what it meant. Our time was running out! It was running out! But I held it all together. The truck was going to stop right there in that furnace! I looked at Marcy, and with all that was going on, she seemed calm. Calm, but not clear thinking enough to consider what the effect would be on those with her that didn't know she had a locomotive horn on her truck. I was already wound up as tight as a watch spring! When she hit that train horn... I wet myself! That... friends and neighbors... was scary."

"Jock, once again, I think you've summed things up for us pretty well! And, we learned some things about you. We didn't know you were a women's college basketball fan, we didn't know you were a WWII Movie buff, and we didn't know you could scream like a 3rd grader at a birthday party when the scary clown jumps out of the closet! Clint, my name is Carlos Santiago and I operate the feller/buncher.

"As for me," Carlos went on, "I was sitting in the sleeper and really couldn't see much of anything. I was taking my cues from the two in the front. For me, I don't think anything will measure up to being there and in that moment. That moment that determined whether a person continues living among us... or becomes a memory. Yesterday, I did things... I was a part of things that before yesterday, I couldn't imagine. What do any of us have to give to another person? We won't know unless we are tested... unless we are tried. If we had stayed on top in the area Jock and I were trying to get ready to serve as a safety zone, our story today would have been much different. I don't know how different. Maybe our story would have been about deploying our fire shelters as the fire burned over us. Maybe our story would be told by someone other than us. Maybe the meeting would have been a memorial service for us because we all died in the fire. Without a doubt, Larry would be dead. I wonder... I wonder. Jock is right though... Marcy went about doing what she needed to do like this was all normal. Who doesn't have a locomotive horn on their truck? I thought I was going to have a heart thing!

"Rick, I don't know about the others... but I think I'd like to talk to you about your faith. You almost sound like you are looking forward to dying... only not in some crazy suicidal way. I don't like the idea of death or dying. I really don't like being in the same room or place with a dead person. If I had thought Larry had died while I was jumping up and down on his chest... one of us would have left that truck and it probably would have been me... fire or no fire!"

Rick smiled and gave Carlos a nod.

"Hey, Clint. I'm Marcy Portman. I drive a transport. I move the dozer around for Jock. I might add, I'm Portman at work on the truck, but I'm all Jones on the ranch!" Marcy smiled and continued. "I think there are things that happened yesterday that will be with us for years to come. I have some experience living with a person who has flashbacks from his time in the military. That is my dad. What we experienced is nothing compared to what he has experienced, but we all deal with what we experience in life in different ways. I don't expect this to have as great an effect on me as it will on Larry, for example. And I'm sorry Carlos if I almost gave you a heart attack. I'm sorry Jock if I made you scream and wet your pants. If I did cause you concern... I hope you get over it soon!" She paused and gave each a big smile.

"As I told Jock and Carlos, my husband is a special person who gets information from God. Yes. I know. And it sounds... unusual. Even more so to me when I say it out loud. But he does. We both have a deep spiritual connection with our creator. As hard as it may be for many people to understand or believe, our God is real and active in our lives. God told Jacody to warn me not to do anything that seemed in opposition to what I thought I should do. Now, I think it was you, Carlos, who asked me when I told you why I knew we were going to make it out alive, why God didn't just tell me directly – why tell Jacody and have him tell me? God has never talked to me the way He does to Jacody. I may know only one other person who God talks to like He does Jacody. You asked... but who am I to question God and how He does His works. We need to listen for God to speak to us whether it is from the Bible, from the pulpit, to us personally, or through another person.

"Jared, I would follow you anywhere, I respect your ability and trust your decisions. My instinct told me not to leave my semi and get in the truck with you. We didn't have time to talk about it. But now, you can see how it worked out. This wasn't the only way Larry could be brought off the mountain... God has a plan for Larry that requires him to be alive. If it wasn't

372

Jock, Carlos, and me, he would have provided another way. I'm humbled that He chose to use us. I was able to stay calm through the whole 'escape'. I imagined Jesus in the sleeper with you Carlos, He was asleep on the mattress... just like it is written in Mark: a great storm came up and was threatening to sink the boat. Jesus was asleep on a cushion in the stern. The disciples woke Him and said, 'Teacher, don't you care if we drown?' Jesus quieted the storm and said to his disciples, 'Why are you so afraid? Do you still have no faith?' So, I was concerned, but if I had been afraid... what good would my faith be? I knew God was in control right there in the midst of the firestorm. I was just trying to do what I thought He wanted me to do."

"Now, Marcy, I heard your words," Jared said, "and I heard what Rick said. I understood those words, but they made no sense to me. It is a miracle anyone got off that mountain alive!"

"You are right, Jared!" Rick said. "It was a miracle! Who do you attribute the miracle to?"

"What do you mean... it's a miracle. That's all." Jared said.

"Well, where do miracles come from? Miracles don't grow on trees!" Rick countered.

"Ok folks," interjected Clint. "I wouldn't be much of a facilitator if I didn't facilitate. This seems to be peeling off into a theological discussion rather than the planned debriefing."

With effort, Clint directed the discussion back to the stressful event from the day before. Each participant was encouraged to share their various opinions questions, and views. When Clint was sure people had talked themselves out, he gave them his perspectives.

"Listening to you all talk, I've heard a variety of short-term reactions to what you all experienced. I've heard shock, denial, anger, some might be bordering on rage even. I heard anxiety, moodiness, sadness, sorrow, and grief. All of these are normal. Knowing it is okay and normal to feel these emotions helps you build a bridge from the event to hope, healing, and recovery. I might add here that you may not realize you need recovery until a certain amount of time has passed. If you start experiencing restlessness, fatigue, sleep disturbances, eating disturbances, muscle tremors, nightmares, flashbacks, heart palpitations...all these physical symptoms may be attributed back to this traumatic event. When you get back home, I encourage you to find a person you trust so you can talk about any symptoms that may appear. Clipped to the pad of paper I gave you, you will find contact numbers of professionals that could be of great assistance to you. Now, don't think you have to be some kind of a superhuman. If any of the symptoms I described start exhibiting themselves, call someone. You owe that to yourself and to the people who care about you. That's all I have for you. Stay if you have any lingering questions or wish to talk with me further. Be safe out there!"

Chapter Twenty
The Road Back
Home

A little after 1500, or 3 PM, Rick and Marcy pulled into the Rim Rock Motel parking area. The CISM had lifted her spirits. Seeing Cupcake with the transport trailer in tow sitting in the stable parking area at the end of the motel raised them even higher! Her three men were hiding from the high desert sun under the shade of a tree at the picnic table. She jumped out of Rick's Forest Service truck and ran jubilantly into Jacody's arms.

"Cupcake is here!" she yelled, as Jacody swung her around!

"It is," Daniel said as they made their way to the parked truck. "We replaced the hoses to the trailer, the engine air filter, and the air conditioner filter. This Diamond Reo is one tuff truck that just keeps going!"

Grandpa Sam said, "Daniel and I are all packed up and ready to roll. We are going to head straight home. Your truck can sit out in our implement yard until we figure out what we are going to do with it. Fixing that sleeper won't be cheap."

"Sure Grandpa," Marcy said. "That'll be fine."

"I never thought I'd be making another run with my boy in this old truck, but for old times' sake, I'm love'n the idea!" Said Grandpa Sam as he slapped Daniel on the back.

"Too bad I don't have a microphone hooked up in the cab," Marcy said. "I'd like to hear you two singing "Six Days On the Road"!

"You know dad, he'll be singing at the top of his lungs," Daniel said, "but you wouldn't hear me. I'll be singing, but dad'll drown me out! I'm kinda looking forward to this trip as well – but not for old time's sake. I like to think it is for new time's sake! I think once we get home, there are some changes I'm anxious to make." He gave Marcy an uncharacteristic hug and a kiss on the cheek. Then he turned, walked over to the truck, and climbed up in the driver's seat, a big smile on his face.

Grandpa Sam followed suit with a warm hug and a kiss, he said goodbye to his granddaughter. After giving Jacody a hug he climbed up in the passenger's seat next to his son.

Jacody and Marcy stood and watched Cupcake idle up past the motel units and pull out onto the highway. Marcy felt a pain when she saw the crumbled corner of the sleeper unit. Still, Cupcake looked bold and beautiful to her as Daniel increased the RPMs and the black diesel smoke blew straight up out of her twin stacks. The truck disappeared, blocked by the motel office. She could still hear the diesel engine rise and fall as Daniel changed gears and the truck gained speed. Soon it was quiet. Quiet as if the truck had never been there.

Jacody wrapped one arm around Marcy and she wrapped both her arms around his chest, laying her head on his shoulder. She closed her eyes. Softly, she said to Jacody, "I want to just stand here like this for a moment."

It felt alien to her now - not having a fire assignment to anchor her to this place. After being under pressure 15 hours a day for the last 8 days, to have that pressure suddenly ripped away felt like being set adrift. Her truck, her whole purpose for being here was gone. She had just watched it drive out of sight. She couldn't explain to herself why she was feeling empty. Moon Ranch had been temporarily put on hold, but Jacody was here now. It was time to make the leap from Marcy Portman, all the way back to Marcy Jones, from Stutler Ridge Fire to Moon Ranch. She just had to recalibrate her mind and fill it with purpose. Opening her eyes and leaning back looking up into Jacodys face... it was done; she was ready. She gave him a wink and a nod. He started moving her towards their room, laying his head over on the top of her head, still arm in arm. In a low voice, he said, "let's get packed and head for home."

"That sounds perfect," Marcy said. "I'm going to sleep all the way!"

Jacody stopped in front of the motel office and Marcy went in to settle the bill with Rhonda. In no time, she was back in the truck. "The fire covered the bill for both rooms. We're good to go."

Heading towards Lakeview, OR, Marcy was asleep by the time they got to Davis Creek. She slept for the next 2 hours or so. Jacody glanced over at her every so often. She was leaning against the door with her head on the pillow they had pulled from Cupcake's sleeper. "Such an angel," he thought, then added, "Is there any limits to her strength?" From what he had gathered from other people's accounts of the previous day, everything around them was going to hell in a handbasket but Marcy remained unrattled. She methodically did what needed to be done without a stumble. Jacody knew she was trusting in God and she hadn't taken it on herself to do the impossible... she left the impossible up to God. He couldn't thank God enough for looking after his wife.

To Jacody, it seemed like the miles were slowly going by. He was cracking sunflower seeds between his teeth and spitting the shells in the empty paper coffee cup he kept in the door's cupholder for just that purpose. Keeping his tongue busy fishing the sunflower kernel out of the shell after it was cracked, spitting the shell out, chewing the kernel, extracting another seed from the half handful stored in his cheek to repeat the process, kept him alert when he might have gotten sleepy. When Marcy stirred, he was happy to have her alert and talkative again.

"So, how was your nap?"

Marcy stretched and yawned, "Good, I guess. I think I was starting to get a stiff neck." Looking at the road ahead, she asked, "where are we?"

"We should be coming into Burns pretty soon. I think we should stop for supper there. What do you think?"

Marcy said, "yeah, I could eat. I think the caterer fed me so much my stomach requires more now for me to feel full. I need to quit eating so much. I'll do that tomorrow but not today!"

"I might be hungry. I can't tell. I've gone through half a bag of sunflower seed and the salt has the inside of my cheeks raw and it feels like a hole is being burned in my stomach. I think packing it with real food would make it feel better!

"Well, you won't have long to wait... it looks like the lights of Burns showing through the twilight in the distance," Marcy said.

"Let's not do a drive-thru," Jacody said. "So no Micky D's or Burger King. Look for something interesting."

Tuesday, and, except for a few fast-food restaurants, it looked like Burns, Oregon rolled up the sidewalks after 8 PM. After passing through most of the town without seeing an eatery that looked promising, they were afraid they would have to go on or turn around to look things over again.

"Oh, look!" Marcy exclaimed. "Do you feel like Mexican? Chilli Willi's Mexican Cantina," Marcy read the sign aloud.

"I'm game if you're game!" Jacody said as he wheeled the pickup into a vacant spot close to the front of Chilli Willi's.

After being seated in a booth, their waiter brought a large bowl of corn tortilla chips, a small bowl of hot salsa, and a small bowl of "not as hot – but still hot salsa. "I can bring you milder salsa on request, here are the menus and I'll give you time to decide what you'd like. I'll be back shortly."

When the two salted margaritas on the rocks they ordered arrived, Jacody said, "Funny, isn't it? I was remarking how all the salted sunflower seeds were making me feel and then I set here eating salty chips and wash it down with a salty margarita!'

Marcy had ordered a grilled chicken, corn and black bean salsa pizza while Jacody had a grilled skirt steak with caramelized onion and red peppers pizza. Candlelight, good food, good drinks, and good company. It was so nice to not have the distraction of driving that they lingered longer than they meant to. Both felt it was worth it. They didn't need to tell Chuck and Chew that they dilly-dallied along the way home.

Back on the road again, the miles seemed to slip by faster for Jacody. Marcy continued to be in a talkative mood. She told Jacody about the CISM she attended. Just like at the meeting, she went over yesterday morning's mad dash for safety. She talked about how surprising it was how all the people saw and experienced the same things but had different accounts of everything they went through.

Eventually, she exhausted that topic and told him about Linda's stalker and her suspicions that he might have been spending time outside Cupcake at night. At first, Jacody was mad because she hadn't shared that with him until now.

"So, what would have happened if I had told you that I felt someone was hanging out below my sleeper unit window every night?" Marcy asked Jacody.

"For one thing, you wouldn't have gotten any better sleep than you did. That mattress is barely big enough for you. If you had told me what was going on... like I would have liked... I would have been right there staying with you! We would have been very uncomfortable... but you would have been safe!"

"Exactly! You would have dropped everything at the ranch when I couldn't even be sure there was anyone out there stalking me. My imagination gets cranked up and I suspect all kinds of things. But you would have been making life miserable for both of us!"

"Safe! You would have been safe! I would have been there!" Jacody insisted.

"Did anything happen to me? No! So I was safe even without you being there!"

"So you thought it was alright to deceive me? I'm not mad or anything.... I'm just asking. Was it okay to deceive me?"

"Well, I don't like the way that sounds. It makes me seem like a... like a..."

"Deceiver?" Jacody offered.

"I was trying to find a different word. One that doesn't make me sound like a 'liar', for example! Let's say... someone who just knew that there was a proper time to tell you... like now... and not then. Then would not have been good. Now, is perfectly fine! This is a good time to tell you!

"Okay. Just so we understand that it is okay to be evasive at the moment with the knowledge that a better time is coming to be open... I won't even add, 'and honest', because that indicates to not be honest is to be dishonest and I know you nor I ever want to be dishonest with each other."

"Well of course not!" Marcy said. "Neither one of us wants to be dishonest with each other!"

Marcy was thinking, "he sure seems to be laying some groundwork for something here. What hasn't he told me and why? Time will tell!"

Jacody was thinking, "she sure seems to be laying some groundwork for something here. What hasn't she told me and why? Time will tell!"

They gave each other a knowing sideways glance... and then a slight look of surprise that they gave each other not one, but then, two similar looks!

Jacody said, "Okay. We seem to agree on that. Back to the point before we got derailed. Why did you think you had a secret admirer hanging out under your window?"

"I had told HRSP D'Angelo about my concern and it was right when the engine crewmember Linda was having her problem that I told you about. He thought that, most likely, the guy pestering Linda could also be the person I thought was watching me. I wanted to believe that, but I kept hearing things that caused me to stay on high alert. Gravel crunching sounds, truck

382

door sounds... it always seemed someone was moving around close to Cupcake. It was wearing me out! Now I may never find out who, if anyone, was staying close to my truck at night. I didn't want relief by way of being removed from the real or imagined peril. That was not how I wanted that to end, but I guess I will have to accept it."

"That may be one of those things we will never know," Jacody was hoping to help Marcy put the whole incident to rest. "Were your instincts right that someone was paying too much attention to you? I think you acted appropriately... better to be safe than sorry. You did all you could. HRSP guy contacted Law Enforcement. It's all over now. I hope you can let it go. Close the book on that chapter. You are home now!"

A big full moon was rising high in the sky as they pulled up to the entrance to the lane that led back to Moon Ranch.

"What... in the world... is all of this!" Marcy exclaimed!

"It is your welcome home surprise, Sweetheart! All the stonework you see here you can thank your dad and grandpa for. They laid it out and built it themselves." Jacody had stopped with his high beams on right at the new entrance to Moon Ranch.

Marcy was looking at the fieldstone walls that her father and grandfather had built to outline the entrance approach area to the ranch. Large fieldstone pillars stood at either side of the opening in the wall for the lane accessing the ranch. Standing erect on the top of each of the pillars was a peeled lodgepole pine pole. They supported a cross pole over the road high enough for a semi trailer van to easily pass under. Above the cross member, the pole on the right extended up another 12 feet, and the pole on the left, another 6 feet. A cable ran from the top of one pole to the top of the other pole. In the middle of the cable was a steel band forming a circle 3 feet across. Held inside the circle was a cream-colored illuminated translucent disk. Between the pillars and below the moon, or disk, an intricate wrought-iron gate blocked the lane. Cut into the vertical bars and positioned along the bottom rails of the gate were 7 life-size wolves: 2 adults and 5 pups. The adult wolf on the left gate half was sitting on its haunches with its head tilted up howling at the moon. Standing on its two hind feet with its front feet on the adult's back was a pup also howling at the moon. On the right side was another pup sitting on its haunches facing the same direction also howling at the moon. Next to the howling pup, was the other adult with its nose down towards three other pups playing with each other with no interest in learning how to howl. Like a jig-saw puzzle, the neck and head of the howling adult wolf on the left extended into the right gate half. The head, shoulders, and front legs of the howling wolf pup on the right half of the gate extended into the left gate half below the howling adult on the left. Wrought iron letters hung under the cross pole above and spelled out, "Moon Ranch".

"Jacody! I'm speechless! This is amazing!"

They got out of the truck so Marcy could get a better look at the estate gate.

"What did Jane Lew say?"

"What do you mean, what did Jane Lew say?" Jacody asked.

"Well, isn't this her gate? You told me you were building her a gate. You sure haven't had time to build two gates!"

"No. This is your gate! And... you are right. I couldn't have built two gates. You see, I wanted to surprise you with the kind of gate you have wanted ever since we moved to Moon Ranch. So, I hated to do it, but I just told you Jane Lew wanted me to build a gate for her because I needed to buy gate material. I expected you might see the charges and start asking questions. I didn't know how else to handle it."

"Look at you! Going to the dark side! What a covert operation! I didn't think anything about it when you first told me the gate was for Jane Lew, but then, a night or two later I ask you about her and you acted evasively. For just a split second, I wondered if something funny was up. But then I thought... this is Jacody, and moved on. I've gotta say though, this... is... sweet!"

"If you recall, we both talked about how we might reserve the truth until the time was best to share it? Well, this is me being truthful. I didn't want you to know until right now and I did hate to deceive you... but it was the only way to surprise you. So I'm glad we got all that 'open and honest' discussion over with on the way home!"

"So this is what that was all about? You trying to make sure I wouldn't have a case against you when I found out you lied to me?"

"I thought we banned that 'lie' word! Besides, you were guilty first!" Jacody was quick to point out.

"Just shut up and kiss me!"

"You always did know how to end an argument in a hurry!" Jacody said as he obliged her.

Marcy snuggled full body up to Jacody running her arms under his T-shirt. She wanted to melt into him. Jacody embraced her and held her tight. Coming home, sharing ... this was a memory she wanted etched permanently in her mind. The homecoming gift, this gate, seemed to establish a monument to their future. Marcy drew back an arm's length and looked up at Jacody's strong features.

"In case I didn't say it before, let me say it now – thank you for the gate! I love it! I think it is incredible!" Marcy said. She had news to share... big news... but this was his moment; his gift to her he had poured his heart and soul into while she was gone. This was not the right time to share it with him – maybe later.

Jacody expected her to be pleased with his gift of the estate gate, but he sensed there was something else brewing here. Ever since they were alone in Jacody's truck after leaving fire camp, it seemed like she was on the verge of sharing something big with him. After talking through the CISM, and the stalker, she had talked about this and that, not staying on any subject too long. He supposed the trauma she had gone through up on the mountain might be to blame. The CISM seemed to be helpful, at least she said it did. And she didn't seem stressed. What went on in a woman's mind he could never figure out, but he was getting ready to take the blame, whatever it was. Marcy really wasn't a flowers kind of woman – he had found that out early. But maybe he should have shown up at fire camp with a big bunch of flowers.

"What's up Marcy? What's going on in that pretty little mind of yours?" He finally asked as the corners of Marcy's mouth belied a grin she might be trying to hide.

"I'm just so overwhelmed right now. Being home. This gift. I think every time I come through this gate it will remind me that I am the alpha female wolf returning to the den with her alpha male! There is nothing... absolutely nothing that will ever come between us... or could ever stop us!"

There was only a hint of dawn seeping into the darkened bedroom from around the window blinds. Jacody's wandering foot told him he was in bed alone. Was it a dream? No, it couldn't have been. He brought Marcy home last night! Through sleepy eyes, Jacody could tell the bathroom door was wide open. He could tell, she wasn't in there. "Oh! Now there's a clue!" The rich aroma of fresh coffee finally penetrated his senses.

Wearing only his boxers, he wrapped the big heavy buffalo robe from the foot of the bed around his shoulders to ward off the slight chill in the air and headed down the hall to the kitchen. Marcy was not there. He got a big mug of fresh coffee and went into the mudroom. Looking out the side door window, he saw her in the dim light sitting on the porch swing with her knees drawn up to her chest underneath her heavy bathrobe.

Still barefooted and near-naked, Jacody joined her on the porch. "So here is where you ran off to!"

"Believe me, lover! I haven't run off anywhere! I woke up and couldn't go back to sleep. Maybe I needed to hear generators starting up and fire engines idling by to stay asleep! So, I got up, went into the kitchen, and made a pot of coffee."

"And yet, here you sit empty-handed," Jacody remarked.

"Odd, isn't it," Marcy said making more of a statement than asking a question. "I made it. Then I didn't want it! Coffee. It made me a little nauseous."

"Should I be worried? We have all met Decaffeinated Marcy before, and she is not a very nice person!" Jacody joked.

"You gotta play with the cards you're dealt, mister! You place your bets and take your chances. Now sit down next to me and share that comfy-looking buffalo rope! I'm getting cold!"

Marcy held Jacody's coffee and leaned forward while he sat and draped the robe around their shoulders. Taking the mug from her, he jumped a little as she leaned against him and put a cold hand on his naked chest. The sun had just hit the mountain ridgeline to the West and was starting its journey down the rock face towards the valley below. Down by the barn, Roho the Rooster started crowing. Up past the corral, a covey of quail started calling from the top of big round bales to assemble their group for the day.

"I could just stay here... just like this... for the rest of the day," Marcy said. "Just sit in this swing and watch the day unwind right in front of me!"

"No coffee. Wanting to sit still and watch the day pass you by – this is different. Do I have to get to know you all over again? Were you abducted by aliens?"

"Noooo. You know me." Marcy exaggerated. "I'm just trying to process the whole experience. There has been a lot happen to me and around me. Did you hear about what all went on at the fire? Have you met my father? Have you seen Cupcake? Have you seen the new entrance to Moon Ranch? Do you know where you are going to put all the things in the small bedroom when we clear it out? See, there just a lot of stuff to think about and process."

"Whoa, whoa, whoa! What was that last thing you said? Jacody asked.

"Stuff to think about and process?"

"No. Before that."

"The small bedroom?"

"Yeah. Why are you thinking about the small bedroom with all the other stuff you mentioned?" Jacody asked.

"All that 'other' stuff happened in the past. We need to clean the small bedroom out for something that's going to happen in the future." She snuggled up close to him. Stretching up she nibbled on his ear and made him jerk. She fastened her eyes onto his. She softly whispered, "you are going to be a daddy."

"What did you say! When? How? Scratch that! I know how!" Jacody squeezed her until it started hurting. "How do you know? How long have you known? I knew there was something you weren't telling me! Oh my gosh! Marcy!"

"I found out when I was at the clinic in Journey." Marcy locked her arms around Jacody's neck and gave him a big kiss. Pulling back, she said, "Ya knocked me up, Gunslinger! And now you're gonna have to pay for it."

"No problem! There isn't a price too big to pay for you giving us a child!" Jacody held her close again. "When will you have him... or her? Oh! I know we've talked about names before, but I just thought about Magnolia! That'd be for a girl of course. We could call her Maggie! What if it's a boy? My mom is going to leap out of her skin! We need to get one of those Red Ryder wagons...."

Marcy jabbed Jacody in the ribs right where it always made him jump. She liked doing that.

Epilogue
Two years later...

The weather was just right for a sweater. Cool breezes and warm sun filtering down through the fledgling leaves made Marcy want to rest back into the cushions on the Adirondack lawn chair. The air temperature was just brisk enough that the throw on her lap and legs kept her comfortable. Marcy was filled with a sense of family, a sense of belonging, being safe, being loved, loving. Her cheeks were warm from the spring sun and her heart was warm from enjoying the sights and sounds of family.

She looked at the woman next to her. Grandma Nellie had stepped in when her mother died. Nellie's snow-white hair fell gracefully down to her shoulders. Her 80-some years may have aged her face but had done nothing to diminish her clear blue eyes and the warm welcoming smile she was so quick to share with everyone.

Marcy shifted her gaze to the woman sitting next to Grandma Nellie, her mother-in-law. Still not her mother, but she couldn't have asked for a better in-law. Randi Mae Jones, Jacody's mother could trace her heritage back through the generations to the Shoshone guide, Sacagawea. When Marcy learned this of her mother-in-law, she quickly attributed Jacody's confident nature to his mother. Just as Sacagawea had guided the Lewis and Clark expedition, Randi Mae guided her family.

Sitting between Randi Mae and Marcy was Lauren. Sweet, beautiful Lauren. Dreamy green/grey eyes and a trusting face, she was a God sent. Lauren was widowed 5 years ago and had become her father's best friend about a year and a half ago. In June, Lauren would become Marcy's stepmother. It didn't take long for the two women to draw close. Neither was expecting a mother/daughter relationship... Marcy said she wouldn't recognize one if it came along. What Marcy and Grandma Nellie had was close enough. A close girlfriend was how Marcy and Lauren described their bond.

Jacody and Grandpa Sam were splitting firewood and feeding a fire in the fire pit. A bed of hot coals was forming. Soon it would be time to start the lamb chops that had been marinating overnight.

Jacody's father, John Jefferson Jones, and Daniel were like two peas in a pod... at the moment, at least. Daniel, a ranch hand with his high school diploma, and Dr. Jones, a college professor with his degrees from Tuskegee University were both reduced to babbling puppets whose strings were being pulled by a powerful little puppet master. They were taking turns high-fiving and tickling their granddaughter, Nellie Mae. One grandfather would get Nellie Mae to high five him. As soon as her hand would go up, the other grandfather would tickle her ribs. She was loving it!

Marcy's heart was melting from the sound of laughing and giggling that came from her precious little girl. Coal-black hair and big dark eyes with a smile that could win over even the sourest of people, Nellie Mae would try to talk to anybody who would listen.

It never ceased to amaze her the changes she had seen in her father since that evening in California a little over two years ago. They had agreed there was no value in going backward to figure out what caused the schism between them after her mother died. Their goal was to work hard each day to make their relationship special, and they had. When Lauren came into the picture, it provided yet another avenue for recovery for Daniel. As a grandfather, Daniel lights up like a streetlight any time Little Nell comes near him. She has never seen him so animated, so affectionate, so much like a father.

Marcy noticed Jacody got a cellphone call. He spoke briefly and looked her way. Then he turned back to the fire and put his phone away. A few minutes later, Chuck and Chew jumped up and went tearing around the house to the front barking loudly. Jacody started ambling after them. She was a little annoyed that after he hung up his phone, he didn't come over and let her know what was going on. They obviously had company and he had allowed them through the gate using his estate gate app on his phone. Well, she was comfortable where she was and would find out who it was soon enough.

A short stout woman appeared followed by a man in a big cowboy hat walking next to Jacody. The cowboy seemed a little nervous that Chuck and Chew were giving him the smell test. As the woman hurried up to Marcy, all of a sudden, Marcy recognized her.

"Sheila! Marcy!" They shrieked in unison. Marcy jumped up, the throw falling to the ground. Instantly they hugged and then, backed up with a shocked look on their faces, looked down at each other's abdomen, and, again in unison, yelled "baby bump!" The two pregnant women laughed and hugged again.

Turning her attention to the cowboy hat she held out her hand. The man took a step forward and, a little jerky at first, took his hat off and took Marcy's hand.

"Larry?" Marcy said incredulously. "Is that you?"

"Well, it ain't that Clint Easterwood feller," Larry said, letting her hand fall.

"Sheila and Larry. Larry and Sheila." Marcy said quizzically.

"I know whut y'all a'think'n," Larry said.

"Good! Because I don't know what I'm thinking!" then Marcy said to the group, "All righty then! Folks, let me introduce you to these two wayfaring strangers!"

Introductions made, she invited Sheila and Larry over to the picnic table under the pergola where they

394

could talk. After they got settled, Marcy said, "First of all... what's up with the baby bump?"

"Let me start a little further back than that," Sheila said. "I always said the first guy that treated me like I was pretty would never get away from me. You were there when Larry said I was cuter than a bug's ear. I punched him right then and there. He didn't know it, but he was mine from that moment on!"

"Y'all were then and y'all even cuter now!" Larry said. "First time I saw Miss Sheila here on that there track with you, I thought to myself, 'self, you ain't never met some woman what wasn't a girly girl. This'un looks different. Then when she slugged me... well no woman ever done nothing like that. I was hooked!"

"And the baby?" Marcy asked.

Sheila showed a nice diamond on her finger.

"Larry! I thought you were a confirmed bachelor! You and Sheila are married?" Marcy asked almost in disbelief.

"Y'all don't have ta be so surprised! I can be convin'cin when I sets ma mind tuit."

"I am just so thrilled for the both of you! And now you're going to be a family! Oh! I am just so happy."

"After we got run off the mountain, I took some time off. I started visiting Larry in the hospital. He had some rehab to do when he got out and I didn't think he'd stick to it if left on his own with just his mother, so, I took on the responsibility to make sure he recovered. That heatstroke weakened his heart and we had to work to get him back into shape. You may notice, he's lost about 30 pounds! I'm so proud of him!"

"Yeah," Marcy said. "I can see that!"

"Now I'm working on getting him to speak above an 'I was raised by wolves' level!" Sheila smiled.

"Yeah... well. We are a try'n, ain't we sweetheart," Larry said.

"You know I love you, Sugar!" Sheila hugged Larry, then focused on Marcy.

"Marcy, we've wanted to come to see you and Jacody for a long time. We've been trying to figure out how to approach you about something - how to deal with it."

"What? Why would you hold back? You should know I'd be happy you guys got married and you're always welcome here."

"Well, at first, we were busy getting Larry back to full speed, but then, we were talking one night about church and why Larry thought it was so important that we got to going to a church. And then..." Sheila sighed.

"Again... what?" Marcy interrupted. "Larry, where'd this come from."

"Jess hush yerself. Sheila'll tell y'all."

"Yeah. I can thoroughly understand why you'd be flabbergasted!" Sheila said.

"I hoped Rick Barron's worship service would take hold, but this is way beyond my expectations!" Marcy said.

"I said it then un I'll say it now. I don't like stand'n round people I don't know with my eyes closed." Larry said emphatically.

"Yes Larry, I think we all know that. Rick's service may have helped but that wasn't what got Larry all fired up for Christ. It was you and things you said and did." Sheila said.

"Me? I intended to try and encourage you, and you, Larry... Jock, and Carlos too... to find the way to eternal life and to live a life based on Jesus while you are still here on earth. But I didn't get to do that. It wasn't me! I think God led you all to Rick's worship service. It had to be Him because I felt I failed." Marcy explained.

"As for me," Sheila said, "I was frustrated and confused about things. I was lonely looking for a friend. You came along and became my friend. I went to Rick's service because I didn't want to disappoint you. Larry here told me he went because I went. I'm sure you remember why Jock and Carlos went – they wanted to see a demon get pulled out of Larry. What a hoot!"

"But you said the worship service only helped, that somehow I did something...."

"Yes," Sheila said. "The day you and Larry were flagging traffic, that big round rock turned up and he said stupid stuff concerning you and your husband, remember?"

"Like I could forget that day!"

"That day, he stayed hot. David D'Angelo gave him a good talking to about the lunch-van girl incident that happened earlier and threatened him with being barred from ever getting on another fire again. D'Angelo didn't say anything about the blow-up you and Larry had had earlier in the day, but just the way D'Angelo talked, Larry felt sure you had. He thought that's why he got such a bawling out with threats of being kicked off the fire."

At this point, Larry turned around on the picnic bench with his back to Marcy. He held his hat in his hand and kept his head bowed.

Sheila went on, "He brooded about it all evening and about the time the generators went down for the night, he walked over to Cupcake where he planned to talk to you about it. As he tells me - and neither he nor I think he could speak about this to you himself right now, that's why I'm telling you - when he got there, he heard you praying in your truck. He heard the pain in your voice. He heard you pray about your father. He said that it felt like a cold icicle had just been shoved into his heart. You see, he lost his father when he was 5 and his mother never remarried. He has always felt he missed being 'normal', for lack of a better word, because he was raised with no male influence. Then you prayed for veterans who suffer from PTSD. He related to that. Next, you poured out your heart on several other things, but the last thing you prayed for dealt specifically with him. You said his name. You told God he was a lonely man with a cold, empty heart. You ask for help in tolerating him and to help you not give up on him. You wanted Larry to find the way to salvation. Well, he was devastated."

"Oh...," Marcy said. "It was never my attempt to hurt you, Larry."

"He knows that. But for the first time, he felt like someone else actually saw him in the same light he saw himself. You were praying about his innermost

398

secret. More importantly, he heard someone praying
to God as if he was worth being saved. He said he
wasn't sure what that meant, but it stood to reason the
opposite of saved is lost. And he didn't want to be
lost... kind of like not having a father... but maybe
even worse. He stayed outside your truck window and
listened to the music you played. Eventually, you
called Jacody and Larry heard your half of the
conversation. It was enough to convince him he
wanted to mean as much to someone as Jacody meant
to you. What's more, he wanted someone to love the
way it seemed Jacody loves you."

"Well, I just don't know what to say! This is all
kind of overwhelming." Marcy said. "When we first
started talking, you were going to become a lesbian.
Then..."

"You were whut!"

"Not now, Larry, I'll tell you later," Sheila said.
"Then, he kept coming back every night to listen to
your phone call to Jacody. He became obsessed and
tried to learn more. He thought maybe you two didn't
act that way all the time, but he found it the same
every night. He could only imagine what Jacody was
saying but he felt he got the tone of the conversation
right. Sometimes he had a hard time hearing you and
he had to stand up and put his ear against the sleeper.
He said Law Enforcement started coming around and
once, they almost caught him in the light of their
flashlight."

Sheila continued, "we had been married for almost
a year before all this came out. If I could have gone
back in time, I would have slapped Larry silly before

he could do any of that stuff! But then, I think of what a difference it made in Larry's life... and what a difference it made in my life! In a way, it prepared both of us for a relationship! Larry and I had been Christians for a while and I think the more we read the Bible, the more he felt convicted about things he had said to you. That's why he unloaded all this on me. Then, when I told him you knew someone was stalking you... well, you felt someone was stalking you by lurking around your truck at night... what he did back then became a heavier and heavier burden for him to bear. You wouldn't believe how many times Larry has told me about this. The longer we have been going to church, the more often he repeats this story to me. He has become more miserable. He has known for some time now, that confessing to me wasn't enough. The only way he could get any relief is to come to you and confess it all, just as I have spoken it."

"Wow! So many questions answered. This means a lot to me. I knew I wasn't imagining things! HRSP D'Angelo and I hoped my feelings about being stalked would go away after that Division Supervisor guy was sent home. Now I know why that didn't change! Larry! You're sitting right here. Couldn't you have said in person what Sheila said?"

At this point, Larry turned around on the picnic table bench to face Marcy. He still held his hat in his hand and slowly let his eyes settle on Marcy.

"Marcy," Larry began, "this is sump'um I gotta say ma own self. It weren't y'all whut saved me outta that fire... it weren't y'all whut led me to Christ... it weren't y'all whut got me'n Sheila here together. But sure as I'm alive... as sure as I'm saved... as sure as ma wife is gonna make me a daddy... God used y'all in a way so mighty... nobody but us'd believe it! So mighty! So mighty! Sheila here is ma witness – I'm a changed man! I love ma Lord! I love ma wife! I love ma soon ta be born child! I love you! I love Jacody! I love..."

Larry became too choked up with emotion to continue. Words failed him. He turned back around on the bench, put his hat back on, and started mopping up his face with a large red bandanna.

Shiela picked up where Larry left off. "The rest of what I know Larry wanted to say was, he is so happy that you and Jacody have been open to what God tells you and you follow through with what God wants you to do. God may never speak as directly to Larry or me, but as you told us, he speaks quite plainly about how we are to live in the Bible. We are determined to follow him."

Marcy said, "I'm so happy for you two. I'm glad you don't credit any of this to me, but to God. Larry, I know it is hard for you to put your thoughts and feelings into words, so the fact that you came here and, between you and Sheila, was able to share what was on your heart, means a great deal to me! Thank you!"

Larry turned sideways on the bench to look at Marcy, "I be like Moses," he said. "I know whut needs ta be said... just not whut words ta use when talk'n ta y'all. So Sheila's ma Aaron, Moses' brother. He dun thu talk'n fer Moses. They dun ok, didn't they? Got them Hebrews outta Egypt."

"Well, yes. It worked well for Moses and Aaron. They were a good team and it looks like you and Sheila have turned out to be a good team."

"Could y'all forgive me?" Larry looked earnestly towards Marcy speaking slowly and carefully. "Know'n whut you know now, will... you... forgive me?"

Marcy was in tears, "Of course I can, and I do... forgive you. I want to thank you so much for telling me all this. You are forgiven!"

"Okay. That's one thing out of the way! Sheila said.

Marcy exclaimed, "One thing? There's more?"

"Yeah, there's more." Sheila sighed. "As I said, Larry was the energy that got us into church."

"I know that's what you said," Marcy replied still not able to take it all in.

"Kinda beats all, don't it." Larry said as though he didn't believe it either.

"This may be hard to explain, but I'll try," began Sheila. "I know I told you, God may never speak to us as directly as He does to Jacody... but up on the mountain that day... not as direct, mind you... but this one time when I thought it all was lost, He kind'a did. You see God let me know I was not going to die that day on Stutler Ridge Fire..."

"Oh, Sheila!" Marcy exclaimed reaching across the table to hold Sheila's hands. "I'm so happy for you. What did He say to you? How did you know? But why are you just now telling me?"

"Hush now. Juss let Sheila talk." Larry said softly. "It's a onerful story."

"Do you remember what Rick Barron said the night we went to the worship service?"

"Sheila, that was over 2 years ago! I know we went, but I don't remember everything."

Undaunted, Sheila went on, "Rick said, 'probably for most of you, this will just be an exercise... but for one or more of you... it may be much more.' He said that just before he had us close our eyes and he talked us through that visualization. Well. I was one. Maybe there were others... but... I... was one... one that it meant much more to! That night, I felt so much hope and potential that I knew, someday, someway, I could find a way to live in the shelter of the Lord. I was going to talk to you about it the next time we were on the track together."

"It was the next morning then. I was with Hank, and he was driving. There was fire on both sides of the road. We were driving slow because of the smoke. It seemed like there was death all around us. The temperature inside the truck was becoming more than I could bear... or so I thought. 'Roll the window down. Roll the window down.' That kept going through my head. That's what you always do when it gets too hot inside. Finally, I couldn't resist any longer! I hit the window button to roll the window down. At first, I was shocked and confused. The cool refreshing air I expected was like a blast furnace full of smoke. The air was scorching my throat and my eyes were stinging and watering. It took me a bit of fumbling around to find the window button again but I got the window back up. It didn't help much though. I was gasping for air and had my eyes squeezed shut. I thought it might be over. Hank and I were going to die right there. Our truck would block the road, catch on fire and no one else would get past us... we would all die. And then... with my eyes closed, I saw Him! Real as life, crystal clear, just as Rick had described him the night before! He smiled at me, and I tried to reach out to Him. But He held up his hands and shook His head 'no'. I felt, and I believe, He was telling me it was not time for me. He was not coming to take me with Him. I would not be dying that day. He was there to see us to safety. I felt reassured and calm. Then I relaxed and started taking short, slow breaths. I thought about what I had just seen and looked out the windows at trees torching and firebrands hitting the windshield. We were still in danger, still in the inferno, but it was different now. I had hope and I had faith. We just kept moving in slow motion. Suddenly, the smoke cleared and we broke out into the sunlight! Drop Point #8 was at the end of the sagebrush flat on our left! We were safe!"

"Oh, what a wonderful experience!" Macy sighed. "Wonderful, even if you were in a chaotic tragedy and could have died. But I'm surprised you didn't tell me and the others about that at the CISM and why you weren't praising God day and night. Why did it take Larry to get you into church?"

"Simply put, after things calmed down a little that day, and I thought about it, I was scared. I was plain scared. It hit me like a ton of bricks. God spared my life. We were in a bad place and my plan was to roll the window down! God came to me and calmed me down; we all got out of there. So. I thought that I

owed God this huge debt. How could I repay Him? I
wanted to stay away from Him because I knew the
price would be high. So I tried to bury all of it.
Meanwhile, Larry had Rick's New Testament and then
goes out and buys another Bible. He was reading and
learning and growing. I was hiding still. The log jam
didn't bust open until Larry and I started having some
heart-to-heart talks. He was able to show me none of
us have what it takes to pay God back for anything!
When I came to understand that, and, more
importantly, believe that – well, I was all in! I'll testify
to anyone what God has done for me!"

"Toll y'all it wus a onerful story!" Larry grinned.

"Larry, when your right you're right! Marcy said.
"You're proud of yourself aren't you big boy?"

"Oh no, Marcy," Larry said. "I'm proud of whut ma
Lord and Savior's done fer me... and with me!"

"I can't tell you how happy I am that you two have
shared all this with me," Marcy said. "It goes to show,
we have no idea who or how God is working with
people. But we can be sure that He is working with
people!"

Sheila gathered up Marcy's hands in hers. "It
seems like it was eons ago now, but back on the high
school track in Journey, California, you said
something so odd, so cryptic, I remember it like it was
this morning. You said, 'Sheila, there's a lot more in
store for you than punching people in the arm. I don't
want you to miss out!' I asked you then what you
meant by, 'miss out'. You said, 'Just remember that.
It will come to you at the right time.' I want you to
know... it did come to me at the right time! I have not,

and am not, missing out. When He came to me through the smoke and firestorm on the mountain, when He led me to the man I was to marry, when He showed me in His word I cannot earn forgiveness but am saved and loved, when I saw the sonogram of our child, each time, I thanked Him and said to myself... I have to tell Marcy! If today is the last time we meet... if I never see your face again... I will always... always... consider you my very best and dearest friend!

Their out-of-town guest left in the late afternoon following kisses, hugs, and promises that they would visit each other again very soon. Shortly after that, Grandma Nellie woke Grandpa Sam up from his unscheduled nap.

"Sam, you'd sleep through anything. Come on," Nellie Portman said. "You won't be able to go to sleep tonight as it is. Let's get ourselves home."

Daniel said, "I can drive you home and Lauren can follow us in my truck."

Grandpa Sam gave Daniel a stern look and said, "You're looking to get your ears boxed, aren't you boy! When's the last time you got knocked down a notch or two?"

"Okay dad, okay. Nobody is taking your keys away... yet. You keep talking that way and it may be sooner than later! Daniel laughed.

Jacody and Marcy walked with her grandparents, Daniel and Lauren out to the parked trucks. There they said their evening goodbyes with hugs and kisses all around. Returning to the backyard fire pit, Grandma Randi was just finishing washing the sticky evidence of S'mores from squirmy Nellie Mae's face.

"Time for you to go to bed munchkin," Marcy told her daughter.

That was met with the expected reply, "I don't want to mama!" Nellie Mae ran over and climbed up in Grandpa John's lap.

"Yes mama," Grandpa John said. "We have a book to read. We can't go to bed yet!"

"Oh! So that's how it's going to be. Two against one, huh?" Marcy said.

Grandma Randi spoke up, "That's right! Nellie Sweetheart, why don't you and I go in the house and get you ready for bed. Then Grandpa John can pick out a book to read to you."

"Thanks, Randi, she's all yours!" and to Nellie Mae, Marcy said, "come give your dad and me good night hugs and kisses!"

"You and Jacody just relax. Once we get Nellie to bed, I think we will turn in too."

Once Marcy had her kitchen straightened up she got ready for bed herself. Then she went to the side porch swing where she knew she would find Jacody. Plopping down beside him, she sighed, "This baby boy of yours is wearing me out!"

"Better enjoy the semi-calm you have now while you can. I bet this kid will be a terror just like his big sister! I can't wait to meet him."

"Yeah... me too. But not today. Today, I'm all in. But what a day it has been! Can you believe it? Larry and Sheila... Sheila and Larry! That whole revelation today has just blown me away! I think Sheila even quoted a line from Steven Winwoods' song, 'Presence of the Lord', 'I have finally found a way to live just like I never could before'. I am so happy tonight!"

Marcy laid her head on Jacody's shoulder, and they sat there quietly swinging gently for a while. A big full moon was rising over the ridge. Off in the distance came the yipping of coyotes. A wave of cooler air from the high country washed down over them. Marcy shivered a little and Jacody pulled her closer to him.

Finally, Jacody asked, "Are you ready to go to bed? I'm bushed."

"Yes, I think I am," Marcy said, "but you know, I was just thinking. All that background noise I've been carrying around from the Stutler Ridge Fire... I think I'm okay now."

"As I've always said," pronounced Jacody, "in the end, it'll be okay. If it's not okay... it's not the end."

Marcy jabbed Jacody in the ribs right where it always made him jump, kissed him on the cheek, and whispered in his ear, "It's the end!"

THE END

LIST OF SONGS REFERENCED

Chap.	Title	Attributed to:
2	Six Days on the Road	Dave Dudley
3	Farther Along	W.B. Stevens
3	The Weight	Robbie Robertson
3	Sweet Home Alabama	Lynyrd Skynyrd
5	Joyful Joyful	Henry Van Dyke
5	In-A-Gadda-Da-Vida	Doug Ingle
7	Love Machine	The Miracles
7	Nights In White Satin	Justin Hayward
7	Fortunate Son	John Fogerty - CCR
7	Walking On Sunshine	Kimberly Rew
9	Good Times	Edie Bricknell
9	I Shall Be Released	Bob Dylan

9	Harvest Moon	Neil Young
10	Nowhere to Run	Martha and the Vandellas
10	Have I Told You Lately	Van Morrison
11	My Back Pages	Bob Dylan
11	Crazy Love	Van Morrison
11	My Guy	Smokey Robinson
14	Chain Breaker	Zach Williams
14	Pass Me Not, Oh Gentle Savior	Francis Crosby
14	Get Together	Chester Powers
15	Staying Alive	Bee Gee's
15	Walk the Line	Johnny Cash
15	Wreck of the Edmund Fitzgerald	Gordon Lightfoot
16	Happytown	Dave Carter & Tracie Grammer
16	Me and Mrs. Jones	Kenny Gamble

Epilog	In the Presence of the Lord	Steve Winwood

Book Referenced

Chap.	Title	Author
14	Mere Shadows	Verda Spice

(Available at: amazon.com)

Made in the USA
Middletown, DE
31 December 2023